Midsummer Night's Magic

EMMA CRAIG
TESS MALLORY
PAM McCUTCHEON
AMY ELIZABETH SAUNDERS

D0126271

LOVE SPELL BOOKS ✦ NEW YORK CITY

LOVE SPELL®
July 1997
Published by

Dorchester Publishing Co., Inc.
276 Fifth Avenue
New York, NY 10001

Printed in the United States of America.

The Trouble with Fairies

Pam McCutcheon

As always, I couldn't do this without the fabulous support of the Wyrd Sisters, especially Deb Stover, Paula Gill, and Carol Umberger, who kept my fairies straight. Special thanks to Linda Kruger for making this possible, and to Johnny and Susan Jackson, whose Welsh Corgi, Candy, inspired Stumpy, the "fairy steed."

Chapter One

"The trouble with fairies," the bartender said, "is they're mighty hard to get rid of."

Nick Fairburn peered at the man through blurry eyes and took another sip of his bourbon. Somehow, after several drinks, that statement seemed almost normal. Almost. "Is that a fact?"

The bartender—what was his name?—oh, yeah, Patrick . . . something. Something Irish.

Patrick Something leaned on the bar with a conspiratorial air. "Aye. If you take the wee folk home with ye, make sure ye set limits."

"Limits?"

"Aye—these fairies are house brownies. They do good work, mind ye, but they'll be everywhere and into everythin' if ye don't declare a space of yer own."

Nick nodded knowledgeably. "A man mus' have his privacy," he said, proud of his continued ability to enunciate. "I wouldn't like 'em in the bedroom with me and m'wife."

7

"Aye, that ye wouldn't." Patrick hesitated and gave him a penetrating look. "Are ye sure about this?"

Somehow, Nick had lost the thread of the conversation. He took another sip. "Sure 'bout what?"

"About taking the fairies home with ye?"

Nick glanced around the bar. No one else was near enough to overhear their conversation—or explain to Nick exactly what the heck Patrick was talking about. "Tell me again," he said, unwilling to reveal his momentary memory lapse, "why I should take 'em home with me?"

" 'Tis the problems with your wife, I'll be thinkin'."

"Oh. That."

The memory of why he'd come here tonight suddenly hit Nick like a sledgehammer. Kate, his beautiful Kate, had been coldly judgmental, saying he was a kid who had never grown up, with no more sense of responsibility than their five-year-old daughter, Cory.

"She wants a sheparation," he said, staring morosely into his glass. "Jus' because the house wass a li'l dirty when she came home. I talked her out of it for now, but Kate's shtubborn."

That's why he'd decided to get drunk, though he'd never had more than two beers in one sitting before. He didn't know why he hadn't—he could hardly even feel the booze.

Patrick wiped a glass with his towel and nodded in sympathetic understanding.

"Not that I'm a mooch," Nick hurried to clarify. "I work at home. I write and lilistrate . . . lustrate . . . li . . . luh . . ." Why wasn't his tongue working properly? ". . . *draw* children's books." He peered at Patrick. "Ever heard of me? Nicholas Fairburn?"

Patrick shook his head. "No, but then, I don't read many children's books."

Nick waved a hand. " 'S okay. Nobody's ever heard of me." Five years he'd been struggling to make a name for himself, to find the one concept that would catch

The Trouble With Fairies

hold and set the imagination of the world on fire. Five years, and he was still no closer to making that big break.

No wonder he had writer's block. But did that mean Kate had any right to lecture him? After all, her career as an accountant in a prominent New York firm was just taking off—soaring, in fact—while his appeared to have hit a dead end.

Nick took another sip. "She said I spent too much time playin' with Cory and Stumpy and not enough cleanin' and workin' on my book."

Patrick gave him an odd look. "Ye named yer child Stumpy?"

"No, no. My daughter is Cory and my dog is Stumpy." He paused as a thought struck him. "Are fairies good with kids?"

"Aye, very good indeed. They dote on the little mites. But what kind of dog do ye have?"

"A Welsh corgi." Nick liked the way that mushed in his mouth, so he repeated it. "Welsh corgi. You know, one of those dogs with the short, stumpy legs. Thass how he got his name."

Patrick shot him a keen glance. "How about cats?"

"No, no cats."

"Good. Fairies hate them."

Nodding in solemn acknowledgment, Nick said, "So does my wife." He fell into silence, staring broodingly into his glass. Maybe he should have another one—he was starting to remember too much. Hadn't he come here to forget?

He pushed his glass toward Patrick, but the bartender ignored it. "Are ye sure about the fairies now?"

Nick wondered at the man's intent expression. "Why you wanna give the fairies away? Why not keep 'em yourshelf?"

Patrick shrugged. "Many brownies came over from the old country, looking for a house to care for. I help them find homes."

A tiny voice in the back of his mind told Nick there was something odd about this conversation, but he ignored it. "Kinda like a halfway house for fairies?" He chuckled at his own joke.

"Something like that. 'Tisn't many who can see the wee folk, or believe in them enough to pay 'em their due. I suspect you're one of them."

"Pay? How much?"

"Naught but a bit of milk left on the hearth overnight. 'Tis the custom, though not many remember it."

"Milk? Thass it?" He could make his household budget stretch that far.

"Aye, but you're not to mention it. The wee folk don't like discussin' anything as crass as payment."

Nick nodded wisely. "Course not."

"But make no mistake, they become mighty testy if ye forget."

"I won't forget," Nick promised. Something Patrick had said earlier suddenly penetrated. "What makes you think *I* can see 'em?"

Patrick cocked an eye at him. "All it takes is a bit of whimsy in your soul and a willingness to believe. Ye have that, don't you?"

Whimsy? According to Kate, he had far too much. That was something he had promised to try to change. Defensively, he said, "What if I can't see 'em? Iss hard to believe in somethin' you can't see."

"Aye, it is at that. They'll help you all the same whether ye can see 'em or not, but ye might be forgettin' the milk if ye don't believe." Patrick locked the cash register and said, "Wait here."

He returned a few minutes later. "Nick Fairburn, I'd like ye to meet Oak of the Wood family brownies." He gestured at the top of the bar.

Nick blinked. There stood a little old man about six inches high, wearing a brown tunic and shapeless pants topped by a brown pointy hat above a gray beard. Nick blinked again. "Are you real?"

The Trouble With Fairies

The little man shot a glance at Patrick. "Ye were right. He can see me."

"Of coursh I can see you," Nick said reasonably. "Can you see me?"

Oak snorted. "Ye're drunk."

Nick thought about it. "Well, I muss be, if I'm seein' fairies."

"Brownies," Oak said, shaking a tiny finger at him. "We're brownies and don't ye forget it."

"Huh?" Hadn't Patrick called them fairies?

"Ye mortals always get us mixed up with those flying flibbertigibbets who haven't an ounce of sense in their pretty little heads," Oak scolded. "If we're to live with ye, ye mustn't make that mistake again, y'hear?"

Nick looked at Patrick, who shrugged. "We've always called the lot o' them fairies," he explained. Then, in a lower tone, he said, "They're part of the fairy kingdom, they just don't like to admit it."

"Aye, and that's part of the problem," Oak said. " 'Tis hard for your average mortal to believe in the likes of fairies, but brownies . . . now there's a concept a man can hold on to."

"He can?" Nick asked.

"Aye. *You* can see me, can't ye?"

"Yeah—unlessh you're jus' a figment of my imagination." Weren't you supposed to see pink elephants after you'd had a few too many? Well, he must not have had enough yet—all he saw was one brown fairy.

"I ain't no figment o' nothin'," Oak declared in a testy tone. "I'm just as real as you."

"Okay, okay. Don' get your knickers in a twist. You're real."

"Ye got that right," Oak said. "Now about this house of yours—what's it like?"

"My house?" Nick repeated dumbly.

"Aye, yer house. If we're to live with ye, I need to know what manner of house ye live in."

Nick glanced at Patrick, who shrugged. *Why not?*

11

Nick described his brownstone apartment from kitchen to master bedroom. Then, at a significant look from Patrick, he added, "But the mashter bedroom is off-limits." He didn't want this little old geezer watching him make love to his wife and, no doubt, criticizing his technique.

Oak gave him an annoyed glance, but didn't say anything.

"Well," Nick asked, "whaddaya think?"

"It sounds a mite small," Oak said, "but I think it'll do."

It would do? Kate had worked hard to afford their home and loved every square inch of it. "Well, you may be shatisfied, but I'm not sure I am yet."

"What?" the little man squawked.

"What you gonna do for me?"

"Why, what brownies always do, o' course."

"Whass that?"

Oak scowled up at Patrick. "Do I have to put up with this ignorant lout?"

Patrick grinned. "Forgive him. He's American—uneducated." He turned to Nick and leaned on the counter. "As I mentioned earlier, brownies will keep yer house spotless, sometimes cook if ye ask nice, and even watch yer daughter for ye."

That was just what he needed to get Kate off his back and give him some extra time to come up with a great book proposal. He stared down at Oak. "You do windows?"

"O' course we do windows," Oak screeched. "We're good brownies, we are." He subsided with a harrumph. "Ye have a wee one, do ye?"

"Cory. She's five."

The man's face softened. "That's all right, then."

"Good. When can you shtart?"

"We can start tomorrow."

A vague concern niggled at the back of Nick's mind.

"We?" It just now penetrated his brain that Oak and Patrick kept using the plural.

"Me and me family," Oak explained. "Ye wouldn't ask me to join ye without bringing me family, would ye? All I have left are me poor orphan grandsons. They're grown boys now, and can do a mighty day's work."

Nick thought it over. What the heck? If one brownie was good, several ought to be even better. Anything to keep Kate happy. He held out his hand. "Okay, 's a deal."

Oak solemnly touched his hand to one of Nick's fingers. "Aye, mortal, that it is. And don't ye be forgettin' it."

Oak turned to leave, but Nick stopped him. "Don' you need directions?"

"No," the little man said with a wink. "Don't worry. We'll find ye."

If Kate Fairburn were the pacing type, she'd be pacing by now. But she wasn't. There seemed little sense in wearing a path in the carpet. It wasn't practical or reasonable and would simply do no good.

Then again, sitting and worrying on the couch wasn't very practical either, but she'd been doing that ever since Nick left. She'd jumped for the telephone every time it rang and leaped up each time she heard a sound at the door.

For heaven's sake, where was he?

Ever since he'd stormed out after their argument, she'd been worried sick. What if he was in an accident? What if some punk decided he didn't like Nick's good looks and took a shot at him? Oh, Lord, what if he changed his mind and decided he didn't want to be married anymore?

No, there was probably some simple explanation for his absence. He was just cooling off somewhere, thinking it over. Yes, that was it. That had to be it.

But . . . he'd never left before. Then again, she'd never asked him for a separation before, either.

A light tap came at the door. Kate sprang from the sofa and ran to answer it. *Nick?* Stumpy beat her to the door and Kate opened it, the expectant look on her face no doubt matching the one on the dog's.

Kate's shoulders slumped and her face fell when she recognized her best friend. "Sarah."

"Wow, thanks for that fantastic welcome," Sarah said and breezed past Kate. "You overwhelm me."

Kate closed the door. "Sorry." She watched dispiritedly as Sarah made a big fuss over Stumpy. "I'm not really in the mood for company right now."

"Nonsense," Sarah declared. "Now is exactly when you need company. You sounded so depressed when I called earlier that I knew something was wrong." She flopped down on the big sofa and ruffled the dog's fur with one hand as she patted the seat next to her with the other. "Come on, tell Auntie Sarah what's wrong."

Despite herself, Kate grinned. *Auntie Sarah?* Sarah looked less like an aunt than anyone she'd ever seen. She couldn't be more than thirty, and was the total opposite of Kate. Where Kate wore her medium-brown hair in a simple bob and favored tailored, classic clothes, Sarah's wild blond mane hung halfway down her back, and her clothing choices were . . . eclectic, to say the least.

Tonight she wore an electric blue broomstick skirt and a tightly fitted powder-blue vest without a blouse. Her shoes looked suspiciously like combat boots and she wore bright, shoulder-dusting earrings with a couple dozen jangling bracelets in all colors of the rainbow. On Sarah, it looked good.

Kate sat on the sofa and cradled her hands between her knees. She didn't know where to begin.

Sarah leaned forward, a concerned look in her eyes. "This isn't just PMS, is it?"

Kate shook her head.

"Then what's wrong? Is it Cory?"

"No, she's fine." Her darling daughter was asleep right now, oblivious to the disintegration of their small family.

"Nick?"

Kate nodded and her face crumpled as she fought back tears.

Sarah moved closer to put her arm around her. "Did he leave you?"

Kate sniffled. "Sort of."

"Oh, no. Why, honey?"

"Because I told him I wanted a separation," Kate wailed.

Sarah pulled back to give her a sardonic look and hand her a tissue. "You want to run that by me again? You're upset because you asked him to leave . . . and he did?"

Kate dabbed at her tears and twisted the tissue in her hands. "It wasn't like that."

"Oookay. Do you want to talk about it?"

Yes, she rather thought she did. Sarah was her only true friend, the first person she'd met when she came to New York. She'd known Sarah even longer than Nick. In fact, Sarah had introduced them and still lived in the apartment above them. "We had an argument," Kate explained.

"I gathered that," Sarah said dryly. "What about?"

"I came home tonight and, for the fifth time in a row, he'd forgotten to clean house and cook dinner."

"That's all?"

"No, that's just the last straw. Last week he forgot to enroll Cory in kindergarten for next month—then we got some nasty notices because he forgot to pay the bills."

"Ah, not so good."

"Right. He promised to be more responsible, but he obviously just said it to appease me. Honestly, I swear he's such a child sometimes."

"I thought that's why you married him—because of his childlike qualities."

Yes, that, and his devilish grin, his whimsical romanticism, and his boyish charm. "Well, that was part of it, but we're both adults now, with responsibilities and commitments. Only I'm the one doing all the work and he just stays home and plays with Cory and Stumpy. Don't you think I'd rather be doing that?"

"Of course," Sarah said soothingly.

"But instead, I'm off in the working world trying to make enough money to support us while Nick dithers at home."

"He hasn't sold any books in a while, has he?"

"No, but I don't care about that. The fact is, he doesn't even try anymore. He says he has writer's block, but I think it's just an excuse."

"I thought you both agreed to this arrangement. I mean, you like working as an accountant, don't you?" Sarah asked in a tone that plainly showed she didn't understand why.

"Yes, but—"

"And this gives Nick a chance to stay at home and do what he likes, plus giving Cory the benefit of having a parent at home."

"I know," Kate said in a small voice.

"So what's wrong? Is he neglecting Cory?"

"No, of course not."

"Money problems?"

"No, that's not it."

"Then it must be sex."

Kate gave Sarah a shocked look. Sometimes her friend's frankness was hard to take. "No!"

"Are you sure?" Sarah probed. "I know you. You wouldn't tell me if you were having sex problems anyway."

"I am *not* having sex problems. That's the only part of our marriage that's working just fine."

Sarah raised an eyebrow. "Then what's the problem?

The Trouble With Fairies

Hell, I'd settle for that kind of relationship myself."

"You would not. I know it's been a while since you had a date, but—"

"Eons, sweetie, it's been eons."

"Whatever. You have to admit even you wouldn't settle for a marriage where the only thing you had in common was sex."

Sarah pursed her lips and thought about it. "Maybe not. But right now, I'd be willing to try." She gave Kate a little shove. "Stop avoiding the issue. If sex isn't the problem, what is?"

Kate sighed. "I'm just tired of being the only adult in this relationship. You know, sometimes *I'd* like to take some time off, be a little crazy, do something a little wild, but I can't."

"What's stopping you?" Sarah asked bluntly.

"Well, someone has to be the grown-up. Someone has to make sure there's food on the table, that we have money to pay the bills, and savings for Cory's education. Nick doesn't worry about any of that, so I have to."

"And you want a separation because of that?"

"No, I don't want a separation."

"Huh?" The expression on Sarah's face was puzzled, to say the least.

"I only *said* I wanted one, to get Nick's attention."

"Whoa, talk about overkill."

"I know, but it was the only way to prove I was serious. I don't want to be separated from Nick—I just want him to change."

Sarah raised an eyebrow. "Big mistake."

"Why?"

"Without you changing, too? It's a little selfish, isn't it?"

That hurt. Kate shot Sarah a dirty look. "I thought you were my friend."

"I am."

"Friends are supposed to help you, not insult you."

17

"I thought I was helping—with the truth. Would you rather I patted you on the back and said, 'There, there'? That doesn't sound very helpful to me, but, hey, I can do that if you want."

"No, that's okay." She couldn't picture Sarah doing that anyway. Kate paused to let her friend's words sink in. "Do you really think I'm being selfish?"

"I don't know. That's for you to decide. But I do know it takes two to make a relationship work, and expecting the other person to do all the changing ain't gonna do it."

"Maybe you're right," Kate said, "but Nick didn't even try to understand."

"You mean he's giving up, just like that, and moving out? That doesn't sound like Nick."

"No, he didn't give up. In fact, he insisted I had to give him a month before I made up my mind for good."

"Well, that's good . . . isn't it?"

"Yes, but then he just . . . left, muttering something about getting some air. He's been gone over four hours and I'm so worried. What if he's hurt and in the hospital? What if he doesn't come back?"

Kate choked back a sob. What if he decided he didn't love her anymore?

"I don't think—" Sarah broke off at the sound of the door rattling. "Is that Nick?"

"It must be—no one else has a key." Kate leaped up and watched the door anxiously. He was taking an awfully long time to open it. Maybe it wasn't him?

Sarah got up with an impatient sigh and peered out the peephole. "It's Nick." She unbolted the door and jerked it open.

Nick peered up at her, still bent over with his key extended in midreach. He grinned up at Sarah, one lock of dark blond hair falling endearingly across his forehead. "Thanksh. I couldn't get it in." He straightened, wobbling unsteadily.

"Yeah, yeah." Sarah leaned away from Nick, fanning

her hand in front of her face. "Whoa, boy, what you been drinking?"

"Jus' a little bourbon," Nick said, slurring his words.

He was drunk? Kate stared at Nick in disbelief. To her knowledge, he'd never been drunk in his life. As she watched in shock, Sarah helped Nick through the doorway far enough so he could lean on the wall for support while Stumpy leaped for joy all around him.

Waggling her fingers, Sarah mouthed, "See you later," and closed the door behind her.

Coward.

"Hi," Nick said, trying to imitate Sarah's finger waggle and failing miserably. " 'Member me?"

"Of course I remember you," Kate said in a cold tone, though she didn't know this side of Nick at all—and wasn't sure she cared to. "Where have you been?"

"At a bar," he explained unnecessarily. "Nice little Irish plashe."

"You've been gone for hours," she said in an accusing tone. "I was worried sick. Why didn't you call?"

Nick staggered over to the couch, where he flopped and rubbed the ears of the ecstatic corgi. "Dint think you cared."

"Of course I care. I'm your wife."

"Yeah?" he asked with a cold look totally unlike him. "But for how long?"

That was unfair. She'd been prepared to forgive and forget, to give him the benefit of the doubt, but he'd come home soused to the gills. Well, if this was the way he was going to deal with the stress in their marriage, to hell with him.

She matched his cold look. "That depends on you, doesn't it?"

When he didn't say anything, she jerked open the linen closet and pulled out some bedclothes. She returned to the couch and dumped the load beside him. "Sleep here tonight. You won't be able to move anyway."

Nick peered up at her. "Fine. Stumpy an' me'll be jus' fine ri' here."

"Good." Kate slammed out of the room into the bedroom, blinking back tears. It was the first time Nick had ever slept on the couch—they'd always been able to work out their problems before now.

She put a hand over her mouth to muffle her sobs. Dear Lord, was this the end?

Chapter Two

Nick woke and immediately regretted it. His head pounded like a jackhammer, his stomach was doing loop-the-loops, and his mouth tasted like a fur factory. He groaned, trying to slip back into the blessed oblivion of sleep, but it was no use. Someone nearby was making too much noise. Way too much noise.

Nick tried to force his brain to function. Where was he and why did he feel so bad? The last thing he remembered was talking to a sympathetic bartender, downing copious quantities of bourbon, and having an intense conversation about . . . something.

Bourbon. Oh. That was what this was—a bourbon hangover. That explained part of it, but . . . where was he? This uncomfortable bunk sure didn't feel like his bed, and there was a heavy weight on his legs.

Nick opened his eyes just a slit and peered around, then shut them in relief. He was home. On the couch instead of his own bed, but still home.

The weight on his legs was Stumpy. Nick cracked his

eyelids open again and the dog whined, wagging his tail. "Good boy," Nick said, patting the dog. "You want out?"

Stumpy wagged even more and Nick wondered vaguely where Kate was and why she hadn't let the dog out yet. A crash came from the kitchen and he winced. Another question answered.

He sat up and moaned as his head spun and the churning in his stomach reversed to take a sickening new direction. Kate stomped into the living room and Nick flinched. Each beat of her heels on the hardwood floor pounded into his head like ten-penny nails, then quivered painfully along his nerve endings. He glanced up and opened his mouth, but she just ignored him and slammed out the door.

Nick groaned, wondering what he had done to deserve such foul treatment. Then, with a jolt, he remembered the reason why he had gone on this bender in the first place—and Kate's reaction to his being drunk.

Great, Fairburn, way to go—that's the way to win your wife back. He would have shaken his head in disgust, but each movement sent his churning stomach into overdrive. *Damn.* How was he going to live through the next few hours without moving his head?

Stumpy whined again and Nick almost whimpered along with him. The dog had to go out, and if Nick didn't let him, he knew the resulting smell would make things worse—much worse. Clutching his head, Nick rose to his feet and staggered to the kitchen to open the outside door.

Cory beamed at him above her bowl of cereal. "Morning, Daddy."

Nick slumped against the door and tried to force his lips to curve upward. No dice. As smiles went, it was a total failure.

"What's wrong, Daddy?"

"Daddy's not"—his stomach lurched as the sweet smell of Cory's cereal reached him—"feeling good."

The Trouble With Fairies

"I'm sorry, Daddy. You got the flu like I did?"

"Something like that," he muttered.

She beamed and jumped up from the table to give him a hug around his legs. "Then I'll take care of *you*."

Nick only nodded. In his condition, someone had to take care of him, and it was obvious that that someone wasn't going to be Kate.

Fear, guilt, and despair assailed him again as he railed at himself. Of all the dumb things to do, getting polluted after their argument had to be one of the dumbest. Well, there was one consolation: at least he hadn't done anything really stupid . . . or had he?

He hoped not, but for the life of him, he couldn't remember. Was that why he'd ended up on the couch?

Stumpy scratched at the back door, and Nick staggered over to let him in before closing his eyes and leaning against the wall.

The doorbell rang and he moaned, grabbing his throbbing head.

"I'll get it," Cory announced, and padded off to the door before Nick could stop her.

Nick then stumbled to the living room to find out why Cory was squealing in delight.

"Daddy, look—fairies!"

Nick usually encouraged his daughter's imagination, but today he wasn't up for their usual game of pretend, especially in front of strangers. He rounded the corner, then stood stock-still and stared in amazement at the four tiny creatures in the doorway. Stumpy halted beside him, whuffing in doggie surprise.

Oh, Lord. This was what he'd forgotten. "Uh, hi," he said, feeling distinctly like an actor in a Disney movie who'd forgotten his lines. The Gnomemobile ought to be along any minute.

"Well," the little old man said, "aren't ye goin' to invite us in?"

"Uh, sure, come on in," Nick said. *Get them in quickly before the neighbors see them.*

Before the neighbors see them? Hell, he ought to be more worried about the fact that *he* could see them.

He closed the door behind them and Cory clapped her hands. "Can I play with them?"

Nick winced at the sound. "No, they're not toys, they're . . ." What were they, again? He wanted to say fairies, but remembered they didn't like being called that for some reason.

"We're brownies," the old man told Cory. "Come to help ye with the house."

"Really? You're gonna stay?" Cory asked in delight.

The older brownie nodded.

"Now wait a minute," Nick said.

The old man speared him with a look. "Ye don't remember me, do ye?"

Like forgetting little men half a foot high was something he could do easily. "A little."

The man nodded wisely. "I thought as much. 'Twas the drink. We'll take care o' that." He turned to the other three. "Off with ye, lads, and fix the man up with our special mornin'-after juice."

The three popped out of existence like vanishing soap bubbles, and Nick could hear rummaging in the kitchen. "Uh, I don't think—"

"I know ye can't," the man said in a sympathetic tone. " 'Tis the drink, but never fear, you'll be all right in a moment."

The other three suddenly materialized, and a glass appeared on the coffee table in front of him. "Drink it," the older one said.

Nick stared at it doubtfully. He wasn't sure he wanted to drink something conjured up by brownies. "What's in it?"

"A bit o' this, a pinch o' that, and a smidgen o' magic."

"Daddy, can I have some?" Cory pleaded.

"No, honey." If Nick wouldn't drink it, he certainly wasn't going to let his daughter try it. He eyed Stumpy

The Trouble With Fairies

with a speculative expression, but the dog slunk away, his head lowered and his tail between his legs.

"Ye have a hangover, don't ye?" the little man asked.

"Yes." *Definitely.*

"The drink'll rid ye o' that. Go ahead, take a sip."

Nick shrugged. What did he have to lose? It couldn't make him feel any worse. He took a sip and grimaced. It was horrible stuff, but his head cleared a tiny bit.

"Go on, drink it all now."

Nick downed it as fast as possible. Like magic, his head cleared up and the effects of the bourbon vanished as if they had never been. With his newfound clarity came recall of everything that had happened at the bar last night.

It wasn't a dream. He really had agreed to take fairies—no, brownies—into his house. In sudden recollection, he pointed at the older brownie. "I remember you—you're Oat."

The little man scowled. "That's *Oak*, of the Wood family brownies. And these here are me grandsons."

The other three stepped forward. Nick had been concentrating so much on the older one that he hadn't paid much attention to the others. He did now.

Unlike the older brownie, the three younger ones were attired in tiny jeans and black T-shirts with the sleeves torn off, and sported the most unlikely hair colors he'd ever seen—pink, purple, and green.

Purple Hair stepped forward. "I'm Cy."

"I'm Sass," said the one with pink hair.

"I'm Syc," said the third.

"You're sick?" Nick repeated. What on earth was he supposed to do with an ill brownie?

"No, dude, my name's Syc. Short for Sycamore." He gestured at the others. "And these guys are Cypress and Sassafras."

Cy snickered. "Yeah. Sassy Sassafras."

Sass glared at him. "Take that back." He didn't wait for an answer, but lit into Cy. In an instant, Cy and

Sass were battling it out on the rug while Syc yelled encouragement.

"Oh, no, Daddy, make them stop," Cory cried.

"That's enough, lads," Oak yelled. "You're upsetting the wee lass."

The "lads" stopped instantly and gave Cory a sheepish look. "Sorry about that," Cy said and straightened his clothes, smoothing back his purple hair. "What's your name?"

"I'm Cory. And that's my dog, Stumpy, in the corner."

"Aye," Oak said in approval, "a fine fairy steed."

"Steed?" Nick repeated.

"Aye. Ye see how the area between his shoulders is shaped like a saddle? 'Tis just the right size for the wee folk. His kind, the corgi, have served me brethren as faithful steeds for centuries."

Nick glanced at Stumpy. The dog didn't seem thrilled at the thought of being taken for a ride.

"Hey, Pops," Cy burst out. "This is great."

"Hush, ye young jackanapes. Mind yer manners."

Nick stared at Cy in curiosity. "Why don't you have an accent?"

Cy looked mortally offended. "I'm as American as you are."

"Oh, sorry, I just thought, because Oak . . ."

"They were born here," Oak explained. "So they never knew the old country."

"I see." Nick stared doubtfully at the younger brownies, wondering about the influence of punk brownies on his young daughter. "I'm not sure—"

"Ah, don't mind them," Oak said, as if he could read Nick's mind. "All brownies love children, and they won't do anything to harm the lass."

"All right," Nick said in a dubious tone. "If you're sure."

"That I am." Oak coughed and gave him a meaningful look. "Ye know, me throat's a wee bit dry."

Oh, that's right. They worked for milk. Oak probably

The Trouble With Fairies

wanted some to seal the deal. But according to Patrick, Oak wouldn't come right out and ask for it.

Nick turned to his daughter, who was watching the brownies in wide-eyed fascination. "Cory, why don't you go into the kitchen and pour our guests a bowl of milk—like you do for your cereal?"

"Okay," Cory said and scampered off.

Oak looked satisfied. "Now, then, we'll just take a bit of inventory and see what ye need."

Cy and Sass disappeared, and Nick could hear them rummaging through drawers everywhere. Syc headed for the bedroom, and remembering Patrick's admonition, Nick called out, "The master bedroom's off-limits."

Syc stopped abruptly, then took off for another part of the house. Good—they kept their word. On this, anyway.

Cory emerged from the kitchen, carrying a full bowl. Very carefully, she set it down on the coffee table and beamed at Oak.

The brownie bowed to her with a courtly air, then took a sip of the milk. He spit it out immediately. "Fah. Ye call that milk? All the life's been squeezed out o' it. Why, 'tis nothin' more than cloudy water."

Uh-oh. Cory must've given them some of Kate's skim milk by mistake. "Is there any of the other milk left?" he asked Cory. "The kind you drink?"

"No, I ate it all for breakfast."

"Uh, sorry about that," Nick apologized to Oak. "I'll go to the store and get some more."

"Ye do that," Oak said, wiping the back of his hand across his mouth. "And while yer at it, ye'll need a few more things."

He gave a shrill whistle and Cy, Syc, and Sass reappeared in a flash. Syc handed him a pen and a pad of paper, and they dictated what cleaning supplies they'd need. Nick dutifully wrote everything down. "You'll need all this?"

"Aye. We can do without, but we'll do a much better job with them. The marvels of modern cleanin', you know."

"Okay," Nick said and stuck the note in his pocket. "We'll get them."

An hour later, he left the house with Cory, closing the door behind them with apprehension. Should he really leave those strange creatures alone in his house?

He shrugged. Patrick seemed to think it was all right, and Nick did remember reading that was what brownies did—they took care of houses. So why did it feel so weird?

He rolled his eyes. Dumb question. Like it was normal to have fairies living with you. Most people would have checked into a psychiatric ward by now. Nick was proud of himself for taking it as well as he had.

He buckled Cory in. "This is gonna be fun," she declared. "Won't Mommy be surprised?"

Nick froze. Yes, wouldn't she? "Uh, Cory, let's not mention the fairies to Mommy, okay?"

"Why not?"

"Well, not everyone can see them." According to Patrick, the only ones who could were those with whimsy in their souls—and Kate had lost her whimsy months ago. "I don't think Mommy can see them. If you talk about them, she might think you're fibbing."

"Oh." Cory thought about that for a while as they drove toward the grocery store. "Can I tell my friends?"

Just what he needed, a bunch of kindergartners telling their parents that Nick Fairburn had fairies living with him. "No, you can't tell anyone."

Cory pouted. "Not anyone?"

"Well, you can talk to me and Stumpy about it . . . and your dolls."

"I can?" Cory brightened and Nick sighed in relief. There was no telling how long she'd remember to be quiet, but maybe she'd keep it a secret for the time being, until he could find a way to explain it.

The Trouble With Fairies

They reached the store and Nick quickly gathered what he needed, adding a couple bouquets of flowers for Kate. After all, that was why he'd taken the brownies on in the first place—so he could win his wife back. In the chaos since their arrival, he'd almost forgotten.

When they got home, Nick walked in the house and smiled. In the short time they'd been gone, the brownies had done wonders—the house positively sparkled, even without the supplies he'd bought.

Stumpy came running up with Sass riding on his back. "Whoa, doggie," Sass yelled and pulled on the dog's collar. He grinned up at Nick, incongruously wearing a tiny cowboy hat on his pink hair. "Howdy, partner."

Stumpy halted and looked up at Nick with a pitiful expression. The poor thing looked harried. Feeling sorry for him, Nick crossed the room to open the door to the bedroom. Stumpy trotted inside and Sass slid off at the doorway as if he'd hit a glass wall.

"Hey, that's not fair," Sass yelled. "My turn's not over yet."

"It is now," Nick said, and was rewarded by a pathetically grateful look from Stumpy, who flopped down in the corner.

Sass left in a grumpy mood, and Nick looked around. The bedroom was still a mess, but the rest of the house looked great. Now all he had to do was bring in the groceries and order dinner from Kate's favorite gourmet restaurant.

He rubbed his hands together in satisfaction. Tonight Kate would have a clean house and a fabulous meal to come home to . . . and Nick would have a great start on wooing Kate back into his arms—where she belonged.

Kate shuffled her papers into neat stacks, then placed each one in its appropriate bin and adjusted the

29

stapler so it was parallel to the notepad and the telephone.

"Going home?" one of her coworkers asked.

"Yes," Kate said and picked up her briefcase. "No overtime for me tonight."

Instead, she needed the time to have it out with Nick. His irresponsibility was bad enough, but last night . . . that took the cake. She couldn't deal with a husband who took to the bottle just because they had an argument, and she was going to point that out to him in no uncertain terms. It was time for Nick Fairburn to grow up.

Decisively, Kate swept out of the office and into a cab, then brooded all the way home about what she'd say. This had been building over the past few months, ever since she'd gotten her promotion.

With the added time she now had to spend at the office, she really needed Nick to take more responsibility for their home and Cory—not to mention his own career. Kate had enough to worry about with trying to protect her rear end from the office back-stabbers while proving to her boss that he'd been right to promote her. She didn't need Nick to add to her aggravations.

Steeling her resolve, Kate opened the front door and stopped in astonishment. The living room positively gleamed. She inhaled. It smelled good, too. The flowers on the sideboard provided a light floral fragrance that gave the air a spring-fresh scent.

Some of her tension melted away. She hadn't realized it until this moment, but the sight of a dirty house made her feel defensive, as if she were somehow responsible for not keeping it immaculate. Even when she knew no one else cared, it bothered her. But this was wonderful.

"Mommy, Mommy," Cory cried and ran to meet her. "You're home."

Kate smiled and leaned down to hug her little girl.

The Trouble With Fairies

"My, don't you look pretty." She did, too, all dressed up in one of her best dresses, and her long blond hair as neat and shining as if Kate had brushed it. She was the spitting image of Nick.

"Daddy told me to—he said tonight's special."

"Did he now?" Kate murmured.

Nick appeared at the door to the dining room, looking positively gorgeous in dark slacks, a white pleated shirt, and a jaunty bow tie. "You're home early," he said.

Before she could reply, he snatched a flower from the bouquet with one deft motion and knelt gracefully before her. He offered her the red rose with a quirk of his eyebrows and a hesitant half smile. "I'm sorry," he whispered. "Can you forgive me?"

Cory giggled.

"Oh, Nick." He was hard to resist when he was in this mood—charming, romantic, and so very sweet. Kate took the rose and rubbed its soft petals against her cheek. "What am I going to do with you?"

His smile widened and he rose to his feet. "You're going to keep me . . . aren't you?"

She shrugged, hedging. She adored him when he was like this, but charm wouldn't solve their problems.

His smile turned rueful. "Come, let's eat dinner."

He tugged her into the dining room, where Kate paused to take in the elegant table. He'd covered it with their best tablecloth, china, and crystal, and left chafing dishes steaming on the table. "This is lovely."

Nick smiled and held her chair out for her, then did the same for Cory. "Thank you. I did it for you."

"I know you did, Nick, and I appreciate it." She had to give him credit—he really was trying.

He seated himself and plucked the cover from one of the dishes. "Soup?"

Kate inhaled in appreciation. Her favorite—a light cream of broccoli. "It smells wonderful."

Nick grinned. "And for the main course . . . Chateau-briand."

Good grief. He had gone all out to impress her. Maybe he really did want to keep their marriage alive. Touched, she allowed herself to be charmed.

Stumpy suddenly zoomed around the corner. He stopped, whining, and looked up at Nick with a pleading expression, then reared his head back and took off again.

"What's wrong with him?" Kate asked.

"Syc's on him," Cory said.

"What?"

"Oh, nothing," Nick said with a warning look at Cory. "She means we, uh, taught Stumpy how to, uh, sic 'em. He's been playing it all day."

"I see."

Cory pointed at the soup tureen and giggled.

"Stop that, Sass," Nick hissed at the tureen.

Kate usually didn't join in their games of pretend, but since Nick was trying so hard . . . "Is the china being cheeky?" Kate asked, grinning.

"Uh, yeah. It's been giving me trouble all day. You wouldn't believe how much *sass* I've had to put up with," he said with a meaningful glare at the tureen.

It must have responded appropriately in his little game, for Nick nodded and his expression turned serene once more.

Kate smiled. "I take it the dishes are suitably chastised now?"

"Uh, yeah, I think so."

"Well, what's next? Are the breadsticks going to jump up and do the cancan?"

"I wouldn't put it past them," Nick muttered. He glared at the breadsticks. "Don't even think it."

Kate chuckled. Nick was really getting into this. "So what's for dessert? Saucy strawberry shortcake?"

Nick swatted at an invisible fly. "No, but how about

some chewy, nutty brownies?" he gritted between his teeth.

"That sounds good."

"Or maybe we'll get a *cat*."

A cat? Puzzled, Kate wondered if she'd missed part of the conversation. "I don't really like cats—"

"Oh, no," Cory said in disappointment. "They're gone."

"Who's gone?" Kate said, bewildered.

"The brownies."

"Yes," Nick said in a rush. "We, uh, got hungry and uh, ate them all earlier."

Cory giggled. "No, we didn't."

"That's all right," Kate assured him. "With this much food, I won't want dessert anyway."

Nick sighed in relief. "Good."

The silliness out of the way, he seemed to relax and enjoy the meal as they chatted about her day and inconsequential things. The meal was delicious, and so was the wine Nick poured so solicitously for her. The only jarring note was Cory, who seemed a little cranky and overly imaginative tonight.

"It's been a hectic day," Nick explained. "She's just a little overexcited. Why don't I put her to bed and take care of the dishes while you take your wine into the living room?"

"All right." Kate smiled. It would be nice to relax for a change. She headed into the other room with her glass, and paused in appreciation. Somehow, Nick had managed to set a romantic mood with candlelight and soft music when she wasn't looking. She seated herself with a sigh and relaxed, letting her mind drift.

This was like the good old days, when Nick had first courted her. He'd been so attentive, caring, and romantic that she'd fallen for him right away—and he for her. Kate allowed herself to dwell on the good times, remembering how sweet he used to be and how much in love they once were.

After a little while, Nick joined her on the couch. She turned to him with a half smile. "When did it go wrong, Nick?"

Stumpy ran by, his nails clicking madly on the hardwood floor. Nick didn't seem to notice. "I don't know . . . a few months ago, maybe?"

Kate nodded. "That's when your writer's block started." Ever since then, he seemed preoccupied—high-strung and obsessed with overcoming it. But somehow no matter how hard he tried, it just seemed to get worse.

"Yeah, right after your promotion."

Kate looked at him in surprise. "Are you saying my promotion caused your writer's block?"

"No, I—"

Stumpy whizzed by again, head held high and a wild look in his eye. "What's the matter with that dog?" Kate asked. "What did you sic him on?"

"Nothing," Nick said, swatting at another invisible fly. "Uh, why don't we go into the bedroom and talk?"

She shot him an accusing look. "Seducing me is not the way to solve our problems."

"I'm not trying to seduce you," Nick protested, sweeping his hand across his knee with an impatient gesture. "I just think it'll be easier to . . . talk there."

"Can't we talk here?"

"Yes, but . . ." He paused to brush at his shoulder with an angry motion. "But I'll be more comfortable in there. Please?"

"Oh, all right," Kate agreed and rose from the couch. Maybe then he wouldn't be quite so distracted, so jittery.

He stopped at the bedroom door. "Hey, Stumpy. Come here, boy."

Kate paused outside the doorway and raised an eyebrow. "Is he going to be part of this conversation, too?"

"No, I, uh, just thought I'd give him a break."

"A break," Kate repeated flatly.

The Trouble With Fairies

"Yeah, the only time he'll . . . stop running is when I let him in the bedroom."

"Then by all means," Kate said in a sarcastic tone. Otherwise the dog might drive her crazy with his constantly clicking toenails.

Stumpy came trotting through the living room once again. He spotted the open bedroom door and his eyes brightened as he increased his speed and galloped toward it. Once he was through, he finally halted his mad dash and sagged with relief. He looked up at Nick with a weary wag of his tail, then went and collapsed in the corner with a sigh.

Strange dog. Kate looked up at Nick. "He must take after your side of the family."

Nick grinned. "No doubt. Shall we continue our talk?"

"Sure—if you think you can now."

"Yes, it's much better in here."

"Good." Kate glanced around. "Looks like you didn't get this far in your cleaning spree."

"Oh, yeah, I forgot. Sorry."

"No problem." She faced him with a smile. "The house looked really good tonight, Nick. And dinner was fabulous. Thanks for trying so hard."

He shrugged and drew her down to sit next to him on the bed. "Kate," he said with a serious expression, "I want to make this marriage work. I don't want a separation."

"I don't either," Kate admitted. "But things can't go on the way they have been. You're right. Everything's been different ever since my promotion. I see that now." She hesitated, then blurted out what was at the forefront of her mind. "Do you feel threatened by my success?"

"No," Nick said indignantly, pulling away a little. "Of course not. I'm proud of you. If this is what you want, then I'm all for it."

"Then what's the problem?"

"You've changed."

"Me?" It was just like Nick to turn the blame on her when he was the problem. "How have I changed?" she demanded.

Nick stroked her cheek with a regretful air. "You've turned into an accountant."

"I *am* an accountant."

"I know—at work. But at home, you used to be more than that. You used to be my wife, my pal, my best friend."

"I still am."

He shook his head. "No," he said in a voice filled with deep sadness. "You're still my wife, but I miss my friend."

She scowled at him. "Nonsense. I—"

"It's not nonsense," Nick said softly. "Tonight at dinner was the first time in months you've smiled or laughed." He smoothed her hair back from her face. "I've been so worried about you, I haven't been able to work."

He'd almost suckered her in, but he wasn't about to get away with blaming his problems on her. "So you think I'm the cause of your writer's block?"

"No, I didn't mean that. I just—"

"Never mind, Nick. Things haven't changed—*I* haven't changed. It's you. You can't handle me making more money than you. That's what's causing your writer's block; admit it."

His face turned stony. "No—it bothers you far more than it does me."

"Me? Don't be silly." She turned away and began to undress. "I'm going to bed."

"Honey, wait," Nick pleaded. "Let's talk this out."

She faced him with a glare. "I think we've done enough talking for one night. When you're ready to admit my promotion bothers you, then fine, we'll talk again. Until then, I'm not going to continue humoring this little fantasy of yours."

The Trouble With Fairies

Nick's mouth firmed into a thin line. She could tell he was angry, but there was also hurt in his eyes.

She couldn't let it sway her. "Good night, Nick," she repeated firmly.

He sighed and shook his head. "Yeah, whatever."

They undressed and crawled into their king-size bed, both staying firmly on their own sides, a vast chasm between them.

Stumpy sighed in the corner and Kate felt like echoing him as she blinked back tears. The evening had started out so well. What had gone wrong with it—and their marriage? And how could she possibly put it right?

Chapter Three

As soon as Kate left for work, Nick shouted, "All right, all brownies front and center."

Oak showed up right away. "What are ye yellin' about?"

"I need to talk to you and your grandsons. Get them here, now."

Though he didn't look pleased, Oak pierced the air with a shrill whistle. Syc and Sass appeared immediately, and Cy came riding in on Stumpy's back.

Arms akimbo, Nick glared down at them. "We need to get some things straight."

"Yeah?" Syc said. "Like what?"

"Like a few ground rules." Nick squatted down so he could stare them in the eye.

Cy snorted. "Rules. Yeah, right."

"I mean it," Nick said. "The reason I took you into my home was so I could win my wife back."

"So?" Sass was equally insolent.

"So I can't very well do that with you popping up like

38

The Trouble With Fairies

jack-in-the-boxes every time I turn around. Kate can't see you—"

"No kidding," Sass said with a roll of his eyes.

Nick ignored him. "It makes it difficult to carry on a conversation with you doing a jig on the soup tureen. Or you"—he turned to Syc—"riding my dog through the house like he's a canine hot rod."

Cy snickered.

"You're no better. I don't appreciate you mooning me and giving me the raspberry when I'm trying to talk to my wife."

"They're young yet," Oak protested. " 'Tis natural for lads to get up to a few hijinks."

"A few? They don't know when to stop."

The "lads" didn't look at all chastened. Oak scowled. "Well, you didn't have to threaten us with a"—he lowered his voice to a whisper—". . . a cat, did ye?"

"It was the only way I could get them to stop. Nothing else worked."

"Ye have a point."

Finally, a concession. While Nick was at it, he might as well give Stumpy a break, too. "And no more riding my dog. You're wearing him out."

"Hey, dude, no way," Syc protested. "That's the only fun we have around this house. Besides, he likes it."

"No, he doesn't."

Seeing the brownies' outraged expressions, Nick relented and gave Stumpy an apologetic look. "Okay, but only one ride a day for each of you—and only five minutes at a time."

The lads griped and complained, but Oak stopped them. "That sounds fair. Besides, ye need to be spendin' more time learnin' the brownie ways, not playin'."

They grumbled some more, but finally agreed to do as their grandfather said.

"Off with ye, then," Oak said. They disappeared and he turned back to Nick. "They're just a wee bit excited. 'Tisn't every day a brownie finds himself a home to take

39

care of—especially one as nice as this." He sighed heavily. "And one where the folk actually believe in ye. It'll be that hard to find homes to place them in, y'know."

So Nick wasn't expected to house them forever? *Good.*

Oak shook his head in resignation. "We were told America was the land of opportunity. For mortals, mayhap, but in all yer chasin' after this 'opportunity,' ye forgot the wee folk." He glared up at Nick with an indignant expression. "No wonder we're havin' problems findin' a place to live."

Despite himself, Nick felt compassion for the little guy. He grinned and tried to cheer Oak up. "Hey, you ought to take your story to Oprah. I bet you'll . . ."

His voice trailed off as he realized what he'd said. What a story concept—a family of brownies who came to America and couldn't find a place to live, so they went on a talk show to plead with viewers to believe in them.

"What's an Oprah?" Oak asked.

"Uh, never mind. Thanks, buddy. You've just given me a great idea for a book."

Oak wandered off as the ideas continued to spin and grow in Nick's mind. This was perfect—whimsical enough to appeal to children, yet current enough to please his editor, who wanted a nineties sort of children's story.

He'd use the brownies as inspiration. After all, Cory adored them—so would other children. And if he added a few curious cats, he had built-in villains. Nick grinned. Finally, his writer's block was broken.

Oak and the boys took care of Cory while Nick spent the morning fleshing out his idea. Finally, in the afternoon, he called his agent.

"Laurel, I've got an idea."

"Well, it's about time," she said with a smile in her voice. "Let's hear it."

He pitched it to her, then waited while she asked a

few questions. Finally, he could stand it no longer. "What do you think? Does it have a shot?"

"It's terrific. I just spoke to your editor yesterday and she was looking for something like this. How quickly can you get a proposal to me?"

"I-I don't know. I just came up with the idea today."

"Do it fast," she urged. "They're looking for a new concept for a series, maybe even some media tie-ins. That translates to big bucks. And if we're the first ones in . . ."

"Okay, I'll get it to you in, say, a month?"

"Make it three weeks. Just a few black-and-white sketches to give them an idea of the concept, plus the story. Can you do that?"

"That's pushing it, but I'll do my best." They said their good-byes and Nick hung up, elated. This was just what he needed to prove he was responsible—and if it paid well, all the better. Maybe then Kate wouldn't feel so guilty for earning more money than he did.

The subtle disapproval of her family and coworkers bothered her more than she'd admit. As for Nick, he didn't care what they thought. But the opinions of others were important to her. And, if they mattered to her, perforce they must matter to him if he wanted to win her back. And he did.

Later that night, after Cory went to bed and the brownies promised to leave him alone for an hour or so, he opened a bottle of champagne and poured two glasses. He handed one to Kate with a smile.

"Mmm, champagne. What's this for?" Kate asked. "Or are you just trying to spoil me?"

"You deserve spoiling. But in this case, I have a toast."

He raised his glass and she did the same, with a quizzical expression.

"To . . . the best damn story idea I ever had," Nick said.

Her eyes widened. "Oh, Nick. Did you break your writer's block?"

"Yes, finally."

They both took a celebratory sip; and Nick told her what his agent had said. "I'm going to have to work night and day for the next few weeks, but I think it's worth it, don't you?"

"Of course. Especially if you can sell it. I'm so happy for you." She set her glass down and gazed at him with a serious expression. "Nick, about our separation—"

He stopped her lips with two fingers. "Please, let's not talk about that." He hated the feeling of panic that swept through him every time he thought he might lose Kate, not to mention Cory and Stumpy. His family meant too much to him. "I still have a month—you promised."

"I know, but—"

"No, Kate, let me show you what I can do. I'll prove I can be responsible, that I have what it takes to make a name for myself—and take care of Cory and the house, too." *Or at least kill myself trying.*

"I know you have what it takes. I just want to make sure you know it, too."

Her tender smile was so irresistible, he couldn't help but kiss her. And wonder of wonders, she kissed him back. Her lips softened under his and the old thrill shot through him. She still cared. Well, at least physically she did.

He pulled away and gazed into her eyes with a smile. "Thanks for believing in me. You won't be sorry."

Kate caressed his cheek and lifted her mouth for another kiss. He obliged her with a quick peck, then leaped off the couch, full of energy and ideas. "I'd better get back to work."

"But, Nicky . . ." Kate drew back her outstretched hand, feeling a little foolish as he headed for his study. She'd thought the kiss was leading somewhere. In fact, she'd been trying to tell him she didn't think a separation would be necessary, but he wouldn't listen.

Finally, Nick had emerged from the funk he'd been in over the past few months. Not only was the house clean and dinner waiting for her when she got home, but he was actually writing again.

And, best of all, he'd shown he really did want to make their marriage work. Thank heavens. So much for Sarah's gloomy prediction—Kate's gamble had worked. But . . . just in case his changed attitude was only temporary, she'd let him wait out the full month.

Kate spent the next couple of hours puttering about the house, paying bills and catching up on correspondence. It was strange how quiet it was with Nick cloistered in his study. She was used to him being around all the time. In fact, she kind of missed him.

When it came time to go to bed, she didn't feel like a second straight night of lonely sleeping. Nick had been working hard all day and all night—he needed a break. She grinned. And she knew just how to give him one.

She rose and went to his study, pushing the door open a fraction. Sure enough, Nick was typing furiously.

While he worked at the computer, she crossed the room to gaze down at the pencil sketch on his drawing board. Four tiny men cavorted in Times Square, making faces at the large people who passed by, apparently oblivious to them. "Nick, this is cute."

He glanced up, distraction apparent on his face. "Huh?"

"This is cute," she repeated. "Is this the story your agent wants to see?"

"Yeah," he said, and continued typing. "Let me just get this idea down. . . ." When he finished a few moments later, he rose to glance over her shoulder. "It's just a preliminary sketch, but I think it's gonna be great."

"So, who are these little guys?"

Settling himself on the chair in front of the drawing board, he explained, "They're brownies. You know, the kind of fairies who keep your house clean and neat?"

"Oh. I see where you got your inspiration."

"You do?" he said with a startled expression.

"Yes, you've been cleaning so much the past couple of days, you probably wished you had some magical brownies to help you."

"Mmm . . . something like that."

"Tell me about the story," Kate urged.

"Well, it's about a homeless family of brownies. One older guy and his three grandsons."

"Good idea—it brings in the current issues your editor wants. Why are they homeless?"

"Because brownies will only live with those who believe in them and pay them in their expected currency—milk."

She chuckled. "Cheap wages. Wish we had a housekeeper who would work for nothing but milk."

"Uh, yeah, me too." He gestured at the sketch. "But no one in today's world believes in them, so they're forced to wander the streets of New York, hoping someone will see them."

"And do they find a home?"

"Of course. Finally, a man sees them and hears their plight. But his wife doesn't believe in them, so he won't take them in. Instead, he gets them on a talk show to ask those viewers who can see them to give them a home."

She hadn't heard such enthusiasm in his voice in a long time. "It sounds like a lot of fun. I'm sure it'll be a best-seller." She stroked the nape of his neck, where his soft hair was just starting to curl.

At her touch, Nick's expression turned to one of mingled surprise and pleasure. Smiling, Kate placed a kiss on his brow and he pulled her into his arms. She settled into his lap with a happy sigh, laying her head on his shoulder.

The Trouble With Fairies

He gave the best hugs—enfolding as much of his body around her as he could, gathering her close as if she were a precious object. She felt safe, protected, as if nothing had gone wrong and never would again.

"I'm glad you like it," Nick murmured.

He nuzzled the hollow of her neck, sending a frisson of anticipation tingling along her nerve endings. "Mmm, nice."

"You like that?" Nick said in a soft, seductive tone. "How about this?"

He cradled her head in his hands and teased her lips with his, then gently parted them to delve deep within. His kiss was tender, loving, with a hint of controlled passion. Snaking his hand up under her blouse, he stroked her breast through the thin silk of her bra. As always, his touch aroused her, making her body sing with desire, craving more.

"Even nicer," she said dreamily. She bent her head to place a kiss just behind his ear—in the exact spot she knew would turn him on.

He groaned. "You know what that does to me."

Kate grinned. "Yep."

Chuckling, Nick unfastened her bra. "Then you're just gonna have to pay the consequences."

He lifted her blouse and took one taut nipple into his mouth, kneading the other with his clever fingers.

"Yes," she said on a breath. It felt so good, so right, and it had been such a long time since she and Nick had felt this closeness, this love.

Abruptly, he pulled his head away and jerked her blouse down.

"What's wrong?" she asked, feeling bereft.

"Nothing. I just, uh . . . let's go to the bedroom." He appeared distracted as he fanned the air above her shoulder.

She smiled, feeling playful. "We don't *have* to use the bedroom, you know." She unbuttoned her top button and gave him a seductive look beneath her lashes. "It's been a long time since we made love anywhere else."

Nick stilled her hands. "I know, but . . . I'd feel more comfortable there."

"Why?" she asked, baffled. Usually Nick was the one to suggest their more adventurous activities.

"The brownies are watching," he blurted out.

Playing pretend, even now? Good grief. Didn't he know when to quit? "Okay, so we'll turn the drawing over."

He shook his head and rose to his feet, sliding her off his lap.

"No, what I mean is . . . this is where I work. The bedroom is where we play. Come on." He tugged her hand, pulling her toward the door.

Cory appeared in the doorway, looking grumpy. "Daddy?"

Exasperated at the delay, Kate asked, "What are you doing up, young lady?"

Rubbing one hand over her eyes, Cory said, "The brownies woke me up."

Kate caught Nick's eye and he shrugged. "I told her about the brownies."

"That's just a story, sweetie. You probably just dreamed about them. Brownies aren't real, you know."

Cory pouted. "Yes, they are." She turned to stare accusingly at Nick. "And you forgot their milk."

"Oh, jeez, you're right. I forgot. I'm sorry, honey. I'll do it right away."

Bobbing her head in satisfaction, Cory said, "Maybe now they'll let me sleep." She trotted back off to bed.

Nick headed toward the kitchen and Kate followed him. "What are you doing?"

Opening the refrigerator, he muttered, "Putting out the milk."

Irritation simmered under her skin. "Don't be silly. You don't need to do this."

He poured the milk into a bowl. "Yes, I do. I . . . promised Cory."

The Trouble With Fairies

Unbelievable. "You really shouldn't encourage her."

She followed him as he carried the bowl into the living room and placed it on the hearth. "Why not?" he asked. "Imagination is good for a child."

"Some, yes, but don't you think you're overdoing it?" Despite herself, her voice rose in annoyance.

"No. You encourage her belief in Santa Claus and the Easter Bunny. How is this different?"

"Because it's an accepted norm—everyone does it. But there aren't many people who believe they have little gnomes living in their house."

"Brownies," he corrected.

"Whatever. I don't want her repeating this to other people. They'll think she's odd."

His voice rose to match hers. "Odd? No, they'll think she's a normal, well-adjusted child with a delightful imagination. What's wrong with that?"

"It's not normal, Nick. You're the only one I know of who has these flights of fancy."

"What about Sarah?"

"Okay, Sarah, too. But I wouldn't exactly call her well adjusted or normal."

"So . . . you want our daughter to grow up and be just like you?" he shot back with a scowl. "Terrific."

Stung, she replied, "What's wrong with me?"

"You used to have whimsy in your soul. You used to join me in my 'flights of fancy.' You don't anymore. Instead, you've turned into a cold fish. A cold, rational fish."

After the way she'd responded in his arms tonight? "I'll give you cold," Kate snapped. "And I hope you like the *cold* comfort of a *cold* bed. Good night, Nick."

She stomped off to the bedroom and slammed the door behind her, glad she hadn't relented on the separation. Nick still had a lot of growing up to do.

Chapter Four

Nick's drawing blurred before him and he put his pencil down to rub his weary eyes. He'd been laboring on the book almost every waking moment for two weeks. Now, after four hours of work this morning, the preliminary sketches were about done. He needed only to finish the story proposal and it would be ready to go.

It was a good thing, too. He didn't think he could stand much more of this pace.

Syc popped in on top of the drawing board and peered down at the sketch. "You made me look like an idiot." He raised his voice. "Hey, guys."

Oh, no, not again.

Cy and Sass popped in behind him, with Oak following at a more leisurely pace.

"Look at this one," Syc said. "I look like a total nerd—and so do you."

They all stared down at the sketch and Oak said, "Well, now, I'll be thinking we look nice."

The Trouble With Fairies

"Nice," Cy scoffed. "He put suits on us. No self-respecting brownie would wear a suit."

"Yeah," Sass said. "Not if he wants to look cool. And look what he did to our hair!" Instead of the spiky punk look the three favored, Nick had given them conservative haircuts.

Nick rubbed his forehead, trying to massage away his burgeoning headache. "Sure brownies wear suits," he said in a weary tone. "If they want to make a good impression on national television."

Three young brownie voices rose in indignant squawks as they competed against one another to see who could talk the loudest. Nick tried to tune them out. It had been like this the entire two weeks. He had finally gotten them to agree to leave him and Cory alone when Kate was around, but that had unfortunately opened him up to relentless harassment when she wasn't.

All four constantly looked over his shoulder as he worked, making caustic comments or providing ridiculous suggestions for "improvement." Just one more week, Nick reminded himself. Seven more days and he could slow the pace, maybe escape from the house for a little while and even find a few moments to talk to his family.

Of course, there was one consolation. At least the little guys were keeping the house clean and taking one worry off his mind—plus they even fixed dinner while he was writing "their" story.

Their voices rose to a crescendo and Nick abruptly cut them off. "Whoa, there. How about a compromise? I'll take the jackets and ties off everyone but Oak, and tone down the hair only a little."

He quickly sketched in what he had in mind and the brownies regarded it with doubtful looks.

"I don't know," Cy said. "We still look like geeks."

"It ain't so bad," Syc said. "But why can't you leave us the way we are?"

"The world isn't quite ready for your sartorial brilliance," Nick drawled.

Sass regarded him with a jaundiced eye. "Was that a crack?"

"Daddy?" came a voice from the doorway.

Nick turned toward Cory in relief. "Yes, honey?"

"Will you play with me?"

"Not now. Daddy has lots of work to do." Work he'd get done a whole lot faster if he could get rid of these pesky brownies. He'd thought about "forgetting" to put out their milk, but the one time he really had forgotten, they'd harassed Cory. It looked like he was stuck with them for a while.

She pouted. "You never play with me anymore."

"I know, and I'm sorry, but I'm real busy right now. In a week or two I'll have time to play, okay?"

"I wanna play now."

Nick sighed. He knew he hadn't given Cory enough attention lately, and she was getting more and more belligerent about it. But she had plenty of playmates in the rowdy brownies. "Sass will play with you."

"But—"

The doorbell rang and Nick went to answer it, gladly leaving the complaints behind.

"Hi," Sarah said and breezed in. She looked like the dancer she was in her gauzy pink dress seemingly made up of a thousand fluttering scarves.

"Hi," Nick said. "Kate's at work."

Sarah dismissed that with a wave of her hand. "I know. I just spoke to her on the phone. I'm here to baby-sit."

"What?"

Sarah pierced him with a disapproving stare. "I told her I would meet her for lunch, but you're going in my place."

"But I have work to do."

"So what? Your marriage is almost on the rocks and

you can't take an hour or two to have lunch with your wife?"

"I'm trying to *save* my marriage."

"By ignoring your family?"

That was unfair. "By trying to sell this book. It's what Kate wants."

"Is it? Then why was she so upset when she called me?"

"I don't know." Nick raked a hand through his hair in exasperation. Who knew what women wanted? Certainly not him. "I don't think she knows what she wants. I can't do it all—clean house, cook dinner, take care of Cory, treat Kate like a queen, *and* write a blockbuster book all at the same time. Especially not when—" He broke off. Jeez, he'd almost slipped and mentioned the brownies.

"When what?"

"Never mind. I'm doing everything she asked me to in order to avoid this damn separation. What more does she want from me?"

"She wants your love."

"She's got that." She'd never lost it.

The look Sarah gave him was full of irritating superiority. "Tell *her* that, not me."

"I'm not sure she wants to hear it. We haven't been communicating very well lately."

"I know. That's why you're going to meet her for lunch in my place. I'll watch Cory."

It would be nice to get out of the house for a little while, and he certainly needed the break. Maybe Sarah was right. Maybe it would help. "All right," he said decisively. "It's a deal. Where do I meet her?"

She told him, concluding, "And you have to meet her at noon, so you'd better—" Sarah halted abruptly, staring behind Nick with an open mouth.

Syc came riding into the room on Stumpy with Cy and Sass running alongside them, whooping encouragement. Cory followed with a giggle.

Sarah's astonishment turned to delight. "Who are they?"

"Uh, Cory and Stumpy?"

"No, of course not, silly. I'm talking about the little guys. What are they, fairies?"

Nick could only stare at her, openmouthed.

Sass glared at her. "We're brownies." He did a double take. "You can see us?"

"Yes, of course. Can't everyone?"

"Nope," Syc said and jerked a thumb at Nick. "His wife can't."

Sarah turned questioningly to Nick.

"Only those with whimsy in their souls can see the little people. Kate can't." His hopes rose. "She wouldn't believe me if I told her. Maybe if you—"

"Not on your life. She already thinks you're loony. I don't want her thinking the same about me."

"Gee, thanks."

Ignoring his sarcasm, Sarah asked, "Why are they here?" She paused, staring in perplexity at Stumpy. "And riding your poor dog?"

"It's a long story." He checked his watch. "And I don't have time to explain. I'll let them do it."

He left the brownies talking to a wide-eyed Sarah and went to clean up. When he was ready, he said good-bye, but no one seemed to notice. They were too engrossed in their discussion.

Shrugging, Nick left to meet Kate. He'd been unsure of his welcome, and was happy to see she didn't kick him out right away. In fact, she seemed pleased he'd come in Sarah's place.

The waiter seated them and Nick smiled across the table at his wife, searching for a neutral topic. There weren't many of them lately. "You look great. I don't think I've seen that blouse before, have I?"

Kate beamed at him. "You really like it? Sarah made me buy it." She glanced down. "But I'm not sure it's really . . . me."

The Trouble With Fairies

It wasn't Kate's usual sturdy beige, brown, or navy blue, that was for sure. But this silky rust-colored blouse brightened her face, made her complexion glow and her hair look shiny.

In fact, she looked the picture of health. Unfortunately, he looked the picture of death . . . warmed over. Their estrangement must not be affecting her as much as it was him.

His lips twisted in a parody of a smile. "I like you this way—you look like you did when we first met." When she was smiling and happy, and hadn't yet bought into the whole accountant persona.

He used to love the way she blossomed around him, coming out of her reserved shell to join in his teasing or crazy stunts.

"Nick, I—"

"Well, hello, Kate," said a big, beefy man who stopped at their table.

"Hi, Stanley. Have you met my husband?" She introduced them, explaining that Stanley was one of her coworkers.

Stanley shook Nick's hand, saying, "So you're the writer. Wow, must be nice to sit at home all day and not have to punch the old time clock."

"I like it," Nick said. It wasn't worth explaining how much work it was. People rarely understood.

"Nick's been working hard," Kate said. "He's got a great idea for a book that's sure to be a best-seller."

"Really?" Stanley looked interested. "What kind of book?"

"A children's book," Nick explained.

If Stanley tried to keep the disdain from his expression, it didn't work. "Oh." He slapped Nick on the back. "Well, good luck with it, pal. Let me know if you ever write a real book."

Nick found it easier to let idiots like Stanley think what they wanted, but Kate leaped into the fray. "It *is*

53

a real book, and it has the potential to make lots of money."

"Yeah?" Stanley said doubtfully. "Well, uh, gotta go. See you."

Nick gave Kate a curious glance. "Are you ashamed of me?"

"No, no." She looked horrified. "Of course not."

"Then why were you so defensive?"

"I just didn't want him to think you were a . . ."

"A loser?"

"You're not a loser," Kate declared.

"I know that. You know that. And I don't care what Stanley thinks, or others like him." But obviously she did.

Her expression turned anxious, pleading. "Are you mad at me?"

"No," Nick said shortly. *Not mad, disappointed.* She seemed ashamed of what he did, no matter how much she protested otherwise. "Let's change the subject."

They ate lunch, chatting about Cory and their work, catching up on what they'd missed in each other's lives. When they finished, Nick paid the check and said, "Well, I guess I'd better get back to work if I'm going to get this proposal done."

"I guess. But I'm glad you got out for a couple of hours. You've been looking so haggard lately, and Cory and I never seem to see you anymore."

Irritation coursed through him. "And whose fault is that? I'm doing everything you asked. Isn't that what you wanted?"

"Yes, but not like this. It's making things worse, not better."

Her expression pleaded with him to understand, but Nick was sick and tired of people complaining when he was trying his damnedest to do everything they expected of him. Why couldn't she just lighten up? "Fine."

He dropped his napkin on the table and stood to

The Trouble With Fairies

glower down at her. "When you decide what you want me to do, tell me. Until then, I'll try to make this book a best-seller so you won't have to defend me to your friends anymore."

He left, fuming. *Maybe then she'll finally get off my back.*

Two hours later, Kate was engrossed in her work when the phone rang. She picked it up with a sigh. The way her day was going, it was most likely an irate client who wanted to yell at her about something.

"Kate? It's Sarah. How'd it go?"

It was worse than an irate client—it was her well-meaning but nosy friend. "Well, it was a nice idea, but it didn't work. The lunch started off a little rocky, then got better, but ended on a sour note."

"Yeah. Nick told me."

Kate absently picked up a paper clip and toyed with it. "He sure is touchy lately."

"I don't blame him."

Bending the clip, Kate said, "Gee, thanks. I love the way you support your friends."

"Hey, he's my friend, too. And I'd be touchy too if my spouse was ashamed of what I do."

"I'm *not* ashamed."

"Well, that's not how it came across to Nick—or me."

"Maybe that's how it looked," Kate conceded, "but that's not how I feel." She twisted the small metal piece more savagely.

"Are you sure?"

"Yes, of course." Kate thought about defending herself, but Sarah wasn't the one she needed to explain it to—Nick was. "What can I do? Everything I say just seems to make things worse."

"Take him to bed," Sarah suggested.

Kate should have known that would be Sarah's recommendation. "Sex doesn't solve everything, you know."

"No, but it can't hurt—and can be a lot of fun if you do it right." Sarah paused. "You do know how to do it right, don't you?"

Stung, Kate snapped, "Nick thinks so." By now, the original form of the paper clip was unrecognizable.

"That's what counts. So do it. Don't talk, don't piddle around the house, don't do anything but make love to each other."

Sarah had a point. Maybe they could recapture some of the wonder and fun that had made them fall in love in the first place. "Well, maybe. But it isn't easy getting Nick alone anymore."

"No problem. I'll take Cory for the night. Stumpy, too, so you'll be all alone." She paused for a beat. "But, uh, make sure you make love only in the bedroom."

What was this fixation people had with having sex only in a bed? "Why?"

"I can't explain, but I know he'll be a lot more comfortable there. Just trust me on this, okay? I have more experience in this kind of thing than you do."

That was true. "Okay," Kate said and smiled as she hung up. It would be nice to have Nick all to herself for a change.

When Kate arrived home, Sarah had already picked up Cory and Stumpy, and Nick was hard at work in his study.

She watched him for a few moments. He might be disheveled and harried-looking, but he was still her Nick. As handsome as the day they first met, Nick still had the power to make her melt with just a crooked smile or a mischievous twinkle of his eyes. Unfortunately, she'd seen them all too seldom lately.

Nick spoke to thin air, apparently arguing with himself. "No, it won't work."

"What won't work?" Kate asked.

Nick whipped around and stared at her in surprise. "Uh, I was just talking to, uh . . . you know how my characters talk to me?"

The Trouble With Fairies

"Yes." He'd explained it before, but she didn't understand. It must be a writer thing.

He glanced down at the board in annoyance. "Well, Sycamore doesn't like the clothes he's wearing in this drawing."

Kate came over to look down at the sketch. "I like it. Makes him look like a brownie with an attitude, but feeling a little insecure, deep down inside."

A slow grin spread across Nick's face and he glanced down at the board with a smug expression. "That's exactly the look I was going for."

"Good." She changed the subject while he was still in a good mood. "Nicky, can we talk?"

His expression turned wary. "So that's why Sarah took Cory for the night—so our daughter wouldn't hear us argue." He turned his back on her. "I'm sorry, but I'm just not up to it right now."

Was that all they did lately, argue? "No, that's not it," Kate protested. She touched his shoulder with a tentative movement, wishing they had their old closeness back. "I just want to be alone with you for a change."

He frowned down at the drawing board. "Then we'd better go to the bedroom."

Was he afraid the brownies were going to watch them again? Though she thought he was taking this characterization thing a bit too far, she let it slide. The bedroom was just right for her purposes anyway. She followed him into their room.

He sank down on the edge of the bed with a sigh. "This is much better."

He certainly looked more relaxed. She chuckled. "What is this? Sort of a free zone where your characters don't bother you?"

"You could say that. But I wouldn't need it if we had a cat."

"Huh?" What did that have to do with anything?

"Never mind." He rubbed his eyes. "What did you want to talk about?"

He looked tired, beat. Kate slipped off her jacket and shoes and knelt on the bed behind him to massage his shoulders.

"That feels good," Nick said. "Don't stop."

"We've spent too much time talking about our problems. I just want to talk about the good times we used to have."

The tension in his neck eased. Taking it as a sign that he was receptive, she rubbed his scalp with one hand and his neck with the other. "Remember when we first met?"

Nick chuckled. "Yeah. At one of Sarah's wild parties. You looked so scared, so out of place, I thought someone ought to rescue you."

"So you did." She paused to place a kiss on his cheek. "I fell in love with you that night, you know."

"Really? I didn't know that. It took me a little longer."

His quirky smile made her heart turn over in remembered affection. "I know. You thought I was boring."

"No—I thought you were out of my league. You were so classy, so . . . perfect. I'd never met anyone like you before."

"So when did you fall in love with me?"

He pulled her onto his lap and gave her one of his special hugs, placing a kiss on her nose. "The night you tried to seduce me."

"Oh." Kate felt her face heat in embarrassment. Naturally, that had been Sarah's idea, too. "But I was so bad at it."

Smoothing her hair away from her face, he said, "You were cute. You were trying so hard to be sexy in that harem outfit."

"That was Sarah's idea."

"I'm not surprised. I was flattered. You were cute and sexy, and so obviously scared out of your mind that I fell in love with you then."

"Hmm," she murmured as he kissed her softly on the mouth. "But it didn't work—you were too much of a gentleman. Remember the first time we did make love?"

"How could I forget? I thought you were going to panic and run screaming out of my apartment."

"But you made love to me anyway," Kate said with a grin.

His hold tightened. "Yes, after I calmed you down. As I remember it, you lost your fear after I . . . touched you." He suited action to words as he gently cupped her breast and kneaded it.

The old familiar yearning seeped through her. "Hmm, I'm beginning to see a pattern here. You're attracted to me most when I'm frightened." She laid down on the bed and pretended to swoon. "Nicky, I'm terrified."

Chuckling, he leaned over to unfasten her blouse and skirt. "Just the way I want you." He leered at her. "Let me ravish you, my pretty."

"No, no," she cried in mock protest as she helped him strip off her pantyhose. "Not that."

"Yes, yes," he said with a dramatic flourish. "Soon you'll be mine—all mine."

She giggled, but when he bent his mouth to her breast, the silliness was forgotten as desire sped through her, weakening her bones and leaving her aching for the feel of him.

Her urgency climbed as she helped him remove his clothes, their hands constantly seeking, stroking. When he finally lay naked beside her, Kate buried her fingers in the downy hair on his chest and sighed as he claimed her lips.

The familiar textures and taste of him took on a whole different aspect, heightened and sharpened by the poignant knowledge that, unless they worked things out, they might never be together this way again.

Her thoughts dissolved into mindless pleasure as he touched her in the way he did best, taking her over the edge to a shattering release. As she lay in his arms, she felt an urgent need to have him inside her, to join together in the most intimate fashion so they would be as one—whole and complete.

She rolled to her back and locked her legs around his waist, thrusting her hips upward to meet his urgency. They merged completely, Nick buried to the hilt in her welcoming body.

He gasped and an expression of exquisite satisfaction spread across his face as he held that position for one endless moment. Then, slowly, he withdrew and advanced, sliding in and out of her with excruciating slowness, holding her close as if she were his lifeline. As if he cherished her.

He'd never held her this close in their lovemaking before, or moved with this slow, intoxicating rhythm. The novelty of it, combined with the sweet friction of their embrace, lent an erotic and exotic air to their coupling. Her excitement increased in dizzying spirals until she hit the peak again and tumbled over it, convulsing around him.

As if her excitement fueled his, Nick's tempo became faster and faster until he cried out her name, shuddering as he emptied himself into her. Spent, he collapsed on top of her and rolled to his side, panting with exertion.

Savoring the way they'd caused each other to lose control, Kate kissed him softly. He exhaled with a sigh and fell asleep with a smile on his lips.

Kate watched him doze. If only it could be like this always—lost with love and lust in each other's arms. But she knew deep in her heart that they still had issues to iron out, problems to solve.

She snuggled up to Nick's warm, welcoming body. Tomorrow would be soon enough to worry about that.

Chapter Five

The three younger brownies played a bizarre game of tag around Nick's study. One would pop into existence next to another, whack him upside the head, then blink out. It made for a disconcerting morning as Nick tried to put the finishing touches on his proposal.

He did his best to ignore them, but it was difficult. Just like the rest of his week. After Kate seduced him, things had gone well for a while, but they'd avoided discussing their problems. Until they did so, nothing could be as it was.

He knew part of the problem was his—he'd been so wrapped up in this book that he hadn't had much time for his family, but that was only temporary. Once the push for this book was over—very soon, in fact—he could concentrate on them, and maybe things could get back to normal.

Sass appeared on Nick's drawing board, startling him. Syc and Cy materialized a moment later and delivered successive blows to the back of Sass's head,

61

sending him sprawling and sliding down the board. Nick snatched his sketch out of the way as Sass shrieked a curse and leaped for his brothers. The resulting free-for-all sounded like a combination catfight and barroom brawl.

As the table rumbled and bounced in the fracas, Cory entered the study, followed by Oak and Stumpy. Oak yelled at them to stop, the dog barked, and Cory began to cry. To top it all off, the telephone rang.

It was too much. "Enough," Nick bellowed.

Everyone froze. There was total silence except for the shrill demand of the telephone.

Nick took a deep breath and spoke in deliberate tones. "I'm going to answer this and you're going to be quiet so I can carry on a normal conversation. Understand?"

They all nodded. Even Stumpy seemed to loll his tongue in agreement.

"Good." Nick picked up the phone. "Hello?"

It was his agent, Laurel. "How's the book coming?" she asked in an excited tone.

He cast a wary eye at the rowdy crew, but they remained silent. Relieved, Nick said, "Pretty good. I'm just putting the finishing touches on it now."

"Terrific. Listen, your editor is going to a couple of conferences and will be gone for two weeks. We have to get your proposal to her today."

"Okay, I can get it to you—"

"No. Not enough time—she's leaving tomorrow. I set up a lunch for the three of us today at noon. You know that new Italian place near my office?"

"Yes, but noon is only an hour away. Don't you want to see the proposal before she does?"

"No, I trust you. Those preliminary sketches you faxed me looked fabulous—and the story is wonderful."

Nick glanced at Cory. He couldn't leave her alone. "I'll have to bring my daughter."

The Trouble With Fairies

"You can't bring a kid to a business meeting," Laurel protested. "How would it look?"

Damn. "Then I'll have to find a baby-sitter first."

"So do it. Your editor will be looking for new talent at these conferences. We want her to see your stuff first. Be there, Nick. It's important."

She was right—he couldn't miss this opportunity. "Okay, I will. But I might be late if I have problems finding a sitter."

"I'll cover for you. Just be there."

Nick hung up and stared down at Cory in dismay. What was he going to do? Sarah was out of town and he didn't know anyone else who could baby-sit on such short notice, except . . .

Kate. Maybe she could help.

He dialed her office and sighed in relief when she answered the phone. Quickly, he explained the situation and asked if she could take a couple hours off to watch Cory.

"I can't," she said.

"Why not?"

"I have an important meeting. I can't miss it."

Raking his fingers through his hair in exasperation, Nick said, "And I can't miss this lunch—it's vital to my career."

"Can't you do it tomorrow? I can watch Cory then."

"No—my editor's leaving this afternoon. It has to be today. Can't you change yours to tomorrow?"

"Not for anything less than an emergency. We've planned this for months and I have to make a presentation. If I back out now, it might jeopardize my career."

"It *might*? Hell, if I miss this lunch it *will* jeopardize mine. Can't you help me out? She's your daughter, too."

"I know that," Kate snapped. "But we have an agreement. It's your job to watch Cory during the day."

Damn it, he knew that, but this was an exception.

"And you just abdicate all responsibility for her, is that it?"

"No—I'm the one responsible for bringing home a paycheck, remember?"

"How can I forget? You remind me constantly."

She gasped. "That's unfair."

Ignoring her annoyance in the face of his own, Nick said, "If they buy my book, I'll bring a paycheck home, too. Isn't that what you wanted?"

"Sure, Nick." Sarcasm practically dripped from her voice. "That's all I want from you—money."

"Damn it, Kate, I need you."

"Well, I'm sorry, but you should have asked me earlier. I have other plans and they're very important."

"Forget it," Nick bit out. "Thanks for your support."

He slammed the receiver down and felt immediately contrite when he saw Cory's lower lip quivering. Gathering his daughter into his arms, he said, "I'm sorry, honey. I didn't mean to upset you."

She hugged him fiercely as Nick searched for a way out of this mess. "I guess I'll just have to take you with me." It would look totally unprofessional and probably blow his shot at the big time, but missing the meeting would be even worse.

Oak stepped forward and peered up at him with a sincere expression. "We'll watch her for ye."

Hope spiked, then took a nosedive. "Yeah, right. You and the tiny tyrant trio. They're too busy squabbling to watch anything."

For a change, they looked sheepish.

Oak gave them a stern look and said, "Not when it comes to the lass. They'll watch over her, never fear."

The threesome nodded and straightened their clothing, obviously trying to look respectable. It didn't work.

Nick regarded them thoughtfully. Then again, the only time they behaved was when they had Cory in their charge, but . . . could he really trust them? "I'm not sure—"

The Trouble With Fairies

"We watch her all day while ye work," Oak reminded him. "Surely ye can leave her alone with us for this small bit o' time."

Could he? He glanced down at Cory. "If I leave you with Oak, will you mind him like you do Sarah?"

"I always do, Daddy."

True, she did. And it would only be for a couple of hours. "All right, I'll do it." He stared sternly at Syc, Sass, and Cy. "But no tricks while I'm gone. And no horsing around. Got it?"

"Got it," they said in unison.

"Good." He paused. What if Kate called while he was gone and asked to speak to the baby-sitter? "Remember," he admonished Cory, "don't tell Mommy. She wouldn't understand."

Cory nodded solemnly, but Nick decided not to take any chances. He took the phone off the hook and checked his watch. He had just enough time to take a quick shower and throw on a suit and tie.

His hopes rose. This was going to work after all.

Kate stared at the receiver. *He hung up on me!*

She banged the phone down. Anger and righteous indignation kept her adrenaline surging for a good five minutes as she paced the office. How dare he treat her like this! What did he think she was—his personal slave?

She couldn't rush to his side at a moment's notice. She had responsibilities, but he'd obviously forgotten that. In fact, she doubted he knew the meaning of the word. That was what had started their problems in the first place.

And this had probably ended it.

She halted in dismay as realization struck. Dear Lord, they'd never had an argument this bad before. In fact, she'd never heard Nick so angry. This must have been very important to him . . . and she'd just blown him off.

She slumped into the chair, covering her face as the adrenaline faded, leaving a sick feeling in her stomach. No wonder he was angry. She would have been, too, if their positions were reversed.

Guilt warred with dread inside her. Nick seldom got mad, but when he did, he didn't forgive easily. Their marriage was doomed.

If only she could take it back. If only she could replay the last ten minutes and do it all over again, somehow finding a way to keep her temper.

Unfortunately, that was impossible. And even if she could, it wouldn't help—she still had to go to this meeting.

Do you? a small voice whispered inside her.

It sounded suspiciously like Sarah. *Sheesh*, even when she was out of town, Sarah still left something of herself behind.

"Of course I do," Kate said, arguing with the little voice.

You could tell the boss it's an emergency.

"But it's not."

Isn't it? Your marriage is going down the tubes. I'd call that an emergency.

Well, if you looked at it like that . . .

And remember, you've expected Nick to change and you haven't done a thing. It's time for you to give in for once.

Definitely Sarah's voice.

Damn it, the voice was right. What did Kate's pride matter if it made her lose the man she loved? Screw the job—her marriage was more important.

The tiny voice in the back of her mind cheered as Kate lost no time in putting her decision into action. She strode to the door and called to her secretary, "Tell Stanley I can't make the meeting—he'll have to make my presentation. I have a family emergency."

That done, she tried to call Nick but the line was busy. He was probably still trying to find a baby-sitter.

The Trouble With Fairies

Well, it would be quicker just to go home and surprise him. It would save time, too, so he wouldn't be late for his meeting.

She caught a cab and hurried home. When she entered the apartment, Stumpy and Cory ran to greet her.

"Mommy, you're home," Cory exclaimed and threw her arms around Kate's legs.

Kate smiled. If only Nick would greet her in the same way. "I came home to watch you for Daddy. Where is he?"

"He left."

Though disappointed she hadn't gotten home in time to offer her help, Kate was relieved he'd made it to the lunch. "Who's your baby-sitter?"

"The brownies." Cory slapped a hand over her mouth. "Oops, I wasn't s'posed to say that."

"That's right, that's just pretend. Where's your real sitter?"

No answer. Cory's face crumpled in distress.

"Never mind. I'll find out." Kate raised her voice. "Hello? Who's here?"

Silence. Kate trooped through the house, looking everywhere, but there was no sign of an adult. What was going on? Had they left? They must have—no one was here.

Damn it, whoever had left her five-year-old daughter alone was going to pay for this. Trying to hide her anger, she squatted down to stare into Cory's eyes. "Honey, what happened to the baby-sitter?"

"Nothin'."

Taking a different tack, Kate asked, "Was your baby-sitter a lady?"

Cory shook her head.

So it was a man. "Where did he go?"

"Nowhere."

"But I've searched everywhere and I can't find him. Where is he?"

Cory squirmed but didn't answer.

Suspecting the sitter had made her daughter promise not to tell, Kate said, "It's okay. You can tell Mommy." Giving Cory a stern look to impress the seriousness on her, Kate said, "Tell me the truth. Who's your baby-sitter?"

Cory's lower lip quivered. "Daddy said not to tell."

Apprehension stole through Kate. Surely Nick wouldn't . . . "He didn't mean not to tell me, did he?"

Cory just looked miserable.

I guess that's my answer. "Daddy's going to tell me as soon as he gets home, so you might as well tell me now." At Cory's continued silence, Kate turned angry. "Tell me now, young lady. Who's your baby-sitter?"

"The b-brow-ow-nies," Cory wailed.

"The brownies." Suspicion crystallized into certainty. "You mean Daddy left you here with only these imaginary brownies to watch you?"

"Yes, but—"

"Thank you," Kate said firmly. "You were right to tell me." She tried to keep her roiling anger from exploding, not wanting to frighten her daughter. Instead, Kate sent Cory off to play and waited for Nick to show up.

He finally did, an hour and a half later. Her anger had turned from fire to ice, but hadn't abated one whit.

When Nick came in the door, surprise and pleasure washed over his face, followed closely by apprehension when he saw her expression. "What are you doing home?" he asked lightly.

"I came to watch Cory," Kate said in clipped tones. "I got out of my meeting to help you."

"Thanks, I appreciate—"

"And what did I find? Cory, left here all alone."

"That's not true—"

He broke off as Cory ran into the room and threw her arms around him. "Daddy, you're home." Then in a loud whisper, she said, "I told Mommy about the brownies. I'm sorry."

The Trouble With Fairies

Nick patted her on the back. "It's okay, sweetie. Why don't you run along and play now?"

When Cory was out of the room, Kate said, "Getting rid of her again? I didn't realize you found our daughter such an inconvenience."

"I don't. But since you look ready to tear my head off, I thought I'd spare Cory the sight of blood."

"Very funny. And I suppose you thought it was a lark to leave her all alone—for three hours—while you gallivanted off to play big-shot author?"

"First of all, I've never gallivanted in my life. Second, it was only two hours, not three—"

"Like that makes it better?"

". . . and third, I did *not* leave her alone."

"Really? Then where's her baby-sitter?"

"They're—" He broke off and raked a hand through his hair. "Look, let's sit down and talk about this." He gestured toward the couch.

She did as he asked, sitting stiffly, arms folded. But if he thought making her sit was going to make her any less ticked off, he was sadly mistaken. "Answer the question, Nick. Where's her baby-sitter?"

He stared at her for a moment, obviously trying to make up a story that would appease her. "Look, this is going to be a little hard to believe, but I want you to keep an open mind. Can you do that?"

"Of course." She'd hear him out, but it had better be good.

"Okay, see . . . the brownies are real." He stared at her as if he hoped she would believe him but knew she wouldn't.

He was right. "Brownies," she repeated.

"Yes." His earnest look didn't waver.

"And you expect me to believe that?"

He sighed. "Not really, but I'd hoped. . . ." He rushed on. "Damn it, I'm not lying and I'm not making it up. There really are brownies living in our house. Where do you think I got the idea for the book?"

69

"From your overactive imagination."

"Not this time. They're real, all of them. Oak, Syca-more, Cypress, and Sassafras."

Exasperated, Kate said, "Listen to what you just said. We have a fairy named Sassafras living in our house? Come on."

"Yes, they're all named after trees and—" He broke off. "Never mind. The point is, they're real, only you can't see them."

"And you can?"

"Yes. Only people with whimsy in their souls can see them, believe in them. You don't."

"Well, it's obvious you have an excess of that. But it's awfully easy to say you're the only one who can see them."

"So can Cory—and Stumpy."

"Cory believes in Tinkerbell, too, and the dog doesn't exactly make a great character witness. Try again, Nick."

"Sarah can see them," he blurted out.

"Well, isn't it convenient that she's out of town so I can't ask her?"

"No, it's damned inconvenient, if you ask me." He turned a pleading look on her. "Kate, you gotta believe me. I'm not making this up. Have I ever lied to you?"

She stared at him for a moment. He hadn't, but there was always a first time. "Either you're lying, or you've lost it. Either way, it doesn't matter. You've made me lose all respect for you." And he'd avoided the issue long enough.

"I'm not—"

"Forget it, Nick." Kate rose to her feet. "You're not responsible enough to care for the dog, let alone our daughter. I want you out of here tonight. Forget the separation. I want a divorce."

Nick looked stunned. "But . . . I did what you

The Trouble With Fairies

wanted. I got the contract. They love the book."

"Good. Then I won't have to pay alimony." She turned to leave, tossing her final comment over her shoulder. "Tonight, Nick. I want you out tonight."

Chapter Six

Kate sank onto the couch with a sigh, promising her-self she'd get up and do the lunch dishes in a few minutes. Right now, she was too exhausted. How had Nick managed to do it all and still have energy left over at the end of the day?

She just wasn't used to it, that was all. It had only been five days since she'd kicked him out. Five endless days in which Nick's absence had left a painful, gaping void she was afraid would never disappear.

Never mind that. Everything would be fine just as soon as she found someone to care for her daughter. And it had better be soon because she couldn't take too many more days off work, let alone survive the stress of continually entertaining Cory, interviewing nannies, and cooking three meals a day.

The problem was finding someone she trusted. No way was her daughter going to be left alone again!

Unfortunately, no one had been able to satisfy either her or Cory with the right combination of responsibil-

The Trouble With Fairies

ity and playfulness. Except for the responsibility part, Nick had set a standard that was hard to beat.

The only bright spot was the house. It was a lot easier to keep clean than she'd expected, though she kept losing things only to have them show up in the strangest places. Like this morning when she'd found her panties in the freezer. She must be more stressed than she thought if she'd put them there. Or . . . was it some kind of Freudian thing?

Cory flopped down beside her and picked at the seat cushion. "Mommy, when's Daddy coming home?"

Her heart sank. Cory asked the same question at least ten times a day. "I told you, sweetie, he's not coming home anymore. He lives somewhere else now."

Her lower lip trembled. "But he hasn't come to see us. Doesn't he love us anymore?"

"He loves you, honey. I'm sure he'll come to see you soon."

Cory began to cry in big, gulping sobs that tore at Kate's heart. Kate cuddled her, crooning softly and wishing she could break down as well. When Cory finally fell silent, Kate wiped her tears away, asking, "All better now?"

Ignoring the question, Cory asked, "Will you play with me?"

Not again. "Honey, I'm a little tired." Cory had worn her out with her endless games. "Can't you play with your brownies?"

Kate shouldn't encourage this fantasy, but she hadn't had the heart to deprive Cory of both her father and her imaginary friends in one fell swoop. Besides, they'd caused so many problems, they might as well take their share of the load.

Cory shook her head. "They won't play when you're here. Daddy told them not to."

Nick again. "Maybe a little later—"

The doorbell rang, saving Kate from further excuses. Gratefully, she got up to answer it. It was Sarah, looking as if she'd just come from a dance audition in a baggy neon pink shirt over black tights.

Kate beamed at her. It was great to see an adult. "Come in."

Cory and Stumpy greeted Sarah with equal enthusiasm, and Sarah leaned down to whisper something in Cory's ear that had her nodding and running off to her bedroom with Stumpy.

They settled in on the couch and Kate asked, "What did you say to her?"

"Just that I wanted to talk to you alone . . . to see if I could persuade you to take Nick back."

"Damn it, Sarah, you had no right to give Cory false hopes like that. I'm not going to take Nick back. I can't."

"Wait a minute. When I left a week ago, you were almost ready to forget about the separation, but when I came back, you'd kicked Nick out and decided to file for divorce. What happened?" Her voice softened. "Do you feel up to telling me now?"

Why not? Maybe then Sarah would realize there was no possibility of a reconciliation. Kate related the whole sordid story, concluding, "I can't forgive him for leaving Cory alone. What if something had happened to her?"

A peculiar expression crossed Sarah's face. "Are you sure she was alone?"

"Of course I'm sure. Oh, Nick had some cock-and-bull story about the brownies watching her, but surely you don't expect me to believe that."

Surprisingly, Sarah was subdued. "The brownies."

"Yes." At Sarah's lack of response, Kate gave her the clincher. "He even said you could see them. Can you imagine that?"

The outrage Kate expected didn't materialize. Instead, with a sickly looking half smile, Sarah said, "I, uh . . ."

"What?"

The Trouble With Fairies

"I . . . *can* see them."

Her, too? "Come on, Sarah. You mean you believe in fairies?"

"Yes, these fairies. Or rather, brownies. I've seen them. Oak, Sycamore, the whole lot."

Relieved, Kate said, "Oh, you mean Nick's characters."

"No," Sarah insisted. "I mean real brownies. Little men, about half a foot high. I've seen them living in your house. I've talked to them."

"Did Nick put you up to this?" It was the only explanation Kate could come up with.

"No, it's the truth. I have seen them."

Was the whole world going mad? "Sarah, stop it. This isn't helping." In fact, it was beginning to tick her off. "Nick insists they're real, Cory leaves milk out for them every night, and now you're saying you talked to them. Come on."

"I'm telling the truth," Sarah insisted. She pointed to the bowl on the hearth. "There. The milk is gone in the morning, isn't it?"

"Yes, but what does that prove? Stumpy probably drank it."

"Okay, what about Stumpy?"

"What about him? He's been sticking real close to me lately." He probably missed Nick, too.

"That's because if he doesn't, the brownies ride him around the house like their own personal pony. Haven't you noticed him acting peculiar?"

"Yes, but what does that prove? Only that he's a strange dog, not that he's fairy-ridden."

Sarah furrowed her brow; then it cleared as she snapped her fingers. "Then explain the house."

"What about it?"

"It's clean, isn't it?"

"Yes, but—"

"How did it get that way?"

"It was clean when Nick left. It just hasn't gotten dirty since then."

Sarah arched an eyebrow. "It hasn't gotten dirty after five days with Cory and Stumpy around?"

That was a little peculiar, but . . . "What's your point?"

"The brownies are doing the work. That's why Nick brought them home. Haven't you noticed the house is cleaner than normal?"

Come to think of it, maybe it was. "Yes, but . . . you expect me to believe little people are doing this? Little people that everyone can see but me?"

"Not everyone. Just those with whimsy in their souls."

Tired of being accused of lacking something so frivolous, Kate snapped, "There must be another explanation."

"Like what?"

"Maybe . . . maybe Nick hired a housekeeper and didn't tell me—a *human* housekeeper."

"How could a housekeeper slip in and out of your house without your knowledge—without Stumpy barking—unless she's invisible, too?"

"Well, maybe it's Nick, trying to drive me crazy." She wouldn't put it past him.

"Yeah, right. You refuse to credit our word that brownies exist, but you believe in invisible housekeepers or an estranged husband who sneaks in at night just to scrub your floors?"

Put that way, it did sound ridiculous. "But you haven't given me any proof."

Sarah stood abruptly. "I'd have them demonstrate their magic, but I can't, because Nick made them promise not to show their faces around you."

Kate's hopes fell. Despite the outrageousness of the concept, she'd been hoping Sarah would find a way to convince her. Too bad she couldn't—or wouldn't—prove it. "Without proof, how can I believe you?"

The Trouble With Fairies

Sarah tossed her hair back with a disgusted expression. "Is it too much to hope you could maybe, like, take our word for it?" At Kate's continued silence, Sarah said, "I guess so. Well, I'll leave you alone to wallow in your misery. Call me if you ever come to your senses." She made a dramatic exit in the way only Sarah could.

Kate sighed. Terrific—that hadn't been very productive. She might as well get back to work and do those lunch dishes. She wandered into the kitchen and paused. There weren't any dishes in the sink. Shaking her head, she left, realizing she must have done them and forgotten about it.

Wait a minute. She hadn't forgotten—she distinctly remembered promising herself she'd do them later. So how did they get done? Surely not . . . brownies.

But what other explanation was there? Kate mentally ran over all the peculiar things that had happened in the past few weeks—Cory's insistence on the brownies' existence, Nick's distraction, Stumpy's exhaustion, the clean dishes, underwear in the ice box. . . .

If you accepted the existence of brownies in the house, it all made sense, but . . . how could she? Quickly, she tried to find some other explanation, some logical, rational reason behind the events, but none of them held up. And if the believable scenarios didn't work, then the only thing left was . . . the unbelievable.

No. It couldn't be true. Could it?

What she needed was more data. "Cory?" she called. When her daughter arrived, Kate settled her on her lap. "Tell me about these brownies."

It was hard to convince Cory that Kate really did want to know, but when she did, everything Cory said tracked with what Sarah and Nick had claimed about the fairy creatures.

Verbal corroboration was nice, she mused, but who was to say they hadn't practiced this story ahead of time? There was nothing like really seeing them herself. "Honey, will you ask the brownies to come, er, talk to me?"

"But they're not s'posed to."

"Tell them I said it's all right."

"Okay." Cory ran out of the room.

When she came back, Stumpy hid between Kate's legs and the couch and whined. Thoughtfully, Kate soothed the dog. Could he see something she couldn't? "Are they here?"

"Yes," Cory said. "Oak is on my knee and Syc, Sass, and Cy are sitting on the rug."

Kate glanced down at the rug. Nothing. "Well, uh, tell them I want to believe in them, but I need proof."

"They can hear you, Mommy."

"Oh, of course."

Cory listened for a moment, then said, "Oak said he's been trying to convince you."

"He has?"

"Yes. By cleaning the house and moving things around."

Moving things around? That would explain the underwear. "Then why isn't the bedroom clean?"

"He said 'cause Daddy put it off-limits." Cory paused. "What's off-limits mean?"

"It means they can't go in there." Suddenly struck, Kate realized Cory didn't know the word.

Is that a shimmer above Cory's knee? Kate shook her head. Her daughter was probably just repeating something Nick had said earlier. Kate blinked and the shimmer was gone.

Then again, it would explain why Nick kept dragging her into the bedroom to talk—and why he and Sarah insisted that was the only place to make love.

Sudden uneasiness assailed her at the thought of four little men watching her and Nick in bed. She shook her head. Ridiculous. She hadn't proven they existed yet.

"I'd like to believe in them," Kate said, "but what do

The Trouble With Fairies

I do? Clap my hands, like for Tinkerbell?"

Cory's mouth formed into an *O* of astonishment. "What is it?"

"You made Oak mad. He said he's not a flittery flying fairy."

Kate's eyebrows rose. Could Cory make *that* up? "Then what should I do?"

"He says you need wh-whimsy." Cory stumbled over the unfamiliar word.

That again. "So how do I get it?"

Cory turned her attention to the rug and giggled. "Syc says you hafta take off your clothes and boogie."

"Like hell I will." There was no way she was going to strip in front of four lecherous fairies. And she was definitely going to have words with them about the proper way to comport themselves in front of a five-year-old girl.

Suddenly, four small forms popped into view, one after the other. Kate gasped. Good Lord, they really *did* exist—and they looked just as Nick had sketched them.

It had to be a hallucination. She closed her eyes, but when she opened them again, the brownies were still there. In fact, she could even hear the older one, Oak, scolding his grandson. ". . . shouldn't say such things in front of the wee lass."

Kate didn't know whether to laugh in delight or check into the nearest funny farm. "You tell 'em, Oak."

He peered up at her, startled. "Eh?"

"See," one of the young ones said, "it worked. She can see us now."

"Ye can?"

Kate nodded and Cory clapped her hands.

"Well, it's about time, ye crazy mortal. I was about to despair of ye."

"Ah, heck," the one with purple hair said. "I hoped she was gonna strip."

Oak scowled down at them. "Off with ye, now. The missus and me have something to talk about."

Cory left to play with the other three, and the little old man scolded Kate at length, explaining what had really happened the day she thought Cory had been left alone. He concluded, looking smug, "I believe you've an apology to make."

Kate's eyebrows rose. What a bossy little man. "Yes, I suppose I do."

"Let's hear it, then."

Annoyed, she snapped, "Not to you—to Nick."

Oak harrumphed in annoyance, but Kate ignored him. Yes, she owed Nick an apology, but . . . would he accept it?

Nick felt awkward ringing the doorbell of his own home. He'd planned to stay away for a full week, wanting to avoid the pain of coming to a home that was no longer his and hoping Kate would come to her senses. But that idea had been shot down when she'd left a message asking him to come by tonight.

Unfortunately, the time she'd specified made it very clear that she hadn't relented yet. It was after Cory's bedtime, so he wouldn't even get to see their daughter.

Kate opened the door and gave him a tremulous smile. "Hi, Nick."

He merely nodded, not trusting himself to speak. She looked fabulous in a bright gold caftan that shimmered with her every movement. Seeing her looking so great just made him more miserable.

Stumpy ran to greet him, tail wagging madly. Grateful for the distraction, Nick leaned down to pet the faithful corgi.

"Come in," Kate said. "We need to talk."

Nick stepped inside reluctantly. He had a sinking feeling she wanted to talk property settlements and child support. He just hoped she wouldn't balk at visitation rights—he knew there wasn't a chance any court would award him custody of Cory once Kate told her story.

The Trouble With Fairies

He headed for the couch, but she stopped him. "Let's talk in the bedroom."

What the hell was going on here? Did she want to seduce better terms out of him? Well, it wasn't going to work—he wouldn't play that kind of game. "No, I think it's better we talk in here."

A peculiar expression crossed Kate's face. "It's just . . . I didn't want to have this discussion in front of the brownies."

That got his attention. "Are you trying to humor me?"

As if they'd heard their names called, the four little guys popped into existence. Kate jumped when Syc appeared on Nick's shoulder, swinging his legs.

"Sorry," she said with a nervous smile. "I'm still not used to them."

"You can really see them?" Nick asked in disbelief.

"Yeah," Sass said, "we done good, huh?"

Nick eyed him warily and removed Syc from his shoulder. "What do you mean?"

"We got you back here, didn't we?"

That remained to be seen. "How long have you been able to see them?" Nick asked Kate.

"Since yesterday."

Unsure what this meant, Nick just stared at her, waiting for the other shoe to drop.

She cast a significant glance around at the curious brownies. "Can we go to the bedroom now?"

"Sure." He didn't want their distraction any more than she did.

He followed her into the room, and Kate closed the door behind him, cutting off Cy's ribald comments. Nick glanced around curiously. The room looked . . . different. Clean and neat, it glowed with the light of a dozen sweet-smelling candles as soft romantic music filled the air. Kate's gold gown reflected the light, blazing like a welcoming beacon, making her beautiful and desirable.

81

If she was trying to show him what he was missing, it was working. Warily, he avoided the bed—avoided even looking at it—for fear of blowing everything.

Kate had no such compunction. She sat on the edge of it and looked up at him. "I-I've been doing a lot of thinking."

Her voice was soft, tentative. Had he imagined that thread of longing? He cleared his throat and attempted to keep the conversation neutral. "I, uh, imagine you did, after you learned the brownies were real."

"Yes, after you and Sarah insisted they were, and the brownies played a few tricks on me, I had to admit there was something to it. Either that, or we were all mad. It was the only logical explanation."

His eyebrows rose. Only Kate would come to believe in something as illogical as brownies by using logic to deduce them. But her initial disbelief still hurt. "Too bad you didn't figure that out earlier."

"I know, Nick. I'm sorry. But you must realize how bizarre it sounded—how unbelievable."

Maybe. "So now that you believe in them, everything's hunky-dory?" What was she getting at?

"No, of course not," Kate said. "But I spent all day yesterday and today thinking about where things went wrong. I think it all started with my promotion."

Nick tensed. Here it came again—the accusations.

Kate twisted her hands in her lap and stared earnestly at him. "I-I didn't really want the promotion."

"Then why the hell did you take it?"

She shrugged. "Partly because I thought I had to in order to keep my job. Partly because it's the expected thing to want to get ahead. And partly . . . partly because I wanted you to be proud of me."

Her soft-spoken admission sped straight to his heart. "Honey, I've always been proud of you, even before the promotion."

She blinked away sudden moisture in her eyes. "But not after. I felt like an outsider, coming home from work to see you and Cory and Stumpy all happy and carefree after a day of playing together. You didn't seem to need me."

Her face crumpled and Nick couldn't stand it any longer. He cuddled up next to her and gave her one of his world-class hugs. "We always needed you."

"For money, maybe," she said, sniffling.

"No, no. For much more than that. Don't you know our day wasn't complete—our family wasn't complete—until you came home and made it so?"

"Really?"

"Really. You were so exhausted you didn't have time for us anymore."

"Oh, Nick, I'm sorry."

"It wasn't entirely your fault. You were right. I did resent your promotion, but only because it took time away from me. I guess I was selfish."

"No—"

"Wait, hear me out. I tried to take more of the load by doing everything around the house, but I couldn't handle it. That's why I kept forgetting things—I'm not as organized as you are."

"Yeah, well, I'm not that organized either. I haven't coped very well these past few days. I don't know how you did it all by yourself." She covered Nick's hand with her own. "I'm sorry. Sorry about everything—that I neglected you, that I didn't believe you about the brownies, that I didn't realize how difficult it is to be a stay-at-home parent. I can see now how you could forget a few things."

"Even paying the bills?"

She looked sheepish. "Yes, I almost forgot them myself a couple of days ago. And with all that stress, no wonder you couldn't write."

"It wasn't just the stress. After these past few days apart, I've come to realize I need outside stimulation to write or my muse goes on strike."

"Oh. So I guess you can write better without us, huh?"

"No, that's not what I meant at all," he reassured her. "I just need to get out of the house more often instead of remaining cooped up like a surly bear."

She picked at the bedspread. "Nick, I've asked my boss to give me my old job back so I can spend more time with Cory." She gazed up at him. "And with you, too, if that's okay. Can . . . can we try again?"

Peace flooded his soul and he hugged her in glorious relief. "God, I hoped you'd say that. I love you. I don't know how I'd live without you."

"Me either," Kate whispered.

They kissed for a long, lingering moment; then Kate said, "With Cory starting kindergarten next week and me being home more, you'll have more time to write—and get away from the house if you need it."

Touched by her obvious desire to make amends, he said, "That's good, I'll need it. My publisher is excited about the book, and Disney is interested in acquiring the rights to do an animated full-length movie—and they want more adventures with the brownies."

Her eyes widened in pleased surprise. "Oh, Nick, that's wonderful. I'm so happy for you."

"But therein lies the problem—the brownies."

She sighed. "I know. They keep the house clean, but they drive me crazy. Syc, Sass, and Cy just have too much energy. They're too hard to handle, and to tell the truth, I'm getting tired of Oak's little sermons. Do we have to keep them?"

"Unfortunately, I don't know how to get rid of them short of finding them someplace else to live with someone who believes in them *and* wants them around."

"Hmm, that's not very likely, is it?"

He hesitated. "There's another way, but I'd hate to do that to them."

"What's that?"

"We could get a cat."

The Trouble With Fairies

"A cat? So that's—"

The doorbell rang and Kate smiled, then grabbed his hand. "Come on, I have a surprise for you."

"For me?"

"Yes, I asked Sarah to bring something by."

Nick followed her to the door, wondering what was going on. Inevitably, the four nosy brownies appeared as Stumpy came trotting up.

When Kate opened the door, Sarah said, "Surprise," holding up a tiny bundle of white fur. "This is for you."

She set the small creature down on the floor and it toddled toward Oak, a look of intense interest on its face.

"A cat," Oak screeched, throwing his arms protectively across his face. "Run for yer lives, lads!" He bolted out the door and dashed down the hall, the younger three running screaming behind him.

"Wait," Sarah called. "Don't leave." She chased after them, shouting, "You can stay with me. I hate cats."

Nick chuckled and closed the door. "You got me a kitten? I thought you hated cats."

"Well, you kept saying you wanted one, so I thought I'd give you one, as sort of an apology."

Nick chuckled as Stumpy licked the puzzled kitten's head in gratitude. "Now you know why."

A comical mixture of relief and remorse crossed her face. "But I feel bad—I didn't know it would terrify the brownies."

"They don't get any remorse from me, not after the way they pestered us."

"Do you think they'll be all right?"

"Sure. Sarah will take them in." He chuckled. "Only I don't know who to pity more—her or the brownies."

She laughed along with him, then wound her arms around his neck. "Hmm, I just realized something."

"What's that?"

Her hands roamed his back. "With Cory in bed, we have the rest of the house to ourselves now." Her eyes twinkled as she began to unfasten his shirt buttons. "What do you say we make love in the study . . . or the kitchen? Anywhere but the bedroom."

Nick enfolded her in his arms, vowing never to let her go again. "Anywhere you want," he murmured, and bent to claim the lips of his lover, his friend . . . his wife.

Whatever You Wish

Amy Elizabeth Saunders

To Betty

Chapter One

No matter what rude or insensitive remark is made to you, there is only one answer allowed in the receiving line at a wedding.

As maid of honor, Meredyth had to remind herself of this law at least two hundred times, hope that her smile didn't look too much like a grimace, and say, "Wasn't it lovely? We're so glad you could be here"— no matter how badly she wanted to bash somebody over the head with her hand-tied bouquet.

"Meredyth, when will it be *your* turn?"

"Wasn't it lovely? We're so glad you could be here."

"Well, Meredyth, it looks like your sister beat you to the finish line."

"Wasn't it lovely? We're so glad you could be here."

"And I thought the oldest sister always married first. . . ."

"You'd better get on it, Meredyth—your biological clock must be ticking. . . ."

"Are you still single, Meredyth?"

"Wasn't it lovely?" Meredyth repeated, through clenched teeth. "We're so glad you could be here."

"Why, Meredyth! Don't you look *darling*! Aren't you married *yet*?"

"Wasn't it lovely," she began to say, until she realized that she was speaking to her brother Mark, who was standing before her in a rumpled tuxedo, a devilish grin on his face.

She leaned in for a hug, and whispered, "I hate you. I hate this dress. I hate liver pâté and pastry swans with almond cream stuffed up their little swan butts. I hate bridal salons and photographers and little matchbooks with names written on them, and I *really* hate ice sculpture."

Mark laughed out loud, gave her shoulders a tight squeeze, and leaned back. "Feel better? Dad said almost exactly the same thing, only everything was prefaced by a *damn* and followed by a price tag." Mark stuck a toothpick between his teeth, narrowed his brows, and delivered a fair imitation of their father. "Damned ice swan. Two hundred and fifty. Damned flowers. Seven hundred and eighty nine. Damned fruity caterer. Four thousand and ten." He removed the toothpick. "And you should have heard him after he found out that the fifteen percent gratuity hadn't been added yet."

"Look out," Meredyth said quickly, "here comes the Wedding Nazi."

The wedding consultant, a very frosted and thin woman who had made her fortune encouraging starry-eyed brides to reduce their fathers' checkbooks, was coming swiftly toward them, wearing her corsage like a war medal.

"Maid of honor, Maid of honor," she chirped, clapping her hands quickly, "keep the line moving."

Meredyth and Mark rolled their eyes. "Wasn't it lovely?" Meredyth recited loudly. "We're so glad you could be here."

Whatever You Wish

Mark choked back a laugh, tugging at his tie. "By the way," he whispered, "you look ridiculous."

Meredyth gave him an insincere smile. "I know. Thanks, honey."

She did look ridiculous. She had come to the conclusion that bridesmaids dresses were designed only for the purpose of making brides look better, by contrast.

She was wearing an iridescent lavender gown that looked like the result of a collision between Glynda the Good Witch, Scarlett O'Hara, and a Christmas tree. Sequins, pearls, and crystals itched around the off-the-shoulder neckline and trailed down the long, tight sleeves. Silver ribbons cascaded from the floral garland on her head that was fastened to her straight hair with a hundred cruel hairpins, all of which seemed to be aimed directly at her brain.

She took some satisfaction in knowing that beneath her hoop skirt she was wearing her favorite jogging shoes, and her dyed-to-match high heels were hidden safely at home in her closet, where they could stay until hell froze over.

Ignoring receiving-line etiquette, Mark stood behind her, delivering whispered commentary as she greeted cousins and uncles and work associates and Melissa's former sorority sisters, all of whom seemed to be wearing engagement rings the size of golf balls.

The ordeal was almost over, and the herd of guests had dwindled to a mere trickle, when Mark leaned forward and whispered, "Who in the hell is *that*?"

"Who?" Meredyth looked up the line, where her sister Melissa stood in white-gowned splendor, her perfect little face glowing with joy and self-importance.

She didn't need to ask twice. The newly arrived guest was a sight. She was an older woman, probably in her sixties, wearing a feathered hat that would have done the queen mother proud, her short, plump body gowned in a caftan of brilliant silk, glowing with all the colors of a peacock's feathers.

She was greeting Melissa as if she knew her, and hugging their mother in a corsage-crushing grip.

"I don't have a clue," Meredyth murmured. "But I'm damned glad to see her."

"Why?"

"Because she looks like the last guest." Meredyth adjusted her floral wreath. "Let's go find the food. If I have to shake one more hand . . ."

"Meredyth! Mark!" their mother's voice interrupted.

"Too late," Mark murmured. "When E. F. Sherborne talks—"

"People listen," Meredyth finished. It was true. Eleanor Frances Sherborne had a way of giving orders that allowed for no argument, and Meredyth hurried to her mother as if she were still nine, instead of thirty.

"Look who's here!" their mother said. "After all these years." She gestured to the woman in the blue feathered hat. "It's Elva! Your godmother, Meredyth."

"I missed the ceremony," the old woman informed them. "My plane was late getting in." She had a soft, pleasant English accent.

"It was lovely," Meredyth told her. "We're so glad you could be here."

The old woman's eyebrows rose, and a dimpled smile creased the plump wrinkles of her face. "How lovely of you to say so." There was a hint of mockery in the voice, as if she somehow knew how often Meredyth had repeated the greeting.

"Have you come to take her back?" Mark asked. "We've been telling her you would."

It was a joke Meredyth had heard a thousand times. Elva had lived next door to her parents for years, and after finding out that bearing children didn't seem to be in their cards, she had arranged, with the help of an adoption agency in her native England, to have two-year-old Meredyth sent to them.

Whatever You Wish

Only weeks after having adopted Meredyth, Eleanor found herself pregnant with Mark, followed two years later by Melissa.

Aside from the fact that she towered like an Amazon over her petite mother and sister, and that she was the only blonde in the family, Meredyth had never really been bothered by the fact that she was adopted. She was practical by nature, not given to whining about problems that didn't exist, and who her natural parents might have been interested her only mildly.

"So you're Elva," she said. "It's good to finally meet you."

Elva had moved away shortly after Meredyth's adoption. Meredyth's only contact with her godmother had been sporadic letters and gifts—odd gifts. Museum-reproduction jewelry from France, cowrie-shell necklaces from Africa, a mummified alligator head from Louisiana, strange perfumes from Egypt . . . all, her mother pointed out, highly unsuitable for a child. Meredyth had loved them.

The old woman took Meredyth's hand in her own, which was small and plump and covered with glittering rings. "How you've grown. And how lovely you are, even in that dreadful gown. Let's go into dinner, shall we? I'll sit with you."

Melissa, whose face had gone into deep-freeze mode at the "dreadful gown" remark, turned to her mother. "But . . . but . . ."

"The seating arrangements," Eleanor said helplessly. "We didn't get your R.S.V.P., and the seating arrangements—"

"I despise seating arrangements," the old woman said cheerfully, in her well-bred British accent. "Don't you, Meredyth?" She gave Melissa a pat on the cheek with her ringed fingers. "I do hope, Melissa dear, that you aren't one of those horrid brides who become dictators as soon as the guest list is written. It's so unbecoming."

Melissa was speechless, and Mark, who had already been forced to cut his hair and shave off his beard at Melissa's demand, laughed out loud.

"Come along, Meredyth." The old woman seized Meredyth's arm with surprising strength, and smiled up at her with eyes that were an amazing shade of blue. "How clever you are," she added, "to wear runners instead of those silly high heels. And almost nobody would notice, would they?"

Meredyth cringed as her mother and Melissa stared at her feet, their faces twin masks of outrage. She could only offer them a weak smile as she followed her godmother to the hotel banquet room, where the old woman tidily threw away every place card on the table she chose.

"Now," she said, "send that nice brother of yours to fetch me some champagne, and we can have a chat. Who is that terrible woman glowering at me?"

Meredyth looked, and laughed out loud. "That's the Wedding Nazi," she said, happy for the first time that day, "and I've got a feeling that the allies are moving in on her territory."

Chapter Two

Elva was wonderful. She had lived all over the world, and was presently living in a little village in England that she described as "so picturesque it's almost sickening." She asked Meredyth to come visit, if ever she had time off from work. She asked Meredyth questions about her family, and her job, and growing up with the Sherbornes.

"An assistant kindergarten teacher. That's perfect. You must like children. Just like Lady Spencer. Are you waiting for your handsome prince to propose?"

"I hope not," Meredyth replied, not bothering to temper her bluntness with courtesy. "I tell you, after a year of Melissa's wedding bells ringing in my ears, I've grown to really despise the whole wedding scene."

Elva nodded, the peacock blue plumes of her hat waving.

As if on cue, the wedding consultant hurried by. "Maid of honor," she whispered, bending down by Meredyth's ear, "you really should be seated at the head table with the rest of the wedding party. One of your duties is to be ready to fetch and carry anything the bride might need."

"Look," Meredyth said, lowering her glass of champagne. "I'm busy. I'm entertaining an old friend of the family. If Melissa needs anything fetched or carried, let Dwayne do it. He married her; he might as well get used to it."

The consultant blinked her mascaraed lashes with an expression of disbelief, and then hurried away to bully the waiters.

"What a tyrant," Elva remarked. "I hope that she's not too well paid."

"She is. Just ask my dad." Meredyth looked across the crowded hotel ballroom, and caught sight of her father hiding behind a flower arrangement with Mark. Probably talking baseball, wondering if the Mariners could afford to keep Griffey another season. She waved, wishing she were part of the conversation.

The Wedding Nazi was making her away across the stage where the band was set up, and gesturing to the photographer to get ready.

"Good evening, and welcome!" she chirped. "It's time to begin the dancing, so if Melissa and Dwayne will take the floor, we can all enjoy watching as they dance their first dance together as man and wife. I'm sure that this dance will be the first of many, and may their life together be as wonderful as this beautiful day."

"I think I'm going to get sick," Meredyth said.

"It is a little much," agreed Elva.

"First," the wedding consultant announced, "the bride and groom will dance. Then the father of the bride cuts in to dance with his daughter, while the groom dances with his new mother-in-law. Then the bride dances with the father of the groom, while the groom dances with his mother. After that the bride will dance with the best man while the groom dances with the maid of honor."

Whatever You Wish

"After that," Meredyth said, "the janitor will dance with the parking attendant, and the sixth cousin twice removed will dance with the assistant caterer."

"It does seem a little ridiculous," Elva agreed. "But just look. Look at Melissa's face. Isn't that beautiful?"

Meredyth looked at her sister, who was circling the dance floor in her new husband's arms. Melissa's face, which had lately been contorted·in the expression Mark called "the Demon Bride from Hell," was soft and radiant, and she had tears in her eyes as she gazed with complete adoration at her new husband. And Dwayne, whom Meredyth and Mark privately called "the Spineless One," was gazing back at Melissa as if she were the most precious creature in the universe.

The flowers, the violins, the young couple gazing adoringly into each other's eyes . . . Meredyth felt her own eyes tearing up. They were beautiful. Somewhere, deep in her heart, she felt a twist of longing.

"Did you really mean what you said earlier?" Elva asked gently, leaning closer to Meredyth. She wore a strange perfume, flowery and mysterious. "You really have no interest in meeting the man of your dreams?"

"It's not real life," Meredyth said. Dating was real life. Boring, disastrous dates, watching Mr. You-Might-Do turn into Mr. Wrong—that was real life. Mr. Right was not part of Meredyth's realistic life plan. Mr. Right was the myth: the nice, good-looking, secure man. Oh, he existed, all right, but only when coupled with a twenty-three-year-old girl with perfect skin and a size five dress.

"My name," Meredyth said to Elva, "is Meredyth. I don't know if you've noticed this, Elva, but Meredyths don't get married. Melissas do, and Ambers and Courtneys and Lisas up the ying-yang, but not Meredyths. Meredyths don't wear makeup. They don't have glamour jobs. They drive old Plymouths and are ten pounds overweight and have split ends on their ponytails and never get their nails done. Meredyths have mean

97

mouths and are bridesmaids. Not brides."

"Good heavens," said Elva. "What a strange and pessimistic view of life you have. I think Meredyth is a lovely name. Do you really believe all that?"

"I know it," Meredyth replied.

Elva leaned in closer, and twisted a ring around her plump, wrinkled finger. It looked like a real emerald, set in a pattern of gold vines. "What if," she whispered, "what if I were not an ordinary godmother, Meredyth? What if I were a fairy godmother, and could grant you three wishes? What would you say then? Would you wish for a handsome prince, to love you forever?"

Meredyth gave the old woman a sharp look. She really was a little off the wall, with her feathers and rainbow-hued New Age gown.

"Sure. Sure, I would. I'd wish for Prince Charming. No, why be greedy? An ordinary knight would do, shining armor or otherwise. Castle in the country, the whole damned happily-ever-after schtick. Why not?"

Meredyth stood up, her rumpled taffeta gown sparkling around her.

"Be careful what you wish for, dear," Elva cautioned her, dimpling. "Oh, I almost forgot. . . ." She offered Meredyth a small package. "I brought you a present. I thought you probably deserved one. It's been a while."

Meredyth hesitated, then accepted the small box. For a moment, she felt like she had when she was a child, and came home to find a brown-wrapped parcel in the mail from Elva, bearing exotic postmarks.

"I never thanked you properly," she said, "for all the presents. It was one of the few things that Melissa ever envied me for. It made me feel . . . special. Like being adopted was a privilege. Thank you. And I'm sorry I was sarcastic with you, just now. I have a mean mouth."

"Were you being sarcastic? Oh, dear."

Meredyth opened the box and withdrew an exquisite necklace. It was silver, a fairy perched on a crescent moon, wearing a flowing gown. Her wings were set with pale pink stones; a round blue one sparkled above the moon, where it was suspended from a slender chain. The fairy held a faceted crystal in her arms, sparkling in magical, iridescent colors.

"Appropriate," Elva remarked, "from your fairy godmother. Don't you think? Here, let me put it on you."

Meredyth bent her head and let Elva fasten the clasp around her neck. The silver felt cool and soothing next to her skin. She touched it softly, and it seemed to tingle beneath her fingertips.

"Thank you," she said, and would have said more, but the Wedding Nazi appeared at her side. "Maid of honor," she chirped, "it's time for your dance. Hurry, hurry."

Maid of honor. Meredyth wondered if she addressed everyone in the bridal party by their titles, or if she just couldn't remember names. "Right away, Wedding Consultant," she answered, thinking turnabout was fair play.

Looking over her shoulder, she saw Elva wink at her, mirth sparkling in her ageless blue eyes.

"Meredyth!" Eleanor Sherborne caught her daughter's arm. "Darling, I left Melissa's overnight bag in my car. Would you be sweet and ask Mark to get it for her?"

"I'll do it."

"But Melissa's getting ready to throw her bouquet. You don't want to miss that, do you?"

"Mom, I'll get the bag."

Eleanor sighed. "Really, Meredyth, you could at least pretend to enjoy it. After all, it's—"

"Melissa's big day. I know, Mom. But I really hate that catch-the-bouquet business. If I miss it, I miss it. I'll go get the bag."

"Meredyth, you aren't going to sneak a cigarette, are you?"

Bu: Meredyth was already gone, hurrying through the crowd of guests, trying not to trample her hoop skirts as she went.

"Maid of honor!"

"Lord help me," Meredyth muttered as the wedding consultant hurried toward her, her arms full of boxes.

"Good timing," the woman sang out, her smile bright and strained. "Now, our bride and groom will be getting ready to go in about a half an hour, so here are your butterflies—"

"My what?"

"Butterflies," the woman repeated, a touch of impatience in her voice. "When our bride and groom leave, the wedding party will assemble on the steps, and each of you will release one of these boxes of live butterflies."

Meredyth took the box, peering into the tiny holes. "There are butterflies in here?"

"So much prettier than rice, and less expensive than live doves. And much more sophisticated than bubbles."

Meredyth held the box to her ear, and imagined she heard the flutter of a hundred wings, trapped in the darkness.

"On the front steps, one half hour," the Wedding Nazi ordered.

Meredyth resisted the urge to salute. She went out into the cool air of the June night, where the parking attendant quickly located her mother's car, and handed Meredyth Melissa's overnight bag.

Meredyth took her time going back, strolling through the manicured hotel gardens. The ballroom windows were bright, and she watched the reception for a few minutes, glad to be away from the noise and confusion.

Melissa, in her pale pink going-away suit, was getting ready to throw her bouquet to a crowd of eager, bright-faced young women. Funny, they all had the same look on their faces—determined, almost fervent, as they crowded for position. Almost as if they believed in the magical properties of the flowers carried by the bride.

The cool spring breeze whispered against Meredyth's cheek, lifting the silver ribbons that hung over her dishwater hair. She held the shoe box–sized container of butterflies tightly against her chest, and had the fey idea that she could feel them flutter against her.

Everything seemed a little strange, almost surreal—the dark, perfect gardens, the tall windows lit like a movie screen, the silence of the hotel garden compared to the obvious noise and laughter within.

The fairy necklace hung heavy against her bare throat. She felt a little light-headed.

"I do need a cigarette," she said aloud. She shifted Melissa's overnight bag over her shoulder, tucked her bouquet under her arm, and retreated farther back into the gardens, safe from her mother's disapproving eyes.

Her feet made crunching noises on the gravel path as she hurried along, and, distantly, she could hear the sound of traffic. The gardens looked lush and perfect in the moonlight.

She stepped off the path onto a perfect circle of lawn, and leaned gratefully against a sturdy tree. Oak. Funny, you didn't see that much oak in Seattle. Most landscaping was done in what Meredyth called "Northwestus Suburbus"—pine, cedar, and juniper, with rhododendrons added for interest and color.

But somebody had bothered planting this small, circular garden with oak, and holly, and small, fragrant borders of herbs that she couldn't recognize in the darkness.

She reached for her purse.

"Damn." It was back in the hotel, her cigarettes and matches zipped securely in the side pocket. She sat on the grass with a heavy thump, beyond caring what happened to the sparkling lavender. It was, after all, not something she would wear again. It was destined to join the seven other bridesmaids dresses in her closet, none of which could be worn again, even if she had the sudden desire to clothe herself in pumpkin chiffon or teal taffeta.

The full moon was high in the dark sky, almost directly overhead. Meredyth stared at it, fascinated by the luminous brilliance. Somehow it made everything seem enchanted.

Perhaps she'd had too much champagne. She felt strange, almost drugged, and at the same time, every detail of the night seemed startlingly vivid. Each blade of grass seemed to shine; the fragrance of the herbs and leaves around her were sharp and distinct. Her skirts sparkled, radiant in the moonlight, and the flowers of her bouquet were brilliant, the scent of the roses and orchids rich and intoxicating. The fairy necklace around her neck felt cold and heavy.

"I'd better go back in," she said aloud. Her voice sounded strange and unfamiliar. She clutched the box of butterflies more tightly, and again had the sensation that she could actually hear them.

Their fragile wings were whirring in their prison as they searched for escape, flying in circles in the darkness. They were flying in formation, a circular pattern, spiraling around and around in the darkness, like fairies dancing in a ring. . . .

No, it was her head. She tried to stand, but the garden around her seemed to be spinning, oak and holly trees rushing past her like the view from a child's carousel.

Wind? The ribbons from the damned flower arrangement on her head were fluttering wildly, the silver silk whipping across her face and throat. But there was no wind tonight; the June air had been still and cool.

But her skirts were fluttering wildly around her ankles, and panic set in as she realized that the earth wasn't spinning, nor the circle of trees. Her entire body was spinning, and lifted entirely off of the ground.

Gravity was gone. She was an astronaut, spinning into space, her lifeline broken. The moon beckoned her, silver and huge, the stars above her whirling like blue fire in the darkness.

The darkness became a whirlpool of lights, flashing and spinning, blinding her with radiance. She thought she felt something catch at her skirts, and had the strange thought that it was the branches at the top of the oak tree as she was lifted higher.

Her mind reached wildly through her panic for any kind of logical thought, but all she could picture was a supermarket tabloid bearing a headline that said BRIDESMAID ABDUCTED BY UFO! or ALIEN BUTTERFLIES ABDUCT SISTER OF THE BRIDE!

She thought she might have laughed out loud, but the laughter was unfamiliar to her. Her last thought, before the lights exploded into darkness, was that it was Elva's laughter, sparkling through the night like a thousand silver chimes.

Chapter Three

The silence was black and solid, and then, gradually, sound intruded. A hushed murmur, a whisper, the distant bark of a dog.

Then sensation began to return. The necklace at her throat felt like ice. The cardboard box of butterflies against her chest was rough against her fingers. The ground felt hard and frozen against her back. It was cold, too cold.

She must have passed out. And it must be late, to judge by the drop in temperature.

She struggled to open her eyes, the ringing in her ears coming and going against the other intruding noises. More whispers, then a hush. A child's voice, high and frightened.

Meredyth struggled again, opened her eyes, and then shut them immediately against the blinding whiteness.

Snow.

No way. Not in June. Not in Seattle.

She opened one eye cautiously, at the same time registering the crunch of footsteps on ice, the undeniable winter freeze against her back.

It was snow, all right. The oak above her was covered, its thick branches sparkling beneath layers of white frosting. She struggled to sit up, her mind recoiling from the absurdity of it. One moment it was June, and now . . .

The oak was the same, and the holly bushes, and the circle of ground between them.

Everything else had changed.

Snow covered everything, billows of sparkling white lying over the ground and trees. The manicured hotel gardens were gone, replaced by forests and a long sloping field. The sky was pale with the light of a winter morning.

And there were people. A crowd of people, watching her, their faces reflecting fascination and fear.

Meredyth stared back, unable to speak.

It was a crowd of extras from an Elizabethan drama. A crowd of peasants and merchants, bundled in winter wools and occasional furs. Heavy capes and more homely stoles of browns and grays and blues wrapped around shoulders, caps pulled over ears, leather boots and slippers showing beneath wool breeches and long skirts.

She stared, fascinated and terrified.

They stared back, old faces with wrinkles and young ones with apple red cheeks, puffing clouds of silent breath into the frosted air, eyes round with fear or narrow with suspicion. Here a gloved hand rested on a dagger; there a bare one clutched a child safe within the confines of a worn shawl.

But real. Real people. If they were made-up extras in a show, the costume and makeup designers were long overdue their Academy Awards.

She shivered, cold in her lavender gown, and tried to struggle to her feet.

"Stay back, fairy!"

She froze instantly, hardly daring to move her eyes. The shout had come from a burly man, his woolen cloak trimmed with rich fur.

"Get the children well away," he ordered, "before she steals them off."

Well. That was a nice greeting. Meredyth's practical mind kicked in, and told her that if this was really happening, she'd better set them straight.

"I don't want your children."

The crowd murmured to each other, their faces flushing with excitement. They seemed surprised that she could speak. She was a little surprised herself.

The burly man, who seemed to be the leader, cleared his throat. His hand never left the dagger at his belt.

"What do ye want then, fairy?" he shouted. There was fear in the gruffness of his shout, but Meredyth decided that, outnumbered as she was, good manners and honesty were the way to go. Her practical mind told her that it was impossible that this wasn't real; but then, neither would she have believed that she would leave a wedding reception by spontaneously lifting and spinning from the earth.

"My name is Meredyth Sherborne," she said, "and all I want is to go home."

There was a stunned silence, and then the crowd erupted into a babble of excited shouts and exclamations of disbelief.

Meredyth tried to make sense of it. There was talk of fairies and kidnapping, of right-born heirs and castles, of full moons and godmothers. And then her name was called out over and over.

"Meredyth! Mine own Meredyth!"

An old woman was pushing her way through the crowd, tears running over her wrinkled cheeks. A shawl of wool covered her gray head; her mittened hands held her full blue skirts out of the snow. Heedless of the arms pulling her back, she hurried through the snow toward Meredyth.

"My own lambykins! My little Meredyth, come back to me, and all these years past."

The woman pulled Meredyth to her feet, ignoring the collective gasp of fear behind her, and stared into Meredyth's face, tears streaming from her watery blue eyes.

"Do ye not remember me, poppet?"

Frightened and unsure, Meredyth shook her head.

"And why not? 'Tis been twenty-seven years since you were taken from me. Why should you remember your old nurse? But I would know you anywhere, though I've not seen you since you were but two years old."

Two years old. The age she had been when the Sherbornes adopted her.

The crowd was fairly shouting with excitement, calling out to the old woman.

"Are thee certain, Alyce?"

"Can it be she?"

"Can ye find proof, Alyce?"

The old woman reached up to touch Meredyth's cheek. The wool mitten was cold and rough against her cheek, but the touch was gentle, and the blue eyes showed nothing but concern and love.

"Of course I'm sure, want-wits! Look at her! Is that not her mother's face, as many of you had seen a hundred times? And here she is, in the very fairy ring she disappeared into so long ago! And look, ye! Look!" The old woman's voice rose and trembled with excitement.

"Look 'round her neck! Is that not the very necklace that wicked godmother gave her as a christening gift, just before she stole her away, and her mother barely cold in her grave?"

The old woman gathered Meredyth into her arms and wept, her warm tears falling on Meredyth's bare shoulders.

"Oh, my little lamb. Taken to live with the fairy folk,

all those years ago, and now come home to your old Alyce. God bless us!"

"How do we know for certain?" shouted the man with the knife.

At that moment, the box in Meredyth's arms came open beneath the force of Alyce's hug, and a hundred brilliant butterflies fluttered out, like yellow sunlight against the ice and snow.

The crowd fell silent, mouths open with shock as the butterflies ascended to the cold skies, searching desperately for their warm home.

Meredyth watched them go, wondering if she, too, could ever follow.

"There!" shouted old Alyce. "What more proof do ye need? Where else could she have found such creatures, but in the fairy kingdom? And look at the flowers! Have ye ever seen such roses? Not in colors like that, and never in January. And what these other flowers might be, they have never grown in England. Not in my lifetime."

Meredyth stared at her bouquet, still fresh and fragrant.

"For whatever reason," Alyce continued, "the fairy folk have sent us back our own, and we dare not offend them. This is Lady Meredyth Sherborne, as I live and breathe."

How strange it was, hearing her name from this unknown woman. And Sherborne, her adopted name. Or was it?

Meredyth stared at the crowd, who stared back at her with expressions of mingled awe and fear.

"Come, lamby," said old Alyce, taking her firmly by the arm. " 'Tis time for you to go home."

"Home?" Meredyth echoed.

"Why, yes. To Sherborne House. 'Tis yours now, and I'll bear witness to it. You were the last of your family, and the rightful heiress, and I'll swear it with my dying breath."

Whatever You Wish

Alyce guided Meredyth through the snowdrifts, and the crowd parted respectfully to let them pass. Meredyth glanced nervously at them, but Alyce gave her a comforting pat on the arm. "Don't thee worry, pet. Do ye think that anybody would be so foolish as to risk offending the fairy folk? Even his mighty self, sitting in the hall as if it was his own. He'll not be able to say naught against thee."

Meredyth was stunned, and it was all too much to take in. At least next to old Alyce she felt safe, as if she had an ally. There was something familiar about the old woman, as if . . .

As if she had known her, and trusted her, long ago.

The townsfolk fell into step behind them, and they trudged through the snow, following the fairy changeling back to her rightful castle.

The procession grew as they went through the village, a fairy-tale town of sloping roofs and towers beneath sparkling snow and icicles. The streets were narrow and twisted, the houses and buildings of dark stone and heavy timbers. Faces appeared at shuttered windows; the smell of smoke from a hundred chimneys filled the air.

Meredyth stared in disbelief as the renaissance world of Shakespeare unfolded before her eyes, not even noticing the cold wind that whipped her iridescent skirts about her like banners in the wind.

The whole village had heard of her appearance in the fairy ring, and neighbors ran to tell other neighbors, who joined the procession as they made their way . . . to where?

Her home, Alyce had said.

"Are any of my family there?" she asked softly.

Alyce looked startled. "Did the fair folk not tell thee, then? No, my poor lamb. Your mother and father were carried off by the sweating sickness before you were taken. You were ill, too, and we all feared that you would be next. But Lady Elva—"

"Elva?" Meredyth's heart skipped a quick beat.

"So you know herself? I thought you might. She was a bad one if ever I saw one. Something not right about her. Your godmother. But I never trusted her, for all that. I thought there was something terrible wrong, there. A fairy changeling, most likely, sent to trick us mortal folk.

"She took ye out of your cradle, fever and all, and out into the dark of night. It was June, sweet and warm, but still no night for a sick child to be out. We found your tracks the next day, leading to the fairy ring, and your silver rattle lying there. But you were gone. Forever, we thought, taken by the fairies. And no trace of you till today, when you turned up in the same place." Alyce shook her head, her breath coming in great puffs in the cold. " 'Tis almost more than can be believed, but there you are, as real as I."

If it was a dream, it was the strangest, most realistic dream Meredyth had ever had, and not something that she would have expected. She was a practical person, not given to fantasy.

"Do ye remember nothing?" Alyce asked, her old eyes anxious. "Nothing of being a wee girl, or your home?"

"I don't think so," Meredyth replied cautiously, too aware of the crowd hovering at a cautious distance.

"What of the fairy world, then?"

Meredyth started to speak, and then stopped as Alyce's grip tightened on her arm.

"There!" the old woman cried. "There is your home, your own birthplace and birthright, Meredyth Sherborne. Do ye have no memory of it?"

Meredyth stared, speechless. It was truly an enchanted castle, three stories high with gabled roofs and at least ten chimneys, tall and slender spires piercing the winter sky. Warm light shone from the mullioned windows.

Whatever You Wish

Huge oak doors with iron hinges waited at the top of a flight of stairs. If there was a drive, or a courtyard, Meredyth couldn't tell. At least a foot of snow obscured everything.

"Wait!" called a voice behind them, and the burly man who had spoken at the fairy ring came forward.

"What now, my lord mayor?" Alyce demanded, putting her mittened hands on plump hips.

"How do we know," he asked slowly, "that she is the true Meredyth Sherborne, and not a fairy changeling sent in her place, to do more mischief? Sir Alex will not thank us if we send an imposter into his home while he is away. Not with his daughter inside, sick abed. She might do harm to the child."

Alyce hesitated, looking at Meredyth for the first time with fearful eyes. Then she brightened. "Don't be thick, man! Give her your knife!"

Meredyth didn't like the sound of this. "Why?" she asked.

" 'Tis iron, of course. Everyone knows that a fairy cannot stand the touch of iron."

The knife was produced, and Meredyth took it in her hand without hesitation, knowing her life depended on the goodwill of these people.

"Praise God!" Alyce cried, when nothing happened. 'Tis she, indeed. As mortal as you and I. Open the doors, and prepare her chambers. Our lady is come home to us."

Home, thought Meredyth, staring at the great castle before her. It looked so strange, and yet there was something familiar there, like a long-ago memory that lay buried in her mind, just out of reach.

She sat shivering before the fire in what Alyce called the great room, seated in the best chair, one with a low back and cushioned seat, carved of dark wood.

It was a beautiful room. The ceilings were high and vaulted, covered with graceful, arabesque woodwork

111

Amy Elizabeth Saunders

and plaster designs, designs that were echoed in the wainscoting that decorated the walls. Everywhere, in the woodwork, Meredyth could see the Sherborne *S*, entwined with and mirroring itself.

The fireplace she sat before was of carved stone, showing heroic mythological figures she didn't recognize, but still impressive in their dramatic stances. Servants brought her steaming cups of wine, and a silver plate of hot beef (which smelled a little off) and a mysterious roasted bird, and nuts covered in sticky, sweet coating, while Alyce stood beaming by her side.

It was not a dream. She could taste the honey and spice in the wine, she could feel the cold drafts from the windows and the raw heat of the fire, she could smell the pungent smell of unwashed bodies as the serving maids came and went, as much to gawk at her as to serve her.

Old Alyce stood proudly at her side, whispering orders to the servants and regarding Meredyth with a mixture of pride and awe. Only after Meredyth had eaten and drunk enough to suit her did she speak.

"M'lady . . ."

Meredyth startled at the unfamiliar address. "Yes?"

"These flowers . . ." And Alyce touched a hesitant finger to the orchids in the forgotten bouquet at Meredyth's feet. "What are they? Where were they grown?"

"Orchids." Meredyth tried to remember the other flowers in the bouquet, but the fact was that aside from the roses, she didn't know.

"Ah, here we are." Alyce hurried forward to meet two maids, who were carrying a heavy, framed portrait. "Just look, Lady Meredyth. I knew this was about somewhere. Your mother's picture. Look at that, and tell me how anyone could doubt."

Meredyth looked, and her heart stopped. It was something like the feeling she'd had when she saw Sherborne House, but sharper. An unnameable, poignant feeling that caught somewhere in her throat. She could no more have described that feeling than she could have described colors to a blind person.

The woman in the portrait was a mirror image of herself—a young woman with ash blond hair, pulled back and covered with a small hood of black velvet trimmed with pearls and gold. The face that rose above the small white ruff was Meredyth's own—strong featured, with a rounded jawline and a firm, full mouth. Amber brown eyes, with naturally dark brows.

Her mother.

Somewhere, in the dark recesses of her memory, she saw gentle, pale hands reaching to stroke her cheek, and heard a soft, husky voice singing, and felt a security, a deep feeling of love and safety.

That was all.

She sank back against the stiff chair, covering her hands with her face, and said nothing.

"My lady?"

Meredyth took her hands from her eyes, and looked up to see Alyce and the two maids watching her.

"Sir Alex's daughter, Lady Katherine, is upstairs, and passing worried. This has been her home for eight years now, and she is fretting. Would you speak to her? Tell her you would not put her out in the snow?"

Meredyth nodded, rose to her feet, and followed Alyce up the long staircase, leaving Melissa's overnight bag and her wilting bouquet by the fire.

Lady Katherine, as she was grandly addressed, was no lady. She was a child, no more than ten, dwarfed by the huge, curtained bed she lay in.

She was pale, with dark circles under her large brown eyes, and a brilliant flush of fever in her cheeks.

The room was hot with the heat of a roaring fire, and stifling with the odor of sweat. The sheets and blankets covering the child appeared none too clean. Neither, Meredyth noticed, did the child herself.

The little girl nodded, and spoke with a dignity far

beyond her years. "I give you God's greetings, Lady Sherborne."

Meredyth nodded back, uncertain. "Hello."

The child looked startled, then repeated the word, uncertainly. "Is that how you greet each other in fairy land?"

Meredyth hesitated, then nodded.

The little girl looked like she might laugh, but only managed a wan smile. Her fingers plucked listlessly at her heavy coverings for a moment before she spoke again.

"It would seem that Sherborne House belongs to you. May I stay until my father returns?"

"Of course. Don't be silly. Do you think I'd throw you out into the cold?"

The little girl seemed startled. She stared at Meredyth, her face pale in its frame of long dark hair. Her hair was lank and oily, and Meredyth itched to wash it.

"Fairies are cruel, they say," she offered at last, her small voice trembling.

"Do they?" Meredyth was startled. "I didn't know that. What else do they say?"

The little girl hesitated, and then said, "Do ye not know what mortals say?"

Meredyth shook her head. "They say that fairies are little tiny people with wings?"

"Oh, no. Not always. Sometimes, they may disguise themselves as such. But they are very strong, and fearsome powerful. They trick travelers off the roads, who then fall into rivers and die. And they steal children away. Like you. And they lure men into ponds and bogs. And if you eat their food, or taste their drink, you are lost forever."

Well. Meredyth had never really paid attention to folktales, and what the child described sure wasn't Tinker Belle.

114

Whatever You Wish

"Is it true?" Lady Katherine's voice was small and shaky.

"Not a bit of it."

The little girl seemed startled and interested. She actually sat up in bed, and her eyes brightened. "Truth? Tell me, then, Lady Sherborne."

As Meredyth started to speak, the door to the bed-chamber opened, and Alyce came in, followed by a man in black robes, a white linen headdress showing beneath a black cap. He was carrying a jar in his hands.

"Time for Doctor," Alyce said, in a strained, cheerful voice. "Let's quit chattering and start your bleeding."

Meredyth stared with horror at the jar in the old man's hands.

Leeches. Slimy, squirming leeches. No wonder the child was so pale.

"The hell you will." She spoke immediately, without thinking.

The doctor stopped, and looked at her with the same awe that the villagers had. Alyce looked shocked.

"But, Lady, she is ill."

"You put those filthy things on her, and she'll get even sicker. Get him out of here."

Meredyth glared at the doctor. He was filthy. Rings of dirt showed around his wrists and neck, and in the fur piece hanging over his shoulder, she was sure she could see bugs crawling. Lice, or fleas.

For that matter, everyone was filthy. The room they sat in was filthy, dark with the smells of sweat and urine and smoke from the fire.

The doctor looked away from Meredyth's face, clutching his jar of leeches, and then fled, murmuring a prayer beneath his breath.

So be it. If she was Lady Sherborne, if this was her rightful home, then she was giving the orders. And if they feared that she would call the wrath of the fairy folk upon their superstitious heads, let them think it. She'd jolly well exploit that fear.

115

Alyce stood by the door, uncertain, looking from Meredyth to the girl in the bed, alarm in her eyes.

"My lady . . ." She hesitated, looking fearful.

"What is it, Alyce?"

"Do you mean . . . do you mean to let our little Kate die?" The question was asked in a piteous whisper.

Meredyth recoiled. "Are you out of your mind? No, not in a million years! But if you let that filthy man put worms on her, she might. It's no way to treat a sick child, believe me."

The child in the bed, who had been lying still and white, brightened with interest. "Do your physicians in the fairy kingdom know more? Can you cure me?"

Meredyth took a deep breath, and had the feeling she might be biting off more than she could chew. She hesitated, and as she did, she saw a flea hopping across the rushes and straw that covered the floor, and climbing on to the child's bed.

She'd do her best, and hope she was dealing with the flu, and not bubonic plague.

"Yes, they know better. A lot better. And the first rule is, the cleaner things are, the less disease can spread."

Alyce looked affronted. "I run a clean house."

By what standards? Meredyth wondered. "Maybe clean enough for you, but not for me. Alyce, when you say this is my house, is it? May I give orders here?"

Alyce bent her plump knee in a quick curtsy. "Of course, my lady."

"Good. Then first things first. Is there a bathtub?"

Blank looks greeted her.

"Oh, boy. All right. First, I need a large tub. Big enough to fit a person in. And warm water. And all this"—she kicked the rushes and straw on the floor with a disgusted look—"goes. Get it out. I want the floors and walls scrubbed."

"All the rushes out?" Alyce looked sick.

"Everywhere. The whole castle. Go tell the servants."

Whatever You Wish

Alyce turned at the door and looked back. "Sir Alex will not be happy, my lady."

"Is it his castle, or mine?"

Alyce fled.

"And now for you." Meredyth settled on the bed next to little Katherine, and laid a hand across her forehead. Fever. But not terribly high. Probably 100 degrees. "Tell me what's wrong—a cough, a runny nose? An earache?"

The child looked at her with awed eyes, and then hesitantly touched the iridescent lavender of Meredyth's gown. She seemed fascinated by the fabric. "Lady Sherborne?"

Meredyth smiled, in her best kindergarten-teacher way.

"If I tell you, will you tell me of the fairy kingdom?"

"Sure. Fair trade."

"I have consumption. I'm tired, and hot, and I cough. It hurts most dreadful. Some days I cough blood. Can thee heal me?"

Tuberculosis. Meredyth's heart gave a sickened thud. Cure her? With no antibiotics, no doctors, no hospitals?

Praying the child was wrong, she gave her a brave smile. "Well, we'll see, won't we? What have they been giving you for medicine?"

The child shrugged. "Cooked veal blood and oranges together, for a physic. And pigeon's blood on the soles of mine feet. That helps a little, I think."

Meredyth was speechless.

"Listen!" Kate cried out, her face brightening. "Horses! My father is home, I think. Go and greet him, Lady Sherborne, and tell him that you are here, and will make me well. And pray, pay no mind if he bellows. He is not as fearsome as he seems."

Meredyth looked out the window, and saw a group of horsemen riding hell-bent toward the house, one well ahead of the others. She'd bet her last dollar that

Sir Alex had already heard of her arrival. And though she couldn't see his face, something about his posture told her he wasn't happy, and that he wouldn't be cowed as easily as Alyce and the others had been.

Chapter Four

"Close the doors, and admit nobody."

Alexander Hartford settled into his favorite chair, threw his gloves to the top of his writing desk, and shed his riding cloak all in one easy motion.

Whiting, his house steward, hurried to close the door of his master's closet, the combination of study and library and bear's den where Alexander spent most of his time.

Alex leaned back and studied the faces of his most trusted men—his house steward, his clerk, Gilman, and Pritchard, his gentleman's servant.

Dr. Horton, his face red under his black hat, stood near the door, trembling with outrage. Alyce Middleton was nowhere to be found.

"Now," he said, his voice calmer than his temper, "tell me again of this changeling heiress, and why she has invaded my house. Whiting, I have trusted you since I came into posession of Sherborne. Explain this to me, and please spare me the prattle and drivel of fairy folk."

Whiting pulled at the small ruff at his throat. "Begging your leave, sir, there is no other way to tell it. She is Meredyth Sherborne, no denying."

"And how did you come to this conclusion?"

Whiting pulled again at his ruff, obviously not wanting to be the bearer of ill tidings, but determined to speak the truth. "I knew her parents well, sir. She is the very image of her mother. Her face, her voice, her way of moving. She even wears the very pendant given to her at her christening. It is most distinctive. I recognized it at once, even though almost thirty years have passed."

Alex plucked at a stray thread hanging from his embroidered cuff. "So," he said at last, "after twenty-seven years, the heiress returns. And my entire household has gone mad, and assures me most earnestly that she has been prisoner of the fairy folk for time between. Explain that—if ye can."

Whiting glanced at Gilman, but the clerk was obviously loath to help. "It would appear to be true, sir. She was in the fairy ring—"

"Superstitious rot—"

"And still warm to touch, though lying on the freezing ground. And bedecked in flowers, as fresh as midsummer; and flowers, sir, such have never been seen!"

Gilman broke in, his ink-stained fingers almost trembling with excitement. "And when old Alyce touched her, sir, the air was filled with butterflies—live butterflies, huge, and yellow as the sun. I would not have believed it, sir, had I not seen it with mine own eyes."

Dr. Horton cleared his throat, and waited for Alex's nod before he spoke.

"If she is, in fact, Meredyth Sherborne, sir, then she has been fairy led. She is no ordinary woman. I would be inclined to believe that she is no mortal creature, but a fairy changeling."

120

Whatever You Wish

"Mmm hmm." Alex stroked his small beard carefully. "How much, Doctor, am I paying thee for the care of my daughter?"

Dr. Horton straightened. "One hundred and fifty pounds in the past year, sir."

"Thou art sadly overpaid. I am paying the wage of an educated man, not a simpleton."

Dr. Horton bristled. "Sir, I speak in truth. The creature who claims to be Meredyth Sherborne, and appears to be, is no woman of thirty years. She is most unnatural of appearance—as tall as any man, and as fresh faced and youthful as a maid of twenty. Her speech is strange and powerful, and she commands your servants in fearsome wicked tones. She has forbidden me from your daughter's chamber—"

"*What?*" Alex's roar shook the room as he rose to his feet. He struggled for a moment to gain composure, and turned away from his servants.

"Bring her to me at once."

His tone was as cold as January, his words clipped and short.

His servants almost tumbled over each other in their haste to obey.

"Sir Alex?"

He looked up, and fell speechless.

It was true. She was as tall as any man, and taller than most. Almost as tall as himself, and he was of a passing height.

And it was also true that she was of extraordinary appearance. He knew very few women free of pox marks or scars, yet her skin had a perfect, radiant glow, as new and soft as the skin of a child. Her hair, free and hanging, showed no traces of oil or dirt, but floated and shone like clean silk.

He rose without speaking, and walked closer, his eyes inspecting every detail of the creature—the gown that molded her figure without the hindrance of busk or stomacher, the fabric that shone with a million little sparkles of light, but without brilliants sewn on, nor a trace of where they might have been woven in.

The flowers that wreathed her head were as extraordinary as he had been told—lush roses in colors of pink and palest purple, and other flowers, fragrant and odd-looking. He touched one with a hesitant finger, and found that it felt like a true flower.

She stood still, her dark eyes following his every move.

He leaned in and sniffed at her, trying to place the light, unusual fragrance that surrounded her. No smell of sweat, or ordinary woman about her. She smelled like a flower herself, though one that he had never known.

"Do I pass inspection?"

He jumped back. Her voice was indeed strange, though her words were common English.

"I beg pardon, lady. Please, sit."

She took the hard, backless stool that was usually occupied by Gilman when they went over accounts together. Alex returned to his usual seat, the expanse of his Flemish writing desk between them.

They regarded each other with wary eyes.

"So you claim to be Meredyth Sherborne."

"I am Meredyth Sherborne."

"And you claim this house as your rightful inheritance."

She sighed, and lifted her hands with a lost gesture. "I don't know. That's what everyone says."

He stared fascinated at her fingernails, which seemed to be painted with a shimmering substance of pale rose. Or perhaps they had grown like that, the talons of some supernatural being, and—

Don't be ridiculous, he thought, annoyed at himself for succumbing to the ridiculous idea.

He noticed, for the first time, the strange object she held on her lap, a cross between a traveling trunk and a purse, made of a green tapestry and trimmed with leather strips of dark green. Strange chains of square, interlocking links ran around it, a tiny lock dangling from one end. He longed to seize it and explore the contents, but decided to tread carefully.

"So, if you are Meredyth Sherborne, tell me where you have been these past twenty-seven years."

He watched the human expressions of uncertainty, unhappiness, and fear flit across her face in rapid succession.

"It's hard to explain. As weird as you think it is, it's just as weird—if not more so—to me. One moment, I was at my sister's wedding, and the next minute I woke up in the snow. Alyce brought me here."

He tried to recall if the Sherbornes had more than one child, and was relatively certain they did not. "Your sister?"

"Melissa," she said, and the name was strange, one he had never heard before. "My adopted sister. I was adopted when I was two."

"By what family, and where did they live?"

Her eyes looked huge and sad. She lowered her lids, and he noticed that they, too, were covered with a strange, shimmering color.

"Mitchell and Eleanor Sherborne," she answered, and her words rang true, though he had been certain that the Sherborne family had died out with the disappearance of their daughter. "And we live in a place called Bellevue. Bellevue, Washington."

Belle View. He had never heard of such a place, or Washington either, though that had an ordinary enough sound about it. He could not place the accent, either, though he had been a seafaring man since his youth, and was better traveled than most.

"Is this Washington a town, here in England?"

She gave a soft laugh and shook her head. "No, it's a state. The great Northwest, the evergreen state."

"I am getting into a state, myself," he said impatiently. "You speak in riddles, lady."

She laughed again, and there was a note of hysteria in the sound.

He saw that she had all her teeth, and they were all white and perfect. He noted the necklace around her neck, shimmering with odd-colored stones. A fairy of silver, leaning on a crescent moon.

"I was granted this house by her majesty, in return for my services to the Crown upon the high seas. If you are proven to be Meredyth Sherborne, what do you propose?"

She tilted her head, her shimmering hair shining in the firelight, and he caught again the scent of her.

"I don't know. I don't know how to prove it, and I don't know why I'm here, or how I came. I don't really want to be here."

He did not believe in fairies, or witches, or sorcery. And yet he knew that she was of a different world. It was undeniable. But she was casting a spell upon him, as surely as if he were fairy led. She had an uncommon beauty, and her body, so visibly fluid and uncorseted beneath the amazing fabric, was fascinating.

His thoughts must have shown in his face, for her eyes met his, startled and aware. A deep rose flushed her unpainted cheeks.

"Damn," he exclaimed. "Forgive my staring. You can hardly expect me to do much else, when faced with such an uncommon beauty. I do almost believe you to be one of the fairy folk, sent to seduce we unwary mortals."

She appeared astounded at this. One slender hand, with its strange, dawn-rose nails, rose to touch her face, as though she could not believe it, and her eyes, fringed with incredibly long and dark lashes, stared bemusedly at him.

Finally she gave a little laugh. "Hot damn," she said. "That was smooth. You're not too bad yourself, Alexander Hartford. I just wish you and your house smelled better."

Whatever You Wish

Only half of what she said made sense, and the part about how he smelled was really terribly offensive.

But suddenly Alex looked at himself, and saw the gray stains on the dingy white cuffs of his shirt, and was keenly aware that he hadn't had a full bath in months, and his skin seemed to crawl beneath the black velvet of his doublet, which made no sense because the damned thing was like new, and he had only worn it twenty times at the most. And yet suddenly it felt filthy to him, and he was seized by the desire to scrub his hair.

The hot-tempered reply to her words died on his lips, and he instead gave the most extraordinary words he had ever spoken.

"Whatever you wish," he said, and left the room in search of a bath.

Chapter Five

Alyce assigned Meredyth a bedchamber: a spacious room, clean of rushes as requested, and with clean linens on the bed.

As soon as Meredyth could, she closed the heavy door behind her, slid the bolt into place, and dumped the contents of Melissa's overnight bag onto the bed.

It all tumbled out onto the taffeta quilt, and Meredyth settled back, the leather mattress supports creaking, and proceeded to take inventory of her survival kit.

The honeymoon nightgown appeared—a confection of sheer white silk, trimmed with Venice lace, seed pearls, and opalescent beads, with a matching robe that wouldn't have kept a hamster warm.

Clean underpants; that would have been nice, if they had been more substantial. Meredyth rolled her eyes at the nonexistent rear end. "Butt floss," she muttered contemptuously. "Come on, Melissa—let's have something practical."

The cosmetic case proved more rewarding—a bottle

of Tylenol, gardenia-scented bath and shower gel, comb and brush, tweezers, an arsenal of makeup, disposable razors, botanical shampoo and conditioner (never tested on animals), a bottle of Liz Claiborne perfume, a personal-size pack of tissues, toothpaste and two new toothbrushes, still in their cellophane, and a prescription bottle.

Meredyth picked up the plastic bottle and peered at the label.

"Ampicillin. Take twice daily, with food, until gone."

She tried to remember why Melissa had them. Sinus infection? Ear infection?

At any rate, they were antibiotics, and better than nothing.

The rest of the bag proved useless. A pair of panty hose, a sundress (size five), and a pair of sandals. A battery-powered tape player and headphones, a Whitney Houston tape, a Best of Mozart tape, and a copy of *Glamour* magazine.

"Way to go, Melissa," Meredyth said. "Ready for any emergency." She flipped to the last page of *Glamour*, and quickly checked out their on-the-street photos of "*Glamour* Dos and Don'ts." Melissa claimed that she lived in terror of seeing Meredyth's picture there, with a strip of black tape over her eyes.

"Not this month, anyway," Meredyth muttered. She swept the jumble back into the bag, zipped it, and stowed it under the bed. She took a quick inventory of her room.

The bed, curtained and covered in a pale green that Alyce had called by the decidedly unattractive name "goose-turd green," a chair, low backed and cushioned in gold brocade, a cupboard with a basin and rough towels.

There was a small room off to one side containing a wooden toilet, with a pan beneath it. A pitcher of water sat alongside, and a pile of linen cloths.

127

"Yuck-o." Meredyth wondered how long she could make the travel pack of tissue last.

A knock sounded on the door. "My lady?"

Alyce. Meredyth hurried to the door, and slid the bolt.

"Sir Alex is sitting to supper, and requests your company."

Meredyth glanced back at her room, and then stepped out into the hall, closing the door behind her.

"Let's go," she said, and followed Alyce through the gallery, down the stone staircase, and to the great room of the house. Maidservants peeked at her from doorways as she went, their glances hurried and fearful.

"Following orders," Alyce said. "The rushes are all out, and the floors are being washed."

Meredyth sniffed. "With what?"

"Vinegar and herbs. I do say, I thought Sir Alex might object, but he did not. 'Whatever she wishes,' he said, meek as a lamb. I cannot think why. Like a man under a spell."

The great room was set for supper. Long cloths covered the enormous table, twenty feet long and three feet wide. Meredyth was surprised at the number of people present, but apparently meals included not only the family, but many employeess, as well. Meredyth noticed that many of those at the table wore the Hartford livery, a gray coat with hanging sleeves, trimmed in dark fur, with silver embroidery showing a crest and a scrolled *H*.

Alyce pointed out, in a whisper, Alex's house steward and clerk, his bailiff and serving man. Little Lady Katherine was there, with a thick velvet robe on, her dark hair hidden under a velvet headdress, and a small ruff around her neck, looking like a miniature adult. Her dark eyes brightened at the sight of Meredyth, and she gave a hesitant smile.

Alyce motioned Meredyth to an empty seat next to Sir Alex, and Meredyth made her way there. All eyes were on her, and the conversation stilled.

Alexander Hartford rose to his feet to greet her. Meredyth drew a deep breath, and sat beside him.

He had a fascinating face. She couldn't decide, at first, whether he was handsome. His face was too contradictory—his jaw was very square, and looked like it might have been broken a time or two. Likewise his nose, which was slightly crooked, but not overly large. But his cheekbones were fine and sharp, and his mouth was perfectly shaped. His eyes were clear and blue, but his brows were dark and a little villainous in appearance.

But he was clean, much cleaner than when she had met him earlier. His hair was deep, rich brown, and shone in dark waves over the back of his collar. His nails were clean. His hands looked as if he'd spent a lot of his life working—not the pampered hands she'd have expected on an average gentleman.

He had changed his clothing for a doublet of deep blue, and wore a small, falling ruff of lace, brilliant white against his tanned skin. He wore a gold ring in one ear.

He looked like a cross between a pirate and a gentleman, she decided.

He seemed equally fascinated by her, and she could feel his eyes on her as she sat and took inventory of her place setting—a linen napkin, a silver spoon, a silver plate, and a tall goblet of gold glass.

"I have decided," he said, "how to resolve our dilemma."

"Fabulous. You're two steps ahead of me," Meredyth told him.

A servant approached and offered her a tray of meat. She hesitated, and indicated some that didn't look too frightening. Chicken, she could recognize.

"We seem to be in dispute over the ownership of the hall," Alex said. "There is only one way to settle such a muddle, and that is legally. We can take your case to the Westminster court, or we can wait for the regional court to meet, which will be in about two months' time. At that time, you may prove your identity, and your lands and house will be restored to you."

"Oh." Meredyth was floored. She had no intention of being here in two months. She had yet to decide how she was getting back, but if there was a way, she was doing it. "That two-month thing, that sounds good."

"Very well. Until then, you are welcome to stay here. I have had my clerk gather the inventory of the house, such as it was when I took possession of it, and the inventory such as it was when the Sherbornes left it. Several years had passed in between, you recall. I cannot be held responsible for any discrepancies. Gilman?"

The thin man named Gilman hastened to bring Sir Alex several large, leather-bound books, which he handed to Meredyth with a bow.

Meredyth caught the clean scent of him, a spicy sandalwood smell that was worlds better than the sweat and horse smell he had reeked of earlier.

"You're not eating," he said suddenly.

"I'm a little overwhelmed. My appetite isn't what it usually is," Meredyth said truthfully.

"Some venison? Or eel, perhaps?"

Eel? "No, thank you."

"You must eat something, madam. Here." He gestured to a serving boy. "Some cheese? And pastry?"

Meredyth smiled, relieved. "That sounds fine, thanks."

The serving boy piled enough for three lumberjacks onto her plate.

"Until we present our cases before the courts," Alex said, turning abruptly back to business, "I suggest that you remain in the house, and that we share the residence in an equitable manner." He glanced at Meredyth with sharp blue eyes. "And by that I mean, you do not interfere with my household, and I will not interfere with you, and whatever strange habits you may have."

Meredyth looked up and saw Dr. Horton's eyes on her, his face smug beneath his flat black hat.

And she saw little Katherine's eyes travel from her to the doctor, and back to Meredyth with a silent plea.

Meredyth decided to take the bull by the horns. "Are you referring to the treatment of your daughter?"

He had been sawing at a piece of meat with his dagger. He stopped, laid it down, and stared directly back at her.

"I am."

Meredyth stared down the table at the child, at her pale, unhappy face that was too thin, and the fevered gloss in her eyes. If they continued to bleed her and stuff their weird potions down her, they would kill her. If they stopped, there was a chance that she would live.

"May I speak to you privately?"

He hesitated only a moment. "Follow me, then."

She followed him from the great room and up the stairs, her hand sliding over the smooth wood of the elaborate banister.

He led the way to the large upstairs room called the gallery, a room with a polished wooden floor and large windows at the far end. Looking out them, Meredyth could see the landscape, barren fruit trees showing their black silhouettes in the snow, and a hill falling down to the black curves of a river.

In the distance, Meredyth could see the spires and rooftops of the village, dark against the rose and gold winter sunset.

"Well, lady?"

He stood beside the fireplace, and the flames reflected on his sharp features and the satin of his doublet and knee breeches.

Meredyth made her way across the room to him, aware, as always, of the way his eyes took in every detail of her person.

"I think I can save your daughter." Even as she spoke, she prayed that she was right. Melissa had quite a bit of medicine in the bag. It might be enough, with proper food and diet, to strengthen young Kate. Perhaps enough to fight the disease.

It was worth a try.

His face showed nothing. It was a perfect blank, the face of somebody hiding his emotions deeply within.

"She has consumption," he said simply, and there was bitter grief in the words.

"That doctor," Meredyth said, "is doing all the wrong things."

"He is very highly recommended—"

"He's bleeding her, damn it!" Meredyth cried. "Can't you see the stupidity of it? He's sapping what strength she has, every day, a little at a time."

"The blood is replaced with a physic—"

"I know. Of veal blood and oranges. It won't work; I swear to you. Has she gotten any better since he started? At all?"

He turned his head and stared into the fire. "No," he said at last.

"She's gotten worse, hasn't she? Weaker, and sicker?"

He looked at Meredyth, saying nothing.

"I tell you, it's killing her. Where I come from . . ." Meredyth hesitated, and then went on. "Where I come from, the doctors are better. They could cure this. Now, I'm no doctor, but I could do better than that quack down there, I'm sure. She has antibodies—chemicals to fight the disease—in her blood, and he's draining it away, a bit at a time."

He appeared unconvinced. "Please try to believe me. Have you ever seen somebody bleed to death?"

He nodded.

"That can happen to Kate; slowly, but it will happen. Please, please let me try to save her."

Whatever You Wish

He searched her face, obviously unwilling to trust her.

"Look, if you let me try, I won't press my case. You can have your house; and everything that came with it. I don't care. But I can't bear to see a child die under these conditions while I stand by and do nothing."

He raked a hand through his dark hair, and said nothing, just stood watching her with glimmering eyes. He turned away.

"Very well." His voice was hoarse, and so low that Meredyth wondered if she had heard him correctly.

He turned around abruptly. "But I give warning, lady, if any harm comes to her at your hands . . ."

"It won't. I'd rather die."

"So thee will," he promised her, his voice cold and calm. "I assure thee."

Chapter Six

She thought that she would never sleep. She tossed and turned in the unfamiliar softness of the goose-down mattress, hating the way it billowed up around her. At last she gave up, rose from her bed, and lit two more candles.

The leather-bound ledgers Gilman had given her lay on the chair beside her bed. She took them back to bed with her, shivering, and began to read.

At first the unfamiliar script was difficult, but gradually she began to get used to it. The first pages were simply an inventory of the household items—not very exciting reading. Lists of beds, cupboards, chairs, and tables. An inventory of the silver plate, down to the last spoon. Every blanket, tester, cushion, and sheet. Then a list of the kitchen inventory, right down to each "firkin" of butter, whatever the hell a firkin was.

The lists of the livestock and stable supplies almost lured her to sleep, and the lists of the lands' tenants and the rents were almost indecipherable, and she dropped them and opened a bundle of papers tied with a faded ribbon of olive green.

There was something familiar about the writing. She frowned, sat up, and held the first paper closer to the light.

My own dearest friend, Frances . . .

Frances. Frances Sherborne, her biological mother. Meredyth looked up at the portrait that Alyce had hung in her room, at the face so much like her own. Like those of so many old portraits, the eyes seemed to follow her.

She turned back to the letter, following the faded lines carefully.

My own dearest friend, Frances,

I am much grieved and frightened to hear of Robert's death, and more alarmed to hear of your fear for your own health, and that of little Meredyth. Do not allow the doctors to bleed you or the little one. I will come to you immediately, traveling from London by barge, and should arrive within days, if travel goes smoothly.

Though I am loath to say it, be sure to put my guardianship of Meredyth in writing immediately, in the event that I am not able to reach you in time.

In the awful event that I have not reached Sherborne by the full moon, do exactly as I have told you. Take the child to the fairy ring, and be sure that the christening gift is around her neck. Keep your hand firmly upon it, and wish with all your tender heart.

Do not fear anything you might see. It will be exactly as I have promised you, and I will follow you immediately. I know that it is hard to understand, but I assure you most earnestly that I have told you true.

Hold fast and true, and pray that I will reach you by the full moon. If not, go forward without fear.

Your loving friend, Elva.

Meredyth read the letter again, her heart beating quickly, and her hand reached up to touch the silver pendant at her throat. The full moon, the fairy ring, the christening gift that even now seemed to tingle beneath her fingers.

Elva. Her fairy godmother. The pieces began to fall together. She could picture it as if she had been there— and perhaps she had.

She could imagine her mother, newly widowed and frightened, feeling the first signs of the illness that had taken her husband, and she could see her sitting down and writing to her dear friend who had promised her the fantastic—another world, where doctors could easily cure the illnesses that so easily struck down the people here.

And she could easily imagine the rest of the story. She knew that Frances Sherborne hadn't lived to see the full moon, or carry her infant daughter to the fairy ring.

But Elva had.

Take the child to the fairy ring, and be sure that the christening gift is around her neck. Keep your hand firmly upon it, and wish with all your tender heart. . . .

Was it that simple? Was that all she needed to carry her home? Just those four things—the necklace, the fairy ring, the full moon, and a wish?

She froze, suddenly remembering sitting at the crowded wedding reception with Elva, looking into her sparkling blue eyes. Hadn't they had a conversation about wishes?

What if I were not an ordinary godmother, Meredyth? What if I were a fairy godmother, and could grant you three wishes? . . . Would you wish for a handsome prince, to love you forever?

And Meredyth, with a sinking feeling, remembered her own flippant answer. *Sure, I would. . . . No, why be greedy? An ordinary knight would do, shining armor or otherwise. Castle in the country, the whole damned happily-ever-after schtick. Why not?*

"Crap." Meredyth raked her hair off of her forehead, looking around her with new understanding. What had she done? Why hadn't Elva warned her? Or had she?

Be careful what you wish for, dear.

"Some warning," Meredyth muttered. She looked around her room again. Her wilting wreath of flowers lay on the floor, next to her stupid lavender gown. Melissa's overnight bag lay next to them, the contents thrown in a disorganized way that Melissa would never have approved of. It seemed like pretty small ammunition to face a hostile century with.

"I wish—" She stopped abruptly. Oh, no. She'd damned well better be careful. Three wishes, Elva had said. She'd used one to get here, and that was scary enough. If she didn't watch herself, she might squander another for something stupid, like a cup of coffee. Or had she already?

She pressed her fingers against her temples, trying to remember every conversation she'd had since she'd arrived.

"Damn!" The word burst from her throat. She had! What had she said to Alex Hartford? *You're not too bad, yourself. . . . I just wish you and your house smelled better. . . .*

And she had been so shocked when he had simply looked at her with those incredible blue eyes, and said, "Whatever you wish."

If only she'd known! But she hadn't and here she was, stuck hundreds of years from home with only one damned wish—and that would have to be her ticket back, at the next full moon.

She sighed and looked up at the portrait of Frances Sherborne, who seemed to look back at her, her amber brown eyes soft and sorrowful. Meredyth studied the picture again, noticing the capable-looking hands, clasped gently together over the skirt of deep blue brocade.

Her mother. She wondered what kind of person she'd been.

"I wish—" She started to say again, and stopped immediately, panic rising. This was too much. How often did people say those words without even thinking? And what would happen to her if she threw away that last precious wish?

After a moment's thought, she took the silver necklace from her neck and hurried from her bed. She hid it deep within Melissa's overnight bag, safe within a zippered side pocket.

She sat there, shivering in the diaphanous honeymoon nightgown that was nothing like the plaid flannel nightgown that she normally wore at home. If she was going to be here until the next full moon, she would have to ask Alyce to find her something more appropriate. Melissa's gown was far too short on her, and she had a feeling that Victoria's Secret was a little risque for old England.

Her bedroom door flew open, and she caught her breath, her hands automatically pulling the folds of the useless sheer robe tightly about her.

Alex Hartford stood there. He seemed as startled as she was. He looked as if he had been about to speak, but he said nothing, just stood with one hand on the door and the other holding a candle, staring at Meredyth as if he had never seen a woman before.

He looked as if he himself had just been roused from his bed. His dark hair was tousled, his white shirt open at the throat, untucked over the knee breeches he had worn earlier with his blue doublet.

Meredyth shivered, and then felt a warm glow against her skin as his gaze traveled over her, almost as if she could feel his physical touch following his stare.

Meredyth wasn't cold anymore. As a matter of fact,

she could feel the heat of her body building and rushing through her veins as Alex Hartford's eyes traveled over her with undisguised desire and admiration, lingering on the swell of her cleavage above the deep cut of the sheer bodice, the line of her legs beneath the translucent fabric of the skirt.

Though he said nothing, his desire for her was clearly written on his face—it was in the sudden glow of his eyes, the almost imperceptible quickening of his breath, the tension of his hand as it tightened around the candlestick he held.

Meredyth had never been so attracted to anybody in her life, or felt the pull of desire so fiercely. But then, she had never seen a face so blatantly sexy. He was the kind of man that you simply couldn't look at without wondering what it would be like, if . . .

"Damn me." He turned away before she did. "I beg pardon for intruding."

Meredyth stood, her legs feeling unsteady beneath her, and yanked the cover from the bed, wrapping it protectively around herself. Her face was starting a slow burn.

"No, it's all right. What is it?"

He glanced quickly, saw that she was covered, and relaxed. "It's my Kate." His voice was urgent; he was all business again. "She has taken a bad turn. I should not have let her come down to supper, but she begged so sweetly. If you think you can help her, please come." He swallowed, then added, "But I would ask you to dress first, lady. I know not what you call this gown, but it would be hard to keep my sanity if I did see you in such a state again."

Meredyth's cheeks and ears felt as if they were flaming. She nodded curtly, looking away.

"I shall wait outside your door," he said, and closed it softly.

Meredyth struggled quickly into the lavender bridesmaid dress, and grabbed Melissa's overnight bag, zipping it closed.

She didn't bother brushing her hair, and laughed as she caught a glimpse of herself in the polished metal mirror.

"This has got to be the only bridesmaids dress that you really *can* wear again," she observed, and hurried to join Alex in the hall.

The little girl was burning with fever. She was so sick that she didn't speak, or even seem to care that they were there. Her eyes glittered with delirium as she opened them briefly, and then she closed them again, her head lolling to one side.

Meredyth reached for the cup at the side of the bed, and then grimaced as she smelled beer.

"Get me water," she ordered, and Alyce looked at her in alarm.

" 'Tis not healthy," the woman protested, and Meredyth thought that she was probably right.

"Bring snow then, as clean as you can find, and boil it. Bring me a whole pot full."

Alyce opened the door, spoke sharply to a maidservant, and turned back to Meredyth for her next order.

"Bring me a tub of water, not too warm. The biggest tub you have, and quickly."

She didn't have a thermometer, but she knew that the child's fever was far past the point of safety, and that she'd certainly go into convulsions soon if it wasn't brought down. Meredyth didn't want to think about convulsions, or the brain damage that could result.

She decided not to wait for the water, and grabbed the mug of beer, struggling to open the Tylenol with the other hand. She threw the cotton to the floor, and shook two capsules into her palm.

"Sit her up," she urged Alex.

He went to his daughter, lifting her shoulders gently. She made a soft, pained sound, and her dark head fell against his chest. A fit of coughing seized her, and the sound was terrible to hear, harsh and painful.

"Katherine. Katherine." Meredyth spoke softly but firmly. "Sweetheart, listen to me. I want you to swallow these pills. Like you did with the one I gave you after dinner. Here." She lifted the mug to the child's mouth. "Take a big drink, and swallow. Please."

She pressed the small caplets into the little girl's mouth. She had never felt skin so hot to the touch.

She tried to get her to drink; Kate choked and coughed, spilling the pills down the front of her night-gown.

Meredyth caught them, and pressed them in again. "I know, honey. But we have to make you better. One swallow, and I'll let you sleep. That's all."

Katherine's eyes opened briefly, feverish and unfocused, and then closed again. Meredyth pressed the mug to the little mouth, poured the beer in, and held her fingers firmly against the fevered lips until she was sure the child had swallowed.

"Good girl."

The child fell back into her father's arms. He lifted his face to Meredyth, and the fear and grief in his eyes were terrible to see.

"It'll be all right." She hoped that she sounded more confident than she felt.

Apparently she didn't, for he gave a weak smile and said, "Thou art no card player, Meredyth Sherborne. Thy fear is writ plainly on thy face."

"Wait and see," she said, unwilling to give up hope.

Alyce returned, leading two servants with a huge metal tub of water. Meredyth felt it. Good. It was luke-warm.

"Strip her down, and we'll put her in."

Alex hesitated, his eyes widening. "Jesu God, lady, it will kill her."

"It will lower her fever." Meredyth spoke sharply, already tugging the blankets away from the child. "I know it seems cruel, but trust me."

It seemed forever that he hesitated. "I meant what I said in the gallery. If you harm her, I will take your life, and answer for it happily."

Meredyth looked full into his eyes, hoping that he could see the sincerity in her own. "Please. Trust me."

He hesitated only a moment longer, and then began stripping his daughter's nightgown from her thin body.

Meredyth almost wept at the sight of the thin, shivering child, grimy with sweat and dirt, her feet still stained with the pigeon blood that Dr. Horton had applied to them. But the sight of it steeled her resolve and confidence. Little Kate had a better chance with her than with the professionals.

"Lift her into the water."

Alex didn't hesitate this time, even though Alyce and the maids set up a cry, protesting that they would surely kill the little one.

Meredyth wasn't in the mood. "Either shut up or get out."

Alyce chose to remain; the maidservants fled.

Alex held his daughter in the water, soaking his shirtsleeves to the elbow. Meredyth had to look away as Kate shivered and cried, begging to be put back to bed.

She dug in Melissa's bag, and dug out the bottle of gardenia shower gel. "As long as she's in there, we may as well take a couple layers of dirt off."

She closed her ears to the sound of the crying, and washed the child quickly. The smell of gardenia soap filled the air, mercifully covering the stale, sickroom odor of illness and sweat.

As gently as she could, she washed the lank, greasy hair and rinsed it, quickly wrapping it in a towel of coarse linen.

Little Kate cried with fear and misery, her teeth chattering, but her skin was still hot in the cooling water.

Whatever You Wish

Alex's face was taut with fear and misery. "How long must we keep her here?"

Meredyth wanted nothing more than a telephone, with a nice, helpful nurse at the other end, giving her instructions. "I'm not sure," she admitted. "Until the fever goes down, I think."

It seemed as if they sat there forever, holding the struggling child in the cooling water, making soothing sounds as she cried, patting her pale arms and legs with anxious hands until Meredyth couldn't stand it anymore.

"How long has it been?" she wondered aloud.

Alex glanced at the table. "About a quarter of an hour."

Meredyth looked for a clock, but saw none. Frowning, she looked again, and brightened. "Oh, the candle," she exclaimed, noticing the rings marked at intervals around it. How clever. Each ring would represent an hour.

"Good enough, I guess," she said, stroking Kate's forehead. Was it her imagination, or was it cooler? "Let's get her out."

They lifted the child out, and wrapped her in a warm blanket before depositing her back in her bed.

She lay there, burrowing gratefully into the warmth of her blankets. Her eyes were closed, her lashes two great fans of darkness against her white skin. She shivered, sighed, and then lay quietly.

Alyce sat on a stool by the door, silent tears running down her cheeks.

Alex bent over his daughter. His eyes were bright with anxiety as he ran his fingers over her face, and touched the pulse point at the side of her tiny throat.

"Her fever has lessened," he said, his voice wondering. "She seems better."

"It will probably go back up again in a few hours," Meredyth told him. "But I'll stay with her, if you like, and give her more medicine."

He nodded, his eyes not moving from his daughter's face.

Meredyth turned to Alyce. "She can't drink beer. Bring me water, water that's been boiled for at least twenty minutes, in a clean pitcher. What the hell, boil the pitcher, too. And a cup."

Alyce glanced at Alex, who nodded.

"And maybe later we can try some chicken broth. But it's to be freshly made. Can we get a freshly killed chicken?"

"Of course. But thee cannot cook a chicken straight-away, lady. It must hang first, at least two days—"

Meredyth interrupted. "No. Hang it long enough to drain it; then wash it well in boiled water, and make the broth."

Alyce twisted her hands in her apron, and looked helplessly at Alex, who nodded again.

Sighing, she left the room.

There was a small cot against the opposite wall, and Meredyth sank onto it, exhausted. She reached for the overnight bag, laid it at the head of the cot, and used it for a pillow. "What time is it?"

"About three."

She had thought that she would never be able to sleep, after the bizarre events of the last twenty-four hours, but she could barely keep her eyelids open.

"Her fever might start to go up at about six thirty. Wake me then."

Her eyes were shut even before she finished speaking.

"Lady Sherborne?"

She was so tired that the name and title meant nothing to her.

"Meredyth?"

She opened her eyes. The room looked very strange to her—the sleeping child in the huge, blue-curtained bed, the firelight dancing off the creamy plaster walls, the tub sitting in a puddle on the floor.

Whatever You Wish

But most of all, she wondered at the dark-haired man who seemed so strange, and yet so familiar to her. He was kneeling by the child's bed, her thin white hand covered with his larger, tanned one. The flames cast dark shadows beneath his eyes and cheekbones, giving him a dangerous look, but the expression on his face as he looked at Meredyth was almost tender.

"My thanks, lady. I buried her mother almost nine years ago, and I feared that my Kate would join her before morning. I know not why you have come here, but"—he swallowed, and glanced away—"for the first time in many a year, I have hope. You have eased my heart as much as you please mine eyes."

It was a dream, certainly. Her eyes closed, and she thought what a great dream it was, where her own fairy-tale knight spoke words like poetry to her. She wondered if he would be there when she woke up, or if he would fade away into the darkness, like all dreams did.

"I forgot to set the alarm," she murmured, and was asleep before she finished speaking.

For a long time after Meredyth fell asleep, Alexander Hartford sat watching her. From time to time he looked away and touched his daughter's face, but her fever did not rise, and her breathing was easy and comfortable.

Meredyth Sherborne. She was fascinating to him. He half believed her to be a fairy, or an angel, or some otherworldly creature.

But he didn't care. He was a man who had learned to trust his instincts, and he trusted her. However outlandish her methods might be, she had acted with Kate's best interests at heart. And succeeded, thus far.

He left his daughter and crossed the room, looking down at Meredyth as she slept. His shadow fell across her face, but she didn't stir.

Gently he reached out a finger and brushed it across

the mysterious shimmering color of her eyelid, and examined his finger. Faint sparkles shone on it. Paint, then, of some sort.

He picked up her hand, and examined her colored nails. It was paint, too. It had chipped a little on one finger. He was glad to know it. She was definitely a mortal woman.

The stuff of her gown was less easily explained. It was as soft and light as silk, but it was stuff that he had never seen before. He examined it carefully, but remained baffled.

Her shoes utterly confounded him. They were bulky, the tops of leather sewn in many pieces, and with dark blue stripes sewn on the sides, and cut high like boots to her ankles, tied about with dingy laces of thick cotton. The soles were thick, like clogs or pattens, with strange circles and triangles beneath, though to what purpose he could not imagine. And they were made of strange, leatherlike substance, but too thick to be leather.

She was sleeping so solidly that he was tempted to peek beneath her skirts, but decency forbade it. He retreated before he was tempted to do so.

And that bag beneath her head! He'd give his teeth to look inside, and discover what mysterious things lay inside.

Yes, she was mortal, but from where he could not imagine. She said she was near thirty years. An age when women were losing teeth, and their bodies beginning to suffer from their daily toil.

But she lay there, as robust and healthy as a young girl, with a bloom of sweet color on her face, and luscious bosoms rising and falling with the deep breath of sleep.

He thought of the thin gown she had been wearing in her room earlier. What fabric! So fine and thin, made to uncover as much glowing skin as possible.

Whatever You Wish

Wherever she was from, they had a fine fashion of night rails. All women should wear them, though he doubted any other woman would look like Meredyth Sherborne, his fairy guest.

Chapter Seven

The two maidservants sat outside little Lady Katherine's room, speaking in low whispers.

"I did see her, through a crack in the door as she undressed for bed, and I tell thee—"

"Oh, Mag—however did ye dare?"

"I did dare, and wish I had not. It was a terrible thing. Her thirty years gone, she says, and still as smooth as a girl. I will tell thee how she does it."

Fascinated, the girl leaned closer. "Tell."

Mag dropped her voice lower still. "She sheds her skin, like a snake! I saw her take the skin of her own legs, and roll it off in one piece!"

Her companion drew back, horrified. "She never!"

"May I be struck dead if she didn't. The skin off of both legs, and rolled it into a nasty little ball of flesh, and the new skin beneath as white as could be."

The two girls contemplated the idea with horror.

"I ran straight away, then," Mag said, "for I was terrible afeared to see more. But she's a bad one. A fairy for sure."

The other maid shuddered. "Does thee think—" she whispered, and broke off abruptly as the door beside them swung open.

They both bobbed quick curtsies as Lord Hartford appeared, handsome as always. He looked tired, but happy.

"My daughter is much improved," he said. "You will bring her breakfast, please. She is to have goat's milk, boiled and cooled, and warm bread, and perhaps some stewed apples. No beer, no wine. And bring another pitcher of boiled water, set to cool in clean snow. And anything else Lady Sherborne asks."

The girls exchanged terrified glances.

"Sir?"

"Do you not understand?" His expression hardened slightly. "Whatever she wishes."

He strode off toward the gallery, leaving the two frightened girls looking after him.

"You see?" Mag said, in a frightened whisper. "He's been fairy led, for certain."

Meredyth could see the terrified looks of the maids who came and went throughout the day, and really didn't care. She had one goal—before the next full moon, when she left Sherborne Castle and returned home, she intended that Kate be well. She had about thirty days to accomplish her goal.

It wasn't much, but she hoped that with the help of Melissa's antibiotics and the change in diet and hygiene, and without the debilitating leeches draining the child's blood, the girl might be able to pull through.

She might have worried more about her own situation, but the best way to deal with stress, in Meredyth's opinion, was to keep busy and not give herself time to worry about it.

So she got busy, and if she ended up causing undue

stress in every other person within the castle walls, too bad.

By the end of the day, there was not a servant within the walls of Sherborne House that didn't have a serious grievance with her.

She ordered that all the floors and walls be swept and washed until they shone, and had poor Gilman, the clerk, order carpets from London. "As if she were the queen herself!" the man reported to the steward, but when they went to complain to Sir Alex, he refused to listen. Whatever "Lady Sherborne" wanted, he told them.

She had the nerve to invade the kitchen, and depleted the pantries and buttery by half, saying that this was spoiled and that was rotten and this had bugs in it and that was unhealthy, and must not be served, until the cook was in a rage, and she berated the scullery maids for not being clean enough. They were already furious at having to boil every dish and pot after it was used.

Even the poor lad whose job it was to empty the closestools didn't escape the wrath of Lady Sherborne; he was told that he could no longer throw the slops out into the garden or against the courtyard walls, but must needs dig a pit some fifty yards from the house, and cover each deposit with earth afterward.

She even took issue with the dogs, who had comfortably wandered in and out of the house at their leisure. They were banished to the stables and gardens, because "Lady Sherborne" had an unnatural aversion to fleas.

Sir Alex listened graciously to each complaint, and nodded and smiled, and refused to overrule the new tyrant.

It was a very dark day, the servants agreed, that the fairy folk had sent Meredyth Sherborne back to them. Nobody, fairy or mortal, could possibly satisfy the woman.

Whatever You Wish

The increase in wages pacified some of the complaints, and the fear of retribution from the fairy kingdom took care of the rest.

And Meredyth, delighted with young Kate's returning health, and happy with her unchallenged position, kept on bullying them all, smiling as she did so.

Meredyth carefully counted the remaining antibiotics into her hand. Though Kate had shown a marked improvement over the past two weeks, she was still far from healthy, occasionally coughing up spatters of blood. She was easily chilled, and her fevers flared up now and then, though never with the ferocity of that first, awful night.

There were enough pills to last six more days. Meredyth knew it wouldn't be enough.

"Lady Sherborne?" Kate was sitting up in bed, her clean hair flowing down her back. "A game of draughts?"

"You bet." Meredyth emptied the pills back into the bottle, tucked it into the bag she now wore tied about her waist, and went to the cupboard. She found the checkerboard, a handsome thing of light and dark wood, and the checkers.

She sat on Kate's bed, and began setting up the game.

"Today I shall win," Kate promised.

"Oh, no, you won't. I'm tired of losing." Meredyth tucked her new skirts of moss velvet beneath her. Actually, new was the wrong word. Alyce made over some of her mother's old dresses for her. They had been stored away in chests. Apparently nothing was thrown away—the price of fabric was too high. So hems had been let down, and seams let out, and at Meredyth's demand, the busks—flat widths of bone inserted into the bodice—had been removed.

And so she had found herself transformed into an Elizabethan gentlewoman, albeit a tall and broad one.

She was less comfortable than she was in her lavender gown, a fact that made her laugh. She had sworn that she would only wear that stupid dress as long as she had to. She'd never dreamed that it would be the most comfortable item in her wardrobe.

"Lady Sherborne!" Kate jumped her checker over Meredyth's. "Are thee woolgathering?"

"Sorry." Meredyth turned her attention back to the game. Winter sunlight streamed across the bed, making bright patterns over the rumpled blue covers, and lighting Kate's brown hair with a golden halo.

"What a cozy scene is this!" The door flew open, and Alex stepped in. He looked as if he had been riding. He was still wearing his high boots, and his dark cape swirled around him as he made a courtly bow. His high cheekbones were bright with cold, and his dark hair looked as if it had been tossed by the wind.

But what Meredyth noticed most of all was the glow in his eyes as he smiled—a smile that embraced her as much as the little girl sitting opposite her.

"What a pleasure," he said, "to see such beautiful ladies in my house. It makes me want to turn away from seafaring, and stay home forever."

"You'd never do it," Meredyth told him, her cheeks warm with the pleasure of the compliment. "You were born to be an adventurer. Look at you—you even look like a pirate."

"Privateer," he corrected, affecting an offended air. "There is a passing difference."

"Like what?" Meredyth demanded.

He winked. "I have the queen's permission to loot and plunder. And speaking of plunder, I have just recently been to inspect my latest takings, and brought New Year's gifts." He presented them from a large bundle from beneath his cape, wrapped in rough paper.

"But it's days past New Year's," Kate protested, laughing.

"Then I shall leave, and take my gifts to someone more appreciative."

Meredyth and Kate protested loudly, and he turned back with feigned reluctance.

"Oh, very well. Here we are. For my Kate, to keep her warm." He threw the paper to the floor, revealing a pile of fur, dark and shining and luxurious.

The child cried out with delight, rubbing her cheek against them.

"Sables from Russia. I am most certain that they were intended for a Spanish princess, at the very least. But they shall suit you well."

Meredyth ran her hand through the dark softness. "They're beautiful."

"And next winter, when Kate is well, she shall wear them out riding with me, and everywhere we go, people shall wonder at her beauty."

Kate giggled, lying back against her pillows and stroking the sables like a cat.

"And for our Lady Meredyth, enchantress of the fairy realm . . ." He reached inside his doublet and presented her with a long golden chain, sparkling with what looked like amethysts and diamonds.

Meredyth stared, speechless. It must be worth thousands of dollars. The chain was at least four feet long, and real gold of exquisite beauty. Hanging from the end was a huge pendant of filigree curves, set with jewels that flashed purple and rainbow fire in the sunlight.

"Come," Alex said, seizing her hand and pulling her to her feet. "Let us see how it suits you." His hands traveled quickly around her waist, with an easy, intimate grace, and he fastened the fantastic belt so that it hung down the front of her gown. "There. It suits thee, Meredyth. A proper lady needs jewels as fine as herself."

Meredyth looked into his face, so close to her own, and her heart gave a quiver at the pleasure in his eyes.

"Oh, Alex—I can't. It's far too valuable for me to accept."

He reached up a gloved hand, which smelled of sandalwood and leather, and brushed a strand of hair from her face with a tender gesture.

"What foolishness. 'Tis little enough payment for my daughter's health." He dropped his eyes, and checked the clasp at her waist. Then he spoke softly, so softly that Meredyth was unsure if she heard him right. "Would that I could chain your heart as easily as your waist, lady. I would keep thee bound to us forever."

He gave her a quick, wistful smile, and left the room, his boots thumping across the shining wood floors.

Meredyth stared after him, her heart racing. Her first wish had come true. She had found her perfect knight, shining armor or not. And in two short weeks, she would have to leave him.

It was inevitable. Her parents were probably out of their minds with grief and fear; the news stations would be showing her picture. Poor Melissa's honeymoon was probably ruined.

"Lady Sherborne?"

Drawing a deep breath, she turned back to Kate, who was lying back in her bed. She looked tired, and her eyes were getting that feverish glow.

"I am passing tired. Will thee tell me stories of fairy land?"

"Sure." Meredyth settled herself on the bed, and wrapped a protective arm around the thin shoulders, stroking the warm forehead. She hesitated to waste any more Tylenol, saving it for only the highest fevers and pain.

"Everything in fairy land is very clean. Even the poorest people have carpets on their floors. There are magical lights in all the rooms, that come on at the touch of a little switch, and are brighter than a hundred candles. And warm air flows in all winter, so you're never cold, and cold air in the summer, so you're never hot."

"And the cities have castles a hundred floors high," the child recited, "and magical lights all along the streets."

"That's right. And you can buy anything you want."

"Flowers in the dead of winter, and fresh fruit as you like," Kate murmured, her eyes heavy. "I only get oranges in the autumn, from Spain." She was seized with a fit of coughing, and Meredyth held her close, wincing at the harsh sound.

"Tell me again of the doctors," the child said. "Nobody ever has pox, or dies from the sweating sickness. And mothers rarely die from birth."

"That's right."

"They could make me well," the little girl murmured, her eyes closed, "in that place."

Meredyth sat silently, until she was sure the child was sleeping.

Then she went to her room, and bolted the door. For the first time since she had arrived, she sat down and wept with frustration.

She had one wish left, and didn't know how to use it to accomplish everything she needed to.

She wanted to go home. The thought of her family's suffering, their grief at her disappearance, tore her heart out. She couldn't bear the thought of being the cause of that much suffering.

And she wanted Kate to live. The child needed modern doctors, and a full course of antibiotics, and to be away from the damp, cold air that no fires could stop.

And she wanted Alex. She wanted to stay near him forever, and to hear his easy compliments of her beauty, and to see his blue eyes shining at her. She wanted to stay in Sherborne House, dressed in velvets and jewels, and be his lover. He wanted her; it became more obvious every day.

And she had only one wish left. No matter how she

tried, there was no way she could fit all her desires, all her needs, into one simple wish. She tried again and again to think of a way, until her head ached with the effort.

Chapter Eight

Alex was sitting at his writing table, looking out the window at the gardens. The snow was brilliant beneath the sunlight. It was the coldest winter he could remember. Even the Thames, the mighty waterway to London, had frozen solid. Sherborne House seemed like a lost island in the barren, frozen landscape.

"Sir?"

He turned. His clerk, Gilman, was standing there, his arms full of papers.

"Gilman?"

"I have prepared our case against Lady Sherborne. I do think we have a good chance. These things are against us—Alyce Middleton, firstly. She is a good witness. She knew the child and the mother, and saw firsthand that cursed pendant. But she is old, and we could discredit her, I think. If the jury is carefully picked—"

"Bought, you mean."

"Carefully chosen, to be modern thinkers who have no silly fancies of fairy stories, then we will have no problem. We can show this woman to be a liar and an adventurer. If worst comes, we might prove her to be a witch, and—"

"God's nightgown! None of that, Gilman." Alex sat up straight, his tone dark with warning. "Jesu God, Gilman, hast thee thought of the outcome of that?"

Gilman rubbed his nose with an ink-spotted finger, looking offended. "Sir, we want to win. Can you really mean to lose all to this creature? She is a fair thing to look on, true, but she will kill your household with her absurd fancies. And yet you follow her, like—" He broke off, as if he had said too much.

"Like what, Gilman?"

"Like . . . like a man bewitched, or fairy led," the clerk muttered reluctantly.

Alex leaned back, his fingers drumming a thoughtful rhythm against the table.

"So," he said at last. "Perhaps I am. Perhaps you are right, Gilman. For I am a learned man, and this story of fairies and magical kingdoms and changeling heiresses sounds like babbling idiocy, even to me." He sighed, taking a drink of warm, spiced wine from the goblet at his side.

"And yet, I think she is Meredyth Sherborne, and no liar. She is a tyrant with mine household, true. And strange to speak to. Her opinions are as harsh and strong as a man's, and her ways a mystery to me. But still, she strikes me as wise and honest."

He set the glass down with a firm motion. "We may yet drop the case, Gilman."

The man stared with disbelief. "But, sir—"

"There yet may be another answer to this riddle, Gilman. What if I were to take Meredyth Sherborne as my bride?"

The poor clerk was struck speechless. He stared at Alex with a face that clearly said that his master had gone mad.

"Is it not perfect and easy? I shall woo her and court

her, and compromise her honor if needs be. That would be a pleasure. And then take her to my side, forever. It would please me, and please Kate."

His mind made up, Alex Hartford dismissed his clerk with a wave of his hand. His years of commanding at sea had taught him to decide on a plan of attack, and then proceed without hesitation. He had learned to trust his instincts, and his instincts were telling him that he would never find another Meredyth Sherborne.

Chapter Nine

Meredyth had never felt so certain that she was lost in a fairy tale. For the next week, everything seemed too perfect to be real.

Kate had never been in better health, Alex told her. The antibiotics seemed to have done their job. She felt well enough to get out of bed and dress, and join them for meals in the great hall, or in Alex's chambers.

Those were the times Meredyth liked best. Alex's rooms were beautiful, paneled in carved walnut and with parquet flooring, with rich rugs from Persia scattered about. The heavy damask curtains blocked out the winter chill, and the fire blazed before the small table that they shared.

It felt like being a family—her, Kate, and Alex, away from the curious eyes of the household, talking and laughing and sharing their meals together.

Alex loved to entertain them with stories of his travels. It amazed Meredyth that in these days, when seagoing was such a treacherous occupation, and most

160

people never went more than seven miles from home in all their lives, that Alex had seen more of the world than she had.

He had sailed to Spain and Holland and Italy, and as far away as Persia. He had, to Meredyth's great surprise, been among the few men that the queen had sent to far-off Russia. He told them stories of the Russian noblemen, the *boyars* in their long velvet robes and beards, who drank like barbarians and spit into golden plates and smashed priceless Venetian glass; men who owned thousands of acres of land and more gold than her majesty's dukes, but who shivered in rickety wooden houses that burned down with alarming regularity.

He was a clever mimic, and his impression of the Russian prince who had been his host reduced Meredyth and Kate to tears of laughter.

She rarely thought of home. It wouldn't do any good, and she hated to ruin her newly found happiness.

It was like a beautiful, fragile illusion, and she didn't want to shatter it. Meredyth was falling in love. And it was a love that was reciprocated. She could see it in Alex's eyes when he touched her hand, or casually smoothed her hair back from her face, letting the fine strands of ash blond fall over his palm as though it were spun gold, watching it with soft eyes.

She could hear it in his voice when he bid her good night, in a gentle, lingering tone that tempted her to stay, and then haunted her sleep at night, filling her dreams with lush, erotic images.

And every day he gave her gifts, with lavish compliments that meant more than the necklace of perfect pearls, or the cape of midnight blue velvet lined with soft fur. He gave her gloves, embroidered and perfumed, and a golden pomander filled with perfume to hang from her belt—though, he assured her, the most costly ambergris would not be more pleasing to him than the scent of her skin.

Meredyth blushed at the extravagance of his words. "You shouldn't say things like that," she said, and her voice was husky.

"Why not?" he demanded, apparently delighted with her reaction.

Alyce had taken Kate off to bed, and they were sitting alone in his chambers, a chessboard of Italian marble on the table between them. Meredyth had just lost the game in an unsurpassed display of poor playing. She couldn't help it; she was constantly distracted by him.

"Why not?" he demanded again when she didn't answer. "Thou art a passing beautiful woman, Meredyth, and deserve to hear it. I have never met a woman could compare to thee for grace or beauty."

Meredyth looked across the table, into his bright blue eyes beneath the dark brows, and was amazed that such a man could ever say such things to her.

"You shouldn't say it," she replied quickly, "because you'll make me fall in love with you. And I couldn't bear it when it was time for me to go."

He reached across the table, the candlelight glowing from the ruby ring on his finger, and caught her chin, lifting her face toward his.

"Then do not go," he said simply. "Never leave us, my changeling love."

The honest emotion showing in his eyes was too much to bear. Meredyth felt her heart melt, and tears sprang into her eyes. She was afraid to speak.

He lifted her hand to his lips and turned it over, placing a lingering kiss on the inside of her wrist. Heat seemed to shoot from the tender spot, and spread through her body like a drug.

"Do not leave us," he repeated in a whisper.

She opened her mouth to protest, but he leaned quickly forward, covering her mouth with his fingers. "You argue far too much, sweeting. Were you never taught to respect your menfolk?" He laughed softly at the look on her face, and then leaned across the table until their faces were almost touching.

"I will take your arguments from your very lips," he whispered, and when he kissed her, Meredyth could no more have objected than she could have sprouted feathers and flown.

She leaned into his kiss, shivering with pleasure at the touch of his mouth against hers, the touch of his warm hand against her neck. Her blood turned to liquid fire; her mind forgot everything but the feeling of his tongue seeking hers, and the feeling of their shared breath.

It seemed forever before their mouths parted. He leaned his forehead against hers, his hand traveling lightly over her neck.

"You have lost the game," he said, his voice low and husky.

Meredyth was dizzy, and his words made no sense. "What game?"

He smiled, and indicated the chessboard on the table. "What, forgotten already? Did we not agree that the loser should pay a forfeit?"

His hand was warm over hers, his fingers stroking her palm with a skill that sent waves of heat to the very core of her.

"We did," Meredyth agreed, wondering what she would do, if he asked the inevitable of her.

He smiled, and blew out the candle that sat on the table. His face was lit only by the flames of the fire, making him look wickedly beautiful. The only other light came from the window, where the damask curtains were thrown open to show the magical sight of the snowy hills beneath the cold light of the moon, hanging low and silvery and—

It was almost full.

Meredyth's heart stopped, and gave a sickened thud. She had one more night, maybe two.

"No need to look so frightened, sweet. I would never ask more than you would willingly give."

She stared at him, wondering how the time had passed so quickly. How could she leave him?

"May I ask?"

"Ask what?" She was torn into a million conflicting pieces, and the sight of him with his eyes glowing with passion and his tender smile tore at her heart.

"My forfeit, of course. I will not ask, if you forbid me."

Meredyth raised her trembling hand to his cheek, and he turned his face into it, planting a kiss there.

"Ask." The word was spoken without further thought. If all she could have was this night, she'd take it without regrets. It would be the greatest one-night stand in history, something for her to treasure forever.

His eyes glimmered with pleasure; his beautifully shaped mouth curved into a smile. He rose from the table, went to the door that led to his bedchamber, and swung it open.

The great bed was curtained in deep blues and golds, like the bed of a king. A single candle burned in a tall stand.

He leaned against the door, long legged and handsome and sexier than any man Meredyth had ever seen.

"Your forfeit is this—I should like to see thee, in my bed, wearing that gown I saw, the first night. The one that seemed to be woven of clouds, and hid none of thy beauty from my eyes. I have dreamed of it since."

Meredyth hesitated, and then felt an answering glimmer in her own eyes. *Why not?*

"You're on," she replied. He might have raised his brow at her odd response, but her meaning was clear.

All night, the candle burned lower, passing one hour mark after another, but Meredyth never slept. Her only provision for the night was that he shut the curtains, hiding the sight of the waxing moon from her eyes. She didn't want to think about it.

She had never thought of herself as beautiful in her whole life. Not bad, but nothing extraordinary, either. But when she appeared in the bedchamber and shed the blue velvet cape, she felt beautiful.

The look in his eyes was all the assurance she needed. He led her to the bed, and watched as she lay down on the soft velvet quilt, his eyes hot with desire.

He ran his hands over the sheer fabric, tracing the lines of her body, whispering words of such tender admiration that she almost wept.

It seemed as if she couldn't welcome him into her body soon enough. If she had thought him handsome in his doublets and capes, she found him even more stunning without, his body hard and wiry from his years at sea.

They fit together perfectly, bodies and hearts and breath mingling together in an anguished sweetness more beautiful than she had ever known.

They made love and rested and made love again. They shared a cup of wine, and then shared their bodies again. They whispered and laughed together, and kissed until they were hungry for each other all over again.

Finally exhausted, Alex drew the heavy bed curtains to shut out the light of dawn, and they were beginning to drift off into sleep when they were startled by a furious pounding on the door.

Swearing, Alex jumped up and went to the door, and came back in a moment, his face taut with alarm.

He tossed Meredyth her blue cape. "Hurry. It was Alyce, and she tells me that Kate has taken a turn for the worse."

Meredyth sat up, instantly awake. Terrified, she thought of the empty bottle of antibiotics that lay on the bottom of the overnight bag.

Gone. Her worst fear had come true. All of her modern medicines were gone, and Kate had relapsed. There was nothing standing between her and death but hope, and what little care Meredyth could offer her.

Chapter Ten

The child had relapsed, and her fever raged throughout the day. There was no Tylenol to ease her pain, no medicine to still the cough that racked her tiny body.

All day long, Alex and Meredyth sat by the bed, sponging the slender child down, laying cool, wet cloths on her forehead. She woke, and asked Meredyth for more physic.

Meredyth shook her head. "It's all gone, sweetie. You'll have to wait till I get more."

The promise felt empty and hollow to her.

"In fairy land?" Kate's eyes were fixed on Meredyth with such a look of love and trust that her heart ached.

Meredyth nodded, unable to answer.

"Take me there," the child begged.

Her father hushed her, stroking her fine, long hair.

"But they have doctors there. They could make me better," Kate cried, fretful and feverish.

"We can do better than that," Alex told her, his voice bright with false cheer. "We have our Meredyth, and

167

she is better than any fumbling fool doctor."

Kate stared up at him, her eyes glazed with fever. "Take me there," she begged, and cried when Meredyth told her they couldn't.

Meredyth left the room, stood in the cold hall, and cried.

All that day and through most of the night, they battled the fierce fever, until Kate fell into a deep sleep. Exhausted, Meredyth lay down on the small cot in the little girl's room, exactly as she had on her first night there, and fell asleep.

She heard Alex come in, and he covered her with a blanket, kissing her eyelids. She smiled, but was too tired to reach for him. She felt him slide a ring onto her finger, and wondered briefly if it was the ruby he always wore. Then she slept, too tired to care about anything.

"Oh God!"

Meredyth sat up straight, shaken from her sleep by Alex's cry of alarm.

It was near dawn. Gray light was showing around the edge of the heavy curtains, falling over the floor and touching the empty bed.

Meredyth stared, aghast, and she and Alex exchanged looks of fear.

"Where is she?" Meredyth climbed out of the narrow bed, her heart hammering, afraid of the answer.

"I know not." He looked wildly around the empty chamber, throwing the blankets from the bed as if the child had somehow flattened herself. He threw open the curtains, letting the cold light of dawn into the room, and rushed into the small adjoining room where Kate's wardrobe was stored.

"Her cloak is gone," he said. "She must be nearby, though. She can't have gone far, in her condition."

Meredyth stared out the window. The moon was still

hanging in the sky, full and magical, rising higher as dawn approached.

"Oh, Alex . . ."

He gripped her quickly, kissing her. "Fear not. She must be somewhere in the house. We'll find her, my love." He rushed from the room.

Meredyth raised a quivering hand to brush her hair back from her face, and then looked at her hand in surprise. Alex's ruby ring was on her forefinger. So she hadn't dreamed it.

She turned toward the door, still shaky from sleep. She could hear Alex calling Kate, and raising the alarm among the servants.

Meredyth stopped in her tracks, her heart pounding.

What if Kate had tried to go to the fairy ring? She had asked so many times yesterday for Meredyth to take her there.

But it was too far for a sick child in the snow. Meredyth ran to her room, throwing open her overnight bag. The fairy necklace was still there, safe beneath Melissa's ridiculous underpants.

She fastened it securely around her neck. She had told Kate the story of traveling through fairy rings with the magic necklace and a wish. Just a bedtime story to entertain a sick child, but she was terrified at the thought that Kate might have gone.

She could hear the servants running through the great house, calling for Lady Katherine.

She was sure of it. The child had tried to go to the fairy ring. Meredyth trembled as she thought of the possibilities. Perhaps Kate was lying in the snow somewhere, unconscious—or worse. She panicked at the thought. Or what if the child had made it there, and had wished herself away in search of the magical doctors who could make her better?

Without hesitation, Meredyth stripped off the cumbersome gown she wore, her fingers fumbling with the ties at the sleeves and stomacher. She couldn't move quickly enough in these stiff and heavy gowns.

The lavender taffeta whispered over her skin, and she tugged the zipper up quickly. She changed her soft leather slippers for her sturdy runners, retrieved from their hiding place deep beneath the bed.

The blue velvet cape tied over her shoulders, she left her room running and took the staircase two stairs at a time.

As she pushed open the front door, she saw two servants staring at her with alarm. "I'm going to look for Kate," she called, and pulled the heavy door closed.

She stopped and took a deep breath. Sure enough, there were the small footprints in the snow, leading toward the village.

Meredyth set off at a run, lifting her skirts from the snow, cursing the heavy drifts that slowed her progress. For a long time she didn't even dare to think, or be frightened. She simply kept on, one foot after the next, her breath huffing and puffing in the cold, dark air of the early morning.

It was very different from the way her progress to Sherborne House had been. She was alone now, the landscape silent. Snow was falling, and Meredyth cursed in eight different ways. She considered turning back and asking Alex for help. But she was already at the village; she was almost there.

"Kate?" Meredyth shouted as she entered the wooded hillside where the fairy ring was.

The white and silent forest gave up no answers.

She trudged forward, gasping with the exertion. Pain lanced through her side, but she ignored it. The day was growing brighter, the moon paling in the sky. She prayed that Kate had been found at home, that she had turned back or taken refuge in the village. Meredyth couldn't find her footprints anywhere. The falling snow had obscured them by the time she had passed through the town.

Whatever You Wish

Uncertain, she paused and looked around. She had been too dazed and frightened to pay attention the last time she had been here. She remembered staring at the people, the slope of hill behind them. . . .

It was this way, she was sure. Her face was numb with cold, and the fear that tugged at her heart was colder still.

She broke into a run as she saw the holly trees and the huge oak, spreading its winter white branches against the brightening sky.

She stepped into the fairy ring and looked around, breathless.

What was that?

Frowning, she bent over to pick up the pale object. A butterfly, pale yellow and frozen stiff. She wondered if it had been here the past thirty days. She tossed it aside, and looked again.

Nothing. Not a footprint. No sign that Kate had been anywhere here. But if not here, where?

"Meredyth!" The call was faint, so faint that she wasn't sure if she had really heard it.

She lifted her head and looked. It was Alex, riding toward her over the white ground on a great brown horse with a white mark on its forehead.

His cape flew around him as he rode toward her through the swirling snowflakes. Her knight. He stopped at the base of the hill and shouted again.

Meredyth frowned, unable to understand.

He waited, drew breath, and shouted again.

"She's found! In the village."

Meredyth raised her fist in a silent hurrah, to show that she had heard.

Alex resumed his ride, his horse picking her way up the hillside, skillfully stepping over fallen trees. The snow fell heavier, and swirled around them like shards of silver.

Meredyth picked up her sodden skirts, and went toward them—

Only to stop short at the edge of the ring, unable to pass through.

The snow dipped and swirled, a thousand flakes dancing around her in the wind.

But there had been no wind.

"No!" The scream that burst from her throat was a raw, terrified sound.

She saw Alex, riding faster, her face creased with alarm as he began covering the final distance that separated them. For a minute, the swirling snow obscured her vision, and she called out to him, panic-stricken.

"Meredyth!"

She tried to move, but her feet felt weightless, as if she were trapped underwater, in the pull of a dark, cold wave. She couldn't breathe; she couldn't see.

She heard Alex shout again, and heard the steady beat of the horse's hooves, faster and closer.

Too late, too late.

She recognized, all too well, the floating sensation, the sight of the sky above her, the sight of the full moon, shining its cold, silver light. The pendant at her neck seemed to reflect the icy glow. Darkness, and then lights.

But I didn't wish. I never wished for this!

From very far away, she could hear Alex calling her name, over and over again, anguish in his voice.

Then there was nothing.

Chapter Eleven

He knelt in the snow, his dark cape falling, and stared around him, shock making his mind slow.

She had been there, and then she was gone.

And that was all.

The circle within the trees was silent. He could hear only the sound of his horse breathing, and his own breath, and the sound of his heart thudding wildly in his chest.

He examined the snow around him. Nothing, save his own footsteps. And yet he had seen her holding her arms out to him, heard her anguished cry.

Something caught his eye, and he bent over, catching it between shaking fingers.

A yellow butterfly, fragile and fantastic, frozen solid.

He stayed there for what seemed a very long time, staring, until he noticed the droplets striking the snow. Rain, at last.

He looked up, and saw nothing but snow, and realized that what he saw were his own tears, falling like rain onto the frozen earth.

Chapter Twelve

"Meredyth!"

She stirred and sat up, her arms trembling with the effort.

"Meredyth!"

She stood, trying to understand what she saw. Dark night, where it had been morning. Perfectly trimmed grass that seemed an incredibly vibrant shade of green. The smell of beauty bark was tart in her nostrils.

"Meredyth—oh, there you are, you bonehead. Why didn't you answer?"

"Mark?" He looked so strange in his tuxedo, with his newly cut hair shining in the moonlight.

"Come on. They're getting ready to leave, and Mom's about ready to kill you. What the hell are you doing?"

"I don't know." Stunned, she let Mark take her arm, and he began pulling her back toward the hotel.

Everything seemed very loud. The whine and rush of distant traffic, the buzz of electric lights, the shouts and chatter of the wedding party as they made their way to the front of the hotel.

Alex. She caught her breath and stumbled.

Mark laughed. "You idiot. You drank too much champagne, didn't you?"

"Something like that." It had been a dream, then; the weirdest, most detailed dream she'd ever had. She felt as if she'd been hit over the head with a brick.

"Here, give me Melissa's bag." Mark seized it from her, pushing her along with the other hand. "She didn't take much, did she?"

"One sundress, one copy of *Glamour*, a pair of butt-floss underpants, two toothbrushes, toothpaste, gardenia soap—"

"Meredyth?" Mark gripped her shoulder. "I don't really care."

"Oh."

"But straighten yourself up and quit babbling, or Mom will know you're drunk."

Meredyth followed him to the front of the hotel, where he steered her through the crowd.

Melissa and Dwayne were coming through, laughing and saying good-bye. The sound of the party hurt Meredyth's ears. Everything felt like a bad dream.

"Butterflies!" The voice in her ear was too loud, and she jumped, turning to see the Wedding Nazi. Her makeup looked very frosty and surreal, her plum lipstick garish around her false smile.

Realizing what was expected, Meredyth tugged open the cardboard box in her arms.

It was empty.

Dazed, she looked up to see if anyone had noticed. They hadn't. All the other bridesmaids, resplendent in their lavender and silver, had successfully released their hostages. Melissa's laughter rang out over the delighted "oohs" and "aahs" of the guests as the air filled with a thousand fluttering monarchs, their yellow wings brilliant in the night.

Amy Elizabeth Saunders

The car was leaving. Melissa was waving out the window. The chorus of good wishes was deafening.

Slowly, Meredyth sat down on the cool concrete of the step. Somebody spoke to her, and she answered without hearing or thinking.

"Wasn't it lovely? We're so glad you could come."

She sat there, watching the crowd break up and drift apart. Her mother fluttered by in a whisper of chiffon; her father patted her head and winked, as if they were sharing a secret.

And then she saw Elva.

The old woman came slowly down the steps, one hand at the small of her back as if it hurt her. Her peacock-hued caftan seemed unnaturally brilliant in the artificial light. Her feathered blue hat was tipped to one side.

"Well." Elva settled down on the step next to Meredyth, and gave her a mischievous smile. "Did you have a nice time, Meredyth Sherborne?"

Meredyth gave a soft, bitter laugh. How was she supposed to answer that?

Elva patted her hand. "The most fantastic things happen at weddings, don't they? All that energy! All those traditions! No wonder brides get overwrought."

Meredyth rested her chin on her knuckles, leaning on her knee and staring across the parking lot. "Elva? Leave me alone, please."

Elva laughed, a high, sparkling sound. "Why, Meredyth! You do have a mean mouth. What's the matter, sourpuss? Did you waste your three wishes already?"

"That's not funny."

"Well. It wasn't meant to be. I was asking seriously, Meredyth. If you had one wish, one chance to get whatever you wanted, what would you say?"

Meredyth sat, staring out at the night, thinking hard. Had it been a dream or not? Did it matter what she said? Was she supposed to stumble around the rest of her life terrified of what would happen every time she said "I wish"?

"I don't know," she cried out. "I don't know. What am I supposed to think? What am I supposed to say? If I wished for everything I wanted to, I could never say it in one sentence. Too much has happened; too much matters! Or maybe it doesn't matter at all. All I know for sure is, I wish everything had turned out differently!"

Silence met her words. She sat, feeling sick, waiting for the skies to open up, for the earth to swallow her, for anything to happen.

Nothing did.

"My good gracious," Elva said. "That's a strange sort of wish. It could mean everything, or it could mean nothing at all. Just imagine."

"I don't want to imagine," Meredyth said. "I'd rather have my teeth removed with a broken bottle."

Elva giggled, and stood up slowly. "Hand me my purse, would you? That's a good girl. Are you going straight home tonight, Meredyth? I'm meeting some friends and going out for a late supper, if you'd like to join us."

"No, thanks."

"Oh, well, I offered. Oh, here's my ride. What a prompt fellow. If you should change your mind . . ."

"I don't think so. I've had all the fun I can stand for tonight."

She watched Elva make her way down to the curb, where a new Saturn had pulled up, the rental ticket still in the window. A small face peered out from the back window, and Elva waved her plump fingers.

"Good night, Meredyth! And if you change your mind . . ."

He was climbing out of the driver's seat, hurrying to open Elva's door for her.

Meredyth sat up straight, her hand flying to her heart.

His dark hair hung in perfect waves over the white collar of his dinner jacket. His hand on the car door was tanned and strong, a single ruby flashing under the lights.

She couldn't breathe.

He turned and looked at her, and he stopped. His blue eyes were bright with interest, his mouth turned up in a familiar smile. He kept staring, a slightly puzzled look in his eyes, as if he knew her but couldn't place her.

Elva turned, and raised a brow. "Meredyth? Are you coming?"

Almost afraid to hope, Meredyth went slowly down the stairs, never taking her eyes off him.

"Meredyth Sherborne, meet Alexander Hartford. Alex, this is my godchild, Meredyth. Alex is a neighbor of mine in England. He's here in town on business, and . . ."

Meredyth didn't hear any more. The warmth of his hand was closing over hers; his eyes were taking in every detail of her, from her head to her toes—and the runners showing beneath her dress. They seemed to amuse him, and his smile felt like sunlight to Meredyth.

"Meredyth will be joining us for dinner," Elva was saying. "And there is Kate, in the backseat. Shall I sit back there with you, poppet?"

Meredyth fought back tears at the sight of the little girl, her long hair hanging in a thick braid. Her cheeks were full and healthy. There were no circles under her bright eyes.

"I'm thrilled," Alex said. "What a delightful surprise. We never know what to expect from Elva, but it's always pleasant, isn't it, sweetheart?"

The child in the backseat laughed and nodded. "Most of the time," she agreed.

Meredyth let him take her hand as he helped her into

178

the passenger seat. She leaned back, hardly daring to breathe.

"Meredyth!" It was her mother, escorting a group of visiting relatives to their car. "Meredyth Sherborne. Just where do you think you're going?"

Meredyth smiled, and leaned her arm out the open window, breathing in the sweet air of the June night. "Where am I going?" she repeated softly. "Wherever I wish."

MacBroom Sweeps Clean
Emma Craig

This one's for everybody on RW-L. If Lily'd had the Internet, she wouldn't have been so lonely.

Chapter One

Angus MacBroom took a pull on his pipe, puffed out three large smoke rings, and chuckled when a family of sparrows darted through them, playing tag. Wee aerial acrobats, they somersaulted away and back again, flitting through the loops from the other direction. Air currents stirred by their wings fuzzed the rings' smoky edges and twisted them into all manner of odd shapes before they dissipated into the atmosphere like wispy clouds.

Neither Angus nor the sparrows minded when their game disappeared. Angus merely blew more rings. The sparrows chirped their thanks and renewed their sport.

Aye, 'twas a fine, fine day. Angus sighed with satisfaction as he strolled along, and his gaze swept the landscape. Good land it was: MacKechnie land, and had been for four hundred years, this being within spitting distance of 1900, and the MacKechnie family having survived the great upheavals in the last century intact. Angus considered it a testament to the clan's strength of purpose and canny management that they had managed to avoid retribution by the English bastards and the Jacobite rebels, both.

A shrewd lot, the MacKechnies. And excellent caretakers, too, which undoubtedly accounted for their continued success. No thrifty Scotsman would exchange a good landlord for an unknown one. This was especially true since most newcomers to the Highlands these days hailed from England. Angus spat, a reaction that had become automatic to him since the evil days of the mid–eighteenth century.

He decided to cease thinking such thoughts, as they were fruitless, disagreeable, and unworthy of such a grand and glorious day. He turned his attention back to the landscape, breathing deeply to rid himself of lingering dismals. 'Twas a sight worth a second glance, to be sure. A number of Caledonian pines broke up a green sward in the long meadow, their mossy sides sparkling amber and emerald in the sun. Wildflowers bloomed in the grass, purple, yellow, and white stars embroidered on a blanket of jade.

Catching sight of sheep grazing in the meadow, Angus smiled at several spring lambs. They were big enough now to frolic in the field while their mothers watched complacently. Highland ponies, their shaggy winter coats a memory today, chewed lazily on tall sweet grass. Cattle lowed a musical counterpart to the birds' happy melodies, and a bull shook his head, showing off his long hair and longer horns.

"Ye'll lure many a lass next spring with them things, me lad," Angus assured the bull, who appeared unimpressed. Angus honored the animal's arrogance. No bull worth his salt needed any help from him, and he grinned in appreciation.

Peaty streams bubbled merrily, cascading over stones on the hillsides and creating a hundred small waterfalls. The cheerful sound was like music to Angus's ears. It spoke of melting snow, long days full of sunshine, and endless twilit nights, of flowers and ferns, market days, and summer fairs; the joy of renewal and the celebration of bounty.

In his mind's eye, Angus pictured young lads puffing out their chests as coy lasses pretended to ignore them and pay attention to the dancers. 'Twas a game as old as mankind, and a jolly one. In truth they'd be worth watching, those dancers, with their legs flashing as they pointed, cut, turned, and lilted to the music of the pipers.

The sky was as blue as a beautiful woman's eyes, and as clear as a baby's conscience. Flowery clouds decorated the atmosphere and brought to Angus's mind the days of his youth. Life had been different then; no denying it. Aye, he'd had a grand childhood. The green men had still lived in the Highlands then; Angus remembered them fondly. Some of his best friends were faeries when he was a boy.

Summer in the Highlands: Angus loved it. And never had a summer begun as cheerfully as this one. Saints be praised, the heat was so intense, Angus even considered removing his woolen cardigan. Since he'd had a cold in his chest for a week or so, he settled for unbuttoning it. He pushed his cap back, though, and unwound his scarf and stuffed it into his coat pocket in deference to the warm weather.

Balmy breezes kissed his weathered cheeks. The sweet sounds of birdsong and rushing water blended with the steady crunch of his heavy shoes and thick walking stick on the stony path. And look there: daffodils had pushed their way up through the rocky, cold-bound earth in late spring and were now about to burst into bloom. Summer heather already blossomed on the hillsides. Truly, this would be a summer to cherish. Angus couldn't recall a day this warm since—well, he couldn't quite remember.

He didn't fret over his lapse in memory, though. Angus was a Broonie and, therefore, as old as the hills themselves. He had more summers to remember than most folk in the Highlands. He did know, however, that this summer showed promise of becoming the most delicious he'd seen in a century or more.

When he heard the sound of a woman weeping, therefore, he stopped short, dismayed. What on earth could a body have to lament about on such a choice summer's day?

Taking care not to be overheard, he crept closer. One could never tell about females, as he well knew. Angus's reflection was borne of no disparaging opinion about the fair sex. Far from it. Rather, it sprang from his respect for women. After all, a body had to use the resources available to it. Since men wielded superior physical and political power and had done since the beginning of time, women had been forced into subtlety. And, as much as Angus loved women—he sighed again, thinking about the bonny creatures—he'd noticed before, that they sometimes wept just out of sight in hopes that the object of their designs would notice their sorrow and offer comfort.

He didn't blame them, although he wished the world were a fair enough place that everyone in it felt free to ask for succor when they required it. And everyone did, occasionally. Need for solace or assistance was a universal condition; Angus had discovered such needs in every living thing he'd encountered in his several hundred years on earth.

Looking about now, Angus saw not another soul in sight. So this poor thing was quite alone in her grief. Whoever she was, then, she'd hidden herself away on purpose and didn't crave discovery. Her sorrow must be genuine, and Angus's heart ached for her. It was a shame for anyone to feel so bad at any time, but it seemed especially unfortunate now, in the glorious summertime.

Angus was old enough to have overcome his compulsion to meddle in the affairs of humans as so many

younger Broonies did. He did, however, possess a
tender heart and a lively curiosity. He hated to hear
anyone sobbing like this woman did, as though her
heart were broken beyond repair. It wouldn't hurt to
take a look into the lassie's problems and see if he
could help her in some way. Carefully, he made his way
through the gorse and grass, climbed up a mossy boul-
der, lifted himself by a pine branch, and settled onto
an outcropping so that he could peek at his quarry
without being seen. Angus wasn't one to barge in
where he could do no good. Some human conditions,
he'd learned long ago, were best left to resolve themselves.

"Och."

The soft exclamation leaked from between his teeth
when he spied the woman. A girl, really, he thought;
she couldn't be more than twenty, if that. She sat on a
rock beside the rippling brook, her legs drawn up beneath her, a plaid shawl snugged about her shoulders.
Angus recognized the colors and pattern as belonging
to the MacKechnies. Although he wasn't sure he approved of this new clan-tartan nonsense the English-
financed woolen industry had foisted upon Scotland,
he did appreciate it now, as it identified this girl as
belonging in the neighborhood.

She wasn't lost, then, evidently, but fretted over
other problems. Refilling his pipe, tamping it down
with his thumb, and lighting it, Angus drew deeply several times and settled down to watch the little drama
being played out on the bank of the bonny brook beneath him.

A slender, pink-cheeked thing, the girl now sniffed
miserably in an attempt to make her tears go away, and
failed. They kept leaking from eyes as brown as the
finest MacKechnie ale. Her complexion was fair, although freckles danced across a nose rosy with weeping. Her deep auburn hair was more brown than red,
pulled away from her face, and tied back with a blue

Emma Craig

ribbon. Escaped curls danced about her cheeks.

Angus thought she was a remarkably pretty little thing, even if she couldn't be called beautiful, since she was far too healthy-looking to exude the fragility fashionable in these strange modern days. To his mind, she was more appealing because of her heartiness. Angus was no fan of modern values. There was an animation about her of which he approved as well. No simpering miss, then, who'd "Yes, sir" and "No, sir" a body to death and never have an opinion to call her own. He'd bet his pipe on it.

He stared at her costume, and realized at once that it had not come from any local needle. Why, the lass wore a dress fine enough for a London debutante. Angus would have to think hard about offering his aid if the girl was English. Not, of course, that this wee thing could be held in any way accountable for the despicable behavior of her ancestors; still, one had to draw the line somewhere. The sins of the fathers, and all that.

As he watched, the lass drew a lacy handkerchief from a deep pocket and blew her nose vigorously. She shook her head, setting her bright curls to bobbing, and said, "Oh, stop it, Lily!"

Angus blinked, surprised. Now where on this wonderful earth did she hail from? She didn't sound like any Scots lass he'd ever heard before; nor an Englishwoman, neither, praise the Lord. He listened harder as the girl took another swipe at her nose, which had turned from rosy to red during her assault upon it with her handkerchief.

"Pa needs you to do this, and you'll just buckle down and do it."

Her firm words seemed to brace her for ten seconds or so. Then, to Angus's regret, her shoulders slumped and shook and she began to weep again. He still wasn't sure what, if anything, to do about the poor dear thing,

MacBroom Sweeps Clean

although his sympathies tilted her way. She didn't *sound* English.

"Oh, Pa and Ma, I miss you so much! And Betty and Bobby Jo and Clyde and Tommy and Artie. And Texas! How will I ever survive here?"

Texas! Why, the wee lassie came from the United States of America!

Angus had never met an American before. From all he'd heard, though, this girl's behavior was atypical. Americans were reputed to be a confident lot. They were said to irritate the very devil out of the British, for which Angus and most other Highland Broonies honored them.

He watched, fascinated, for several more minutes, having long ago stifled any tendency to rush in where angels feared to tread. And, as there didn't seem to be any angels hovering over this poor wee lass at the moment, Angus supposed they'd all had second thoughts. He wasn't surprised.

He'd never harbored much respect for angels, who seemed to devote most of their time to folks who didn't need them. After all, how much assistance could one offer a good Christian who never strayed from the straight and narrow path? Such folk were worthy, surely, but not often in need of help.

As for himself, Angus preferred a good sinner. Oh, not the vicious kind who robbed, pillaged, and looted. No. He had no use for mean folk, except to teach them a hard lesson every now and again. But Angus felt kinship with those poor humans who tried and failed; who erred occasionally; who succumbed to greed and then felt guilty; who spoke ill and regretted it; who had a fault or two to make them interesting.

"Stop it, Lily!"

The girl's stern admonition to herself drew Angus's consideration from his ruminations to her again. He puffed on his pipe, determined to wait a while longer before he made a move.

She sat up straighter and pulled her woolen shawl more tightly around her shoulders. Then she patted her curls, a feminine gesture that made Angus smile. No matter how unhappy she was, any lassie worth the name gave a care to her appearance. A female's face, after all, was more often than not her fortune. 'Twasn't fair, but 'twas life, and Angus harbored a deep respect for practical people.

"No matter how awful the prospect, you have a job to do, and you'll do it. You promised your family, Lily Munro, and a Munro doesn't go back on her word."

Lily Munro! So she was a Scot, after all. Angus remembered a family Munro who'd had to emigrate to America after the Great Rebellion. He wondered if this lassie was one of them.

Well, no matter. Angus's decision was made. He tapped out his pipe on a rock and stuck it in his pocket. Then he heaved himself to his feet, using his heavy walking stick as a prop, and carefully negotiated his way down the rocky slope to the brook's side.

Lily heard the sound of footsteps and hastily dried her cheeks again. *Oh, Lord,* she prayed without hope, *please don't let them find me here. Not until I've composed myself.*

In that endeavor, she leaped to her feet, forgetting to be careful about where she put them. They sank in the muddy bank, reminding her in no uncertain terms of one of the reasons why she was so unhappy.

Attempting to ignore her wet feet which, she was sure, would now freeze and cause her to succumb to a cold if not a fatal inflammation of the lungs, she turned to greet the intruder with equanimity if not with dignity. It was difficult for one to be dignified when one's feet were caked in mud, one's eyelids puffy with weeping, and one's nose bright red.

Lily took another swipe at it, hoping to repair some of the damage her tears had caused. She didn't harbor much confidence in her success.

Chapter Two

When she got her first glimpse of the visitor to her secluded brook, Lily forgot for a moment to be miserable.

Since her arrival in Scotland the first of June, she'd seen many unusual-looking people. At least they were unusual to her. Lily was used to seeing men dressed in the rugged high-plains garb of the western American frontier. She was accustomed to the cowboys who worked on her father's southeast Texas ranch; men in high-heeled boots and spurs wearing denim or buckskin dungarees, leather vests, and chaps, with broad Stetson hats and broader Texas accents.

In her entire life, until she arrived in this cold and hostile land, she'd not seen a man in a skirt. For heaven's sake, any man who dared dress thus in Texas would be ridden out of town on a rail. Probably tarred and feathered first. Maybe shot. But the men here in the Highlands didn't think twice about donning kilts and bonnets, with their infernal thistles hanging about their ears, and that shocking thing they called a sporran dangling right in front of a portion of their anatomies Lily was too much of a lady to name, even to herself.

The fellow tramping down the rocky hill toward her wore a kilt, bonnet, and sporran. He had a shock of stark-white hair under his plaid cap and must have been no more than five feet tall, although something about the way he carried himself told Lily his size wasn't important to him. Or to anybody else.

His kilt wasn't made from the MacKechnie plaid, Lily saw at once. She hadn't yet sorted out all the tartans these people seemed so proud of, but she could at least spot the MacKechnie plaid when she saw it. It was about the only thing she'd done right since her arrival, as a matter of fact.

Because she knew where her duty lay even if she didn't want to do it, Lily tried to smile, failed, swallowed, and said, "Good morning, sir."

"Aye, 'tis a fine morning, lassie," the man replied.

He had a nice voice; it sounded merry to Lily, and she was surprised she didn't resent it. She wished she could be merry. His blue eyes were remarkably bright for a gentleman with as many years under his belt as he appeared to have. Lily had more often encountered faded eyes in the countenances of elderly people. He was as spry as a spring lamb, too, which almost, but not quite, made her smile. She wasn't sure what to do next, so she stood still, her hands at her sides, and waited.

Back home in Texas she'd know what to do. She'd offer this fellow some down-home Texas hospitality, complete with barbecue and beans, and conversation would never flag in this uncomfortable way. It had been impressed upon her quite forcefully, however, that the Scottish people didn't consider silence uncivil as Texans did. Oh, a Texan knew when to speak and when to be still. Lily knew full well that on trail drives the men sometimes didn't speak for days on end, but that was primarily because there was nobody around with whom to talk. Even when they weren't talking to each other, the cowboys always sang to the cattle.

But in social situations, Texans conversed. Lily knew how to hold up her end of a conversation as well as anyone. Indeed, David MacKechnie was forever asking her not to chatter. Which reminded her of why she'd sought out this sequestered bank and made her sniff indignantly and swallow again. Chatter, indeed!

"May I share your wee rock, lassie?" the stranger asked when he got closer.

"Of course you may." Lily stepped aside. Honesty and unhappiness made her add, "It's not my rock."

The old man laughed, a creaky sound so jolly that Lily almost smiled in spite of herself. Her misery was acute, however, and her smile died before it made it to her lips.

"Aye, I don't reckon it belongs to none but God, lassie."

After sniffing again, Lily said, "God and David MacKechnie." Then she could have kicked herself for sounding so sarcastic. This wouldn't do at all. These people all considered David as close to God as made no matter. She knew she had to mind her tongue.

"Aye." The old man nodded. "Good fellow, Master Davy. His father and grand'fer was good men, too."

"So I've heard."

Lily suddenly found herself being scrutinized by a pair of exceedingly sharp eyes. She dropped her gaze and fiddled with her shawl. It was so cold here in the Highlands. Sometimes she thought that if she could ever get warm, she might not look upon her future with such dread. It was difficult to be sanguine about the uncertainty facing her when she lived in constant fear of frostbite.

"Ye know our Davy then?" the old fellow asked.

He took a black briar pipe out of his pocket. The pipe

looked about a hundred years old. So did he, as a matter of fact. He tapped the pipe on a rock, reached into his sporran, pinched out some tobacco, packed it into the pipe, and lit it. His movements were deft and sure even though his fingers were twisted with age, and Lily was fascinated.

"Yes. Yes, I know David."

The old man took a deep draw on his pipe and blew out a smoke ring. "Ye're wearing his plaid," he observed.

"Yes."

Lily was charmed by that smoke ring. She watched as it lifted into the air—for once unmarred by gale-force winds—hovered over the little man's head like a halo, and feathered out to evaporate into the sky. As soon as it was gone, the old man made another. She watched that one, too.

"Ye like the smoke rings, do ye, lass?"

When she looked down at him, she discovered his eyes twinkling up at her like two bright blue stars. She felt a little embarrassed. "You make them very well. My grandfather used to blow smoke rings from his cigar. I used to pretend they were bracelets and stick my hands through them." As soon as the words left her mouth, homesickness hit her in the stomach like a fist.

The old fellow must have seen her flinch, because he patted the mossy rock beside him and said, "Sit yourself back down here, lassie, and tell old Angus all about it. It helps to share your woes with one as has no call to care about the outcome."

Immediately, Lily's heart cried out to unburden herself to this kind old soul. But because she'd been taught good manners, she demurred. "Oh, thank you very much, sir, but I don't want to bother you with my troubles."

"Nonsense, lass. I'm old enough that nothin' ye can say will astonish me much. And who knows?" He winked at her. "Ye might even find your troubles aren't so heavy if you share them. Angus MacBroom has shoulders broad enough to carry your woes and more."

This, coming from a man a good three inches shorter than Lily herself and very slightly built, made her smile at last. He seemed like an awfully sweet old gentleman. His eyes were so merry and his aspect so compassionate, Lily discovered herself doing as he'd asked. Smoothing her skirts, she sat on the rock without even wiping it off first, a breach of etiquette David would deplore. He was such a stuffy old stick. Young stick.

Angus grinned and blew another smoke ring. To Lily's amazement, it drifted through the air and right to her hand, where it circled her wrist like a bracelet. Her delighted laugh was entirely unconscious. She'd been so dejected for so long, she couldn't remember the last time she'd laughed. Angus laughed with her.

"What's your name, lass? Ye're new to these parts, I'll warrant."

Brought back to her present miseries, Lily sighed. "My name is Lily Munro, Mr. MacBroom. And yes, I'm new to the area. I'm from the east Texas plains in the United States."

Nodding wisely, Angus blew out another ring and said, "Missin' your home, are ye?"

"Oh, yes!" Lily's eyes filled with tears, and she tried without success to keep them from falling. Annoyed, she grabbed her wrinkled hanky out of her pocket and blotted them away.

"Homesickness is oft the worst kind o' sickness, dear heart," Angus said softly. "Aren't ye plannin' to go back home again?"

Lily heaved a huge sigh. "Oh, I imagine I'll be allowed to return for a visit someday. It's—it's . . ." Tears leaked out again. She scrubbed at them mercilessly. "It's so far away."

Her handkerchief had performed valiant service today, but it wasn't designed for such rough use. By this time it was soaked through and wrinkled into a tight little ball. Lily was startled when Angus produced a large linen handkerchief. She didn't see where he'd come by it, but she supposed it must have been secreted about his person somewhere.

"Here, Lily-lass, use this. It's clean, and it's big enough for the job." He winked at her.

She took the handkerchief gingerly, uncertain if she should. She needed it, though, so she said, "Th-thank you, Mr. MacBroom."

Angus's grin broadened. "Call me Angus, dear. Everybody does."

Lily was unused to calling elderly people by their first names. Nevertheless, she said, "Angus," because she knew the ways of the Scots to be strange to her.

"Now tell me, Lily-lass, why is it ye'll only be payin' visits to your dear Texas home from now on? Ye're here for more than a short stay, then?"

"Yes."

More tears. More embarrassed swipes, this time with Angus's handkerchief.

"Your folks aren't here wi' ye?"

"No. I've come here for my wedding."

"Your weddin'! Why, that's wonderful, lass! I should think ye'd be happy as a lark instead of sittin' here by the brook with old Angus, cryin' your eyes out."

"I suppose so." Lily sounded as unhappy as she felt. "Actually, Angus, I didn't realize how much I'd miss my family and Texas when I agreed to the match." If she'd told the truth, she'd have said she hadn't anticipated this weakness in herself and was heartily ashamed of it.

"Aye. I understand, lass. It's hard to leave your home, and the feelin' of loss is something a body don't expect."

Lily believed he did understand and felt minutely better.

"So, who're ye marryin' with, lass?"

"David MacKechnie."

MacBroom Sweeps Clean

Angus's eyes opened wide. His mouth dropped open and the pipe would have fallen from his lips if he'd not caught it.

"Our own Davy MacKechnie! Ye'll be lady of the manor and of all the lands for miles hereabouts. Why, Lily-lass,'tis a match made in heaven!"

It was too much. Guilt and misery propelled Lily up from her rock. Wringing her hands and feeling worse than she'd ever felt in her life, Lily cried, "It's *not* made in heaven. I miss Texas! I miss my family! I miss the people there! They're warm and friendly and as open as the sky. I hate it here. It's freezing cold and damp and windy. The sky doesn't even get dark at night, the people are as cold as the weather, and—and David MacKechnie *hates* me!" The last came out in a little wail.

Although he didn't rise, Angus reached up and touched Lily's hand. His touch calmed her.

Taking a deep breath and commanding herself to stop her stupid crying, Lily said, "I'm sorry, Mr. MacBroom. Angus. I—I didn't mean to sound so rude."

"No need to apologize, lass. Ye seem a sweet girl, in spite of your feelin's about my own lovely Scotland."

She hung her head, ashamed of herself for her weakness and rudeness. He patted her hand.

"There, missy, sit ye down again and let's us talk about this."

She sat meekly, bowed her head, and prepared for the lecture she knew would come. She deserved one, for sure.

Angus surprised her. He only asked mildly, "It's warm in Texas, is it?"

Slipping him a sideways glance, Lily found him watching her as if his only interest at the moment was the weather in Texas. As though he didn't disapprove of her. Lately it had become a novel experience, not to be disapproved of.

She nodded. "Yes. Yes, the weather is very warm

where I live. And it's dry. It—it doesn't rain all the time like it does here. In the wintertime, sometimes we'll have a little bit of snow, but it usually doesn't stick on the ground for long."

" 'Twould be a good place for old bones, I'll warrant."

"I suppose so. It gets dark at night, too." She was embarrassed by how sullen she sounded. But good grief! Nighttime was supposed to be dark, wasn't it?

"Aye. The days are long here in the summertime. P'raps I'll have to give Texas a try one day."

His expression was so solemn and his eyes so twinkly, Lily found herself smiling. After a moment, he grinned back.

"So, Lily-lass, ye're not fond of our weather."

"Well, not very." She left it at that, fearing a detailed account would lose her a new friend.

"I see. And ye find the folk hereabouts not to your liking?"

"They—they seem cold and withdrawn to me. People in Texas are friendly and warm and open and—well, I guess I'm just used to them."

Angus nodded. "It's difficult to get used to a new set of folk; I understand. But I confess ye wrung my heart when you told me our David hates you. I've known the MacKechnies these many years, lassie, and I never knew one of 'em to be a bad sort, or mean tempered. Is our David so very terrible to ye?"

Lily felt awful. She wished she'd never opened her mouth. Shaking her head, she mumbled, "No. I don't suppose he's terrible."

Another pat on her hand told her Angus didn't think poorly of her. She appreciated him in that moment more than she could express.

"Tell me about it, Lily. If I don't understand, I'll at least try to."

"Thank you," she whispered.

"What makes you say David hates you?"

Experiences over the last month tumbled through

Lily's mind, making her more sad than angry. "He—his manner is aloof. He never smiles." She sucked in another deep breath, the truth making her heart ache. "He disapproves of me and considers my behavior inappropriate. I can't seem to do anything right."

"No?"

Angus's eyes sparkled like the brook rushing past, but his expression remained more kind than Lily expected she deserved. After all, she'd be inclined to resent anybody who invaded her own beloved Texas and disparaged it. Or her father or mother or brothers and sisters. Then again, her father and mother and brothers and sisters weren't stuffy, disparaging monsters of coldness who found fault with everything a body did, either.

She shook her head. "No. When I speak, he frowns. When I laugh, he'll even get up and walk out of the room. When I ask him questions, he tells me I needn't bother. When I chat with the maids, he tells me not to be familiar with the servants. Why, I was having a nice chat with his bailiff about horses, and David actually told me not to visit the stables again!"

Angus shook his head and tutted. "A monster, sure," he said. Lily could tell he was joshing her and she didn't appreciate it.

"Well, he was mean! What am I supposed to do? Sit in my room all day long and dress my hair? Or knit? Or read?"

After scratching his head, Angus said, "Well, 'tis what I've most often seen ladies do, lass."

She gave a very unladylike snort. "Well, I guess I'm not a lady then. I'm used to being busy, to riding, to taking an interest in my father's business. Besides, David doesn't even approve of the books I like to read!"

"Och. That's bad."

They sat in silence for a moment or two, Angus blowing smoke rings. Lily picked up a piece of bark and began making a moss bed on its curved, smooth inside surface. While Angus meditated and watched, she crafted a tiny village on the mossy bed.

After a moment, he pointed to her handiwork. "Ye've got hands made to be busy, lass. I can see why idleness don't become ye."

Her hands stilled. "I suppose so."

"Tell me why ye came here to marry up with our David. Surely it wasn't your choice."

Lily said in a stifled voice, "I didn't object when the subject was broached to me."

"But 'twasn't your doin'?"

"Not exactly. My father and David have joined together in a business enterprise. My father's family was from this part of Scotland originally, but had to leave sometime in the last century."

"Ah, 'twas what I supposed, then." Angus nodded as if it all made sense to him now.

"They've begun bringing sheep into Texas. A lot of the cattle ranchers don't like it, but my father says the longhorns are becoming less profitable as new breeds are introduced, and the land is better suited to sheep than cattle, anyway. He and David formed a business partnership a few years ago. They decided a marriage between our families would help strengthen the partnership."

"And you agreed to it?"

Angus's surprise was patent, and Lily bridled even though she couldn't blame him in her heart. "I love my family, Mr. MacBroom," she said haughtily. "I wanted to do my part to help them."

With a big grin, the old man said, "Och, spoken like a true Munro, Lily-lass."

"Well, I am a Munro." She felt silly about her show of defensiveness.

"Aye. I can tell ye are." Angus drew deeply on his pipe. "Ye'll do, y'know, lass. Ye'll do."

Whatever that meant. Lily's shoulders slumped again.

MacBroom Sweeps Clean

"But ye'd better scoot on back to the manor house now, girl, before they miss ye and set up a search party. Reckon our David'll be worried about ye."

"I doubt it." She felt mean and petty as soon as her words hit the air. Rising from her rock again, she shook out her skirt. "But you may be right. I suppose I'd better get back."

Peeking down at her muddy shoes, Lily suddenly realized how cold she was, and spared a moment to be surprised the cold hadn't hit her before. Generally, she was half-frozen twenty-three hours out of every day. The other hour of the day was spent in front of the roaring fire in the parlor after supper at night. It was all the time David allowed her, believing it improper for a lady to sit up late.

"Thank you for your time, Mr. MacBroom. Angus."

Angus rose creakily from the rock and held his gnarled hand out for her to shake. Lily had the strangest sensation that he meant it when he said, "Ah, Lily-lass, 'twas my great pleasure."

Chapter Three

Angus sat down on the rock again and watched, puffing on his pipe, as Lily made her way across the meadow, headed for the huge stone structure rising from among the trees in the background. A castle, folks in the village called it. Having seen a castle or two in his day, Angus would have called it a very large manor house. He didn't argue, though; he knew how much folks here in the village of Lochlydh in Strathclyde liked to think they had a castle in the neighborhood.

This one possessed the requisite turrets and a crenel or three, and presented a fine prospect. Well kept, too. For all the faults Lily found with David MacKechnie, he wasn't one to ignore his land, his home, or his duty to his tenants. David had proved his mettle years before and deserved a castle if anyone hereabouts did. For Angus's money, though, the best part of Castle MacKechnie was the old brewery out back, built more than a century ago and still producing fine ale.

Meditating on the tale Lily had just told him, Angus

MacBroom Sweeps Clean

watched her sprint, light-footed as a deer, across the meadow, her plaid shawl fluttering out behind her. Grinning, he decided he didn't wonder at David's doubts, although he thought the young man must be awfully stodgy to find grievous fault with her. At the very least, David must be sorely inept in handling her.

Granted, Lily Munro didn't behave like a Scottish lady—leastways no lady Angus had ever met would run hotfoot across a field—still, that was what was so appealing about her to his mind. Like a breath of fresh air, Lily was.

He hoped the heavy burdens David had had to bear in his life hadn't damaged or hardened him. Worse, perhaps the MacKechnie blood had thinned so much through the centuries that young Davy, slave to duty that he was, pined for a stiff-lipped, bloodless bride. Angus knew Englishwomen to be a cold lot; heaven protect Lochlydh from one of those. The mere thought of an Englishwoman presiding over Castle Mac-Kechnie and the surrounding neighborhood brought a chill to Angus's old bones. He'd take that sprightly Texan over a Brit any day.

"Och, what's the matter wi' ye, Davy boy?" he muttered. "And what's the matter with our darlin' Lily, that she can't see the good in ye?"

Giving a thought to MacKechnies past, Angus smiled. There'd been dozens of 'em, and all possessed of fire and humor, goodwill and charity. When he'd last seen David, Angus had thought him to be a good-hearted young man, albeit reserved and somewhat stuffy.

Angus knew the poor boy'd had reason to be serious, given the problems he'd faced in his short life. But perhaps the seriousness Angus perceived in David was really indifference, and the clan spirit was dying out; the notion sent a ripple of sadness through him.

Well, he guessed he risked nothing by going to Castle MacKechnie and taking a look into the matter. In spite of her assessment of his beloved homeland, Angus had found Lily to be a sweet girl. He thought she'd be an asset to any young man's life. She was certainly refreshing to his own old bones.

Pushing himself to his feet, he clamped his pipe between his teeth and set out across the field, using the path Lily had forged through the tall grass. "Compromise is what's needed here, I'll warrant. Those two young people can't see it yet. Poor wee Lily's mournin' her lost Texas and her family, and silly David's believin' himself to be saddled with a hoyden." He shook his head and chuckled. "Youngsters!"

"There's an old gentleman askin' to talk to ye, lady."

Lily looked up from the book she was reading, in defiance of David's edict that detective fiction was unfit for gentle ladies' eyes.

As usual her aunt Minnie, who was ostensibly her chaperon, had pleaded headache, dined in her room, and still rested there. Lily knew her aunt to be full of beans. A hedonist to her core, Minnie was too much a slave to comfort to leave her room unless it was absolutely necessary. Minnie swore this drafty castle was going to be her death, and she wasn't about to let it get the best of her. So she stayed in her room, drank single-malt Scotch whiskey—to ward off the germs, she said—and taught her Scots maid to play poker. Lily loved Minnie dearly, but she couldn't give her high marks as a chaperon.

Lily blinked at the maid who stood in the doorway. "An old gentleman?"

"Aye, lady."

"I wonder who it could be." Lily glanced at David and found him frowning at her. What a surprise. Her heart pulsed painfully; she didn't know how she was going to endure a lifetime of his disapproval.

David rose, rattling his newspaper as if he didn't appreciate this interruption. "I'll see to it."

Lily rose, too, irritated by his presumption. "That won't be necessary. Apparently the fellow asked to see me."

"Aye, he did," the maid confirmed. "He's in the kitchen."

"The kitchen?" Lily was surprised. Most visitors came to the front door.

"Aye, ma'am."

"Very well, Alice," David said, dismissing the maid. "I'll see to it."

As soon as the door closed behind Alice's back, Lily said, "I'll go, David. It's me he's asking for." She made no effort to moderate her tone, which was sharp.

So was David's. "Stay here, Lily. I'll see what the man wants. It's improper—"

"Oh, bother impropriety!" Lily felt her cheeks flame. "I'm sick and tired of your notions of propriety, David MacKechnie!"

And with that, she flounced out of the room. After gaping speechlessly for several seconds at the door she'd slammed behind her, David slapped his newspaper down and headed after her.

Lily knew he'd follow her; he couldn't risk allowing an insult to his precious dignity to pass by unremarked. No; she was in for a lecture, at least.

Because she wanted to see what this caller wanted before David butted in, she hastened down the hall, across the gallery lined with portraits of MacKechnies past, and dashed down the back steps to the mammoth kitchen. She'd been surprised by its size and its crude facilities at first; now she knew the ancient kitchen to be part of MacKechnie history and, therefore, inviolable. David wouldn't allow a modern appliance to sully his ancestral home no matter how much it might ease the cook's job. Lily considered it one more indication that the man was impossibly old-fashioned. Not that the cook wanted her territory modernized. She was as old-fashioned and stuffy as David, and she objected to Lily even more than David did.

Thrusting through the big double doors into the kitchen, she stopped short, startled.

"Angus!"

He twinkled and nodded at her from his seat beside the fire. "The very same."

Mrs. Fleming, the cook, stirred a pot and looked grim. "Come knockin' at the back door, he did, mistress. Says he's hungry."

Lily cried impulsively, "Oh, Angus, why didn't you say something earlier? I'd have invited you to dinner!" The door swished open behind her and she knew David had heard her.

"Thank ye, Lily-lass. Reckon your young fella there'd have had somethin' to say about my takin' dinner wi' the family."

She sniffed and shot a glare over her shoulder. "I suppose so." She admitted it grudgingly.

"Good evening," said David.

His greeting surprised Lily, because it sounded quite kind. Taking a deep breath, she said, "David MacKechnie, this is Angus MacBroom. We met earlier in the day."

"How do you do, Angus?"

"I'm doin' well, lad, thankee," Angus said with a sparkle in his eye.

David looked smug when Lily glanced at him, as if he were glad to prove to her that he wasn't the pompous fellow she thought him to be. Lily was unimpressed.

Walking over to the chair by the kitchen fire, David shook hands with Angus. "I'm sure I've seen you in the neighborhood, Angus, although I don't believe we've ever been introduced."

"Aye," affirmed Angus, "I've lived on MacKechnie lands all my life—which is a lot longer than either of you have."

MacBroom Sweeps Clean

He chuckled. His good humor was so infectious even Mrs. Fleming grinned, astonishing Lily, who had found the cook to be one of the dourest of the dour Scots employed at Castle MacKechnie.

She felt ill at ease now that she knew David wasn't going to throw Angus out, as if she'd been foolish in her show of defiance. Surely David could have handled this matter. With an internal sniff of disdain, she decided she couldn't have known that. For all she knew, he'd have sent the poor man away without seeing to his needs first. If she hadn't defied him in coming to the kitchens, he'd probably not have bothered even to ascertain what those needs were.

Squaring her shoulders, she turned to Mrs. Fleming. Back home in Texas, she never had to adopt this lady-of-the-manor attitude the people around here seemed to expect. Back home, she was on friendly terms with everybody, from the kitchen help to the cowboys.

When she'd made her first foray into the kitchens at the castle, hoping to swap recipes with Mrs. Fleming and establish some kind of rapport, she'd been treated to icy monosyllables. She wasn't sure she'd ever get used to the infernal formality prevailing at Castle MacKechnie.

In the most patronizing tone in her repertoire, she said, "Mrs. Fleming, will you please see to it that Mr. MacBroom is fed some soup and bread and butter?"

"Got no soup."

Mrs. Fleming didn't bother to make her declaration polite. Lily bridled.

"What's in that pot you're stirring?"

"Bones."

Lily rolled her eyes and tried again. "Are you making a soup stock?"

"Aye."

"So it's not ready yet?"

"Nay."

"Well, there must be *something* in the larder a man can eat!"

"Aye."

Well and truly annoyed now, Lily said, "Will you please prepare Angus a plate of something? I don't know the prevailing custom in Scotland, but back home in Texas we don't send hungry men away from our doors unfed!"

Mrs. Fleming looked up from her stock pot. Lily detected resentment in her gaze, and told herself she didn't care. She wouldn't put up with surliness in her staff.

Deliberately turning to David, the cook asked, "Master Davy?"

"Of course, Mrs. Fleming." He turned and smiled at Angus as if nothing at all unusual were happening. "We'll have your belly filled full of Mrs. Fleming's good cooking in a shake of a lamb's tail, Angus."

"Thankee, Master Davy."

Without another word, Mrs. Fleming turned to do her master's bidding.

Fury blossomed in Lily's breast. She clenched her fists and felt utterly impotent. Angry tears burned her eyes. She blinked them back resolutely. She wouldn't allow this horrid woman to reduce her to tears in front of David and Angus. She wouldn't!

Very interesting, Angus thought. Very interesting, indeed. Poor little Lily-lass. With the entire castle staff set against her,'twas no wonder she was so unhappy. As he sat at the kitchen table and ate cold mutton and bread and butter and washed it down with a mug of good dark MacKechnie ale, he pondered how such a thing could have come to pass.

Later, after he'd had his fill of Mrs. Fleming's good cooking and bad company, he meandered outside. As familiar with Castle MacKechnie as with the back of his own hand, he understood the habits of its inhabitants well. He strolled to the garden, where he knew David was inclined to wander of an evening. He'd been doing so a lot lately. Now Angus knew why.

Sure enough, there he was, pacing back and forth in front of the rosebushes. His head was bowed, his hands were clasped behind his back, and he looked gloomy in the moonlight.

"Evenin' again, Master Davy. Thankee kindly for the mutton."

Looking up, surprised, David smiled weakly. "You're more than welcome, Angus." His smile tipped upside down. "We don't hold with turning hungry folks away unfed at the castle, you know."

Angus chuckled at David's salty words. So he believed he had to defend himself against Lily's earlier obvious accusation, did he? "Aye. I know it, Master Davy."

He lit his pipe, comfortable with the silence that fell between them. He'd noticed, however, that Lily took these stretches of silence amiss. A voluble lot, Texans, he reckoned.

After his pipe was drawing properly, he observed, "Lively, pretty girl, Miss Lily."

David's expression turned from one of unhappiness to one of disapproval. "I understand you met earlier in the day."

"Aye, we did, by the brook yonder."

"She didn't tell me."

Although he couldn't be sure, since he couldn't read minds, Angus thought he detected an element of hurt in David's small sentence. Keeping his tone mild, he said, "No? Well, I expect she'd have if you'd asked. She don't seem like a liar, our Lily-lass." He chuckled to rob his words of any sting.

"No. No, she doesn't lie." David sounded as if he made the admission reluctantly. Again, Angus detected the hint of hurt feelings. His heart warmed toward this poor man, who obviously didn't know what to make of his wild Texas Lily.

"She told me all about Texas."

"Did she?"

"Aye. 'Tis warm there, I understand. Loosens folks up; makes 'em feel free and easy-like."

"Makes them act free and easy, too," said David, obviously deprecating the fact. "I can't seem to make her understand that things are different here."

With another chuckle—to keep things light—Angus said, "Aye. Them Americans. A talkative, reckless lot, I've heard."

"This one is; that's for sure."

"Don't behave like our own Scots lassies, I'll warrant."

"She most certainly doesn't." Evidently David didn't appreciate, it, either.

Angus blew out a smoke ring. "I reckon they don't understand what it's like here, them Americans. Reared to thinks folks are equal, they are. Have no understandin' of the distinctions between classes. Why, I understand that in America the lowest coal sweeper can make somethin' of himself, and folks'll treat him as if he'd been born to the purple. I 'spect it's money makes the classes in America."

"Hmph."

David apparently didn't approve. Angus couldn't help but smile. He truly had become a stuffy fellow, Davy MacKechnie.

"Aye," he said. "P'raps you'd be better off takin' an Englishwoman to bride, Davy. Them English folk, they understand classes. Better'n most, I'll warrant, since they invented 'em."

Shocked, David cried, "No! Why, I'd be boiled before I'd marry an Englishwoman, Angus!"

Angus said nothing. He took another puff on his pipe and sent a series of tiny rings into the night sky.

Apparently his silence pricked David's pride. "Surely

you can't believe the master of Castle MacKechnie would marry an Englishwoman, Angus. Why, I couldn't do such a thing to my tenants. They'd be horrified. It's bad enough we have the blasted English queen running loose in Balmoral half the year. The English damned near ruined the valley a decade or so ago. I'd not sully the sensibilities of the citizens of Lochlydh by marrying one of them!"

Deliberately making his eyes twinkle, Angus said, "A Texan's better'n an Englishwoman, even if she is a bit lively, eh?"

David frowned. "I suppose so."

Angus sighed lustily and said, "She's a sweet thing, Davy."

David looked at him sharply. "Is she?"

"Aye. Didn't ye see the way she stood her ground against Mrs. Fleming? Took guts, that did."

David's frown deepened. "What do you mean by that? For the love of God, Angus, Mrs. Fleming's a servant. She'll do as she's told by the mistress of the house."

"Aye, I expect she will. Servants can say more with silence than most of us can say usin' words, though, I've noticed. She don't respect our sweet Lily. I saw it."

"Well, if the girl didn't behave in such a wild manner—" David stopped speaking abruptly and looked embarrassed.

"Aye, a wild woman she is. Rantin' and ravin' and pullin' out her hair and causin' you no end o' grief, I'll be bound."

"Of course she doesn't do that."

David drew himself up straight and looked every inch the laird. Angus smiled and puffed some more. After a moment, just as Angus knew he would, David spoke again.

"She's too free with the servants, though, and that's a fact. Visited Mrs. Fleming right off and asked her to make some foul American dish called *chili con carne*.

Wanted to exchange recipes, for the love of God."

"A sin, that." Angus shook his head in mock sadness. "Wouldn't want anything new to pass the master's lips."

"Well, no decent Scots lady would exchange recipes with her cook."

Nodding, Angus said, "Aye. They're born with 'em, cooks are. Them recipes is in their brains and blood from birth." He tapped his head and looked wise.

David's embarrassment grew. "Well, of course they aren't. Lily was simply too familiar, is all. Her familiarity put Mrs. Fleming off."

"Aye. It would. Especially with you tellin' the poor lass so in front of the other servants, who raced right downstairs to report your lecture to Mrs. Fleming, who hasn't said a kind word about another soul in forty years."

Angus saw his words hit home. Then he saw David draw himself up for a defensive maneuver and smiled to himself. He hadn't had this much fun in a hundred years or more.

"She wants to change everything, too."

"Och, that's bad."

"Well, Mrs. Fleming doesn't want a big fancy new stove in her kitchen. She likes the old ways."

"Aye, she would prefer cookin' her meat over a peat fire in a fireplace big enough to roast an ox whole, now that she has the hang of it, I'll warrant. One of them stoves regulatin' the heat and all would be a right bother."

David cast him a sharp glance. Angus kept his expression bland. "And I expect the kitchen boys'd have nothin' to do if they didn't have to sweep out the ashes every day, nor the maids if they didn't have to scrub soot off the walls all the time."

Since he knew good and well David's laborers were always griping about their sons and daughters being taken away to work in the kitchens when they were needed with the shearing or planting, Angus didn't expect an answer. He wasn't disappointed. David glowered and huffed, irked to have his obstinacy shown to be foolish.

Angus let him think about it for a minute. Then he rose and stretched. "Well, I wish ye happy, Davy. I think ye have a peach in our darlin' Texas Lily, but I expect men's tastes differ regardin' womenfolk." With a grin, he added, "If they didn't, we'd all want the same woman to wife, wouldn't we? And that would never do."

David's chuckle was slow in coming, and reluctant, but chuckle he did.

Angus stayed in the garden for several minutes before he went on about his nightly chores. They were both good folk, David and Lily. Neither of them had hesitated so much as an instant before they offered a hungry beggar food. Smiling, he decided there was hope for them yet.

Chapter Four

Lily hung her head and looked more forlorn than David had ever seen her. As she'd seemed dejected since shortly after her arrival, that was saying something.

"I—I don't think I can go through with it, David."

Even though he'd been expecting her to say something of the sort for days now, her words struck him to the heart.

"I know you've been unhappy here, Lily."

She nodded and dashed a hand across her eyes. He could tell how hard she was striving to keep from crying, and wished he could unbend: take her in his arms and soothe her or something. He'd had to work so hard for so long at being strong, though, that he'd all but forgotten how not to be. During those stressful years spontaneous expressions of physical affection had become as foreign to him as Lily was now. Unable to break free from the restraint binding him, David had to settle for watching her and aching inside.

"I—I was hoping I'd be able to get used to life here."

Her voice sounded utterly miserable. David could tell this admission was being wrung from her very soul.

"I was hoping you could, too," he said, and wished he'd kept his mouth shut when she stiffened.

"Yes," she said, resentment singing in the syllable. "I know you did."

David wondered why he couldn't seem to do or say anything in a way Lily could understand. It was as if they communicated on two separate planes and those planes never met anywhere, even by accident. He sighed his frustration.

She took his sigh amiss, too, which didn't surprise him much. "Well, you certainly didn't do anything to make my stay tolerable, did you? You—you disapprove of every single thing I do!"

Shaking his head, he said, "Not everything, Lily." Again, it was the wrong thing to have said, as he recognized immediately when her eyes blazed with fury. He sighed again and muttered, "I'm sorry."

"I'll write to my father tomorrow."

David bowed his head. She was right; he knew it as well as he knew his own name. Yet something screamed inside of him not to let her go; something told him that if she left him, she'd be taking his one hope for happiness with her. He licked his lips. "I—I wish you wouldn't, Lily. Not yet."

Her eyes were as clear as the summer sky outside. "Why not? Do you really think there's hope for us?"

He heard the hurt in her words as clearly as if she'd spoken it aloud, and honesty made him say softly, "I don't know. I only wish you'd wait a little longer, Lily. Maybe—maybe something will happen, and we'll figure out how to—how to—"

How to what? David didn't know, and his thought died before he found words to express it. Lily finished it for him.

"How to get along together?"

That wasn't it. Frustrated, David shrugged. "I guess."

For a long time, Lily merely looked at him warily, as if he were some sort of alien being with which she'd had no prior experience and didn't know what to do. Which, he supposed, he was. The thought made him sad.

At last, she said, "All right. I guess a little longer won't matter. Heaven knows, Aunt Minnie won't mind. She loves it here." She loved the free Scotch whiskey, was what she loved, but Lily decided she'd be better off not saying so.

"Thank you."

Lily nodded, lifted her chin, and silently left the room.

David watched her go as defeat, black as a winter's night and bitter as wormwood, washed through him.

Perhaps the MacKechnie line would die with him. He tried to feel sad about that, but at the moment he hurt too badly about losing Lily to worry about the succession. Which made no sense at all. After all, they didn't get along. She didn't like anything about Castle MacKechnie or the land of his ancestors. Or him. He resented her for that and felt ill-used by her.

She didn't understand what he'd had to do to keep this place. Thus far she hadn't even tried to understand how hard it had been, how he'd had to fight and scratch and be cleverer than any six blasted Texans. Texans didn't have to fight the British government tooth and nail to preserve their homes and keep their tenants alive.

Of course, it wasn't his place to tell her, either. After all, he was a man, and a man didn't boast of his accomplishments. Besides which, in truth, David wasn't proud of himself for merely doing his duty. A man did his duty, and David was a man.

Nevertheless, a compulsion with which he was entirely unfamiliar struck him, and he had to restrain himself from running after Lily. Immediately he told himself not to be stupid. He told himself that Lily

MacBroom Sweeps Clean

Munro was a wild American female who didn't know how to behave herself. It was entirely possible that even if she tried—and David wasn't convinced she'd tried at all—she'd never fit into his life. He told himself that it might be better if she did go home to her precious Texas. He reminded himself that she hated life here; hated the weather; hated the people; hated him.

The last point made him hang his head and wish he were still a boy so he could cry.

David crinkled his paper. Lily glanced up from where she'd been brooding over her porridge. Her aunt was taking breakfast in her room. Or drinking it. David suspected the latter.

For the first time, he noticed how pale she'd become. Her skin hadn't been that ashy when she'd first arrived here from her wretched Texas. When she'd first entered his home, smiling and friendly, he'd thought her quite the prettiest girl he'd ever seen. Then, after observing her for a day or two, he knew he'd have to quell her spirits some or she'd never do. No, never do at all for the laird of Castle MacKechnie.

The words Angus had spoken last night rolled back through David's brain, and he frowned. A stuffy Englishwoman, indeed! Why, all David wanted to do was curb Lily's tendency to be loud and rambunctious. Overly familiar.

A good Scots lady would never clap her hands in the impulsive way Lily had, for instance. Or scoop a child right up from the walkway and bestow a smacking kiss upon her cheek just because she'd presented Lily with a welcoming bouquet. Although, David remembered, his eyebrows dipping, the child, Mariah Kelly, had gone quite pink with pleasure. For the first time, he allowed himself to wonder if what Lily had done was so awful. He himself had grown used to presenting a rather grim demeanor to the world; had created it, in fact, to counter the effect of his own extreme youth when he'd had to assume his responsibilities.

He cleared his throat. Determined to make an effort—this would be his last chance, after all—he said, "Do you eat porridge for breakfast in Texas, Lily?"

She looked at him as if he'd grown a second nose on his face. David was struck by the realization that he'd never asked her such a question before. He didn't indulge in idle chatter at the breakfast table. Or anywhere else, for that matter. Perhaps it was because he'd not had anybody to converse with over breakfast for more than a decade. Perhaps it was a quirk he'd developed in his determination to be strong. Maybe he'd been a little hard on her. After all, Lily had no idea what sorts of tribulations David had endured through the years. He shook out his paper again, folded it, and laid it beside his empty bowl.

"No."

She didn't elaborate, and David's heart smote him when he saw the defensive air she adopted. Surely she wasn't afraid of him, was she? Why, he'd never hurt a woman!

Refusing to be defeated without a fight, he asked, "What do folks eat for breakfast in Texas? Cows' livers and rattlesnakes?"

She stiffened up like a poker and said, "No," again.

David saw her press her lips together, as if she were holding her temper in only with great effort. So she'd misunderstood him again; believed him to be making fun of her home. For some reason, that made his heart hurt, too.

Although he'd never recognized a need to apologize to her before, he found himself saying, "I'm sorry, Lily. 'Twas meant as a joke."

Immediately, her rigid attitude softened. David's feeling of relief surprised him. Before the moment passed, he hurried to say, "Angus said you told him all about Texas when you two met yesterday."

"Did he?" Her voice was small, cautious.

MacBroom Sweeps Clean

A sudden vision of Lily as she'd been when she first arrived in Edinburgh smote him. He'd gone to meet the train she'd taken from London. She'd told him all about her trip from the United States, bubbling over with news and excitement, full of stories about life on the ship, her fellow passengers, the sights she'd seen, and brimming with the joy of life. She'd made him laugh with her word portraits. He couldn't remember the last time somebody'd been able to make him laugh.

David didn't generally feel any particular joy in his own life. He'd spent most of his days since his seventeenth year worrying about his businesses and his tenants. Lily had transmitted some of her own joy to him that day, and he'd been enchanted. She'd been as bright and friendly as a new puppy—and pretty, too. He'd wanted to marry her then and there and bed her at once, and he'd been glad she'd agreed to their marriage.

His pleasure hadn't lasted long. Her ways were so different from his; she and he seemed to rub against each other constantly. He still wanted to bed her—after all, he was a man—but he didn't much want to have to live with her.

She'd changed, too. In the month since her arrival, she'd drawn inside herself. It was as if she were trying to protect an essential part of herself from being wounded. He certainly hadn't meant to stifle her, if it had been he who'd done it. He'd only meant to teach her how the wife of David MacKechnie was expected to behave.

As a rule, David wasn't particularly interested in the inner woes afflicting his fellow man. He let other people do that: the local clergyman, Mr. McTavish, for example; or old lady Elliott, who took care to know everyone else's business.

As for himself, David had hundreds of people depending upon him for their livelihoods: for the food they put in their mouths and the roofs standing over

219

their heads. That was enough responsibility for him, and something he understood. He left his dependents' spiritual requirements to others better qualified to deal with them than he.

This morning, however, he experienced a compulsion to understand this girl, this Lily Munro, who had come here to become his wife and who now seemed as unhappy about the prospect as he. If there were only some way to preserve the essence, the liveliness, of her, yet maintain the dignity of the position she was bound to assume, they might still suit. It seemed an impossible task, though, and David felt glum.

The notion of Lily returning to Texas, however, offended not merely his keen sense of honor, but also gave him a dismal ache in his guts, as if he'd be rejecting something precious; something he needed. He persisted this morning, therefore, and had a feeling Angus would be proud of him.

"Aye. Angus said it's warmer in Texas than 'tis here." David sucked in a breath and took a chance, asking softly, "Have ye been so very cold here, Lily?"

She dropped her gaze. Staring at the glossy table, where she'd been ignoring her porridge in favor of drawing circles on the wood with her fingertip, she murmured softly, "I've been a little cold. Yes."

"Your blood's thin from livin' in Texas," David said with a very small grin. His life had been built on work, not gaiety, and he was unpracticed in the art of smiling.

He was sorry to see her stiffen again, as if he'd just slandered her homeland, or slapped her. Good heavens, what had he done to create this defensiveness in her?

Or had it been he? Perhaps she was just defensive by nature. Another memory, of a laughing, smiling, sweet-tempered, open-handed Lily, came to him, and he knew this leery attitude was not natural to her.

He sighed deeply, wishing he were good with fancy

words. If his tongue were glib and easy, he supposed he could put her at ease and be off about his business, ignoring her. The good Lord knew, he'd seen men charm women before with honeyed words. Such behavior in others had always struck him as dishonest, though, and David had never learned it.

" 'Twas another joke, Lily. I'm not very good at 'em."

After staring at him cautiously for several seconds, Lily said, "I'm sorry I took it the wrong way." She gave him a little smile, and he felt some emotion quiver in his chest. "I'm not used to you joking with me, David."

He wanted to keep looking at her. She was a wee, perky thing; Angus had been right about her spirit and liveliness. Today those attributes didn't strike him as inherently wrong the way they did most days. Of course, right now, at the breakfast table, her behavior wasn't embarrassing him in front of his tenants or his staff, either. Sighing again, he looked away. "No, I reckon you're not."

Keeping his tone guarded, he said, "Would you like to go ridin' with me today, Lily? It's time for me to pay a call to some of the farmers."

"You wouldn't mind?" Her astonishment was patent, and David flinched inside. "I thought you didn't want me in the stables."

"Well, I don't want you in the stables. For heaven's sake, Lily, you're to be the lady of the manor, not a servant."

She went as rigid as a setter on point, and he knew he'd said the wrong thing again. Even if he'd meant it. He hastened to make amends. "That's not to say I don't want you ridin', Lily. As long as you go with me, or take a groom along wi' you, I'm sure ridin' will be good exercise."

"I don't need a groom!"

"You do so, Lily. It's not fittin' for a lady to be gallivantin' all over the countryside with nobody to accompany her." He tried to keep his tone patient. As he was used to dealing with people who obeyed him instantly, patience wasn't a virtue he'd cultivated, and he wasn't altogether successful.

"For heaven's sake, David, I know how to ride. My father taught me how to ride when I was a baby, and I've ridden all my life. I don't need a groom. How on earth do you think I got around on the ranch?"

"This isn't Texas, Lily, and this isn't your father's ranch."

He saw her withdraw into herself at once, and sighed again. He was doing this all wrong. "Lily," he said, striving to keep his voice mild, "in Texas, you knew your way around, and everyone knew you. Life is different here."

She sniffed with disapproval and he felt a ripple of anger shoot through him. He refused to react.

"I know you don't like the differences, but truly, lass, my tenants expect their master and his lady to behave in a certain way. It doesn't do to be puttin' up people's backs." He took a deep breath and another chance. "Your father must ha' taught you that." He was surprised when she jerked as if somebody'd pinched her.

David's remark struck Lily to the heart. *These folks are relyin' on me, Lucky, and I'm relyin' on them. Don't you go rilin' 'em, hear?* She heard her father's jolly admonition in her head, clear as day, and almost sobbed. Oh, how she missed being her daddy's Lucky Lily!

And oh, how she hated knowing David was right. It almost killed her to say, "I understand," in a voice so small she barely heard it herself. Gathering her pride around her like a shield, she added defiantly, "I shall try not to disgrace you, David."

Was it her imagination, or did his eyes go soft for a moment? The moment passed, and Lily decided it had been her imagination. David MacKechnie harbor a soft emotion in his breast? Heaven forbid!

He stood and gave her a look that set something in her own breast to fluttering. She felt terribly attracted to him in that instant; she recalled the feeling as one she'd felt when she'd first met him, as well.

"I'm sure you shan't. I'll tell old Hamish to saddle up that pretty white mare and meet you at the front door, if that's agreeable with you."

She gulped, not having anticipated the excitement bubbling up in her bosom like champagne in a fluted glass. "Yes. Yes, that will be fine." Feeling as though she were making an enormous concession, she added, "She's a beautiful horse, David."

"Aye, she is."

He gave her another one of those looks, and she swallowed. He had lovely eyes: deep blue and thoughtful.

"I knew your father'd have taught you about horses, and I expected you'd want nothin' but good horseflesh under you. I bought her as soon I learned you'd be comin'."

This time, Lily knew it wasn't her imagination. David's midnight blue eyes held something warm, almost hot, as he watched her. When he looked at her in just that way, she had a mad impulse to fling herself into his arms and beg him to be kind to her, to please not send her away. She told herself not to be idiotic.

"Oh," she said softly. "I didn't know that."

The moment passed. David dropped his gaze and straightened his cravat. "Well, 'tis the truth. Can't have the lady of Castle MacKechnie ridin' around on a slug, now, can we?" He gave her a small smile to let her know he was attempting humor again.

"I wish you'd smile more often, David."

Lily felt herself flush as soon as her thought, which she'd meant to keep to herself, smote the air.

David looked at her again, quickly. His smile froze momentarily and vanished. "Aye. Well, perhaps I'll smile more often when there's cause."

Remembering all the reasons she had to feel sorry

for herself, Lily stood, too. She didn't look at him. "I'll run upstairs and dress."

"No need to run." David's voice was as dry as Texas in August when she fled out the door.

Because she didn't want to annoy him—not for his sake, but for hers, because she wasn't sure how many more of his black moods and stern lectures she could endure—Lily dressed quickly and ran downstairs. She waited for David on the massive front porch of Castle MacKechnie, fidgeting with her riding crop. She discovered Angus next to the porch, sweeping up.

"Good morning, Angus." She deliberately made her voice cheerful.

"Beautiful mornin', Lily-lass."

Taking a glance around, Lily had to agree. It wasn't Texas, but these Highland vistas were quite lovely, and they were certainly green. "Yes. Yes, it's a beautiful morning." Another sweeping look prompted, "And it's not raining for once, either."

Angus trudged up the porch steps, propped his old hands on the broom, and chuckled. "The rain makes everything green, lass. Don't you like green?"

Remembering her promise to try one last time, Lily felt herself blush. She said hastily, "Of course I like green, Angus. I didn't mean to sound disapproving."

Angus eyed her costume and twinkled at her. "Goin' for a ride with our Davy, are ye, lass?"

"Yes." She sniffed for form's sake.

In truth, Lily wasn't sure what her mood was this morning. Until David spoke to her at breakfast, she'd been feeling quite dejected. Now her frame of mind alternated between depression and acceptance, but with such rapidity that she couldn't seem to catch hold of an emotion and stick with it. Which was just as well, as neither appealed to her much. What Lily wanted was to be happy again; to feel free and easy and light-hearted and gay: the way she used to feel in Texas.

MacBroom Sweeps Clean

"Ah, but ye're not in Texas anymore, are ye, lass?"

Lily's heart skipped and she felt her eyes pop open. "Angus, you're not going to tell me you can read minds, are you?" She kept her tone light, but the old man's perceptiveness had shaken her.

He gave her a roguish smile. "Hearts, lass. Your heart's as plain to read on your pretty face as if 'twere print in a book."

"Oh." She bowed her head and pretended to fiddle with her riding crop.

Angus offered up an elaborate sigh and stared at the distant hills, which sparkled with the snow melting on their peaks. "Aye, 'tis a woeful life, lass, being wrenched from your lovin' family and dropped in the Highlands with Davy MacKechnie, as glumpish a lad as ever lived. Never a good word to say for anyone, our Davy. I reckon you're right, lass. He's a stick, and there's no doin' anything with him. 'Tis a wonder the folks hereabouts haven't run him off long since."

She knew he was ribbing her and wasn't pleased. "Well, he is stuffy, Angus. And dreadfully disapproving of anything he's not used to."

"Aye. A regular hobgoblin, our Davy."

Chuffing out an irritated breath, which she noticed dismally, hung in the frigid morning air like a cloud, Lily said, "It's not my fault I'm used to people who smile and laugh and treat people in an easy manner, Angus."

"Course not, lass." He gave her a wink. "But I gather you hold Davy accountable for what he's used to."

Lily opened her mouth to retort, then closed it again. Angus was right; Lily wasn't happy to have to acknowledge it. Since she was an honest young woman, however, she had to. "I suppose that's what I've been doing. I'm sorry." Her heart gave a tremendous throb. "But it's so hard, Angus!"

Clucking in sympathy, Angus patted her hand. "I know it is, lass. Ye needn't apologize to me, ye know."

Lily sniffed and swallowed. "Do—do you think I need to apologize to David?" A month's worth of grievances lined up like soldiers in her mind's eye, and she felt her lips quiver with indignation and hurt. She wasn't sure she could apologize to David if she wanted to.

"Och, lassie, I didn't say so, did I?"

"I don't suppose so. Not in so many words."

Still gazing off into the distance, Angus said, "P'raps the both of ye just need to get to know each other better, lassie. P'raps you might want to observe him for a while, without judgin'. It's been my experience that females are able to do that better than fellows are." He gave her another wink. "Ye women are smarter than yer menfolk, Lily-lass, as a rule."

She remembered her mother telling her much the same thing. She wished she believed it. "I haven't felt very smart lately, Angus," she admitted unhappily.

"O' course not. Ye're far away from home and feelin' cold and alone and sad. But ye're not without friends, lass."

By this time, Lily was so near tears, it was difficult to hold them in check. "Th-thank you, Angus."

He gave her hand another pat, and she felt better.

"Och, Lily-lass, ye'll do our Davy proud. Ye just wait; ye'll see."

"I guess I'll just have to wait, won't I?"

Angus laughed much more heartily than her miserable little jest deserved. David rode up then, so she couldn't say so.

With a nod for Angus, David lifted Lily into the pretty sidesaddle perched on her white mare. His hands felt warm on her waist, and she had a momentary wish that he'd leave them there. It would be nice to have a hug right about now. She told herself to stop being foolish and deliberately turned her thoughts to the saddle. She wondered if he'd bought it especially for her as he had the mare, but didn't feel comfortable asking.

If he had, it was a nice thing to have done and·she'd like to tell him so.

On the other hand, she didn't want to give him more credit than he deserved.

After waving good-bye to Angus, she rode off beside David, who looked quite magnificent on his big black gelding. She felt as confused as ever.

Chapter Five

"Master Davy!" Mrs. Malcolm dropped a dish towel and clapped her hands to her plump cheeks, which turned scarlet. Her face donned a huge smile, and she ran to open the gate so the horses could pass into the yard. Chickens scattered, squawking, and geese scolded the intruders in no uncertain terms.

David was pleased by Mrs. Malcolm's gratifying display of delight at his arrival. He shot Lily a sideways glance, and was also pleased to note her expression of surprise. *Ha! Foolish girl.* Believed everyone thought as little of him as she did. Well, they didn't, and he aimed to show her so.

His purpose in suggesting this trip, in fact, was to prove to her that his dependents liked him, even if she didn't. They knew he was a good landlord and a good master. They respected him and his authority. They didn't defy his every request or question his every word. They didn't behave in the wild manner Lily'd been suffered to do in Texas.

MacBroom Sweeps Clean

And, what was more, they had reason to harbor good feelings for him. He *was* a good landlord. He'd worked like the devil since his seventeenth year to make these lands and the people on them flourish, and despite the long odds, he'd succeeded.

The tenants on MacKechnie lands didn't labor under the neglect many of the other Highland farmers did. David kept their cottages in repair, gave them employment, managed his lands well so that everyone on it benefited, and paid attention to the needs of his people. He knew them all by name and could even remember a good number of their children's names, too, what was more.

He nodded at the farm woman. "Good morning, Mrs. Malcolm. How're ye this fine summer day?" He noticed that Lily had pulled her collar up to her chin to ward off the cold and fought his frown.

"Well. We be well, Master Davy. But come in and have a cup o' tay." She gave Lily a good once-over and added, "And bring yer fine lady wi' ye."

In spite of Lily's obvious chill, David felt vastly pleased with himself. "Thank you, Mrs. Malcolm. I believe we shall." Because he knew Mrs. Malcolm didn't expect it from the laird, he didn't smile. The British smiled as they savaged the land and starved the people. The Highland Scots had lived hard and knew the value of a master's smile.

A little boy ran out of the thatched dwelling and, looking both shy and important, took charge of the horses. Lily, who smiled easily, did so now, and said, "Good morning." The lad's chest puffed out even as a blush stained his cheeks.

Mrs. Malcolm frowned at her son. "Take care o' them horses, Billy." The admonition was unnecessary, as he'd already begun to do so.

"I'm sure he'll do a fine job of it," said Lily, making Billy's blush deepen. Mrs. Malcolm harumphed and looked on with narrowed eyes, studying Lily closely.

"Well done," David whispered into her ear as he lifted her from the saddle. He still didn't smile.

It was the first time he'd ever said anything to her that smacked, even faintly, of approval. Rather than feeling good about his praise, however, Lily experienced a rush of irritation. As if it were up to him to approve of her! She gave him a frigid glare, which seemed to take him slightly aback. Resentment throbbing in her breast, she looked pointedly away from him.

As soon as she saw Mrs. Malcolm staring at her in patent shock, she was embarrassed by her show of pique. *You're being childish, Lily,* she told herself. *You'll never get anywhere this way.* To make up for her lapse, she gave Mrs. Malcolm one of her sunniest smiles.

"A cup of tea sounds delightful, Mrs. Malcolm."

The older woman hesitated for just long enough to give Lily the distinct impression that she wasn't approved of. She figured it was for daring to show any sign of spirit to the local laird.

"Aye, well, ye'd better come in, then."

Lily's heart seemed to shrivel, and she found herself resenting Mrs. Malcolm, too. Why were all these people set against her? They didn't even know her! And what did they all see in David MacKechnie? Was it merely that they were accustomed to him? Did his countenance, which showed about as much animation as a plaster statue, appeal to something in them that craved solidity? Stolidity, Lily would call it, rather.

Perhaps they feared him. Immediately, Lily knew she was being unfair. Aloof, David MacKechnie certainly was. And cold and reserved, and he pricked her own pride constantly with his disapproving looks. She'd never once, however, seen him behave cruelly to anyone. Still, she didn't understand why he couldn't be more friendly.

She didn't know what his appeal was to these people. All she knew was that by the time they'd taken tea and oat cakes at Mrs. Malcolm's weathered kitchen table, Lily was still sure Mrs. Malcolm found her sadly lacking. The farm woman seemed glad to be rid of her, although her leave-taking from David was cordial. She even whispered something in his ear that made him smile slightly.

"Thank you, Mrs. Malcolm," David said afterward.

Lily's heart ached as they rode away from the small farm, and it wasn't merely because she expected a scolding from David.

Oh, how she wanted to be accepted by these people! She'd come here expecting to spend the rest of her life with them, and her heart ached when she considered giving up in defeat and going home. Lily was a Texan, and Texans didn't take defeat lightly.

Yet when it came to these stubborn Highlanders, she was going about earning their approval all wrong, knew it, and didn't know how to rectify her lapses. She wished she were back on her rock by the brook, where she could be miserable in peace. Or, better yet, in Texas where she understood what was expected of her and knew how to achieve it.

Their next stop was at McBain's farm. McBain, too, invited them in for tea and he, too, watched Lily like a hawk. It seemed to Lily that he was hoping to catch her doing or saying something wrong.

And so it went. All morning long, Lily met David's tenants. All morning long, they inspected her. All morning long, she felt herself come up short in their estimation.

"I felt like an insect pinned to a board, Angus," she said gloomily after luncheon that afternoon.

Miracle of miracles, David had gone to the village without lecturing her on her behavioral missteps. Lily had changed from her riding dress into a green woolen gown that would have done quite well for a winter's day back home, snatched up her woolen MacKechnie plaid shawl, and meandered to the brook, feeling chilled to the bone and very much alone. She was glad to find Angus already there, a string tied to his walking stick and dangling in the brook. He was fishing.

Angus chuckled and pulled in his line. He frowned when he found it empty of fish, but dripping a long strand of river weed. He plucked it off and flung it back, saying as he did so, "Aye. I expect you did, lass. You're new here. Folks in the Highlands haven't had much luck with newcomers in the past, y'know. They've learned to be a cautious lot."

His explanation made Lily cock her head to one side. "I hadn't thought about it that way."

"Well, 'tis the truth, lass." He tossed his line back and chuckled again. "Last newcomer we had who wasn't English was Roland Birnie. The farmers have accepted him pretty fair."

"New Rolly?"

"Aye. That's the one."

"How long has he been here?"

Angus shrugged. "Fifty years, more or less."

Lily sat up straight. "Fifty years? And they still consider him a newcomer?"

"Aye, that's it, all right."

"Good heavens! I thought there must be some other explanation for his nickname."

"Nay. 'Tis 'cause he's come new to these parts."

"He's been here fifty years, Angus," Lily said severely. "After fifty years, he's not new any longer."

"Reckon that depends on a body's perspective, Lily-lass."

Lily gave a meaningful sniff. "Well, it seems to me that people are just being silly. For heaven's sake, if we used your standards, almost everybody in Texas would be newcomers."

"Aye. I expect they be."

She shook her head. "That's silly, Angus."

"Well, now, that's not to say a newcomer can't be

accepted into the community, lass. New Rolly was accepted right off, more or less."

Lily watched the water where Angus's line had entered. Ripples, a series of sparkling rings, circled it, getting bigger and bigger the farther out they got, and for some reason they reminded Lily of gossip. "I wish I knew how he did it," she said, feeling quite sad.

A puff of smoke from his pipe drifted up over Angus's head, looking like a halo and making Lily smile. Now he had rings at both ends, she thought.

"Well, lass, 'tis possible that New Rolly already knew what life was like here before he moved."

"Maybe."

"And 'tis also possible that he didn't mind the weather, bein' used to the cold and damp and so forth already."

Lily pulled her shawl more tightly around her shoulders. She would love to be warm again for twenty-four hours in a row. It seemed like such a little thing to complain about, yet the persistent cold nipped at her until she wanted to scream. The cold was pesky and irritating, like the mosquitoes during the summers back home that used to torment her.

She opened and closed her gloved hands several times. "My fingers always feel stiff and clumsy, Angus, like they're frozen all the time."

He shook his head in sympathy. "Have ye told our Davy about your problem, lass?"

Her gaze flicked to the trees in the distance. Castle MacKechnie rose from among them, looking like a medieval fortress. "Sort of. I asked him if we couldn't light a fire in the breakfast room. Or in the book room during the day."

"And what did he answer ye?"

She sighed again. "He looked at me as if I were crazy and said it was summertime. He said there'd be plenty of fires lit when the weather turned cold."

Again Angus chuckled. "I was thinkin' that very thing the day I met ye, lass."

"You met me yesterday, Angus," Lily reminded him with a small smile.

"Did I? Well, there. You see? I lose track o' time at my age, Lily-lass."

It was on the tip of Lily's tongue to ask him how old he was but good manners prevailed, and she didn't. She wished David could have been there to appreciate her forbearance.

They sat in silence for several minutes. The fish didn't seem to be biting. Lily figured it was because they hadn't thawed out yet from winter, but she didn't say so. She ran over the events of the morning in her mind, and realized she was puzzled by more than her own failure to win the approval of David's tenants.

"How many people do you suppose depend on him for their livelihoods, Angus?"

He slanted her a look. "What 'him' are ye talkin' about, lass? David MacKechnie?"

"Yes."

He shrugged. "On towards a hundred and more, I expect."

A hundred. A hundred people, all depending upon David's management for their livings. "That's—that's a big responsibility."

"Aye."

She licked her lips and then regretted it when the chilly wind nipped them. They'd be chapped by evening. At least here, in sheep country, there was plenty of lanolin to spread on chapped lips and hands—which seemed a very good thing to Lily, given the bitter state of the weather. "He seems to be a good landlord. The people all welcomed him when we were out today, and thanked him for a variety of different things he'd done."

"Aye."

"I guess when Mrs. Malcolm's son was ill, he brought the doctor from Strathclyde himself."

"Aye. I recollect that. Mr. Malcolm was down in

Glasgow on business and wasna there to go himself."

After a moment or two, Lily said almost grudgingly, "That was nice of him."

"Aye."

Then she sniffed again. "Although I suppose it's no more than he ought to do. After all, these poor people aren't even allowed to own their own land."

"Aye."

As if some imp inside her wouldn't allow David MacKechnie an inch of slack, she added, "And I imagine he likes to keep his tenants healthy. After all, a sick person can't do much work."

"Aye. A prudent sort of lad. That's our Davy."

Angus sounded sly, and Lily's glance sharpened. He looked as innocent as a newborn lamb. Not that Lily had ever seen a newborn lamb, although she was evidently going to get the opportunity to see any number of them in years to come. If she stayed. She sighed yet again.

"I can't imagine not being able to own land if you wanted to."

Angus shrugged. "I expect folks who have a cravin' to own land can always take themselves off to America."

"I guess." Lily had begun to poke the pebbles at her feet with a stick.

"The rest of us poor benighted Highlanders'll have to depend on lairds like our Davy."

"Mmmm."

" 'Tis a good thing some of 'em take the job seriously. I reckon if Davy didn't, little Mariah Kelly and her ma would have been in the soup good and proper."

Lily looked up, her interest caught. "Mariah Kelly's mother has problems?"

"Aye. I reckon you can call a dead husband a problem."

"She lost her husband?" Lily pictured as if she were still standing before her the shy little girl who'd given

Emma Craig

her such a pretty bouquet of flowers. Sad that Mariah should be without a father, she asked, "How did it happen?"

"Accident," Angus said succinctly.

"What kind of accident?"

Exhaling a cloud of tobacco along with a deep sigh, Angus said, "A carriage ran him down."

"Ran him down! Good heavens! How did that happen?"

"An Englishman who come here to fish didn't think our Samuel got out of his way quick enough."

Lily tried to digest this news, but it gave her a stomachache. "And David helped his family?"

"Aye. Sent in doctors for Samuel. They tried to save the poor bugger, but couldn't. Without Samuel to work in the fields, o' course, the Kellys like to starve, even with folks helpin'. 'Sides"—Angus gave Lily a long look—"most folks hereabouts don't hold with acceptin' charity. Pricks the pride to be unable to care for your own. So our Davy gave Sarah Kelly another job."

"He did?"

"Aye."

"What kind of job?"

"She does the sewin' for the castle now. She makes the curtains and the tablecloths and mends things."

"Oh." Lily plucked a long stem of grass and chewed on it thoughtfully. "Who did the sewing before?"

"One of the girls at the castle. Lass name of Becky."

"Oh, yes, I know Becky. She's a sweet girl. Works in the brewery."

Angus nodded. "She does now. So does Matthew Kelly."

"Little Matthew?" Lily remembered the young fellow who carried buckets of water from the stream. At the time she'd wondered why so small a boy had been put to work, even though he'd looked rather proud of himself. Now she guessed she knew, although at first she'd considered his employment merely another example of

236

Scots insensitivity. Being an American and accustomed to American ways, she believed little children should attend school.

"Aye, that's the lad."

"So, in effect, you're telling me that David created a job for both of them to make up for the loss of Mrs. Kelly's husband."

"Nothin' can make up for that, lass. But he gave 'em employment so they wouldn't have to beg in the streets or take charity for the rest of their lives."

"That—that was very nice of him."

"Practical, lass," Angus said. "I'm sure he knows it pays to keep his tenants happy. They produce more that way, don't you see?" He gave her another canny look. "O' course, if you want to fit our Davy with angel's wings, I don't reckon too many of his tenants would find fault wi' ye on the score."

"Humph," said Lily, although with less vigor than usual.

Angus had given her a lot to chew on. At the moment, it was making her feel rather sick.

"O' course," Angus continued, without giving her a chance to do more than consider the Kellys, "If ye were to ask around in the village of Lochlydh, you might hear tales about how our own David MacKechnie saved the valley, but I don't know as how I'd go that far myself."

"Saved the—"

A hearty "Good afternoon, Angus. Good afternoon, Lily," startled her nearly out of her wits and brought her springing up from her rock. She turned, alarmed, to see David MacKechnie himself striding down the slope to the book's bank. He carried a package with him and looked every inch a man who belonged in this rugged country, in his tweed walking coat, twill trousers, white shirt, jaunty hat, and plaid scarf.

And he was the man who'd saved the valley? Oh, how

she wished she could ask Angus about his artfully dropped bombshell.

There was no time to do so, though, so Lily smoothed her skirt and patted her hair in place, and hoped to heaven David hadn't heard Angus and herself gossiping about him.

Chapter Six

"Any luck, Angus?" David asked, sounding friendlier than Lily'd ever heard him.

She watched, fascinated, as David negotiated the rocky path, surefooted as a mountain goat. She was struck, not for the first time, by how handsome a man he was. His looks, in fact, set her insides to trembling. When—if—she married him, she'd at least have a husband who appealed to her on a physical level.

Not, of course, that Lily knew much about such things. Her feelings of propriety rebelling, she gave herself a mental shake and told herself to cast her mind upon higher matters.

David was a man obviously at ease out-of-doors. Lily felt more comfortable thinking about his affinity for the great outdoors.

When she'd first arrived in England and stayed with some friends of her father's, Lily had feared her future husband might be one of those foppish sorts who eschewed country life and never stirred outside before noon—and then did so only to take a carriage to his club. Since she loved taking long energetic walks, delighted in horseback riding, and even enjoyed fishing and shooting, the notion of a soft-bellied, card-playing, snuff-taking indoor husband didn't appeal to her much, although, for the sake of her family, she would have compromised her desires if he were affable enough.

When she'd met David and recognized in his tanned face and trim body a man who spent a good deal of his time out-of-doors, she'd been rather more encouraged than not. At first. Until she realized he was a cold fish and she couldn't do anything to please him.

"Caught me a wee, sweet lass," Angus said, winking in Lily's direction. "But the fish aren't as cordial as our Lily-lass."

Giving a thought to the people she'd met earlier in the day, Lily knew her smile must look anemic. She expected David to say something sarcastic.

Instead, he said, "Aye," surprising her. "And speaking of such things, I dropped by Mrs. Kelly's house in the village to see how she and little Mariah are getting on. She asked me to give ye this, Lily, in thanks for being kind to her wee bairns."

"She did?" Lily sounded every bit as flabbergasted as she felt. *Was I being kind to Mariah? All I did was give her a thank-you kiss for the pretty bouquet.* She'd believed David had deprecated her impulsive gesture. He'd certainly frowned heavily enough at the time.

She took the brown-paper-wrapped package David handed her, feeling shy. "Oh!" she cried when she opened it up to find a long scarf knitted from soft green wool and decorated with a delicately knotted fringe. "How pretty."

"Very nice," said Angus, nodding his approval.

"Almost as pretty as the lady it was made for," affirmed David, drawing Lily's immediate attention. She encountered a look so warm, it made her insides sizzle.

MacBroom Sweeps Clean

At once she dropped her gaze again. Had he just complimented her? If she'd been alone, Lily would have smacked the side of her head to clear her ears of impediments. And that smile of his . . . She wanted to look again, to see she'd been mistaken about reading such warmth into it. But what if she had been mistaken? She wasn't sure she could stand it, and felt a momentary, instantly banished, sting of tears behind her eyes.

"I should be thanking Mrs. Kelly," she murmured. "She's the only one of your tenants who doesn't seem to hate me."

"*Hate* you?"

David's astonishment was so plain, Lily looked up again. He was staring at her, his deep blue eyes wide with incredulity. She heard Angus chuckle, but didn't spare him a glance.

"Don't they?" she asked in a small voice, her attention all on David. His answer, she knew instinctively, would be one of the most important she'd receive in her life.

Taking a step toward her, David put a hand on her shoulder. His touch had an alarming effect on her, and she sucked in a deep breath, hoping he'd complete the gesture with his other hand and draw her to his chest. She could scarcely believe herself capable of such shocking urges and wished her mother were here so she could discuss them with her. The good Lord knew, she couldn't talk to Aunt Minnie about them. Aunt Minnie was not only a maiden lady, but tiddly nine-tenths of the time, to boot.

David must have misinterpreted her gasp, because he let his other hand drop to his side and only kept the one resting lightly on her shoulder. "Do you know what Mrs. Malcolm told me when we left her farm today, Lily?" he asked softly.

His gaze held hers captive. She couldn't have looked away if she'd tried; nor could she seem to speak. She swallowed and managed to shake her head, mouthing a no.

"She said you're a pretty lass with spirit, and that everybody in the valley had feared I'd take an English-woman to bride. They're pleased to have you, Lily."

Angus cried, "No!" in a horrified voice, effectively breaking the spell. Lily blinked. David's gaze finally left her face. He was actually smiling when he turned to look at Angus.

"Aye, Angus, and ye needn't look at me that way. I know what ye're thinkin'."

Angus grinned around his pipe. "I doubt it, laddie."

David dropped his hand, leaving Lily feeling oddly bereft. She was from a hugging family. She missed being hugged, and wondered if she could teach David to be more spontaneous if she tried. Then she wondered where her wits had gone begging.

"Well, I'm needin' Lily at the house, Angus, so we'll leave you to your fishing now."

Tipping his woolen cap, Angus said, "If I catch any-thing, I'll take it to Mrs. Fleming." He smiled broadly at the two of them.

"Good man," David said with an answering grin.

"One cold fish to another," murmured Angus.

Lily choked. David burst out laughing, startling Lily nearly out of her skin.

Then he completed her astonishment when he took her hand and began to lead the way home. A thrill lodged in her heart and for the first time in weeks, she felt a tiny flicker of hope.

"I got this for you today in Lochlydh, Lily."

David watched Lily's cheeks turn pink when he handed her the package he'd brought home with him, and wondered why he'd never brought her a gift before. He wasn't a stingy fellow by nature; he just hadn't thought about it.

"Thank you." She took the package, then stared at it

as though she weren't quite sure what to do with it.

"Open it up, Lily," he urged. "If you don't like it, I can take it back and get another."

Her hands trembled when she fumbled with the string wound 'round the package. David hadn't seen her look so nervous since he'd first met her. When she unwrapped the brown paper, he was nervous, too. This had been an impulsive gesture on his part. David was unused to giving in to impulse, and hoped he hadn't made a damned fool of himself by doing so today. He didn't think he had.

Since his seventeenth year, when his parents were carried off in an influenza epidemic that had swept the valley, he'd been forced to live his life prudently, giving great thought to his every move. The responsibility for many lives had rested on his boyish shoulders, and he'd sworn to himself and the memory of his parents that he wouldn't neglect it. Over the years, he knew, circumstances had ground away at his gaiety. He'd not had cause to regret the fact until Lily was thrust upon him. Before his world had turned upside down with his parents' death, he used to be a jolly enough fellow.

After his chat with Angus last night, though, David realized for the first time that he didn't so much deprecate Lily's spontaneity as fear it. He'd allowed Lily's freedom of expression to prick him as if he were still a lad of seventeen and fighting to appear grown-up to the people who depended upon him. The sudden insight had given him food for thought. Today, when he'd learned the valley folk had expected him to wed an Englishwoman in spite of their great love for him, he understood how far from necessity his serious disposition had taken him.

So, when he and Lily had taken their ride this morning and he'd noticed her shivering, not for effect or to spite him, but because her Texas blood and bones were accustomed to a warmer climate, he'd formulated his determination to visit the village. He'd been full of glee when he set out after luncheon today. At the moment, he wanted to rub his hands in anticipation. Or bite his fingernails in anxiety.

"Oh, David!" she cried when she pulled out the fur muff. "Oh, David!"

Immediately, she brought the muff to her cheek and rubbed against it like a cat. He could see tears in her eyes when she lifted her face.

"Thank you, David," she said, her voice as soft as the sable fur of her new muff. "Thank you so much!"

He clenched his hands to keep from succumbing to one more impulsive gesture. If he grabbed her and drew her into his embrace as he wanted to do, he was pretty sure she'd slap his face at the very least.

"I'm sorry you've been cold, Lily. I'm sorry I didn't realize sooner how different our weather would be from what you're used to."

"It's not your fault, David," she said, surprising him. He'd begun to believe she considered everything his fault.

She surprised him further when she said, "I-I'm sorry I haven't tried harder to—to fit in."

"Ye fit in fine, Lily," he assured her quickly, uneasy with confessions of this nature. He licked his lips. "Ye're doing fine. I've—" He cleared his throat. "I've been too quick to find fault wi' ye. I know it, and I'm sorry." Intimacy had been denied him for more years than not, and it made him edgy. He offered her the apology with great difficulty.

He was horrified when the tears standing in her eyes splashed over onto her cheeks. Putting out his hand, he cried, "Here, lass! There's no need for that."

He fumbled for a moment at his breast pocket and drew out a handkerchief, then took a step back and dangled it out in front of her, trying to distance himself, uncomfortable with her display of emotion. Such displays were foreign to him, and they worried him.

She snatched the handkerchief from his hands and

mopped her cheeks. Then, in yet another impulsive gesture, she almost shocked him senseless when she threw herself at his chest and wrapped her arms around him. He stood, stupefied for a moment, before his reserve dissolved in a wash of emotion.

A small woman, Lily was yet a woman, and a well-filled-out one. David had noticed her figure right off, before he'd become preoccupied by what he perceived as her failings. Now he wasn't so sure they were failings. He believed Angus was right, and that he'd been too hard on her, forgetting to allow for differences between the wild Americans and the steady, stable Scots.

His arms closed around her of their own accord, and he thought perhaps a fine figure in a woman could atone for a good deal that might otherwise be difficult to take. "There, there," he murmured. He nestled his cheek on her soft curls, and wondered if this was what cats felt like when they stretched and rubbed.

Perhaps he'd lived too much in his head these past years. There was no fault in that, he supposed, but it might be time to explore his other senses. There was a time and place for everything, and now seemed to be time to experience more earthly pleasures. And, with that decision out of the way, David gave in to sensations of the flesh.

When the door opened several minutes later, he and Lily had traveled to the sofa. Lily sat on David's lap, her hair tumbling around her shoulders. His hand was exploring inside her unbuttoned bodice, and hers was investigating a fascinating, hard ridge that had grown in his trousers.

Neither of them noticed that their sanctuary had been invaded until a short, sharp screech smote their ears.

Alice, the maidservant who had opened the door, dropped her dust rag and fled, slamming the door behind her. Lily lifted the hand that had lately been tormenting and delighting David and pressed it to her cheek, which flamed with embarrassment. David withdrew his own hand from Lily's bodice. He did so reluctantly. Her bosom was even more enticing in the flesh than it had seemed when modestly covered with several layers of fabric.

Expelling a heavy breath, he dropped his head back against the sofa cushion as Lily scrambled from his lap. His state of arousal was acute and his frustration intense, but his sense of well-being had shot up at least a hundred percent.

After a moment, he opened his eyes and sought Lily. He discovered her standing in front of the fireplace. Her back was to him, but he could tell she was fumbling madly with her front buttons. Some imp of mischief with which he'd entirely lost touch in the twelve years since his parents' deaths propelled him from the sofa. He walked stiffly to Lily and gently turned her around.

"Here," he said, panting, "please allow me."

And he removed her hands from her buttons. Then he thoroughly kissed the flushed flesh of her perfectly spectacular bosom. When he was through doing that, he continued her job and, with extreme reluctance, refastened her bodice.

Then he hugged her hard, cradling her head to his shoulder. With something akin to awe, he decided his future didn't seem so bleak after all. In fact, if he could convince her to stay with him, he might even rejoin the human race.

Chapter Seven

Lily still suffered from acute embarrassment about the prior afternoon's indiscretion when she sat down to breakfast with David the following day. She could barely recall supper last night. In fact, she'd almost succumbed to her mood and supped in her Aunt Minnie's room. Pride had prevailed at last, though, and she'd taken the meal with David in the dining room.

She had no idea what she'd eaten. All she knew for sure was that she and he had dined in silence, and she'd escaped to her room without even warming herself by the drawing-room fire. She'd been astounded to discover a fire burning in the grate of her own bedroom, so she'd sat in front of that fire, hugging herself, and wishing the arms around her were David's. She hardly knew what to make of herself.

This morning, her cheeks felt hot, although they were nowhere near as hot as the rest of her. And here she'd thought she'd never be warm again. Ever since their interrupted interlude, her insides had been fairly steaming.

"Thank you for having a fire prepared in my room, David."

"Certainly, Lily. I hope you were warm last night."

"Yes, thank you. I was."

"I was fair to boiling all night myself."

She shot him a keen look and glanced away again just as quickly when she saw his broad grin. His obvious enjoyment of her mortification did nothing to help her regain her composure. And here she'd been deprecating the fact that he had no sense of humor and never smiled. This would teach her.

Although it strained her natural expansiveness, she assumed a pose of rigid dignity as she served herself from a platter of kedgeree, a dish she could barely pronounce, much less digest. This morning she didn't even spare a thought for the breakfasts she missed back home.

"Thank you," she said to the serving maid. Unfortunately, it was Alice, the same maid who had interrupted her torrid embrace with David the day before. Lily felt her blush deepen. She was not mollified when David's deep chuckle smote her ears.

Since she couldn't think of a single thing to say that would put him in his place, she decided to endure the meal with fortitude and carry on as if nothing of an embarrassing nature had happened between them. With her back as straight as an iron rod and her chin tilted at an angle calculated to depress levity, she said, "Angus said you might be thanked for saving the valley, David. What did he mean by that?"

She was pleased to see David's saucy grin vanish. It was replaced by a flustered expression Lily had never seen on his face, which generally displayed extreme confidence and stoical calm. She felt a surge of satisfaction. *Ha! Let him be uncomfortable for a while. It would serve him right!*

MacBroom Sweeps Clean

"That's foolish talk, Lily, and nothing of any matter."

He, too, took a serving of kedgeree and nodded his dismissal to Alice, who left after casting one significant glance at Lily. The maid's look spoke worlds to her. She tended to pay attention to it rather than David's modest words.

"I don't believe you, David," she said, and was amazed at her own temerity. "And I don't believe Angus would have said such a thing unless it were true. So please tell me. How did you save the valley?"

"Och," he said, reminding Lily of Angus himself. He sounded annoyed, flapped his hand as if to dismiss the subject, and took a bite of his spicy breakfast.

She was intrigued now, though, and wouldn't be dismissed. "Well? If the man who may yet be my husband is a hero, I'd like to know about it."

Her astonishment trebled when she saw a flush spread up David's neck and invade his cheeks. She could think of only one reason to account for his discomfort. Putting down her fork, she exclaimed, "You *did* save the valley, didn't you? Oh, David, please tell me about it!"

"Nonsense!"

"If you don't tell me, I'll ask Angus. Or the reverend Mr. McTavish or Mrs. Elliott." With a sly look, she added, "Or Alice."

Lily had never teased David before, and was rather confounded to hear herself do it now. Until he'd kissed her so thoroughly, she'd tried to hide her natural sense of humor from him, believing him to be absent any human emotions. Now he looked up at her with eyes both twinkly and reticent, and her heart flipped over and began hammering hard. Goodness, she couldn't be starting to *care* for him, could she?

"Truly, it was nothing," he said. "Nothing that anyone else wouldn't have done under the same circumstances."

"Which were?"

He huffed out an enormous breath. Lily thought it was sweet that he seemed shy about accepting praise or trumpeting his own achievements. She'd grown up in Texas, around men who delighted in telling tales of their own valor and who basked in the acclaim of others. Bravado was part of a Texan's legacy. David's reluctance either to boast or to brag charmed her.

"Oh, I just gave 'em a little hand when they needed it, is all."

Lily squinted at him for a full minute. David ate doggedly and refused to catch her eye. She said, "That's not all, David MacKechnie, and you know it. If you expect me to remain here, you must tell me this story. I know it's important to the valley, and if it's important to the valley, it's important to the lady of Castle MacKechnie." Somewhat triumphantly, she added, "As you've told me at least a hundred times yourself."

David heaved a big sigh and sat back in his chair. He settled his fork on his plate and looked as though her insistence provoked him. Lily wasn't surprised. Nor was she to be rebuffed. She merely continued to look at him, hard.

At last he said, with obvious reluctance, "Well, the men in the valley were losing jobs to the woolen mill on the other side of the loch. As you may know, it's run by an English firm. All the managing positions are held by British men. Folks in the valley, if they were hired at all, were only allowed to hold menial positions."

Lily could tell what he thought of the British by the way he explained the business. She didn't quite understand what he was trying to tell her, though. "But there's a mill on your land."

He took another bite of kedgeree, chewed it thoroughly, and swallowed it before he said, "Aye. There is now."

She blinked at him as his words sank in. "You mean you built that mill and bought all the equipment and so forth just to provide your tenants with work?"

He was paying very close attention to his meal and put another bite of it into his mouth before she'd finished asking her question. Since his mouth was full, he merely shrugged. Lily got the distinct impression he'd stuffed his mouth deliberately and that he didn't want to discuss the matter anymore. She was intrigued now, though, and wouldn't let it drop.

Her own fork clattered when she set it on her plate. "Wasn't that dreadfully expensive?"

He shrugged again.

"It must have been an awful gamble, too, David, what with a fully staffed mill already operating on the other side of the loch."

Conversations that hadn't made any sense to her in Texas dribbled back into her mind. She remembered her father, tears in his eyes, holding a letter and telling his mother about the great and noble risk a young man of his acquaintance was taking, and how her father wanted to help him. She hadn't paid much attention at the time, believing her father to be referring to an American business acquaintance. Besides, that was several years ago. She sat up straighter.

"When was this?" she asked.

She was too quick for him and asked her question before he could cram more food into his mouth. He took a drink of water before he answered. Then he shrugged again and said, "Oh, about eight years ago."

Eight years ago. She'd have been thirteen. No wonder she didn't remember the particulars. She did know, however, that around that time she began hearing her father and mother discuss "the mill." Eight years ago. She cocked her head and gazed at David, who still wouldn't meet her eye.

"How old were you when you did this, David?"

He shrugged again, but Lily insisted. "David Mac-Kechnie, answer me this instant! How old were you when you did this?"

He looked annoyed. Lily didn't care. Things were

starting to settle in her mind. She looked upon him intently.

"I was about twenty-one or twenty-two when I decided to go on with the project." He lifted his glass in a gesture oddly resembling a toast. "I couldn't have done it without the help of your father and a good many other people in the United States. They were much more willing to help me than the Scots bankers in Edinburgh and Glasgow." In a bitter undertone, he added, "Damned money-grubbing British shills."

Lily sat back and dropped her hands to her lap. "Well, for heaven's sake."

He lifted a brow. "Don't give me too much credit, Lily. 'Twas the folk in the valley who made the mill work. The English mill could have paid 'em more. At first."

Silence fell between them. Lily wondered if she'd been part of the deal struck between her father and David. She thought about asking and then decided she didn't care. However he'd done it, whatever bargains he'd struck, David had saved the valley. Her heart filled, and suddenly she felt proud almost to bursting.

Her pride must have shown because David said irritably, "It was an awful chance I took, Lily."

"I suppose so."

"Now that I look back, I wonder at my audacity."

So did Lily. She had a hard time picturing the stiff, unsmiling David MacKechnie risking everything he owned for the sake of the people who depended on him. Then again, maybe she didn't.

"I staked everything on that mill. I could have lost the castle that's been in my family for hundreds of years."

"I suppose so."

"The whole enterprise could have crashed down around my head and ruined us all. Everybody in the valley and me, too."

"But it didn't."

After a moment, he said, "No. It didn't. But it could have."

"Well, I think what you did was special, David, and I don't blame the folks in the valley for thinking so highly of you."

Her words must have stunned him. Lily saw his jaw work uselessly for a moment or two before he uttered a strangled "Thank you."

She smiled and nodded. Then, feeling better than she had since shortly after her arrival, Lily dug into her breakfast. It almost, but not quite, tasted good to her.

"There are several men from the village outside, Master Davy. They say they have a large delivery for you."

It was several days after David's revelation about how he'd saved the valley. He hadn't made any further references to his heroism, and he hadn't kissed Lily again. Although she still couldn't claim to have conquered her qualms, Lily didn't feel as alienated from him as she had formerly.

Surprised by the interruption, she looked up from the book she was reading to see Porter, David's ancient butler, frowning at David from the doorway. She sat in the library in a big chair by the fireplace while David worked at his desk. She'd started coming in here after breakfast, finding she rather enjoyed her perhaps–future husband's silence, which she'd come to understand stemmed from concentration on his work rather than a deliberate attempt to ignore her. He'd also begun requesting a small fire to be lit in the room. Since her Aunt Minnie was certainly no company for her, she enjoyed these hours with David. She expected she would have if she'd had six Aunt Minnies here in Castle MacKechnie with her.

Porter looked as though he didn't appreciate this distraction from his daily routine.

"Ah, thank you, Porter."

David rose from his chair and stretched. Then he cast a somewhat apprehensive look at Lily and mumbled, "I'll just see what's going on, Lily. You needn't bother."

Before she could answer, he scooted out of the room as if he couldn't do so fast enough and closed the door behind him.

"Well, for heaven's sake."

Lily had never taken kindly to being excluded from mysteries, as she possessed a lively curiosity. She didn't take it kindly today, either. Leaping up from her chair, she set her book aside and dashed after David. He had disappeared from sight, but after a determined search she found him at last, outside on the front porch and delivering instructions.

"Take it around to the back of the castle, Charlie," David was saying to the burly man at the reins of an ox-cart. Three large men who looked as though they might be Charlie's sons crouched in the bed of the wagon next to a huge, blanketed object. "After you and your boys unload it, I'll have Mrs. Fleming pull ye all a pint."

Charlie tugged his plaid cap. He didn't smile. Lily understood by this time that these Highlanders were exceedingly spare with their smiles. She no longer believed their severe expressions betokened unfriendliness, however. Rather, she'd learned their dourness stemmed from a wry humor that delighted in understatement. Her Texas expansiveness, she decided, was the natural by-product of a warm climate.

Impulsively she put a hand on David's arm, and he gave a start. He'd obviously not expected her to disobey and follow him, although why that should be Lily had no idea. She'd never obeyed him blindly in the past. He frowned, and she could tell he wasn't happy to see her.

"I told ye you needn't bother, Lily. I'll take care of this."

"Aye," she said, trying out a Scottish accent for fun.

"I know ye did, Davy, me lad, but I chose to see for myself."

For a moment his expression hovered somewhere between annoyance and amusement. Annoyance won—or maybe, Lily thought with something of a start, it was embarrassment—and he huffed, "Well, stay out of the way, then. These men have work to do."

"I wouldn't dream of interfering," Lily said virtuously. She smiled when he glared at her.

Then David hopped onto the back of Charlie's wagon and she was left to scowl after him as the wagon rattled off. She resented his cocky grin and his nonchalant wave as he rounded the corner of the castle in a puff of dust. Well, he wouldn't shake her off that easily. Lily was nothing if not resourceful.

Chapter Eight

David didn't expect Lily to be daunted by his slick escape for long, although he couldn't help but hope. This could prove to be embarrassing.

By the time Charlie and his sons got his enormous purchase unloaded, she hadn't yet found her way to the kitchen. David thanked the saints for small favors. He figured he'd have enough to do in soothing the feelings of Mrs. Fleming without having to deal with the triumph Lily was sure to feel as soon as she discovered he'd bought a monstrous modern stove for the castle's kitchen.

At the moment, the cook was eyeing the huge metallic contraption as if she were looking into the face of Satan.

"Och, and what's that?" she asked, suspicious.

"It's a grand new stove, Mrs. Fleming," David told her, making an effort to keep his voice hearty and his mood jolly. He spread his arms wide and gestured at

MacBroom Sweeps Clean

the appliance much as if he were showing a champion ram at the sheep fair in Strathclyde.

"And what am I to do with it?" demanded she.

"Why, you're to cook the castle's meals on it." In a wheedling tone he could scarcely credit as coming from his own throat, he added, "Ye're already the best cook in the Highlands, Mrs. Fleming. Just think what masterpieces ye'll be able to create on this grand new thing."

"Oh, David!" he heard from the doorway, and cringed. "You bought a new stove!"

Lily had found him. He rolled his eyes heavenward and hoped she wouldn't set the cook irrevocably against the new invention she was eyeing with such malevolence. Mrs. Fleming resented Lily, and had done from the moment Lily first set foot in the castle kitchen and tried to talk recipes with her. David held himself responsible for the cook's animosity, too, although he hadn't admitted as much to Angus and had only done so to himself in a moment of uncontrollable honesty.

"Aye," he said, trying for a severe tone. "It's time to drag the kitchen of Castle MacKechnie out of the Middle Ages and into the eighteen nineties."

He didn't appreciate the gleam of amusement he detected on Lily's countenance. Even less did he appreciate the bitter look Mrs. Fleming cast at Lily.

"I didn't know ye were dissatisfied, Master David." Mrs. Fleming's voice conveyed a world of hurt feelings.

"Of course I've not been dissatisfied!" David cried, shocked at the very idea. "But ye must admit your life will be easier with such a masterpiece of modern convenience, Mrs. Fleming."

It didn't look to him as though Mrs. Fleming wanted to admit any such thing. Indeed, the woman appeared at the moment as if she didn't know whether to throw a temper tantrum or fall weeping onto the kitchen's cold stone floor. David looked from her to Lily, who was beaming at the stove as if it were on the order of a second coming, and knew a moment of utter perplexity.

He said uncertainly, "And it'll free up the kitchen lads to work in the fields, too, Mrs. F. The boys are sorely needed there."

Mrs. Fleming looked at him as if he'd just denied the existence of God, and David could have bitten his tongue. He wished he knew what to say now, but he hadn't a clue.

He'd ordered the stove to prove to Lily that he wasn't the benighted, old-fashioned fuddy-duddy she evidently believed him to be. Now that it was here, he wasn't at all sure he'd done the right thing, particularly if it meant alienating Mrs. Fleming. The cook had been one of his staunchest supporters over the years.

It was Mrs. Fleming whose phlegmatic countenance David recalled when he looked back upon the days of his youth. It was Mrs. Fleming who used to sneak him trays of sandwiches when he'd been sent to bed without his supper for misbehaving. It was Mrs. Fleming whose good soups had nursed him through colds and measles and broken bones. It was Mrs. Fleming, more than anyone else except his parents, whom David thought of when he remembered his childhood.

As he watched, the cook circled the stove. She kept her arms crossed over her chest, as if she were loath to touch the metal monster. Minutes crawled past, each one feeling like an hour to David. Lily stood beside him and gripped his arm as though she, too, felt the suspense of the moment.

At last Mrs. Fleming spoke. "How do it work?"

How do it work? David looked helplessly at the stove. Then he looked at Charlie, who shrugged. So did his boys. David asked, "Did it come with instructions?" Again Charlie shrugged. Another age seemed to limp by.

MacBroom Sweeps Clean

Then, into the silence, Lily spoke. "I'll help you learn how to use it, Mrs. Fleming."

David looked at her, astonished. Mrs. Fleming looked at her, too, but her expression was hostile.

"You know how to use one of these things?" he asked.

This time it was Lily who shrugged. She looked more than a little timid. "I used to cook at home all the time. This stove is very like the one we had on the ranch. I'm sure it can't be that much different."

Yet another eon trudged past.

"It will be a black day," Mrs. Fleming said at last, her words hard, her cadence measured, "when the lady of Castle MacKechnie dirties her hands in the kitchen."

David saw a flash of annoyance pass over Lily's face. She drew herself up straight. He could almost see her gather her pride and deliberation around her; then she used them both to create a smile that appeared almost genuine.

"Nonsense," she said brightly. "Why, a modern woman has to know how everything works, from cooking to politics. I'll be happy to help you learn to use this stove, Mrs. Fleming. Once you grow accustomed to it, I'm sure you'll be ever so happy. Look there; see that valve? It regulates the temperature to a turn. And," she added on a note of pure inspiration, "you'll find, I'm sure, that the walls of the kitchen won't get nearly as dirty with soot and smoke now."

David could have kissed Lily then and there. If there was one way to reconcile Mrs. Fleming to a modern contraption, it was through the lure of clean kitchen walls. His earliest memories were of the kitchen maids complaining about having to scrub soot off the walls. Mrs. Fleming was a beast for cleanliness. She was also a beast when it came to Lily, however, and she glowered at her now.

Taking the biggest chance he'd taken since he decided to open the woolen mill, David said, "There you go, Mrs. Fleming. You have a built-in tutor right here, in our own Texas Lily."

For a long moment, it seemed to David as if his very future hung in the balance, strung taut between these two strong-willed females. Lily smiled sunnily at the cook; Mrs. Fleming glared with malice at Lily. David had a sudden vision of this kitchen—his future—without Lily, without the enormous gleaming stove. In his vision the kitchen was bare, and his future was, too. It seemed to stretch on forever, a blank, bleak, endlessly barren horizon.

He didn't want the brightness surrounding Lily Munro to leave him, he realized with a pang. In that moment, if he'd been forced to choose, he'd choose a future with Lily by his side and leave the past, the castle, his tenants, and Mrs. Fleming, in the dust. He wasn't sure what that spoke of his character and didn't care to investigate it too closely.

The tension in the air snapped suddenly when Mrs. Fleming abandoned her position, centuries of class-consciousness making her bow to the woman David had all but declared to be his bride. The past ceded to the future when she dropped her gaze and said sullenly, "Very well, then. I'll try."

David expelled his breath and realized everybody else in the room had been holding theirs, as well. He glanced at Lily, who looked as relieved as he felt. She didn't pause to gloat. She clasped her hands together, carefully avoiding touching the already touchy cook, and cried, "Wonderful! Then perhaps you'll show me how to prepare kedgeree. You know, I've never tasted anything like it in my life. We don't have such things in Texas."

Since David knew for a fact that Lily hated the dish, which had been introduced to the castle a century or more ago by a cook who had learned his craft in the British East India Company, he all but gaped at her.

MacBroom Sweeps Clean

His heart filled, and he knew in that moment that he loved her.

How odd, he thought, that it should be a lie about food, of all things, that tipped the scales. His feeling of oddness gave way to amusement as he watched Lily pointedly ignore Mrs. Fleming's black look, don a big starched apron, and say merrily, "All right, let's just see what we have here."

He looked toward the doorway to find most of the outside staff gathered to watch the showdown between Lily and Mrs. Fleming, and he sighed. He might have known his employees would understand the importance of this stove, even though it had eluded him entirely until now.

One wizened face drew David's attention. Angus winked at him, and suddenly David's heart felt light.

Lily wondered what possessed her even as she made her astonishing offer to Mrs. Fleming. She hated to cook, and she hated kedgeree. What was more, she didn't like the cook, and the cook didn't like her. Mrs. Fleming, more than anyone else, had been her enemy since Lily had set foot in Castle MacKechnie.

Then Lily looked at David and knew what had possessed her.

She smiled and gave him a little nod, as if to assure him that she'd do her best to smooth Mrs. Fleming's ruffled feelings. He'd bought the silly stove for Lily; she knew it, to prove that he wanted to please her. She also knew in that moment that she loved him.

Lily was proud of herself. She didn't stamp her foot or raise her voice once during the exhausting morning, but endured Mrs. Fleming's barbed hostility with her smile intact. While the cook scowled, arms still folded over her chest, Lily investigated the stove and realized at once that she hadn't been mistaken. It was very like the one she'd been forced to learn how to use back home. This was the first time she'd been glad her mother had insisted she learn to cook.

"You never know what life will bring, Lucky," her mother used to tell her.

"I'll just eat sandwiches," Lily used to answer back.

"Nonsense. All young women should know how to cook."

Eager to be outside on the back of her horse—eager to be doing anything, really, rather than be bored to death in the kitchen—Lily had endured her mother's cooking lessons, sulking all the while. Mrs. Munro had endured, too, and Lily had learned how to use the stove. Right now, Lily appreciated her mother's incredible patience more than she could say. During those interminable lessons, Lily must have behaved very much the way Mrs. Fleming was behaving now.

Mrs. Fleming was nothing like Mrs. Munro. Lily missed her mother terribly that day. She intended to write her that very evening and thank her for not giving up on her during her many episodes of childish rebellion.

She sat down to luncheon after her ordeal, with her cheeks flushed from heat and her body trembling from nervous exhaustion. She was worn to a nub, what with having spent the morning in the huge kitchens trying not to shriek at Mrs. Fleming while attempting to master the castle's new stove. She felt much as she expected raw recruits must feel after having endured their first taste of war. She'd had to race upstairs and change in time to eat the meal she'd just helped prepare and now didn't want to eat. Panting, she made it to the dining room in time and sat in a flutter of petticoats.

"I see you survived your ordeal."

She looked up to find David watching her, his smile as warm as her cheeks. This time she knew she wasn't imagining the heat in his expression.

"Yes. Barely." She made a funny face and was pleased when he chuckled.

Lifting his glass in salute, he said, "You performed a noble service today, Lily, my girl. Thank you."

She lifted her glass as well. "Thank you, David." They drank, never breaking eye contact. When they put down their glasses, it was more than Lily's cheeks that felt hot.

Although by this time Lily was sick to death of the mutton chops she'd already had entirely too much to do with, she began to cut her meat into bite-size pieces, having been struck by an unaccountable attack of nervousness.

David chewed thoughtfully for a moment before he pronounced, "Very good, Lily. You'll make some fellow a fine wife someday."

Lily dropped her fork. Immediately she was embarrassed and snatched it up again. Her heart thumping painfully, she made her voice airy when she said, "I'm sure that's true."

"Aye. You'll be a prize to be treasured, Lily-lass. Not only will you bring your own pretty self into a marriage, but ye'll be bringing these astonishing cooking skills." He smiled and popped another bite of mutton into his mouth.

With David's second comment, feelings began rocketing about Lily's insides like shooting stars. It was an effort, but she managed not to holler at him. She wanted to demand to know what he meant. Did this mean he was no longer interested in her as his own bride? Or was he teasing her? Oh, how she wished these dreadful Scots were as easy to read as her native Texans. She considered this dryness of wit they so prized a true flaw in them.

She wanted to say something witty in her turn, but couldn't find her wits. She said instead, "You think I'm pretty?" and could have smacked herself. *Stupid Lily!*

In spite of her embarrassment, however, she prayed he'd answer in the affirmative.

He'd been inspecting his luncheon plate as if he intended to memorize its contents. Now he lifted his head and cocked it to one side, transferring his inspection from his plate to Lily's countenance. After a moment he said, "Oh, aye. Ye'll do, Lily-lass. Ye'll do."

"I'll do?" Irritation of nerves propelled her words and they came out too loudly. She felt silly.

He cocked his head to the other side, as though he were reconsidering his prior assessment. Lily wanted to throw her napkin at him. Then he nodded. "Aye."

Lily sniffed. "Thank you so much."

"You're welcome." David tipped his glass toward her and then sipped from it.

Lily wished he'd choke on his wine. Annoyed, she paid attention to her own luncheon. It didn't taste nearly as good now that she knew what went into producing it.

Her nerves continued to jump as she doggedly took another bite. She waited for David to continue his monologue on her looks, cooking skills, and suitability as a mate, but he didn't seem inclined to do so. The longer the silence lasted, the more edgy she became. After several moments that were among the most tense she'd ever endured—although David seemed perfectly at ease, damn him—Lily deliberately set her silverware down.

"All right, David, what do you mean?"

He looked up and blinked at her. "What do you mean, what do I mean, Lily?"

"Just what do you mean that I'll make somebody a good wife someday?"

"Why, exactly that, lass. I think you'll make somebody a fine wife. I had no idea you could cook and ride a horse and handle temperamental family retainers, and all the while look so pretty. I apologize for misjudging you."

MacBroom Sweeps Clean

She waved his apology aside, uninterested. She didn't even pause to consider how bitterly she'd longed for an apology of this nature from him as little as a day or two ago. "You know what I mean, David Mac-Kechnie, so quit beating about the bush."

"Beating about the bush? Me?" He donned a blank look which, if Lily didn't know better, she'd have taken as one of perfect innocence. She did know better, though. He was teasing her again, the wretch.

"Yes, you! Answer me right this minute, David MacKechnie: For whom will I make a fine wife?"

His slow, hot smile robbed her of breath and made her feel light-headed.

"I reckon that'll be up to you, Lily-lass," he said softly.

Lily gripped the edge of the table, afraid if she didn't she'd slide from her chair and onto the floor. "What—what do you mean it's up to me?"

David's smile died. "I mean just that, Lily." He drew in a deep breath. It was no deeper than Lily's, but David used his to say, "I'm sorry your introduction to Scotland and my home wasn't happier, Lily. I didn't realize how many things would be different for ye, and I didn't take the proper care of you. I love you. I hope you'll reconsider your decision to leave me."

"You—you love me?" Lily's voice had taken to squeaking.

David nodded and stared at her apprehensively. Then he licked his lips. "I-I don't expect ye to return my regard, Lily, but I'll do my best to be a good husband for ye, should you choose to honor me wi' your hand."

Relief and happiness flooded Lily so suddenly, her eyes filled with tears. David sat up straight, appalled. "Here, now, there's no need to cry, Lily-lass. If ye can't find it in your heart to forgive me, ye needn't cry about it!"

In spite of her tears, Lily laughed. She used her napkin to scrub at her tears. "Oh, David! How silly we are."

He swallowed. "We are?"

"Yes. Oh, yes, we are."

Obviously unsure what he was supposed to do or say now, David sat as still as a stone for several seconds. Then, after one or two false starts, he said, "So I'm still not sure, Lily. Is that a yes or a no? Will ye marry me, lass?"

All at once Lily jumped up from her seat at the table. Startled, David leaped to his feet, too. It was fortunate he did so, because he was just in time to catch her when she hurtled into his arms.

"Yes! Oh, yes, David! Oh, I love you so much!"

Through the dining room window, David caught the hint of a glance of Angus, who had apparently been watching the drama David and Lily enacted. Right before he buried his head in Lily's bouncy curls, David saw the old man tip his hat at him.

Chapter Nine

Lily sighed deeply and snuggled more closely to David's side. She'd drawn the curtains back from the window before they went to bed because she liked to look out into the vast twilight of her new home. She still wasn't used to nights that didn't get completely black, although David assured her the Highlands would make up for the summer's lack of nighttime darkness come winter. Lily could hardly wait to see the Northern Lights he'd told her about.

David's big bed was feather-soft and as warm as toast, and his arms felt like heaven around her. Her mother slept just down the hall, in a room next to Aunt Minnie's, and her father and David's uncle Andrew were undoubtedly still arguing over sheep in the sitting room below. They'd taken to each other as soon as the Munros landed in Scotland, and might have been long-lost brothers, to judge by the way they were always together. Heaven alone knew where her brothers and sisters were. Probably in the village, entertaining the locals with tall Texas tales.

Lily could only be sorry her parents would remain in the castle for just one more month. At least she no longer harbored fears about her future. She knew she'd be happy here; in fact, she guessed she'd be happy anywhere, as long as David was with her.

Her mother and Mrs. Fleming had spent a fruitful morning swapping recipes. Lily'd had a hard time believing her ears when she'd heard Mrs. Fleming asking Mrs. Munro how to make Texas chili. She'd also scarcely believed her ears when she'd heard her mother ask Mrs. Fleming how to make kedgeree. She shuddered now, in fact, and spared a moment from her overwhelming happiness to feel sorry for the cowboys back at the ranch. Now they'd not merely have to endure sheep, but kedgeree as well. Poor fellows.

David sighed, too, and Lily kissed his cheek. Since their wedding two weeks ago, they'd been spending a good deal of their time in bed, where David had been teaching her the marvels of the marriage act. Tonight's lesson had been particularly inspiring.

David had already promised Lily that he'd invite her family to visit when the wee bairns began to arrive. He assured her he'd do his best to make sure she wouldn't have to wait long to see them again. Lily was pleased to hear him say so.

"Ye're a wonder, Lily-lass. A pure wonder. Your father must be right about Texas ladies."

"And just what exactly did he say about Texas ladies?"

"Why, that the alarmin' heat in Texas makes ye wild, o' course."

Lily giggled and smacked him lightly on the chest. He grabbed her hand, drew it to his lips, and kissed it.

"I love ye, Lily."

"And I love you, David."

MacBroom Sweeps Clean

"Ye're a good, wee lass, in spite of your wild Texas ways."

"And you're a fine, brawny lad, in spite of your dour Scots ways."

"Aye, we make a pair, all right."

"A good pair."

David demonstrated how much he agreed with her until Lily was breathless and sated, and he was, too.

Afterward, he plumped the pillows at his back and sat up, drawing Lily into his arms again. They sat wrapped in each other and the deep silence of the night for several minutes. Then David stirred.

"I haven't seen Angus since before the weddin', Lily."

"I haven't, either. I was sorry he didn't come to the church to see the ceremony. After all, it was he who brought us together."

"Aye." David was quiet for another several seconds. Then he said musingly, "I wonder . . ."

"You wonder what?"

He gave a small shrug. "I wonder about Angus, is all."

"What do you wonder about him? You wonder what happened to him?"

"Aye, that. And another thing, too."

"What other thing?"

"Well, ye know how sma' he was?"

"Yes. He was short, all right."

"And how old."

Lily laughed softly. "He looked about a hundred and twenty."

"Aye. Except for his eyes."

"Oh, yes, his eyes. He has the brightest blue eyes I've ever seen. They're remarkably youthful for such an elderly gentleman."

"Aye, they are. I wonder . . ."

Lily kissed him once more. "You're back to wondering again, but you won't tell me what it is you're wondering about."

"Ye'll think I'm daft if I tell ye, Lily-lass."

"I already think you're daft, David, so it won't make any difference."

He chuckled, a deep sound that sent a thrill through Lily. She could hardly believe her luck in uncovering the worth of David MacKechnie. If it hadn't been for Angus, she never would have, either. It was Angus who'd made her look beneath David's stuffy surface to discover the wonderful, kind, brave man underneath. She didn't think she could be happier if she tried.

"Have ye ever heard o' the wee fellas, Lily-lass?"

"Wee fellows? You mean like leprechauns?"

David pulled away from her and pretended to take offense. "Leprechauns? Lily-lass, ye should be ashamed o' yourself, comparin' our wee fellas with those devilish Irish leprechauns."

She giggled again. "You mean Scotland has wee fellas, too?"

"Not *too*, Lily," David said severely. "The Broonies aren't pesky devils like those nasty little Irish creatures, who trick and fool folks and make them ridiculous and steal their gold and goods. Our wee fellas always come in the form of an old beggar man wi' bright blue eyes and a wee white beard. They don't play mean tricks, like the leprechauns do, but come to visit folks in order to teach them lessons about life."

Lily contemplated this for a moment. "Well," she said at last, "Angus fits that description to a T, except for the beard."

"Aye. He had no beard."

They subsided into silence again, hugging each other and relishing the life they'd chosen to live together. After several minutes David sighed again. "Still," he said, "I can't help but wonder."

Lily sighed, too, in contentment, staring out at the almost-starry night. And she wondered, too.

The Fairy Bride
Tess Mallory

This book is for the real *Erin, Heather, Ydroj (Jordy), and Ekalb (Blake), and for my father, whose wonderful stories about Puff and Mousey and Phoebe the fairy started me on this journey in the first place. This one's for you, Pop...and for J. Boliver Thud.*

Much thanks also to Helen Eisaman for sharing her experience at the Blarney Stone, as well as her books, reference materials, and as always, her kindness.

Chapter One

"You must travel to the Outerworld and find your mortal bride."

King Connal of the house of Tain considered the wizard's words, then rose from the huge, ornate throne and walked to the edge of the crystal platform on which it sat. Slowly the platform lowered itself to the floor of the great hall below. Connal's dark auburn hair brushed against the blue-green tunic covering his broad shoulders as he paced across the stone floor, his face a smooth mask of contemplation. The walls behind him were golden, studded with jewels. The windows were hung with gossamer curtains spun from spider's webs.

Pausing in front of a high, arched window open to the cool breeze, his gaze fell on the pale lavender mist of early morning in the valley below. The castle sat perched upon one of the highest hills in Tir Na nOg. Built eons ago, the white stones were kept smooth and clean and strong by the magic within them.

Connal's gaze shifted across the valley to another, distant hill, where a castle of equal proportions looked back at his own. The house of Dar. Prince Tynan lived there in seclusion, practicing his magic and harboring his jealousy toward Connal. The king sighed. Why the good Dagda had appointed *two* ruling houses to guide Tir Na nOg he would never understand. The house of Tain had ruled the land for countless thousands of years. The rule of Tir Na nOg could only be remanded to the house of Dar if the reigning king had no heir. As a result, the nobles of the house of Dar had no part, no function in the ruling of Tir Na nOg. Could he count on Prince Tynan to support them now, in their time of need? He wished he felt more certain.

"You do not respond, Connal," the voice behind him said. "Do you refuse the quest?"

Iridescent gold wings, previously lying dormant upon the king's back, now slowly unfurled, stretching to their full, magnificent length, shimmering in the predawn light, reaching well above his head.

"I have resolved myself to do it," Connal said softly, still staring out the window.

The wizard tapped one finger thoughtfully against his long, aquiline nose before speaking. "We of the Sidh tend to think that because we are immortal, we are also infallible."

His silver, waist-length hair drifted against the long blue robes designating his high office as he crossed to the king's side. Wrinkles painted a map across his long, thin face, and as Connal looked down at his friend he realized Moragh was getting old, even for a fairy. He was always distracted and scatterbrained, but his mind seemed to wander even more as of late.

"We are not infallible," Moragh went on. "Our blood weakens just as any other race's must from millennia to millennia. That is why every ten thousand years the king or queen's mate must be chosen from the mortal world.

The Fairy Bride

In this way, our bloodline is strengthened, as is the magic that guards our world."

"Mortals have no magic, and they are selfish, greedy creatures by all accounts," Connal said, his green eyes wary, his dark brows furrowed. "How, then, can marrying one add to our strength?"

"Some mortals are indeed selfish, greedy, and much worse," Moragh agreed. "However, the woman you seek is none of these. Many mortals possess courage, cunning, and a stubborn perseverance that will not be shaken by circumstance. Our people, on the other hand, rise above humans in the areas of pureness of heart, honor, and logic, but tend toward the fragility of melancholy when presented with overwhelming odds."

Connal bristled. "I am not melancholic," he objected. "Nor have I ever been so."

"Ah, but that is because of the blood of the mortals which imbues your magic, the magic of us all— through your family's blood. Without the periodic infusion of the more noble characteristics of humans, we would eventually fall prey to our own weaknesses." Moragh continued, "Our borders grow weaker every day, and now that we are on the verge of war with Lodan, our magic must be strengthened."

"Goblins! Bah!" Connal whirled from the window and strode across the room and back. "I'd like to destroy every one of them. All right. I understand the why of it. Now tell me the how. How will marrying a mortal bring the power back to us?"

The wizard's eyes brightened as he spread his hands apart eloquently. "First of all, the joining of a mortal and fairy in love will imbue Tir Na nOg with a surge of magic which will strengthen its borders. The child of such a union, the heir to the throne, will possess a greater magic than you or anyone else in Tir Na nOg. The magic of the ruling house is what determines the amount of power that surrounds our land and protects it. This is why such a union is so important." His face darkened. "Especially now."

"A child." Connal's gaze softened, his lips curving upward gently. A moment later the smile faltered. "But what kind of life can a child have if raised in a home where there is no love?"

Moragh chuckled and clapped one hand on Connal's shoulder. "Have you not yet learned that magic without love is of the weakest variety?"

"What do you mean?"

"It is the magic of love that will lead you to the woman who is to be your bride."

Connal continued to stare out the window, Moragh's last words falling heavily on his tortured mind. The sky, usually a deep purple, had of late faded to a paler shade of lavender. All the colors in the kingdom had paled in recent days, a symptom, Moragh had told him, of the fading power of Tir Na nOg's magic. He turned away from the window, his jaw set.

"You are a romantic fool," he said. "Just tell me what must be done."

"You must cross through the portal in the fairy ring, to the Outerworld. In the passing you will lose your wings and become the size of a mortal man. Once in the mortal's world, you will begin your search for her."

Connal crossed to his side, his hands clasped behind him. "It seems impossible. She could be anywhere. How will I ever find her?"

"I told you, you will be magically drawn to one another by your love."

The king raised one dark brow in cynical disdain. "How will I know for certain when I have found her?"

"You will know. However, if you need concrete evidence, something you can see with your own stubborn eyes, then know that when you touch her, a lavender aura will appear around the two of you, affirming your choice."

"What if she won't come back with me?"

The Fairy Bride

The wizard shrugged, his gray eyes like silver. "She already loves you—you must simply find her and make her realize this. However, she must come with you willingly or the magic of your union will be tainted."

"What about my own magic? Will I be able to use it in the Outerworld?"

The wizard hesitated. "Your magic will go with you but it is not as strong in the world of the humans because of their unbelief in such things. It is weak and limited. You must use it only when it is absolutely necessary, for once you've exhausted that supply of power, there will be no more to be had until you return to Tir Na nOg."

"What if I am followed?"

Moragh shot him a look. "I have sealed the palace from invasion. Lodan will not know you have gone."

Connal shook his head, then weighed his words carefully before he spoke. "I hesitate to remind you, but your own magic has grown weak as well, my friend. Lodan may follow me. And what of Prince Tynan? If he hears I am gone, he may cause trouble. I fear he will use this war as an excuse to seize the throne."

Moragh twisted away from him in obvious frustration, his long robes flapping about his feet as he paced.

"I will take care of Tynan, but you are right about the goblin king. My magic is weak, and if Lodan follows you to the Outerworld, he may try to kill you and your bride. He retains the full extent of his power there, for humans believe in evil."

"I will be careful," Connal promised.

The hesitation in the wizard's eyes was still apparent. "Connal, do not underestimate the power of your enemy. If I am able to join you, I will. But you can't let down your guard."

Connal gave the wizard's shoulder a reassuring squeeze. "I promise you, I will not. Where is Eky?"

The king crossed the great hall to a large window and opened it, sticking his head halfway out.

"You aren't thinking of taking him, are you?" Moragh asked, his voice a mixture of amusement and tolerant disdain.

"And why not? He can use his cloak while we're in the Outerworld. Will his magic be altered as well?"

The wizard considered, tapping one finger thoughtfully against his chin. "I confess, I do not know." He frowned, then waved his fingers in the air. "My mind, my magic, are not what they once were." He sighed. "I fear I am growing old, Connal. You are wise to question my words. You should think of finding another high wizard upon your return."

Connal looked back at him. "My friend, you have protected Tir Na nOg and my family for countless years. Don't you realize that your magic and your thinking suffers more than the rest of us, because your very being is tied to our land? If it is fading, are you not fading also?" His gaze softened. "You are high wizard of Tir Na nOg, and so it shall ever be, until you yourself decide to step down."

"Thank you, Connal." Moragh's knobby Adam's apple bobbed up and down, the tendons in his neck flexing visibly as he fought for composure. He cleared his throat loudly. "Oh, very well, take your little pet," he said in a loud, scathing voice. "I know the creature's presence calms your nerves."

Connal raised one dark brow in Moragh's direction, then laughed and turned back to the window. He whistled once, twice, three times, and suddenly there was the sound of wings beating against the wind outside the casement. Connal held out his arm, and when he drew it back within the castle walls, a small, winged dragon, pale green, clung to his forearm like a falcon. Its wings were a darker shade of green and it blinked in the daylight, its light purple eyes heavy with sleep.

"Hello, Ekalb," Connal said, stroking the dragon's back. The ribbed scales arched beneath his hands as the creature began making a low, rumbling sort of

The Fairy Bride

noise in its throat. Pale wisps of smoke drifted from the two wide nostrils at the end of the graceful nose. "Are you ready for a new adventure?"

"One thing more," Moragh said, stepping forward. "We of the Sidh cannot remain in the Outerworld for long without suffering dire consequences. You must return to us after two days or you may not be able to return at all."

"Do not fear, Moragh," Connal said, stroking Eky's wings. "I will find my bride, and the magic of Tir Na nOg will be restored. I swear it."

The wizard nodded, satisifed. "We go now to the fairy ring."

Moragh lifted both arms skyward, and Connal felt the familiar surge of the wizard's power flood around them. His vision blurred as the castle disappeared, shifting into another picture, another place. The wizard lowered his arms and they stood at the top of a gently sloping hill, a ring of beautiful heather encircling the edge of the mound. A tree grew from the very center of the circle. The wizard glanced at the sky, at the quickly lowering sun of Tir Na nOg, then back at Connal.

"Sleep here beneath the tree and let the magic take you through the portal. When you awaken, you will be in the Outerworld."

"Worry not, Moragh. All will be well. I shall return."

The wizard held out both arms and Connal clasped them with his own. The two smiled, then Moragh turned and, lifting his arms, disappeared.

Connal sank down beneath the tree and stared at the disappearing sun as he reached up to scratch Eky behind one ear. The little dragon began to rumble.

"So it begins," Connal murmured. "The quest for my bride." He leaned back against the tree. "Sweet smoky dreams, little one."

Connal watched the sun sink slowly behind the distant purple hills of Tir Na nOg. What would she be like? he wondered. Beautiful? Passable? Tall, short, fat, slim? Blue eyed or green? And most important, would she truly love him enough to give up her life in her world and join him in his?

There were too many unanswered questions, and Connal wished he had asked Moragh more. It was too late now. He could feel the magic of the ring beginning to lull him, to permeate his being. He allowed it, and felt his consciousness slip away. The king of the Sidh slept, confident that the morning would bring an answer to the woes of Tir Na nOg.

In the shadows below the hill, an ugly creature not of the fairy kingdom, a creature whose skin boasted a faint sheen of scales, waited and watched the king slumbering inside the fairy ring. At sunrise, when the king's form shimmered and glimmered and quietly disappeared, the goblin-spy slithered soundlessly away to report that King Connal had indeed gone to the Outerworld in search of a mortal bride.

Chapter Two

"Damn the Irish!"

Erin McKay glanced up from the map she held to see yet another herd of sheep blocking the road in front of their rented car. Her fiancé leaned on the horn, the blaring sound sending the fleecy creatures scattering and earning the visitors an uncharacteristic shake of a fist from the Irishman driving them along.

"There is such a thing as patience, Reggie," Erin said, tossing an apologetic smile at the shepherd as they passed.

She threaded her fingers nervously through her short, honey blond hair, her hand traveling over the recently shorn locks. Reggie had asked that she cut her hair after he learned that he had been appointed to a modest teaching position at Oxford. He intended to climb the intellectual ladder of success, and his wife must help him set the tone, the mood, and the level of approval he wished to attain. Waist-length hair, it seemed, was too trendy for the wife of a professor. She had cut it just before they left on their pre-wedding trip to Ireland. He hadn't wanted to go to Ireland at all, and so she had made a deal with him: her hair in exchange for the trip. She was slowly learning how to handle Reggie.

Handle Reggie? Erin felt the alarm ring through her as she turned toward the man she had pledged to marry. Would she spend her life *handling* her husband? She'd always thought marriage would be a partnership. Her gaze raked over him as he shifted the sports car into a lower gear, his eyes fixed firmly on the road ahead.

Reginald Francis Barrister III was thirty-eight and as handsome as a model with his dark hair and his brilliant sky blue eyes. His jaw was well chiseled, his chin stubborn. She had met Reggie outside of London, when her rented car broke down and he stopped to help her. A whirlwind courtship had followed, and she'd fallen for the soon-to-be Oxford professor.

She hadn't even planned to go to England. For years she and her parents had planned to visit Ireland, had read volumes of travel guides and books on the country. The trip was to be a way for them all to celebrate the completion of her doctorate degree. But one week after her graduation and two weeks before the trip was to begin, her parents had been killed in a terrible car accident. Unable to deal with her grief at home, Erin had decided to take the trip anyway, at the last minute changing her plans and stopping over to sightsee in London before going on to Ireland.

She glanced down at her engagement ring. A huge garnet surrounded by diamonds, it had belonged to Reggie's grandmother. Erin thought it was the ugliest ring she'd ever seen.

He was older than she—eleven years older, to be exact—and when they'd first met, his mature, calm, self-possessed air had felt like a balm on her shattered senses. Reggie's proposal of marriage had rescued her from ever having to return to her parents' empty home, and had offered a security Erin couldn't turn down, even if now, after being in his exclusive company for three weeks, she had begun to have doubts about their compatibility.

"Why do you detest the Irish so much?" she asked aloud, carefully folding the map, her eyes on the cool white paper between her fingers.

"Why are you so enamored of them is the question." Reggie's gaze darted toward her as his dark brows arched upward in a familiar gesture of disdain. "It's a backward country filled with backward people and yet you are fascinated with them."

Erin flushed. "There are many ways of being backward," she muttered under her breath.

"What's that, dear? You're mumbling again. You really must break that habit; it's most disconcerting."

"I wasn't mumbling; I was talking to myself."

"Yes, well, you know what they say about people who do that. Now, what was your observation of my comment?"

"Nothing. I didn't say anything."

She folded her arms across her chest and gazed out at the beautiful green countryside, trying to ignore her growing frustration. The glory of Ireland spread before her. Erin took a deep breath and let the fresh scent of the earth, the peat, the heather, and the emerald grass permeate her senses. Sea air mixed in with the perfume, for they were only a few miles from the ocean. Stone walls broke the color of the sweeping emerald fields, along with picturesque thatched cottages and herds of grazing sheep.

Erin smoothed her hands down her blue-jeaned legs. They had argued about that, too. Professors' wives didn't wear jeans; they wore neat little linen or tweed suits with silk blouses even when on holiday. She grudgingly admitted that he looked better than she in his dark gray slacks and navy blue blazer. Atop her jeans she wore a beige fisherman's sweater she'd purchased in Dublin when they'd first arrived there. Casual versus proper. Erin felt the panic well up inside her again. They were from two different worlds.

"This trip is important to me," she said at last, "and I feel like you don't understand that."

"Darling, I do understand, but you need to realize that the Irish are hotheaded drunkards for the most part."

"Don't forget, my family's roots are Irish," she said, her voice cool. "Your bigotry frankly concerns me, Reggie."

"Very well." Reggie snapped the words out, a defensive mask settling over his features. "I will endeavor to keep my thoughts concerning the Irish to myself. Let's just get back to that blasted bed-and-breakfast you've booked us into."

They traveled in silence for a moment, but at his mention of the place they were staying, Erin couldn't help but voice something that had been on her mind all night.

"Are you attracted to me, Reggie?"

He looked at her, startled, then laughed uncomfortably. "Well, of course I am. Whatever do you mean?"

"I guess I was just surprised when you wanted to have separate rooms at the bed-and-breakfast." She felt the warm flush of embarrassment crawl up her neck as Reggie's eyebrow arched upward.

"Oh. I see. You thought we should cohabitate like the common rabble do in America," Reggie said. "I'm sorry to disappoint you, Erin, but I am an old-fashioned man with old-fashioned ideals. Can you accept that?"

Erin closed her eyes against the fresh air plowing into her face and sighed. "Of course, Reggie. It's a very admirable attitude."

You are a stuffy old man! she thought silently as the little car flew down the road toward Dalkey. Immedi-

The Fairy Bride

ately her own honest nature scolded her. She had always been just as old-fashioned, and was probably the only twenty-seven-year-old virgin left in the world. But she'd never been engaged before. She'd just assumed— she pushed the thought away. She should admire Reggie for his moral fortitude even if his clinical approach to love seemed somewhat cold and emotionless.

They wheeled into the small town of Dalkey, and Reggie pulled up in front of the two-story house. Erin loved it as fervently as Reggie hated it. She loved the sprigged rose wallpaper and old lace curtains at the wide windows in her room, the worn, pink-edged rug gracing the white board floor, as well as the creamy lace coverlet adorning the old white four-poster bed. Erin had entered the room with a sigh and a feeling of having come home at last.

Reggie had been given a similar room in blue, but had spoiled everything by complaining incessantly about the inconvenience of having to go down the hall for the bathroom, and the lack of having a queen-size bed. She had almost told him then and there to forget everything—the trip, the marriage—everything. But she hadn't. Something had held her tongue.

"I'll park the car," Reggie said, bringing the car to a stop. She nodded and climbed out, hurrying into the house and rushing upstairs to find the comfort that awaited her in her room. Once inside she sank down on the bed and felt the truth settle around her heart. She didn't really love Reggie, not like she should. She should end their relationship, give back his engagement ring, and tell him it had all been a mistake. Then she would fly back home and pick up the pieces of her life.

Alone, she reminded herself. *Don't forget you'll be alone.* The pressure of her doctorate studies had meant shutting out most of her old friends. She'd only had time for her parents, and now they were gone.

A soft tap at the door wrenched her anguished

thoughts back to the present as Reggie poked his head inside the room.

"May I come in? I have a surprise for you," he said.

"Of course, what is it?"

He pulled a chair up beside the bed and sat down, then held out two thin pieces of cardboard.

"Tickets? To what?" As she took them from his hand and read the writing inscribed on the green cardboard, her face fell, her heart along with it.

"A tour of Ireland by bus," he said proudly. "When I was parking the car I saw a sign across the way at the travel office. I wanted to prove to you that I am aware of the importance you place on this trip."

His lips stretched into a smile and Erin felt her heartbeat quicken. He was so handsome. He could be so sweet. Their life together would be orderly, secure, calm, peaceful. She needed peace, craved an end to the pain that still pierced her heart. Was she really willing to throw this man away just because he had high standards and an unreasonable hatred of the Irish?

"Won't it be grand? This way we can see everything worth seeing in this wretched country in just a few days and then be on our way home again." He picked up her hand and kissed it. "I love you, Erin," he said simply.

As he leaned toward her Erin let the tickets fall to her lap, fighting tears of disappointment as he covered her lips with a chaste kiss. A set-up tour of the country was the last thing she wanted. She and her parents had planned for years how they would see Ireland—and it wasn't by tour bus! He moved away from her and she opened her mouth to tell him, but nothing came out. There was a new light of uncertainty in his eyes she had never seen before. He looked almost vulnerable.

"I say, won't it be grand, Erin, love?"

He'd never called her *love* before. *Darling*, yes, *dear*, but never *love*.

The Fairy Bride

Alone.

The voice echoed into her mind, and, biting her lower lip, Erin forced herself to smile.

"Yes, Reggie," she said softly, "it will be grand."

Chapter Three

Connal stood at the edge of the city and blinked. He had journeyed to the Outerworld before, but it had been thousands of years ago. Much had changed. Upon awakening in the fairy ring on this side of the Outerworld he had made Eky cloak himself and then, risking a little magic, had flown across Ireland, landing at a town called Waterford. He didn't know how he knew his bride-to-be was there, but he did. It was part of the magic Moragh had described, he supposed.

Connal headed into the town, Eky riding invisibly on his shoulder, when suddenly he realized that the road beneath his feet was incredibly hard and even, unmarred by rocks. As he leaned down to touch it, something big roared by him, almost knocking him down. When he regained his equilibrium he looked up and saw that some kind of monster had stopped only inches away from him. It was huge, boxlike, with gray and white stripes, two large eyes that staring at him glassily, and wheels instead of feet. Astonished, Connal saw that it

The Fairy Bride

was full of people. *Swallowed? Imprisoned?* All at once the side of the monster burst open and Connal jumped back, feeling Eky's claws digging deeper into his shoulder as he did.

The people came clamoring out of the beast, laughing and talking. Connal relaxed. Apparently they were in no danger from the monster in whose belly they had ridden. They scattered in different directions, a few giving him curious glances.

"What do you think of that, Eky?" he said softly. "Is it alive, do you think? What? No, I don't think you should challenge it. Moragh might have mentioned these creatures. I'm afraid he *is* getting a little scattered in his thinking. Now, where should we look first, do you suppose?"

All at once Connal saw that he was fast becoming the center of attention as more people disembarked from the monster and paused to stare at him. Why? He closed his eyes with a groan as comprehension came. His clothing. His blue-green tunic and tight green leggings, the soft forest green boots, as well as the golden girdle at his waist, were apparently completely out of place in this world. Another little detail Moragh had forgotten to mention.

"Oh, look," a feminine voice cried out, "a medieval costume—they must be doing a reenactment somewhere around here. Let's talk to him and find out where."

It was so easy, after all. He glanced up from contemplating his clothing and looked into the blue, blue eyes of the woman destined to be his bride. How did he know? That, too, was simple. He looked into her eyes and saw their hearts intertwined. He saw her in his arms, saw her laughing at his side, saw her walking beside him through life, saw her bearing his children. He didn't know her name but he knew how her lips tasted, the softness of her skin, the warmth of her body beneath his. His heart and soul cried out to hers, and in that moment frozen in time, as their gazes locked, her heart and soul answered him.

The woman hesitated, then approached him, her brilliant smile sending a warm rush throughout his body. So this was love. He'd never thought it possible to fall in love in a matter of seconds. But no, he had not fallen in love with her so quickly—he had always loved her. Now he understood Moragh's words: *You will be magically drawn to one another by your love.* He gazed at her, drinking his fill as she stared up at him, her eyes opened wide, as if in stunned surprise.

Short hair, cut like a pixie's, the color of winter wheat in Tir Na nOg, danced over her ears and brushed the nape of her neck. Her creamy, heart-shaped face was defined by high, sculptured cheekbones whose sweeping blush led his wandering eyes immediately back to hers. Almond-shaped, as blue as the mortal sky, fringed with dark lashes, they gazed back at him, mirroring the sense of amazement he himself felt. He wanted more than anything to step forward and take her into his arms, to press his lips against her soft, full, pink ones that were parted as if she wanted to speak, but could not. He took a step forward. Eky's claws brought him back to reality just in time.

"Hello," she said, her beautiful smile widening.

A voice like an angel, like a sonnet, Connal thought as he continued to stare down at her. She came only to his shoulder. Just the right size. They would fit together perfectly, in every way. She wore leggings of some kind, blue and thick, as well as a cream-colored tunic that resembled woolers, a covering the elven spiders often spun for him from wool.

"Are you all right?" she asked, her smile faltering as a dark-haired man stepped up beside her, his hard gaze sweeping over Connal.

Connal shook himself out of his trance. "I beg your pardon," he said with a small bow. "May I be of service to you, milady?"

290

The Fairy Bride

The woman laughed and the sound swept over him like an invigorating breeze from the ocean. "Oh, you're good at this. Tell me, are you performing anywhere near here?"

"Really, Erin, please come along," the man beside her said in an oddly flat tone of voice. "I am exhausted, and I would think you would be too after riding on this accursed bus all day. Thank God there's only two more days left. Pardon us, old boy, but our supper at the hotel must be getting cold. Come on, Erin." He steered the woman away from Connal and toward a tall building.

"All right, Reggie," the woman said, and Connal noticed faint lines of strain around her lovely mouth. Suddenly she pulled away from her erstwhile companion and turned back to him. "Would you like to have supper with us?" she blurted. Her eyes widened as if she hadn't meant to voice the invitation aloud. Her gaze flickered back to the man beside her almost fearfully.

His dark brows met fiercely over harsh blue eyes. "Erin, really, I'm sure this man, whoever he is—"

"Connal O'Tain," Connal said, cutting off his protest. "I'd love to have supper with you. I—" He stopped and cocked his head toward his shoulder. "What's that? Oh, yes, I should change my clothing first. Shall I meet you inside?"

His gaze locked for a long moment with the woman's as the dark-headed man glowered at her side. At last she blinked and laughed self-consciously.

"Of course," she said, "we need to change, too. We'll meet you in the hotel restaurant in a few minutes." They turned and walked toward the tall building, and Connal was left standing beside the gray-and-white monster, his heart soaring.

"That's her, Eky," he whispered. "Even her name bespeaks the ancients. Erin. The name of this isle that houses the portal to Tir Na nOg. But I must be sure. I

291

must find some way to speak with her, to touch her. I dare not risk using my magic again for something that is not essential. Try your magic and see if you can give me some proper clothes."

Eky rumbled softly and Connal felt a familiar rush as the dragon's magic swept over him. Glancing down at himself, he saw he now wore a pair of strange blue trousers similar to those Erin wore, as well as a wooler the color of the Irish hills.

"Thank you, my friend." He turned to go to the hotel, but Eky dug his claws into his shoulder. "What is it now?"

A leather drawstring bag materialized and dropped into the king's hand. Inside he found strange silver coins and pieces of green paper. He examined them carefully, then grinned up at his friend.

"I see. It's the currency of the Outerworld. Excellent."

He headed for the large building across the hard roadway, then stopped abruptly. What if she was already married to that pompous twit? The thought sent a surge of apprehension through his veins. If she were already married, could he in all good conscience take her from her husband's side? What if there were children? Connal closed his eyes. This was growing more complicated by the minute. A soft breath of warm air brushed against his ear.

"You're right, Eky. One thing at a time. No sense in creating problems where there may not be any."

He squared his shoulders and headed up the steps to the hotel.

Reggie wouldn't speak to her. She didn't know herself why she had done it. The man was probably some kind of kook; after all, look at his costume and the fact that he talked to himself. Erin suddenly just wanted to go home.

"Reggie, I'm sorry. It was just an impetuous gesture. We'll have supper with the man, have an interesting conversation, and that will be the end of it. There's no need to get so angry."

"I am not angry," he said, biting off each word. He picked up the menu and opened it, effectively blocking her view of his face.

She looked up just then and saw their dinner guest entering the restaurant. Her breath caught in her throat as their eyes met. She had the most incredible feeling she knew this man. Not that she had met him before but that she *knew* him, as an intimate acquaintance. That was ridiculous, of course, but the feeling persisted, and was now intensifying as he smiled and waved, crossing the rich carpet of the hotel restaurant to their table.

"May I introduce myself again?" he asked, stopping directly beside Erin's chair and offering his hand. "I am Connal O'Tain." Reggie stood and intercepted the handshake.

"Of course. Reginald Barrister, London," he said flatly.

Connal shook the man's hand, his gaze lingering on Erin's face. She looked up at him, her heart suddenly beating a staccato rhythm as his green eyes quickened with warmth and his full lips curved up into a smile. She gave a little start under his scrutiny, her cheeks flushing with color, yet she couldn't seem to look away.

"I'm Erin McKay," she said.

"Delighted to meet you." The man dropped Reggie's hand and extended his toward her. Mesmerized, Erin placed her small hand in his larger grasp. Instantly she felt a shock—like a mild electrical current—pass between them, and saw a lavender aura flash around the edges of their hands. An instant later it was gone. The man's smile broadened.

Erin stared up at him, feeling stunned, her hand still in his. "Did you see that?" she asked, her voice scarcely more than a whisper.

"See what?" Reggie demanded, sinking back down

in his chair. "For God's sake, Erin, do you intend to hold Mr. O'Tain's hand all night? Sit down, O'Tain, since you seem fated to join us."

Erin blushed in earnest this time, jerking her hand out of Connal's grip and staring shamefacedly at her knees. What was wrong with her? Who was this man and why was he having this effect on her? Had she really seen a flash of lavender color when they touched? Had she really felt the current of power? As if some invisible force compelled her, she lifted her head and looked up at him again.

It was crazy. As he gazed down at her it seemed that she could hear the distant lilt of Celtic music, could see the two of them walking hand in hand across fields of lavender and blue. His eyes were warm and filled with understanding—and something more. His eyes were filled with promises, promises of forever.

Chapter Four

"Are you Irish?" Barrister asked, shaking out the napkin in his lap. "Or Scottish? Can't quite place your accent."

"Well, actually I live in Ireland *and* Scotland," Connal said, taking a seat beside Erin. "In a manner of speaking."

Reggie frowned at his enigmatic statement, but Erin smiled at him, her creamy features flushed with color. "Oh, I love Scotland. I mean, I had planned to visit there also, but I don't think we'll have time." Connal saw the shadow of disappointment in her eyes.

"You must," he said decisively. " 'Tis a beautiful place, wilder than most of Ireland, more mysterious. Not as much sun there though, and a wee bit more rain."

While he'd never actually been to Scotland, Loch Ness was one of the several connecting portals between their two worlds. Nessie, a Celtic waterhorse who had wandered into the mortal world long ago and

decided to stay, visited frequently in Tir Na nOg. He'd
had several informative conversations with the old girl.
Thinking of the creature who had so beguiled mortals
over the centuries made him remember his own wee
beastie, and unconsciously Connal reached up and
scratched Eky behind the ear.

"Are you all right, Eky?" he asked softly.

Erin's eyes widened and Barrister cleared his throat
noisily. Connal dropped his hand back to the table,
aware he had committed a tactical error.

"Do you do medieval reenactments all the time?" she
asked. "Your costume was wonderful, so authentic."

"No, not all the time," he said, lifting the glass of
wine the waiter had deposited by his elbow and taking
a sip.

Her gaze swept over him, and Connal burned beneath her perusal. Damn this man who sat beside her.
Were it not for his presence, Connal would sweep her
into his arms and spirit her away to a private place
where he could confess his love for her. Claws tightened on his shoulder and he smiled grimly. Well, perhaps it was a good thing Barrister was along—for the
moment. The last thing he wanted to do was frighten
his bride-to-be.

"Yes," Barrister interjected, lacing his fingers more
securely through Erin's as she continued to stare at
Connal. "We might want to take in one of your shows
before we leave on our honeymoon."

"Honeymoon?" The word was unfamiliar, but it
linked the two of them in some intimacy. He frowned.
"When will this be?"

Erin laughed and he could hear the tension she was
trying to mask. "Next week after we return to England.
We're to be married on May the twentieth."

"Married? The two of you are going to be married?
To each other?" Connal felt his heart squeeze painfully.

"Yes, old boy, that is how it's usually done," Barrister
said with a condescending laugh. "Are you going to

order?" He handed him a large, boardlike piece of paper. "I warn you, these places tend to be quite expensive." His false smile widened. "I know how it is with you laborers, Irish or Scottish. Always trying to stretch your meager paychecks until the next one comes along. That is, unless you drink it away first."

Connal's temper rose at the intentional insult, then he felt Erin's embarrassed gaze on him. He would not shame her by acknowledging the man's rudeness.

"Thank you for worrying about me, but I am not a laborer."

Barrister's lips tightened imperceptibly. "Excellent, excellent. Er, what line of business did you say you were in, Mr. O'Tain?"

Connal hesitated. "I don't really have a line of business, Mr. Barrister," he admitted. "Shall we just say that money is not a problem in my life?"

Connal picked up the large boardlike paper and stared at it with unseeing eyes. They were to be married. She was engaged to this twit of a man.

But she doesn't love him.

The certain knowledge of this truth seared into his brain and left him with a breathless kind of joy. She did not love the man beside her because she loved him—Connal, king of the Sidh. She just didn't know it yet.

Chapter Five

After the meal was over Erin ordered coffee and tried not to stare at the man sitting across the table from her, nursing a solitary glass of whiskey. Reggie had already had three to Connal's one. She knew her inability to take her eyes from Connal O'Tain was making her fiancé increasingly angry.

It was hard not to stare at Connal. Reggie had a nice body. He worked out and took care of himself. But Connal . . . Connal had a body that transcended working out in the gym. Connal was broad shouldered, broad chested, with arm muscles stretching the boundaries of the green sweater he wore, his legs long and muscular.

He sat now with his auburn hair waving around his face, his dark brows raised quizzically as he stared around at the luxurious restaurant. It was a typical upper-class hotel restaurant, with blue velvet curtains and dark tables and booths. Erin noted Connal acted as though he'd never been in a hotel in his life.

The Fairy Bride

Well, maybe he hadn't, at least not one this expensive. In spite of his claims to be wealthy it was obvious to her he had been playing the age-old male game of one-upmanship with Reggie. She didn't blame him in the least.

But what if it wasn't a game? What if he was a little— off? After all, he did talk to himself.

So do you! a little voice in her head said. She ignored it and tried to ignore Connal as well. Her gaze fell on his hand, large and square, lying near hers on top of the pristine white tablecloth. Not the hand of a laborer, that was true, but neither was it the hand of someone who spent his time allowing others to do for him. All at once Erin wanted to touch him, to wrap her hand around his and feel its warmth. She almost gasped out loud at the thought.

What was wrong with her? She had spent a ridiculous amount of time changing her clothes upstairs before they'd come down, finally settling on a semiformal dress of sky blue silk that brought out the color of her eyes and clung to her slim form in a flattering sarong style. Reggie had complimented her, in his own way, by telling her she was looking "well." Connal, on the other hand, told her with his eyes she was the most gorgeous woman he had ever seen.

She looked up from her coffee just then and her breath caught in her throat as her gaze collided with his. She knew him. She knew the smell of him, a combination of musk and heather, knew what it would be like to stroke the wide, well-defined jaw with her fingers, then run those same fingers through his long, auburn hair. Erin knew how his lips tasted and how he kissed, knew what it felt like to possess this man, and to be possessed by him, and she had seen the same knowledge flash within his eyes, eyes the color of Ireland. Clear and green, fringed with dark lashes long enough to be a woman's, those eyes gazed back at her from under dark brows perpetually arched, as though everything he encountered in life was a new and delightful surprise to him. So unlike Reggie, whose attitude toward everything struck her more and more as that of a bored, petulant child.

She cleared her throat and tried to still the trembling of her hand as she lifted her cup to her lips.

"Do you have family here?" she asked, after taking a sip.

"Yes, O'Tain," Reggie said dryly, rolling the shot glass of whiskey between his fingers. "Just who are you? Not royalty or Lord somebody or other we need to bow to, are you?"

Connal's lips curved up mysteriously, and Erin found herself smiling at the secretive twinkle in his eyes. "Funny you should mention that."

Reggie laughed shortly. "Don't tell me you're claiming to be of the nobility. That's impossible, old boy."

"And why is that?" Connal said, the humor fading from his eyes.

"Because you said you were Irish. Now there's an oxymoron for you—Irish nobility." He tossed back the whiskey he held, and his eyes, already bleary and red rimmed, began to water.

"My father was a king," Connal said.

"Oh, a king—of lower Slobbovia, no doubt."

"Reggie, please stop being so rude," Erin said between clenched teeth.

Reggie ignored her and held up his glass. The waiter hurried over and filled it to the brim once again. "Pah! The Irish are all a bunch of bloody fairies! Don't you agree, O'Tain?"

Connal frowned and Erin bit her lower lip, ready to duck out of the way of flying fists. But the man didn't look angry; he looked confused. To her surprise he agreed with Reggie.

"Aye," he nodded. "I've known a few who are."

"A bunch of bog-trotting imbeciles who don't know their arses from their elbows."

The Fairy Bride

"Well, I wouldn't say that."

"Why don't we call it a night and go upstairs?" Erin interrupted hastily. "I really am exhausted."

"But we haven't found out what kind of nobility O'Tain is, darling mine." Reggie sneered at Connal and lifted his glass in his direction. "We must toast to his royal highness. You said your father was a king—here's to Prince Connal, long may he wave!"

Connal stood. "Come, lad, let me help you to your room before you embarrass the lady."

Reggie tilted the glass to his mouth and swallowed half of the drink. He coughed a little, then cleared his throat. "Well, that would be a switch, now, wouldn't it? Usually it's the other way around, you know."

Erin sat back, speechless and stunned. All at once Connal was at her side, his face next to hers, his voice low.

"Stay here, lass," he said gently. "I'll help your friend up to his room."

Erin stared up at him, then found herself nodding. Connal tucked one hand under the man's left arm and hauled him to his feet. Reggie looked up at him dazedly.

"I say, old man, who the hell do you think you are?"

"I'm the king of the bloody fairies, you pompous twit," Connal said softly. "Now come along like a good boy or, so help me, I'll change you into a frog. Come along, Eky."

He moved away from the table as Erin sat with her mouth open, watching him move the drunken man deftly through the tables with a grace she'd have thought impossible. What had he said? He was the king of the fairies?

He'd said the silly words with such—sincerity. Not as if he were making a joke, but rather as though he were stating a fact. As if he had said, "I'm a bricklayer in Sligo," or "I'm the head of IBM." What did he mean? Then he'd said that name again—Eky? What did it mean? Suddenly she was afraid. What if this guy was crazy? What if he took Reggie upstairs and slit his throat? Her mother had always said she was too trusting. Jumping to her feet, Erin grabbed her purse and hurried out of the restaurant. She ran across the wide foyer just in time to find Connal standing in front of the elevator, frowning at the glowing button beside the doors.

"I'd better help him myself," she said, moving to wrap her arm around Reggie's waist.

"That's all right, I have him," Connal said, refusing to relinquish his load. "He's passed out cold and is very heavy. Wait for me down here, but, er, first could you direct me to the stairs?"

"I'll help you," Erin insisted. She pressed the up button and stood nervously beside the tall man.

The elevator doors slid open and she wondered at the amazed look on the man's face. They stepped inside and the doors closed behind them. Erin pressed the button for the fourth floor, then realized, too late, that she was virtually alone in an elevator with a man she knew nothing about.

"Why are you afraid of me?" he said softly.

The gentle lilt to his voice, not quite Irish, not like any Scot she'd met on this trip, sent a thrill down her spine. She looked up at him, ashamed that her fear had been so obvious. She was probably making a lot out of nothing.

"I'm not. Don't be silly."

His lips twisted in amusement, and he nodded. "Good, that's good, for I'm the last person in the world you should fear, Erin." He gestured toward Reggie with his head. "Now this lout, that's another matter."

The doors opened, saving Erin from commenting on Connal's observation. She led him down the hall and together they managed to get the Englishman into his bed for the night. Erin walked Connal to the door of the room and he turned to her abruptly.

"Come back downstairs with me, won't you? I think

you and I have earned one of those whiskeys your boyfriend is so fond of."

"No, really, I think I should stay with Reggie," she said with a forced smile. She held out her hand without thinking. "Thank you for your help."

Connal took her hand and she gasped as the electric current coursed between them again and the flash of lavender outlined their hands. She jerked away from him.

"Do you see that?" she whispered. "Do you see what happens when we touch? Or am I totally insane?"

"Do you mean this?" Connal lowered his lips to hers, and the now familiar power surged into her flesh again, this time reaching down inside of her. His kiss was as familiar as her own name. As his lips, soft and full, burned into hers, Erin opened her eyes and saw the lavender color encompass them fully. When Connal deepened the kiss, his arm around her tightening, Erin pulled away.

"What is happening to me?" she said, feeling her heart pounding in her throat as he continued to hold her close. "Who are you, Connal O'Tain? What do you want?" she asked, gazing up into his clear green eyes.

"I want you, Erin McKay," he said softly.

Erin sat in a booth in the hotel restaurant, contemplating the breakfast menu. She had made Connal leave immediately after that searing kiss and had spent a mostly sleepless night on Reggie's couch, berating herself for allowing such a thing to have happened. She had fled the room before her fiancé awakened, unable to face him. His behavior the night before was inexcusable, but he would explain it all away, no doubt, and end up making it all her fault—as he usually did. She lowered the menu and sighed.

"But if I don't marry Reggie," she whispered to the menu, "what will I do?"

"Marry me."

Erin whirled around and found to her chagrin that Connal was in the booth behind her, leaning his forearms against the back of her booth, his chin on his hands, a smile on his handsome face.

"What?" she almost shouted the word. "Are you out of your mind?"

He slid from his booth and moved toward hers, gesturing to the empty space beside her.

"May I sit with you?"

"No, you may not."

His face fell and Erin felt a twinge at the sight of his disappointment.

"You're angry with me," he said. "Because of the kiss?"

"I don't know what kind of morals people have over here, Mr. O'Tain," Erin said, brushing an imaginary speck of dirt from her sleeve. "In my country men do not try to hit on women who are engaged."

"Hit on?" He frowned. "I did not hit you. I would never hurt you, Erin."

Erin jerked her startled gaze to his, then sat, transfixed by the sultry look in his dark-lashed eyes. Unconsciously she ran her tongue across her lips, remembering his kiss. His eyes followed the movement, and, with a start, she realized she was doing it again, falling for Connal O'Tain's charm.

"It's an American term," she went on, averting her eyes. "It means to come on to someone, to try to seduce them."

He nodded. "Ah. I see. Please, could I sit down? We have much to talk about."

"No." She bit out the word. "I have nothing to say to you."

Connal released his breath explosively and ran one hand through his long, auburn hair. It waved sexily down to his shoulders, caressing the green sweater he wore again today.

The Fairy Bride

"Very well," he said, with an odd little bow. "I am sorry if I have offended you."

He turned and walked away and Erin felt oddly disappointed.

"Don't be ridiculous," she scolded herself aloud.

"I beg your pardon, miss?" The waiter stood next to her table, balancing a silver tray on his hand.

"Nothing, nothing at all," she muttered. "I just want coffee, thank you."

"Certainly, miss."

A man in a booth in front of her flagged down the waiter.

"Cigarettes," he said brusquely. "American. What? Don't care what brand."

She tuned out the conversation between the two men while wishing all European restaurants had non-smoking sections like their American counterparts. A few minutes later the smell of tobacco wafted across to her booth and she coughed involuntarily. The waiter returned with her coffee, and as she glanced up she saw that Connal had taken a table across from her.

She ignored him, pouring cream into her cup and stirring in three teaspoons of sugar when she usually only took one. What was the matter with her? Why didn't she just go back upstairs? She was going to marry Reggie. Never mind the qualms she had about it. She had made up her mind and that was that. She didn't want to go back home and face her parents' empty house. She didn't want to be alone. Reggie was a good man and he loved her. That was enough. It would have to be.

Erin sneaked a look over at Connal's table. He was staring directly at her. The sadness she saw reflected in his green eyes sent a sharp stab of regret through her. She turned away as he waved the waiter over to his table.

"A pack of American cigarettes, please," she heard him say. "I don't care what kind."

Oh great, she thought. *Not only am I attracted to a stranger who has a few screws loose, but he's a smoker.* Erin hated cigarette smoke—the smell, the taste, everything about it.

The waiter brought a tray with a pack of cigarettes on it and placed it in front of Connal. He looked down at the object as though he'd never seen such a thing before, then slipped a cigarette out of the package and put it in his mouth, filter tip away from him. He glanced over toward his shoulder.

"What?" he said to himself. "It goes the other way?" Connal deftly flipped the cigarette around, then turned his head toward his shoulder once again. Erin felt a wave of pity sweep over her. It changed to astonishment as all at once *the cigarette lit by itself.*

Erin's mouth dropped open as she stared at the man. He took a deep drag on the lit cigarette and immediately began to cough, hacking loudly, almost spilling his water as he grabbed for the glass and then drained it. A flush of embarrassment crept up his neck as he crushed out the cigarette and turned to his shoulder again.

"Well, *you* smoke," he said, an edge to his voice. "Yes, I know your kind of smoke is different," he muttered, then reached up and scratched the air. "It just looked like fun, Eky."

"All right, brother, that's it." Erin rose, grabbed her purse, and stalked across the room to Connal's table.

"Who are you talking to?" she asked bluntly.

Connal looked at his shoulder in that maddening way, then looked up at her.

"Just myself," he said.

"How did you light that cigarette?" she demanded. "I want some answers, Mr. Connal O'Tain. How did you do that?"

His mouth slid up in a lopsided grin. "Magic?" he ventured.

The Fairy Bride

Erin rolled her eyes. "Thanks for making this easy. Good-bye."

"It won't be good-bye just yet, Miss McKay," Connal said. "You see, I've joined your tour."

Erin froze at his words. "Just stay away from me, do you hear?" she hissed. "If you don't I'll tell Reggie what you did last night."

She turned and almost ran out of the restaurant, the heels of her shoes clicking decisively across the polished floor of the foyer. There always seemed to be something wrong with the beautiful ones. Connal was crazy. Reggie was stuffy. Why couldn't a man just be normal? she wondered as she punched the elevator button and prepared herself to face her fiancé.

Well, at least this put the question of Mr. O'Tain to rest. He was not royalty. He was not a rude hustler trying to pick her up. He was just certifiable.

Somehow the conclusion brought her little comfort.

Chapter Six

"I tell you, Moragh, it's a lost cause."

The king of Tir Na nOg slumped down in the plush chair of his hotel room and rubbed one hand across his forehead wearily.

He had joined the tour and they had traveled on the monster called a bus to a town called Blarney. That afternoon they were scheduled to visit an ancient castle and kiss a rock called the Blarney stone which promised the gift of gab to those who risked the venture. Connal had grinned when the tour guide explained it. Everyone knew that particular gift could only be granted by water kelpies. He tried to tell Erin, but she turned away, ignoring him completely, sending a stab of pain through his heart.

"She thinks I am mad." Connal sat up, hands stretched out in front of him in exasperation. "She's told me to leave her alone. She's going to marry that bloody Englishman!"

Moragh had just arrived. He fingered the blue material of his robes thoughtfully. "Perhaps if you saved her from some sort of danger—that appeals to women."

"No!" Connal sprang to his feet. "I will not have it, Moragh. Erin is not to be placed in any sort of danger."

"Not real danger, a magical danger that I shall create. You can save her from it and become her hero."

"I thought you said we couldn't do much magic out here."

"No, I said our magic is limited out here, but I am not the one who must save my magic in case of an emergency." He shook his head, and the long, silver hair brushed the blue robe. "Time grows short, Connal. You have only one day left."

"I know, I know." Connal paced the room, wishing he had not been such a fool in his encounters with Erin. He stopped in his tracks. "Very well, do your magic. Create a situation I may save her from and perhaps then she will no longer think me a madman. I should have never spoken to Eky in public."

Moragh's smile broadened and he gave his king a wink. "I told you to leave that dragon at home."

Ekalb, perched on Connal's shoulder, gave the wizard a withering look, smoke curling softly from his nostrils. Connal glanced over at the creature and his face split into a wide grin.

"You think Moragh looks like a what?" He chuckled. "Yes, now that you mention it, I believe he does."

"Well, if you're going to be rude about it—" Moragh lifted both arms and, in a burst of blue smoke, disappeared.

Connal laughed again, scratching Eky behind the ear, his amusement fading as quickly as fairy dust.

"This might be our last chance, Eky," he said softly.

Erin stood at the top of the stone edifice called Blarney Castle, looking out over the quiltlike countryside, feeling properly awed. The castle itself was little more than a shell of its former self, but it was beautifully picturesque, with its mossy walls and its towering countenance.

She stood with a handful of others from the tour on the narrow ledge ringing the top of the hollow castle that led to the infamous Blarney stone. She held on to the metal wire that served as a guardrail and looked down, her stomach turning queasily. They were three stories up from the ground, and from where she stood, the drop was straight and unbroken. On the bottom level an auburn head suddenly came into view. Connal O'Tain turned and looked up at her. He grinned and Erin looked away, stepping back against the seven-foot wall framing the ledge.

The line was advancing and she obediently followed. Reggie had stopped on the bottom level, presumably to buy postcards, but she suspected he had a fear of heights he didn't want to disclose. His face had paled when the tour guide had explained they would have to climb to the top of the castle and then hang by their legs upside down in order to kiss the Blarney stone.

Erin risked a peek over the edge again and saw Connal was still gazing up at her, smiling. Her own lips curved up involuntarily. Well, Connal O'Tain wouldn't have any need to lay his lips on the cool ancient stone. He had enough blarney to spare. The thought of Connal's lips sent a disturbing flush of heat up her throat and across her cheekbones. He looked incredibly attractive today. The soft Irish breeze lifted his long auburn hair to dance against his face, drawing her attention to his eyes, as clear and green as the sea. He was dressed in blues and grays today, and, with a start, Erin realized she was too. She wore a gray sweater almost identical to his with a sky blue blouse beneath it. Gray pleated trousers, also much like his, completed her ensemble, along with a gray shoulder bag.

The line moved forward again, and Erin resolved to

The Fairy Bride

forget about Connal O'Tain and lose herself in the history of this incredible place. Cromwell had once attacked this castle. Centuries of pathos and excitement lay dormant within the stones. She glanced over her shoulder and gasped. Connal O'Tain stood beside her.

"Are you really going to marry Barrister?" he asked abruptly. "You know you don't love him, Erin."

Erin glared up at him. "Of all the—What makes you say that?"

"Because you love me."

Erin dropped her purse. He bent and picked it up, handing it back to her with a gentle smile.

"You are a sick man," she said, fighting for control.

"What are you afraid of?" Connal moved closer, spanning the short distance between them. His hands slipped around her waist, bringing her suddenly, firmly against him, and Erin's voice caught in her throat. She couldn't speak, couldn't tell him to let go of her, couldn't demand that he release her. She could only stare up into his face, her heart pounding rapidly as he held her. He brought his mouth closer to hers, and Erin knew she had to say something, do something before this madman kissed her right here in front of the world. Reggie might show up at any second! But she couldn't. She could only sink into the green of his eyes as her bones turned to water.

"Are you worried about hurting Reggie?" he whispered. "Don't be. He'll have you replaced with someone more suitable for him and his life before you can blink an eye."

Erin blinked her own eyes at his words and something inside of her snapped back to reality.

"How dare you?" she hissed, jerking away from his touch. "I told you to leave me alone and I meant it!" Horrified to find she was on the verge of tears, Erin spun away from him. "If you don't leave this instant I'm going to tell the guide that you tried to molest me! And I mean it, I—" She glanced back and he was gone.

"Are ye ready, mum?"

The line of people waiting to kiss the stone had dissipated, and suddenly she was the only one left. A short, squat man sat at the edge of a sheer drop-off. He patted the stone floor next to him. "Just sit ye down here and I'll take hold of yer legs and give ye support, like."

He had the ugliest face she'd ever seen on a human being. His features were squashed up as though he'd been made from wax and left out in the sun too long. His eyes were so squinched up she couldn't tell what color they were. Still, he was smiling—at least she thought that was a smile.

"Well, mum?" he growled. "Do ye want to kiss the stone?"

Dazed, Erin walked over to him. The Blarney stone was embedded in the wall of the castle about three feet below the ledge on which they stood. A hole had been cut in the ledge at some distant time, allowing visitors to lie down and, with their legs supported by a guide, lean backward, headfirst, dangling three stories in the air, to reach the legendary stone. In the wall on either side of the stone were metal rails, which offered further support for the person braving the ordeal.

Examining things a little closer, Erin realized there was very little danger involved, really. The ledge would support her back and the guide would hold her legs. Only a small portion of her body would actually extend over the opening, and by holding on to the metal rails on either side of the stone, it would be virtually impossible to fall unless someone pushed her.

Erin got down on her knees and turned around, letting the little man position her over the opening. She found herself hanging backward, staring straight down at the faraway ground. She grabbed hold of the metal rails, pulling herself toward the stone, when all at once a loud explosion shook the castle. Erin started to pull herself up, but suddenly the steady pressure of the little man's hands changed. Instead of holding her legs, he was pushing her down, over the precipice, into thin air.

Erin screamed as her legs were flung over the ledge. The motion wrenched one of her hands from the metal bars near the stone, and she dangled by one hand over the wide expanse of space below her.

"Help!" she shouted, even as her fingers began slipping from the bar. Suddenly a strong hand encircled her wrist and Erin felt herself being lifted, pulled up, back onto the ledge. She didn't realize she had her eyes closed until she opened them and found herself gazing up into the terrified face of Connal O'Tain.

"Lass, are you all right?"

"Oh, Connal—someone pushed me!"

He held her against him and Erin flung her arms around his neck. Here was safety. Here was comfort and reassurance. She clung to him, the top of her head grazing the underside of his jaw.

"Did you see him? A short, ugly little man—he was holding my legs; I thought he was one of the guides. But there was an explosion and then he *pushed* me off the ledge!"

"Whist," Connal said softly, cradling her, "I believe you."

She sniffled, brushing frightened tears from her face, then glanced around and was relieved to see that they were completely alone. "Where is everyone?"

"The explosion drew everyone's attention. I heard you scream."

"Please don't tell anyone about this, all right, Connal?" she pleaded, her fingers curling into his sweater front.

"But why? The authorities should be told—"

"No, I—I'm afraid he'll be embarrassed."

Understanding dawned in his green eyes and Connal nodded. "Ah. The boyfriend. He's still downstairs. He heard you scream, Erin," he added softly.

The cold, clammy hand of truth clutched her heart.

Reggie had heard her scream. He hadn't braved the staircase to help her or to find out what had happened.

"I'd better go down to him," she mumbled. Connal helped her to her feet and she started around the ledge, her throat aching with unshed tears. Behind her she heard his voice, soft and low.

"I'm going to kill Moragh," he muttered. "What, Eky? Yes, I shall let you blister his toes."

Erin fought back a sob and began to walk faster.

"What do you mean, you didn't do it?" Connal said in a hushed voice, glaring at the silver-haired wizard sitting calmly in front of him. They sat together in a pub near the hotel, Moragh dressed awkwardly in mortal clothing. Connal lifted a glass of dark beer to his lips, fighting to control his anger.

"I mean exactly what I said. I did not cause your bride to fall at the castle."

"You are telling me that you did not disguise yourself as a guide, place Erin in a dangerous position, then disappear?"

"Pah," Moragh said, "don't be insulting. Do you possibly imagine I would initiate such a bungled piece of magic? I told you I would not place her in any real danger." He scowled at the king. "I know I am old, Connal, but I am not befuddled. If you don't think me capable—"

"No, no." Connal held up one hand to stop his words. "I'm sorry, Moragh. It's just that when I heard that explosion—which turned out to be no explosion at all, just a sound that came out of nowhere and drew everyone's attention—then heard her scream, saw her fall . . ." He shook his head. "Forgive me, my friend. Then what—" His face paled. "Goblins."

Moragh's brows collided. "That could be possible. Lodan's forces are gathering in the borderlands. He knows you are gone and I fear he means to attack any day now. He may have sent his thralls to kill her. You must bring her to Tir Na nOg, Connal."

"Yes," he agreed, staring down into the foaming glass he held. "In the meantime send a messenger to Tynan. Ask for his help."

Moragh frowned. "Is that wise? To place yourself in a position of asking for help—"

"I will not let my pride stand in the way of saving Tir Na nOg," Connal said. "Go to him. Tell him of Lodan's forces. Ask him to send his own warriors to stand guard with mine on the border until I return."

"What if he joins with Lodan instead?"

Connal rose from his seat, his gaze on a world he could not see. "Then may the good Dagda have mercy on his soul."

Chapter Seven

Erin slept restlessly that night in her luxurious hotel room, dreaming of Connal and Reggie and love gained and love lost. Once she'd awakened and thought she saw soft smoke curling from the corner of the room and two purple eyes watching her. She dreamed again, this time about dragons. It was funny, but the dream gave her an odd sense of comfort—and resolution. She awoke knowing exactly what she had to do. She rose and bathed, then dressed in the rattiest pair of jeans she owned, donning the cream-colored sweater she loved. Waiting for Reggie downstairs in the foyer of the hotel, she wondered absently where Connal was. His rescue of her at Blarney Castle and his unfailing kindness had caused her to reach a decision: she was going to be friends with Connal O'Tain even if he was crazy. Maybe she could help him.

"Hello, love." Erin turned and tried to smile as Reggie pecked her on the cheek. He looked handsome this morning with his oh so proper shirt, tie, and vest ensemble, and as his left eyebrow lifted and he gazed askance at her own outfit, she felt suddenly relieved. She had made the right decision.

She reached into the pocket of her jeans and pulled out the garish engagement ring. His face fell. Quickly, before he could speak, she took his hand and placed the ring in his palm, curling his fingers around it.

"Good-bye, Reggie. I'm sorry it didn't work out."

Reggie looked down at the ring, the cool mask she had come to know and hate sliding over his perfect features. "You'll regret this, Erin, and when you do, it will be too late. I won't take you back."

A slight smile tugged at the corner of her lips. "I understand, Reggie. Good luck with your job at Oxford and everything."

He glared at her icily, then without another word, spun on his heel and stalked out of the hotel. Erin closed her eyes, feeling as if a five-hundred-pound weight had been taken from her shoulders.

A touch at her shoulder sent her spinning around. Connal stood smiling down at her, his green eyes glowing with hope.

"Did you mean it, Erin? Are you really through with Barrister?"

"I—yes, I meant it."

"Thank the gods." Connal took her hand and pressed it to his lips. Lavender sparks danced across her skin, and Erin was amazed to realize the sight had begun to seem almost normal to her. "Are you ready to go, then?"

Erin laughed. "Go where?" Now that she was free of Reggie she wanted to get to know this strange man. She wanted to trust him. In fact every part of her being cried out for her to trust him—almost every part. The rational part of her brain told her she was crazy, a fool, an idiot to trust a man who talked to imaginary people and lit cigarettes as some kind of lame magic trick to impress women.

"What did you have in mind?" she asked, feeling a

little breathless as she gazed into his green eyes.

"I know a place that is more beautiful even than Ireland. I'd like to show it to you, if I may."

"A place more beautiful than Ireland? I can't imagine that." Did he mean Scotland? she wondered. Some people thought Scotland the most beautiful spot on earth.

"Will you allow me to take you there?" Connal said. As she continued to hesitate, he squeezed her hand, his eyes never leaving hers. "I promise you, Erin McKay, no harm will befall you. I, Connal of Tain, swear it."

Erin opened her mouth to regretfully decline. "I'd love to go," she said, then turned to see who had spoken.

Connal smiled. "Are you sure?"

Erin hesitated, then nodded.

"Close your eyes, lass, for I've little time to spare."

"Close my eyes?" she asked. "What for?"

" 'Tis a surprise." He took a step toward her and gently put his arms around her waist, then laid one hand over her eyes until they slid shut. "Now, no matter what happens, no matter what you feel, don't open your eyes or the surprise will be spoiled."

"Just promise that when I do you won't hand me tickets to another bus tour," Erin said dryly.

Connal chuckled. "I promise."

A sudden gust of wind must have broken through the hotel lobby's front door, for suddenly Erin heard a whoosh and felt a frenzied breeze dance up and down her skin. She shivered, then laughed.

"I must look incredibly stupid standing here in the lobby with my eyes closed and my hair flying."

"I think you look beautiful," Connal said, his voice almost a whisper. "Now, open your eyes."

Erin opened her eyes, expecting to see Connal pull from behind him a big bouquet of roses or some other such romantic nonsense. Instead, she found herself standing on a hill overlooking a distant, mist-filled

The Fairy Bride

valley. She was stunned, then enraptured. Flowers of heather encircled the top of the hill, creating a perfect circle. In the center was a large tree. She stepped out of Connal's arms and sank down into the velvety softness of the dark, emerald green grass, feeling overwhelmed.

Connal plucked one of the purplish pink flowers from the few growing within the circle and dropped it into her lap. She picked it up and stared at it with unseeing eyes. Minutes before she had been standing in a hotel in Blarney. Now she was suddenly in the middle of nowhere. This was impossible—absolutely impossible!

Connal sat down beside her and took her hand in his. The lavender aura surrounded them and she drew her breath in a little.

"We are still in Ireland," he explained. "This is just a stopover on our way to our final destination."

"How did you do this?" she asked. She was trembling, and as Connal moved toward her she shrank away from him.

"Don't be afraid." He brushed the back of his hand against her face. "Please don't be afraid of me."

"I am afraid," she said, reaching up and stopping his loving touch, "but not of you. I should be, I know. Just tell me how you did this—how did you bring me here?" She saw the hesitation in his eyes, and realized he was battling with himself to keep from telling her the truth. "Tell me, Connal," she implored.

"Magic," he said, so softly she wasn't sure she heard him correctly.

"Did you say magic?" Erin sat back on her heels and felt the anguish wash over her. He was truly crazy, but then again . . . She stood and walked around the breadth of the circle. How *had* they gotten here? Had he drugged her somehow? But no, she'd never been unconscious. She circled back to him, hands on her hips, striving to keep her voice calm. "I see. That must be how you lit the cigarette in the hotel, too, with your magic."

"Well, actually that was with Eky's fire," he said, rising and running one hand through his auburn hair, obviously disconcerted by her questions. "But we can talk about that later because—"

"No. We will talk about it right now. And who or what is Eky?" she demanded, clasping her arms around herself and pacing back and forth. "I want to know what's going on, Connal."

He took a step toward her, his hands knotted into fists. "Erin, there are many things I need to tell you, things that you will find hard to believe—"

"Like your magic."

"Like my magic and like . . . my dragon."

Erin stopped in her frantic pacing and spun around, her mouth open. She couldn't have heard him right. She couldn't have.

"Dragon?" she whispered.

"It's just a miniature one; he's perfectly harmless. Do you want to see him?"

Erin swallowed hard, then nodded.

"Are you sure?"

"Yes."

"Are you—"

"Connal!"

Connal nodded, glancing at the fast-fading sun. "We haven't got much time left. Very well, Eky, show yourself."

Erin gasped as something began to materialize on Connal's shoulder. First his wings appeared, dark, iridescent green, fluttering in the Irish wind. Next came his tail, rowed in silvery spikes, then his face, a long snout and gleaming purple eyes. The rest of his body quickly solidified and Erin sat back down on the ground as if her legs had become suddenly boneless.

"Ekalb, this is my lady, Erin McKay. Erin, this is my dear friend, Ekalb out of Merrowagh, son of Finn."

The Fairy Bride

Connal reached up and stroked the dragon lightly across the tail. "What? Yes, I think you could."

The little dragon stretched his wings and effortlessly lifted himself from Connal's shoulder. He fluttered down to land beside Erin, who stared at him, her mouth open, her eyes blank with wonder.

"He—he was in my dream," she whispered.

"I don't know about that, but he was in your room. After the goblin tried to kill you, I left him to stand guard."

Erin nodded as Eky snuggled his snout into her open hand. She flinched, then tentatively stroked his nose. "Yes, of course. That was very nice of you to—" She jumped to her feet again, sending Eky scurrying out of the way. "Goblin! What in the name of reason is going on here?" Fear choked her as she shifted her gaze to Connal's face. "Who are you?"

Connal held out his arm. Eky flew back to him and took his position once again at his shoulder. For a moment Connal looked so regal Erin believed he might truly be royalty.

He cleared his throat, lifting his chin in a gesture that somehow separated her from him. His voice changed as well, became that of a man in charge, in command, in control. Erin watched his face and was suddenly struck by the strength she saw there.

"I am Connal of the house of Tain, of the land of Tir Na nOg," he said. He took a deep breath and released it slowly, his eyes sliding shut, as if he dreaded saying his next words. "I am the king of the Sidh."

Erin took a step back from him. "Pardon me? Cheer nah nog? The *shee*? Is that some kind of obscure country or something?" She stared at him uncomprehendingly. What kind of a—Wait a minute. She had taken a course in Irish literature during her doctorate studies. The *shee*. The *sidh* were the fairy folk. *The fairy folk?*

Her mouth twisted angrily and she crossed the short

321

distance between them, skewering him in the chest with her index finger.

"Are you telling me, Connal O'Tain, that you are the king of the freaking fairies?"

Connal's laughter was the last thing she expected. Furious, she stomped her foot and turned away, heading down the hill. If she kept walking she would eventually come to a town, a village, something. She'd had enough of Connal and his mind games.

Connal reached her in two swift strides and caught her around the waist, swinging her into his arms.

"Think it's funny, do you?" she said, struggling against him. "Let me go! Joke's over!"

"It's no joke, I promise you. I couldn't help but laugh at the look on your face."

She wrenched away from him, but he wouldn't let go of her arm. "You're nuts and you're making me nuts! Let me go!"

Connal pulled her back against him and she went suddenly still. The lavender sparks were going wild around them and she felt dizzy with his nearness.

"Erin, darling," he said softly, his breath warm against her face, "think about it a minute. How could I manufacture all of this? How could I invent a pet dragon? How could I transport you from Blarney all the way to here? I am the king of the fairies."

Erin looked up at him. It was impossible, and yet— what possible explanation could there be for what she'd experienced? She felt suddenly as though the rules of reality no longer applied to her life.

"You are the king of the fairies." She repeated his words softly, her face only inches from his. "And what do you want with me?"

"I want you to come back with me to Tir Na nOg and be my wife. Only with you by my side can I stop the war with the goblin king."

"The war with the . . ." Erin leaned her head against his chest and closed her eyes. "Of course, of course."

The Fairy Bride

Her eyes flew open and she threw her head back. "I'm ready to wake up now, Mr. Sandman or whoever is in charge of these things. Yoohoo! I'm ready to wake up now!"

Connal's hands slid to capture her face, effectively silencing her as he lowered his lips to hers. Erin shuddered beneath his touch and responded, curling her arms around his neck. His lips touched hers with a sweetness almost too intense to be borne. They melded together, and Erin had the sensation that they had once been one person, part of one another; that somehow they had been divided, and only now were the two separate parts of themselves being brought back together. His arms bound her to him; his thighs burned into hers as his hands slid down the length of her back, his lips tracing a firy path down the side of her neck.

"This isn't a dream," he whispered against her, "but now, if you'll let me, I'll take you where dreams come true."

Chapter Eight

"This has to be a dream."

"But it isn't." Connal led her to the tall tree in the center of the circle of flowers, the dragon's tail moving back and forth across his shoulders in time to their footsteps. "It is almost sunset. We cannot stay inside the fairy ring unless you are willing to journey with me to Tir Na nOg."

"Tir Na nOg?" Erin said, feeling a gentle lethargy stealing over her. She sank down on the soft green grass. "Why do you call it such a strange name?"

"It is the ancient fairy tongue. Some of the Celts living in the Outerworld still use our language." She lifted both brows and Connal sighed. "It means 'Land of Youth.'"

"So does that mean you'll never grow old?"

She found herself staring at his face again, at the rugged features that were paradoxically also gentle and kind.

"We grow older, but have the power to appear any

The Fairy Bride

age we wish. At least, until we reach our twenties."

"Your twenties?"

"After we reach the age of twenty thousand of your years it becomes a little harder to maintain a youthful image."

Erin took a deep breath, half-afraid to ask the next question. "And will I remain young if I go with you?"

"After you become my wife, your life will be governed by the physical laws of our land. You will become as immortal as any fairy."

Erin closed her eyes, leaning her face in her hands, feeling a wave of dizziness overwhelm her. "Connal, please tell me this is some huge hoax, that this is some strange way you have of picking up women on the weekend."

"Pick up women? Why would I pick up a woman, unless she fell down and needed help?"

Erin looked up into his puzzled eyes and burst out laughing. His green eyes quickened with warmth and her laughter stopped abruptly.

"Or unless I was carrying her into our chamber on our wedding night?" he said, his voice husky as he gazed into her eyes.

Erin's breath caught in her throat. "The point is, this is impossible. You can't have a miniature dragon riding on your shoulder, and you absolutely cannot be the king of the fairies. It's crazy."

"What about this?" he asked, touching her shoulder lightly. The lavender aura shimmered around the outline of their bodies, then disappeared. "How do you explain it?"

"Special effects, maybe," she said, feeling panicky. "A magician's tricks. I don't know. I just know this is impossible."

"Do you know what the aura means, Erin?" he asked, drawing her next to him.

"That you have on electric underwear?"

He laughed softly and rested his chin on top of her

head, cradling her in his arms. "It means that you are the one chosen to be my bride. You are the one chosen to return with me to Tir Na nOg, where we will be married and where you will bear the child who will save my kingdom."

"Suppose I say I believe you—how would our child save your world?" She felt a subtle thrill at the thought of having a child with this man. He had to be crazy, and yet she felt more drawn to him than to anyone she'd ever known. And there was no way around the fact that he did have a dragon sitting on his shoulder. .

"A child born to a fairy and a mortal possesses far greater magic than any other creature in our world. The magic of Tir Na nOg is drawn from that of the ruling family. It sustains the land, the people, everything."

Erin's eyes slid shut as she let herself lean against his broad chest and listen to his insane words. Wouldn't it be wonderful if it were true? Wouldn't it be marvelous just to slip away to another world, where fairies and dragons and unicorns lived? She opened one eye halfway and peered out. "Do you have unicorns there?"

"Of course."

"Of course. Okay, just checking." Reaching out, she touched his lips gently with her fingertips. "How can I believe this?"

"I can prove it to you easily. Stay with me tonight inside the fairy ring. This is the portal to our world. In the morning, if we aren't in Tir Na nOg, well, then I will admit that I am crazy. What do you have to lose?"

If you only knew, Erin thought, feeling her insides beginning to melt because of his nearness. "How do I know you won't murder me in my sleep?"

Connal cocked his head at her, and Erin had the grace to blush. "All right, I guess I don't really believe you'd do something like that."

The Fairy Bride

"If I didn't know that the magic of our love is already present within us, I'd tell you that you *are* crazy to trust me. But it is that very magic which compels you to trust me, to stay with me, to take this chance."

"The magic of our love? A little premature, aren't you?" Erin scoffed. She stood and began walking around the tree, kicking at the ground, keeping her eyes on the green grass swiftly turning paler in the waning sunlight.

"There is one thing you must know before you agree. If you stay with me tonight and journey to Tir Na nOg, you can never return to your world—at least not permanently." He smiled up at her. "You never did get to see Ireland, but you can visit the Outerworld for a day or two at a time, and I promise as soon as we're married, I'll show you places in Ireland no one has ever seen."

"There's nothing to go back there for anyway, not permanently," she said, smiling to herself. Now he had her talking as though his mad words were true.

"Nothing?" Connal asked, rising and moving to her side. He leaned one hand next to her head, the other holding another flower of heather. "No one?"

Erin's lips parted of their own accord as she gazed up at him. "Nothing," she whispered, suddenly sadly aware of how true the words she spoke were. "And no one at all."

"Poor lonely lass." Connal caressed the side of her face with the flower. "I promise you this: you will never be lonely again. And I promise you, if you'll come with me to Tir Na nOg, I will make all of your dreams come true."

His voice was deadly serious. The situation was totally ridiculous, as ridiculous as the fact that she loved him. She loved this crazy man who claimed to be the king of the fairies. But what about the dragon? her mind insisted. She shrugged to herself. Automated puppets—electronics—who knew? She just knew it couldn't be true. What about the quick trip from Blarney? Again she pushed away the questions. She couldn't explain how these things had happened, but just knew there had to be a logical explanation.

She tugged at the short ends of her hair. "My dreams come true, eh? Can you make my hair grow back?" she asked. "I cut it for Reggie, you know. What a waste."

A smile split Connal's handsome features and he straightened away from her, spreading his hands apart. "Come with me and you can have your heart's desire. Stay with me this night and I swear before the good Dagda that I will not touch you, save to keep you safe from the night's cold." He held out his hand. "Agreed?"

Erin hesitated. She would stay with him, and in the morning, when nothing had changed, she would take him to a doctor. Maybe his delusions were treatable. All she knew was that she couldn't leave him. She smiled back at him and placed her hand in his.

"Agreed."

The lavender aura shimmered against their skin, binding them together beneath the pink and gold of the sunset sky, as together they watched the red-gold orb sink like silk into the emerald green of Ireland.

Erin awoke in Connal's arms. She didn't open her eyes but instead savored the moment. They had talked most of the night, Connal spouting such insanities about his world that after a time Erin listened in rapt fascination as she had when as a child her father told her fairy tales. He described his kingdom, the war between Tir Na nOg and the goblin king, Lodan, Prince Tynan—whose family somehow was entitled to the throne of the Sidh, but only every ten thousand years—until it all began to sound real to her. Eky had sat in the tree above them, his purple eyes glowing in the darkness, smoke curling down toward the two of them. Then she found herself telling Connal of her life,

The Fairy Bride

about growing up in a small Texas town, about graduate school and losing her parents and her fateful trip to England.

"I'm sorry for your grief," he'd said, that wonderful lilt clinging to his tongue as he tightened his arm around her shoulder, hugging her to him. "Your parents sound like wonderful people. I am lucky to still have mine."

"Where are they?" she had asked dreamily, staring up at the full, golden moon.

"They live in another kingdom, quite distant from Tir Na nOg, near the ocean. They oversee the silkies and the mermaids."

"Ah, of course. Silly me. It was too much to hope they were rocking on your front porch, I suppose."

Connal laughed. "I'm sure what you're saying makes sense to you. Maybe you'll explain the meaning to me."

And so she had told him of rocking chairs and how the elderly were disdained for the most part in her world, and then he began to tell her how the old were revered in Tir Na nOg for their wisdom and experience. Soon her eyes had drifted shut. She dreamed of castles and kingdoms, of unicorns and dragons, but most of all she had dreamed of Connal, aware in some still cognizant part of her mind that she was headed for a fall. She cared much too much about him.

She'd slept so wonderfully that she hated now to open her eyes and face Connal's disappointment when she pointed out to him that they were still in the "Outerworld" and not in his fairy kingdom. Or would he know the difference? Would he claim that they *had* journeyed to Tir Na nOg?

She opened her eyes slowly and stretched her arms above her head. Connal stirred beside her and she gazed for a moment at him as he slept, resisting the urge to brush her fingertips along his jawline. He was so beautiful. She sighed. How was it possible to feel so content when she knew what must lie ahead for her—

loneliness, guilt over Connal. She turned her gaze upward, toward the lavender sky glimmering through the blue-leaved treetop above her now budded with large pink flowers.

How beautiful Ireland is, she thought. *I don't ever want to leave. Maybe I can get a work visa, teach at a university in Dublin or Galway; then I can keep an eye on Connal while he's in therapy.* Erin rubbed her eyes and sat up a little straighter.

Lavender sky?

Blue-leaved treetop?

Her mouth dropped open and she jumped to her feet, looking in awe at the sights before her. The grass beneath her was a mixture of pale blues and lavenders. The tree under which they had slept was gray barked, with huge blue leaves and giant pink flowers. The sky was a lovely shade of lavender, and turquoise clouds floated in a wispy parade across the open space. In the distance a huge castle sat upon a purple mountain, and, turning, Erin saw an almost identical one on a similar mountain across the valley.

"Connal . . ." Her voice came out raspy with shock. She turned to run toward him but stopped, her eyes widening even more as he stood and smiled at her.

Iridescent, golden, gossamer wings unfolded from his back and spread in a glorious display behind and above him. He was dressed in gold as well, a medieval-style tunic shimmering in the early morning sunlight. Emerald green velvet edged the round collar and ends of the sleeves and made a sash at his waist, where a long silver sword hung at his side. Green leggings and soft, golden boots completed his ensemble. Erin stared at him openmouthed. He was no longer Connal O'Tain. He was a king.

His auburn hair was the only thing familiar about him, that and his green eyes—but even they had darkened until they were almost the same emerald color as his sash.

The Fairy Bride

"Welcome to Tir Na nOg, milady," he said with a bow. "I trust my gift is to your liking." He gestured toward her and Erin looked down at herself, then gasped.

She matched his colors, gold and green. Her gown was deep emerald and it clung to her as though it had been especially made for her. Wide gold trim edged the V-necked collar and the long sleeves dragging the ground. A golden girdle encrusted with jewels encircled her waist, and she had her own small dagger in a scabbard at her side. Her hair hung in a long braid over one shoulder and—*a long braid over one shoulder!*

Erin lifted her hands to her head, running her fingers over her scalp, down the back of her head to the neatly braided locks. Moving with fevered passion, she ripped the gold binding from the end of the braid, which reached almost to her knees, and unbraided the mass of shining honey blond hair, letting it cascade around her shoulders.

"Connal," she said on a breath.

He took a lock of the golden tresses between his fingers and smiled at her as he wrapped it around his fingers, the movement drawing her closer to him.

"This is Tir Na nOg, the land where dreams come true, remember?" He lowered his head to hers and Erin felt the last ebb of resistance flow away. Or was it her sanity? She didn't care anymore. She melted into Connal's arms, Connal's embrace, and prepared to accept whatever came next. Funny, she hardly even noticed the lavender glow anymore. It seemed entirely natural as it flickered around them.

It was Connal who broke the kiss, reluctantly, but with a joyous look on his face. He then swept her up into his arms and spun around. Her hair streamed out behind them and his wings fluttered gently in the breeze he created.

"Now, shall we go?" he asked her.

"Where?" she whispered, overwhelmed.

"To my castle. I'm sure Moragh is anxious to meet you." He glanced back over his shoulder at Eky, who still sat perched in the tree. "No, I haven't forgotten you, Eky. Come along. We have a wedding to plan."

Erin clung to Connal, her nails biting into his shoulders as his great wings began to move rhythmically, lifting the two of them from the ground. Eky stayed at their side as they rose into the air and soared across the valley. Erin stared up at Connal's wings, feeling the lump in her throat enlarging by the moment.

He gathered her closer as they rode the wind. Erin held out one hand cautiously to feel the rush of the air against her fingers. They were directly over the castle now. Glancing down, she saw an elderly man dressed in blue robes standing at the top of one of the castle walls. He had long, silver hair and was smiling from ear to ear.

"Connal, is this real or am I crazy?" she whispered.

"It is real," Connal said, caressing her hair. "As real as this."

His mouth claimed hers, and for a moment the sky, the wind, the castle below disappeared for Erin as Connal gently seared his claim upon her. Erin opened her eyes and found herself floating downward toward the castle. Above them Eky executed a series of loop-the-loops that could only be described as joyous. Erin threw back her head and laughed, shaking her long hair in abandon. This time she kissed Connal, burning her own claim upon him, upon her love, the king of the fairies.

Chapter Nine

"Erin McKay, may I present to you Moragh, high wizard of Tir Na nOg."

They stood on the flat roof of the castle, the wind buffeting them as Connal introduced his bride-to-be. Erin smiled but twisted her hands nervously together. What was the proper protocol when meeting a wizard? she wondered.

"My lady Erin, it is a great honor to meet you," he said softly, bowing before her. "If you will follow me, I will personally show you to your room. We have much to do."

"First, I'd like to show her the throne room." Connal winked at Moragh. "I think she'll find it rather interesting."

The wizard's gray eyes twinkled. "I'm sure she will, but take care not to overwhelm the child too much on her first day," he advised.

Connal tossed the elderly man a grin and led Erin into the castle. As they passed down one corridor after another and moved through elegant room after elegant room, covered with shimmering tapestries and filled with elaborate furniture, Erin felt her anxiety growing by leaps and bounds. The king stopped at last before a large, wooden door that stretched up toward the ceiling. He waved his hand in front of it and it opened. He bowed before her. She suddenly noticed that his wings were gone.

"Milady, this is where we shall be wed on the morrow."

"On the morrow." Erin repeated his words, stunned, and walked through the doorway. An ornately carved wooden throne sat on a crystal platform floating in midair. Golden walls were studded with crystals and precious jewels. Gossamer curtains hung at the windows, looking as if they'd been spun from moonbeams. Probably they had been, she realized.

"Good grief," she whispered aloud.

"You shall have a throne beside mine, of course," Connal said. He lifted her face to his and kissed the tip of her nose. "Now, you must lie down and rest awhile, for the spinning fairies will soon be here to measure you for your wedding gown."

"My . . . wedding gown." Erin blinked and shook her head, forcing the fog from her brain. She pulled her face from Connal's touch. "Connal, this is all moving too fast for me. You've got to give me more time."

Connal's dark brows darted upward. "We don't have more time, Erin. The magic of Tir Na nOg is failing even as we speak."

"I can't help it." She moved away from him, gesturing at the room. "I have to—to digest all of this! You don't even know if I love you."

"Don't I?" His arms encircled her and Erin felt the heat between them even before his lips seared into hers. All at once she knew he was right. She loved him.

The Fairy Bride

She loved Connal O'Tain, lunatic, gentleman, king of the fairies. She had always loved him.

"I-I still can't marry you tomorrow," she whispered.

"At last, someone in this castle who has a little sense."

Connal groaned aloud. Erin spun around at the sound of the voice behind them and saw the silhouette of a man at the back of the great throne room. He stepped out of the shadows and she caught her breath at the beauty of the intruder's face.

His hair was dark and reached halfway down his back. His blue eyes reminded her of the color of bluebonnets back in Texas. His jaw was firm, his lips full, his nose aristocratically straight. He was an imposing man—but no, he wasn't a man; he was a fairy, too, for great wings stretched behind him, silver with iridescent blue streaks that matched the blue tunic he wore. His appearance was simply breathtaking, and Erin couldn't help but stare, even as Connal moved to put his arm possessively around her shoulder.

"Hello, Tynan," the king said. Erin could feel the tension in his body as his fingers tightened against her skin. "What are you doing here?"

"Why, I've come to sign the treaty promising my troops will join with yours to fight Lodan." His bowed toward Erin. "I didn't dream I would have the opportunity of meeting your bride-to-be. Milady." He straightened. "I am Prince Tynan of the house of Dar. Please feel free to call upon me at any time. If you are ever in need, I will hasten to your side."

"That won't be necessary," Connal said. Erin glanced up at him and saw he was holding his temper in check with great difficulty. "I will take care of Erin. She has no need of you or your 'protection.'"

"Connal, if you don't mind, I'm very tired," Erin interjected, hoping to forestall any further arguing between the two. "I'd like to go to my room."

Tynan pulled his angry gaze from Connal and his

eyes softened as he turned to her. Before she could move, he took her hand and brought it to his lips. His breath brushed against her skin, and she had to admit the experience was not unpleasant.

"Rest, lovely lady," he whispered. With a final squeeze to her fingers, he spun on his heel and stalked out of the throne room.

Erin sighed with a relief that was short-lived as she looked up at Connal, standing woodenly at her side. His green eyes were focused on the doorway where Tynan had exited, his lips pressed tightly together.

"Connal? What is it?"

Connal blinked and drew in a deep breath before turning to her. He dragged one hand through his auburn hair, pulling it away from his temples.

"He's up to something. I feel it. Stay away from him, Erin."

Erin's left brow arched. "Is that an order, King Connal?"

He took her hand and pressed his own lips against her flesh, as if to sear away the invisible mark left by Tynan's boldness.

"Aye," he said softly. "Though I'm not usually one for issuing orders, this time I will. Stay away from him, Erin. He means to destroy me, one way or another, sooner or later, and he just might try to use you to do it."

"Thinks he can order me, does he?"

Erin threw a pillow across the room and wished she could bear to throw one of the beautiful glass sculptures of unicorns and dragons scattered around the lovely room she'd been given. She was so angry she wanted to smash them all, but she just couldn't bring herself to destroy something so beautiful. Instead she fumed and stomped and cussed within the confines of her chamber, railing at Connal at the top of her lungs.

"First he tricks me into coming here—yes, that's exactly what he did, making me think he was some poor lunatic who'd lost his medication! No, no, first he tried to seduce me! No, first he tried to break my engagement to Reggie, in which he succeeded beautifully—" She stopped in her tirade as her own honest conscience prodded her. "All right, so I wanted to break up with Reggie—but what I wanted was to see Ireland! Damn! I still didn't get to see Ireland, not much anyway, and now I am trapped in fairyland—fairyland! Trapped forever! And I'm supposed to marry him tomorrow! Tomorrow!"

"You are repeating yourself, my love," a deep voice from behind her said.

Erin whirled around. Prince Tynan lay on his stomach across the wide, king-size bed in the center of her room, his chin propped on his palms, his blue eyes twinkling with mischief. His wings were gone, but what appeared to be fairy dust glistened in his long, dark hair.

"How did you get in here?" She held up one hand before he could respond. "Never mind, I know. Magic. Well, I suggest you get out of here before I start screaming and King Connal lets his pet dragon play ball with your head."

"Connal's bark is much worse than his bite, my love. Haven't you discovered that yet?"

Erin rolled her eyes and pressed her fingers to her temples. "I'm really not in the mood for your little games, Tynan."

"Games? Why, I don't know what you're talking about."

"Of course you do. You're here because you know it will make Connal furious, just as you knew it would make him angry when you kissed my hand and made those insinuating remarks about protecting me." Erin crossed to the bed and stood glaring down at him, her hands on her hips. "Now, get off my bed and whisk yourself somewhere else."

Tynan laughed, the sound deep in his throat, then rolled to a sitting position. Sitting cross-legged on the tapestry spread woven in rainbow colors, Tynan gazed at her, ignoring her entreaty.

"You really are beautiful, you know," he said. "Connal has done well."

"Thanks. Now will you please go?"

"I am here for a reason, Lady Erin, a very important reason. If you'll let me have my say, I promise afterward I will disappear in the twinkling of an eye."

Erin released her breath explosively and sank down into a lovely silk-and-satin-striped chair next to the bed. "Oh, all right. Just make it snappy. I don't want Connal to find you here."

"Of course." Tynan paused, his dark brows furrowing together. "Connal has told you, I'm sure, of the impending war with Lodan."

"Yes," she said impatiently, "isn't that why I'm here? If he marries me, then the magic of Tir Na nOg will be strengthened and our child will renew the magic for thousands of years."

"Exactly. But what he hasn't told you is that there is another way to restore the magic of Tir Na nOg, one that will not involve such a supreme sacrifice on your part."

Erin stood slowly. "What are you saying? That Connal lied to me? I don't believe you."

"No, no," Tynan said, sliding off the bed in one smooth movement and crossing to her side. "My own high wizard, Nord, only recently discovered that there is an alternate way to aid Tir Na nOg. If a mortal comes to Tir Na nOg and takes upon himself—or herself—a quest from one of the high wizards, and completes it, the magic of Tir Na nOg will be restored. My wizard has devised one for you, and if you complete it, you will be spared from marrying Connal."

Erin walked away from the man to stand at one of the long windows studding the chamber. Turning one of the silver handles set in the frame, she pulled the window open and took a deep breath of the clean, clear air of Tir Na nOg. *Leave this beautiful place? Leave Connal?* She smiled and all of her anger dissolved into nothingness.

"Your story is certainly fascinating," she said, gazing at the beautiful world before her. "I might even say creative. However, I am not a fool. You see, I love Connal of the house of Tain, king of Tir Na nOg, and I have every intention of marrying him—after he apologizes, of course." Her grin widened at the thought and she turned to confront Tynan. "So why don't you—"

Tynan's handsome face was no longer smiling with cocky humor. In fact, his blue eyes glinted like steel. Erin lifted one hand to her throat unconsciously. On either side of him stood three manlike beings with squashed-up faces, red eyes, and long, razor-sharp nails, exact duplicates of the thing that had tried to kill her at Blarney Castle. The thing Connal had said was a goblin.

"Tynan . . ." she said softly, shaking her head. "Don't do this."

Tynan moved swiftly to her side and spun her around, pulling her hands behind her. He waved his hand and suddenly she couldn't pull her arms apart.

"I am sorry, milady. I didn't want to bring you to Lodan at all, but now I must do what needs to be done. Cooperate and you will not be harmed."

"Connal will kill you for this," she cried. "How can you do this, Tynan? How can you betray your own king?"

He spun her back around, his fingers biting into her arms as he glared into her face.

"My king! Do you know that if it were not for Connal I would be king? And if it were not for you as well!"

"How is that?" Erin asked coolly, marveling at the calm in her voice when she was shattering inside.

"If Connal remained unwed—which he must if his

mortal bride refuses him—then he will have no heir. It is the law of Tir Na nOg if the ruling house has no heir, the rule automatically shifts to the other."

"So if you get rid of me . . ." Her voice trailed away.

"No, I do not intend to hurt you, milady. I thought to send you out on a quest and keep you busy and keep you away from Connal while the magic of Tir Na nOg ebbed away. Then Lodan would attack and the kingdom would be mine." He brushed one finger against the side of her face. "I plan to make you my own queen."

"This is all ludicrous," Erin said, jerking away from his touch. "Connal will stop you."

Tynan smiled. "How? In a matter of seconds I can have you in Lodan's camp."

"Oh, yes, of course, your magic. But I doubt you can do it before—"

The room around her suddenly shifted, and Erin fell to her knees as a terrible vertigo seized her. When she opened her eyes the luxurious bedchamber was gone. The castle was gone. She knelt on a cold stone floor, her hands still bound behind her back, staring up into the face of the most hideous creature she had ever seen. He was over eight feet tall, covered with dark gray scales. His arms reached to his knees. A murky tail lashed back and forth as he turned and moved toward a throne formed from some kind of dark and twisted wood, his movements reminding her of a snake's.

He wore a tattered brown robe that made his olive-skinned face look even muddier. He had the same melted-wax kind of countenance as his minions, but longer, drawn out instead of squashed up. His eyes gleamed red and his long, sharp nails tapped on the armrests of the throne as he gazed down at her. Erin dared a glance around and saw she was now in a dank, dark hall, in a castle whose stones seemed to be crumbling even as they formed the moldy walls around her. Tynan stood beside the thronelike chair.

The Fairy Bride

"You were saying?" His blue eyes were devoid of emotion.

Erin ran her tongue across her lips, swallowed twice, and at last found her voice.

"Are you Lodan?" she whispered.

The being's eyes burned a little brighter; then the wide, flat lips opened and he spoke, his voice like the sound of a man whose throat had been half-torn from his body.

"Kill her," he rasped.

Chapter Ten

"He has taken her."

Moragh spun around at Connal's words, his silver brows knitting together. The king had knocked on Erin's chamber door a few minutes after she slammed it in his face, only to find she had disappeared.

"What are you saying?" Moragh asked, tapping one long finger against an ornately carved sculpture next to Erin's dressing table. "That Lodan somehow spirited her away from here without my knowledge?"

"Moragh, I mean you no disrespect, but she is nowhere to be found."

"There could be another explanation."

"Yes, but—What's that, Eky?" Connal cocked one dark brow toward the dragon perched on his shoulder. "Tynan? When?" He turned to the wizard. "Eky says that Tynan was here in this room. He senses the remnants of the essence of his magic."

"Tynan? But he—" Moragh broke off, shaking his

head. "Yes, of course. I feared he might join with Lodan."

"Either that or he has taken Erin for himself." Connal pressed his lips together, forming a hard line. "I saw the way he looked at her today."

"More likely he wants to stop the wedding. If he can keep you from marrying her and producing an heir, he can take the throne from you without needing the help of the goblin king."

"Aye." Connal ran one hand through his long hair. "The question is, has he taken Erin to his castle or to Lodan?" The thought of Erin being at the mercy of Lodan made his flesh crawl.

"So, lad, what will you do now?" Moragh asked softly.

Connal glanced at the little dragon on his shoulder and, reaching up, rubbed the end of the animal's long nose.

"Find reinforcements."

"If you kill me, King Connal will hunt you all down and destroy you," Erin said defiantly. "He'll never rest until you're all dead!" She glared at Tynan through her tears. He stood to one side, arms folded over his chest, his handsome face a stark contrast to the ugliness of the goblins surrounding him on either side.

"My lord," he said, suddenly stepping forward and making a slight bow to Lodan, "I must remind you that the immediate death of Connal's bride-to-be was not our plan."

"You"—Erin spat out the word—"you call yourself a prince? You don't care about your world. All you want is the throne. But answer me this—what good is the throne if Tir Na nOg is turned into a goblin's wasteland? You are an idiot, Tynan!"

Tynan's angry gaze darted away from her, but she thought she saw uncertainty glimmer there before he looked away.

"Ssssilence!" the goblin king commanded, standing and pointing at her with one long, talonlike fingernail. "I will do the sssspeaking and there will be no discussion with you, woman-creature. You will not be killed just yet. When I destroy you it will be before all of Tir Na nOg. Once the fairies ssssee their future queen die before their eyes, they will give up their paltry attempts to resist my forces."

"King Connal will never give up!" Erin shouted, leaning forward in her fury, straining against the magic binding her wrists. "He'll never hand Tir Na nOg to you without a fight!"

"Not even if I promisssse to give you back?"

Erin froze. Would Connal fall for such a ruse? Surely not. He was too smart. He wouldn't trust the goblin king and risk his world.

"He'll never believe you."

"No, not me, but he might believe hissss dear friend, Tynan."

She shot the man a scathing look. "Tynan is no friend of his."

"Sssstill, he might believe he could convince a fellow fairy of the error of hissss way, hmmmm?"

The goblin king stood and crossed to stand in front of her.

"Take her, Tynan, and if Connal does not ssssurrender his forces by ssssunset, I will attack all of Tir Na nOg, including your sssstronghold."

Tynan stepped forward and took her by the arm. Erin looked up into the strong face and wondered how someone so refined, so noble, could stoop so low.

"Tynan," she whispered, "if you help me now, Connal will forgive you."

His fingers tightened around her arm. "Quiet," he commanded, shoving her down to her knees. "It is I who will not forgive Connal." He lifted his arms, and Erin felt the magic swirl around her, taking her away.

* * *

The Fairy Bride

Connal hesitated before entering the Enchanted Forest. All of Tir Na nOg was enchanted, but this was where the most dangerous, as well as the most powerful, of the fairy creatures lived; the most mischievous and the hardest to control. Brownies and kelpies, renegade fairies, dragons and unicorns, as well as various sorcerers who dabbled in arts that were not fully condoned by the high wizard, used the forest as a refuge.

Connal wasn't afraid to go inside, he just dreaded the meeting that was about to take place. He had sworn he would never ask help from Ydroj again, not after their last argument. Now he had to put his personal feelings aside for Erin's sake. Ekalb puffed some smoke from his vantage point on the king's shoulder, and Connal reached up to pat him.

"Aye, I know. But we've little choice, my friend."

They entered the misty twilight of the forest. Connal parted the dark rainbow branches of the trees, pushing through, his feet making hardly any sound at all on the soft emerald green carpet of the forest floor. Nowhere else in Tir Na nOg was grass green. Connal smiled, remembering the grass in the Outerworld, then shook away the friviolous thought as the thick foliage he was struggling through suddenly opened into a wide clearing.

A large cave nestled between two giant trees, their rainbow-streaked leaves hanging down in front of the wide rock opening. Smoke curled softly from the interior, and Connal released his pent-up breath in relief.

"He's home. Come on, Eky."

They had almost reached the cave's entrance when a sudden blast of fire ripped through the misty atmosphere, almost singeing Connal's boot tips. He staggered backward as Eky took flight, circling above him, screaming his indignation with the shrillness only a miniature dragon could produce.

"All right, Ydroj!" Connal shouted. "There's no need

345

to roast us like spitted pigs—a simple 'go away' would suffice."

A sudden movement in the cave sent the king's hand to the hilt of his sword. The tip of a long snout appeared first around the edge of the entrance. The rest of the face followed, strong jaws, sharp teeth protruding on either side of the long mouth. Purple eyes gazed balefully at the king, while the sharply pointed ears twitched in his direction. Blue-green scales dipped down into the dark green forehead of the creature. He crossed two huge muscled forearms under his chin and, settling his head on them, proceeded to gaze silently at Connal.

The king shifted under the dragon's perusal, then sighed in exasperation. "Very well, Ydroj, you will not welcome me—will you at least speak with me?"

Ydroj lifted one scaly brow and spoke, his voice as deep as thunder. "Doth the king of Tir Na nOg deign to speak with one as lowly as I? Zounds! 'Tis a day I shall long cherish in mine memory." Eky squawked in protest from above, still circling, and the huge dragon sent a tiny spurt of flame in his direction. "Bring thy minion down before I melt the scales from off his scrawny back."

"Eky, come down," Connal commanded, keeping his gaze on the larger dragon. "It's been a long time, Ydroj."

"Aye. Why art thou here, Connal of the house of Tain?"

Connal gazed at him for a long moment, then lifted one hand in dismissal. "Never mind. It was a mistake. I thought I could come to you and speak to you as your king. I thought perhaps we could put aside our difference for the sake of our world. But I can see that nothing has changed. You are still the same stubborn, rebellious creature you ever were. Come, Eky, we must find another way to save Tir Na nOg." He turned to go.

The dragon had been chuckling softly, but at Connal's last words he stopped laughing and lifted his large head. A brief thread of fire darted between Connal's legs, bringing him to a standstill.

"Whist," the dragon said. "What is this of Tir Na nOg?"

Connal turned back, his tone nonchalant. "Oh, nothing you'd be interested in, Ydroj, just the utter destruction of our world by the goblin king and Prince Tynan." He walked on, then smiled as he felt the fire whip past him again.

"Not so fast," Ydroj rumbled. "Sit down, my king, and tell thy tale. Mayhap I will listen."

Connal grinned. Dragons were notoriously curious creatures. He sobered before turning to face his onetime friend. "Time is short. I have none to waste unless you are willing to help save Tir Na nOg from destruction."

The dragon settled his head back on his forearms, curling tendrils of smoke rising from each nostril to form a misty crown around his blue-green head.

"Tell thy tale, Connal of the house of Tain," he said again, "and then perhaps we shall negotiate the terms of my assistance."

Connal groaned aloud. "Perfect. Blackmailed by a dragon. Can this day get any better?" He flung himself into the dirt at the dragon's head and began to speak.

Tynan paced the chamber, his hands clasped behind his back, sword at his side. Erin watched him move in swift, sure strides, back and forth, like some caged animal. She didn't really believe Tynan was as bad as he made himself out to be. It was obvious he was having second thoughts about what he had done. Guilt was written across his features as openly as if the word were painted on his forehead.

He had taken her to this tiny room at the top of his castle and there bound her magically to a golden chair and placed her near the large fireplace. He had waved his hand and a small fire had appeared, but she still felt chilled to the bone. With fear, no doubt. After dispatching a note to King Connal, he had begun to pace, and now, two hours later, he was slowly driving Erin crazy.

"Tynan," she said, "why are you doing this? I know you must love Tir Na nOg as much as Connal does."

He stopped in his pacing and glared at her. "Do you know how it feels to grow up, your entire life, knowing that you are nothing more than a caricature?"

Erin blinked. "I'm not sure I understand what you mean."

"I mean that I am a caricature of a king—a buffoon—the worthless heir to a throne that I will never inherit."

"But eventually you'll inherit the throne, won't you? Connal told me that the ruling power switches every ten thousand years."

His blue eyes darkened as he turned and suddenly advanced on her. Erin gasped as his hands closed around her upper arms and he shook her, his face only inches from her own.

"Not if he marries you and produces an heir! Then his child will inherit the kingdom. That is the law. The power only changes every ten thousand years if the present king remains childless! If Connal has a child and his child grows up and produces an heir, I might never rule Tir Na nOg!" His fingers bit into her flesh. "I did not want to join forces with Lodan, but it is my right—my right to be more than an imitation noble laughed at by all of Tir Na nOg!"

His face was flushed, his voice ringed with desperation, and yet Erin felt suddenly calm. This was not some power-crazed dictator bent on destroying his world. This was a man who had no purpose in his life—a life that in Tir Na nOg lasted forever. This was a man who could possibly be reasoned with.

"I'm sure the people of Tir Na nOg don't laugh at you."

The Fairy Bride

"Ha!" He released her and began pacing again. "You don't know. Since I was a small child they have laughed at me. Prince Tynan—Prince of what? I am nothing. I sit in my castle and I practice my magic—but for what? I will never use it to defend Tir Na nOg, to rule Tir Na nOg!"

"You could use it now to defend your world," Erin reminded him. "You could help Connal defeat the goblins."

"Why should I?" he shouted, spinning around. "Why should I help him? Let him fall, be captured by Lodan and then perhaps—" He broke off and his eyes met Erin's. She was surprised at the shame she saw mirrored there and suddenly she understood.

"You wish him dead," she whispered. "But he told me—aren't all of you immortal?"

Tynan moved to stand in front of the fireplace, one wrist balanced on the wooden mantel as he stared into the flames. The fire sent eerie shadows across his face, and Erin shivered involuntarily as he answered her, his voice hard.

"Yes. But there are worse fates than death. Lodan has the power to place Connal in a state of suspension for an indefinite length of time."

Erin's hands began to tremble against the arms of the chair. "Surely, you wouldn't allow such a terrible thing," she choked out, fighting back tears at the thought of Connal being trapped for all eternity.

"It is not what I want," he said, his voice low, "but how else may I gain the throne? How else may I regain my pride? How else can I still the laughter of Tir Na nOg?"

"Tynan," Erin whispered, "don't do this. It isn't too late. Tell Connal what you've told me. I'm sure something can be done, something can be worked out."

Tynan turned, his face once again a stony mask. "Tell Connal? And have him laugh at me as well? And what can we work out? Will he give me his throne?"

"There are more important things at stake here than a throne!" Erin said, anger rushing through her. "Stop worrying about yourself and start worrying about Tir Na nOg. If you don't release me and help Connal stop Lodan, there isn't going to be a kingdom left to fight over!"

"I can handle Lodan," Tynan scoffed. "Having nothing to do for a few thousand years has given me time to develop my magic and raise my ability to a level that Connal and the goblin king can only dream of attaining."

"How can your magic remain strong when the magic of all of Tir Na nOg is fading?"

"My alliance with Lodan strengthens my magic. How can I put it? It feeds my own ability. Lodan's magic is very powerful."

"Then use your magic to help your king!" Erin bit her lower lip as Tynan stiffened at her words.

"He is no longer my king," Tynan said, his hand dropping to the hilt of the sword he wore at his side as he paced away from her. "Or at least he will not be once Lodan has finished with him."

"What are you going to do?" Erin felt the breath rush out of her as he swung around, determination in his stony blue eyes.

"I'm going to use you to lure Connal here. Once he is inside these walls my magic will hold him captive until Lodan arrives to seize him. Then you and I will rule Tir Na nOg together."

"But I wasn't chosen for you," Erin said in a choked voice. "What about the magic of love?"

"When Connal dies," he whispered, head bowed, "the magic of your love will die with him."

He jerked his head up and spun away from her, crossing to the high, narrow window. Erin fought back a sob, wondering if she only imagined the regret she saw hidden behind the steely mask the Prince of Nothing wore.

Chapter Eleven

"Interesting. Fascinating even." Ydroj said, then yawned, his breath bathing Connal with a wave of heat as the king finished his story. "But what does it have to do with me?"

"As much as it pains me to admit it, I need you," Connal told him. "The magic of the house of Tain is fading, and unless I marry Erin by tomorrow morn I fear I will not be able to stop Lodan from destroying Tir Na nOg."

"But we are safe in the Enchanted Forest. Our magic is not dependent upon thine, O King."

"Perhaps more so than you think," a voice said from behind Connal. The king spun around and saw with relief that Moragh had arrived, his blue robes billowing around him, his silver brows making an angry vee across his forehead.

"Thou didst not say thou had brought the rabble of the kingdom with thee, O King," Ydroj said with a sniff.

"Connal, are you out of your mind, asking for his

help? You know what happened last time." Moragh
darted a scandalized glance at the dragon. "Chaos! Ca-
tastrophe! Cataclysms!"

" 'Twasn't all that bad," Ydroj murmured. "I got the
job done."

"Now, Moragh, much of that episode was my fault,
I'm afraid. After all, I did tell Ydroj to give a demon-
stration of his firepower."

"Yes, and in all fairness to his majesty I must admit
that neither of us thought the folk of Firnaree would
think I intended any harm to them," Ydroj said
thoughtfully. "Thou sayest thou wert wrong, O King?"

Connal grinned. "Indeed I do, old friend. Shall we
make peace?" Ydroj's purple eyes held his for a long
moment, then the dragon nodded.

Moragh folded his arms across his chest irately.
"Just what do you intend to do with this big tub of
lard?"

"Careful, little man. I can fry thee where thee stand."

Connal stepped quickly between the two. "I know
what I'm doing, Moragh. Return to the castle and have
everything in readiness for the wedding."

"Oh, very well, but I'm telling you, you are making a
mistake, placing yourself in that one's debt again."

Moragh lifted his hand and a sudden poof of smoke
covered him. When the blue haze cleared, he was gone.

"Dramatic." Ydroj yawned again, tapping his claws
lightly against his mouth. "Always said old silver-hair
was overly dramatic."

"Will you help me, Ydroj?" Connal asked anxiously.
"We must hurry."

The dragon smiled, his mouth stretching a half yard
on either side of his jaws, his sharp teeth gleaming in
the pale light of the Enchanted Forest.

"Of course, my King," he said. "What shall it be?
Fire? Destruction?"

Connal set his mouth grimly. "I'm afraid it has come
down to that."

The Fairy Bride

"And of course thou hast no qualms about killing the innocents that may get in the way. After all, thou canst not worry about such things when so much is at stake."

Connal ran one hand through his hair and released his breath explosively. "All right, Ydroj, I know that tone. What are you getting at?"

"Nothing at all, O King, only—"

"Only what?"

"Hast thou never considered the fact that Prince Tynan is in constant rebellion against thee primarily because he is an intelligent man with nothing to do?"

Connal blinked at his words. "Nothing to do? He has plenty to do. He oversees his land and those within its realm."

"Ah, but he does nothing for Tir Na nOg. Think thou for a moment, O King. If it wert thou who must sit in a castle for a dozen millennia, knowing thou wert of royal blood, knowing thou had no say, no role, no part in the running of Tir Na nOg, how wouldst thou fare?"

"I would not like it," he admitted. "But I am king. I cannot share my throne, Ydroj. Tynan is too unstable. We would be at constant war with one another over whatever decision I made."

"No, no, I did not mean to let him rule. Thou art the wiser. Only, perhaps there is other work Tynan would be well suited to, work that could use his talents, work that would satisfy his pride."

Connal sat down beside the dragon again and folded his arms across his chest. "Just what do you have in mind?"

Erin sat on the cold stone hearth, shivering as Tynan continued to stare out the window. He had at last released her from her bonds, then flung her down near the fireplace. It was strange how cold Tynan's castle was, cold even in front of the roaring fire. Erin held her hands in front of the flames and felt no warmth. It

353

was as though the fire wasn't there. She spun around, eyes wide with sudden insight.

"Tynan—your fire has no warmth! Your magic is fading, too."

Tynan turned, his dark brows darting downward with impatience. "What? Don't be ridiculous."

"See for yourself." Erin gestured toward the fire.

Tynan crossed to her side and knelt on one knee, extending his hand. The flames flickered and leaped as he pushed his fingers nearer and nearer, then, with an oath, plunged them into the fire.

"Tynan!" Erin shouted, grabbing his arm and pulling him back. "What are you doing?"

"It isn't hot," he whispered, sitting back on his heels abruptly. "It isn't hot at all. But Lodan promised—" He stopped speaking and Erin laid one hand on his shoulder.

"Lodan promised what? To keep your magic safe? To *feed* it, as you said? Don't you realize that you can't trust him? Once he has Connal he'll squash you like a— a firefly!" Erin said, well aware that she was risking Tynan's wrath. "You're a fool, Tynan, and it's sad, because I believe that deep inside of you there is a good man—I mean, fairy—I mean—oh, you know what I mean! Give up this awful plan!"

"And go back to being Prince Tynan the laughable?"

"Better than being Prince Tynan the fool—or Prince Tynan the traitor. Lodan is not going to let you rule the kingdom, you idiot! He wants it for himself."

"I know that. I am not as stupid as you think. But with my magic—"

Erin interrupted him, her lips twisted sardonically. "You mean the magic that can't even heat your castle?"

Tynan's face flushed scarlet as he stood, his hand encircling Erin's wrist as he jerked her to her feet. "You should learn when to be silent, human."

"And you should learn to listen when someone is telling you the truth." A deep voice said from behind.

The Fairy Bride

Tynan spun around, and Erin almost wept with relief. *Connal!* He stood smiling at her from across the room, Moragh at his side, Eky on his shoulder. The sight of his dear face made her knees weak, and she wanted to rush across the room and throw herself into his arms. She took a step forward, but Tynan tightened his grip and pulled her back to his side.

"Connal. How did you pierce the shield around my castle?"

" 'Twas an easy matter with Moragh's help. Your magic is as weak as the rest of Tir Na nOg."

"No! It cannot be."

"But it is." Connal's smile disappeared. "Now, Tynan, surrender my wife-to-be and I will not exile you. In fact, I will make you a proposition of a sort."

Tynan grabbed Erin and drew his sword from the scabbard at his waist. She gasped as he held the blade to her throat. "You and your propositions can go and fling yourself into the North Sea in the Outerworld! I will not surrender her to you, Connal. Why should I? So that you can drive me away in disgrace? So that I can lose what little I have?" He shook his head. "Nay, I will kill her and take this kingdom."

"And what will you do with Moragh and Eky and my army of loyals?" Connal asked softly, taking a step toward the prince. "I tell you, Tynan, once the people of Tir Na nOg learn what you have done, you will have to send them all into limbo to keep them from overthrowing your rule. Why not listen to me instead?"

Tynan's fingers tightened around the hilt of his sword, and Erin's mind raced frantically. Should she stomp on his instep? Ram her elbow into his stomach? That would give Connal the chance to grab him, but she had no doubt that it would also mean her immediate death.

"If I give her to you, you'll exile me," Tynan said.

"No, I won't." Connal took another step. "There is another way. Tell him, Moragh."

The high wizard nodded, then cleared his throat. "I am growing old, Tynan. I have finally admitted it to myself, and to my king. In all the years I have been high wizard I have never taken on an apprentice. I was too proud, I suppose, too sure that I needed no helper, no aide. Now, however, I see that when I am no longer able to perform my magical duties, I will be leaving my king without a high wizard, and thus will be leaving Tir Na nOg virtually unprotected."

Tynan let the sword he held sag a little, lowering it from Erin's throat to her waist. "What are you trying to say?"

"I want Moragh to make you his apprentice," Connal said.

His green eyes were intense, their expression confident. Erin bit her lower lip. The king was inching slowly forward. Would he take her from Tynan by force? She heard the quick intake of breath behind her.

"I don't believe you. Why would you do such a thing? I am your enemy! I am threatening the woman you love with death!"

Connal cocked one auburn brow toward him and nodded. "True. However, I don't think you'd do it. I believe you are a man driven by desperation and jealousy, but I don't believe you are a murderer. You are an excellent magician, Tynan, and Moragh and I both think that with his guidance, you could become the most powerful high wizard Tir Na nOg has ever known."

"Why?" Tynan demanded. "Why would you trust me with such power?"

"Because I see your heart, my boy," Moragh interjected. "Because I have the ability to know the truth about you, and that truth tells me you are not evil, only . . . misguided." The wizard walked toward him and Tynan lifted the sword again. The old man waved one hand in disgust. "Tish, tosh. Put down your weapon and talk to your king. He *is* your king, you know,

The Fairy Bride

Tynan, whether you like it or not. Are you going to throw away your chance to finally be a part of Tir Na nOg?"

Erin waited, her heart in her throat, as Tynan hesitated, gripping her more tightly around the waist until she thought she would faint from the pressure.

"Do I have your word on this, Connal?" Tynan asked, the sword wavering in his hand. "The word of the king?"

"Do you now acknowledge that I am the king—your king?" Connal's gaze sharpened, then grew soft with the prince's next words.

"Aye," he said. He lifted his chin as if to remind Connal that he was not defeated, only appeased. "I acknowledge it."

"Then I give you my word."

In an instant it was over. Tynan had released Erin and resheathed his sword even as Connal crossed the short distance between them and gathered her into his arms. With a cry of relief, Erin threw herself against him, and the lavender glow shimmered. Connal tilted her head up to his and kissed her deeply, his mouth burning into hers, bringing tears to her eyes with his gentle possession.

"And now, my lady, we have a wedding to attend."

"Yes, my king," she agreed in a husky whisper. "I'm ready when you are."

Erin stared around the great hall of Connal's castle, once again was mesmerized by the brilliance of the golden walls and the precious jewels embedded there. Gossamer threads in silver and gold stretched in gentle garlands over the heads of their guests, which included most of the inhabitants of Tir Na nOg. Flying creatures sailed overhead, giggling and dipping down from time to time to peck the new queen on the cheek. At first she'd tried to dodge their mosquitolike bombardments, but at last she had given up and accepted their pestering with good humor.

Erin glanced down, admiring her wedding gown, marveling at its beauty. A deep cream color, it was made from the purest silk, spun by the kingdom's finest silkworms. Dewdrops hung magically at her neck and her ears as jewelry, and a tiara of the same glimmered gloriously atop her hair. A gauzy veil woven from cobwebs sparkled with more dewdrops. A sense of awe swept over her, and for a moment she once again teetered on the stark edge of reality and fear.

How could this be happening? How could this be possible? She shook her head. She didn't know. She only knew that it was possible, it was happening. She had found Connal—no, he had found her—and had been rescued from her loneliness by the man who would hold her heart, her soul, throughout time. Forever with Connal would truly be exactly that, for once she married the king of the fairies, she, too, would become immortal. *No regrets*, she thought suddenly. *I have no regrets*.

"Are you ready, my lady?" Moragh said, appearing at her side.

Erin took a deep breath and nodded. Immediately a thousand birds above her broke out in a chorus of triumphant sound, then gently faded to a softer song as she took Moragh's arm and began walking toward Connal. The king stood in front of the great crystal platform, which had lowered itself to the floor for the occasion, and Erin thought she'd never seen him look so wonderful. He, too, wore creamy white silk, white leggings, white boots, and a long golden cape. For the wedding he had forgone his wings, and his auburn hair lay in burnished waves to his shoulders.

As she walked the length of the great hall, she kept her eyes fixed on those of her beloved until at last she placed her hand in his. Lavender sparks. Electrical current. She smiled. How long ago it seemed that his

The Fairy Bride

touch had first created such a stir inside her soul. Connal gazed down at her, his green eyes dark with love.

"I love you, Erin McKay," he said softly as the lavender aura danced around them. "And I promise, from this day forth, to make all your dreams come true."

"You already have, my love," she answered, her gaze never leaving his. "You already have."

"All right, all right," Moragh grumbled under his breath, moving to take his place as the offical magistrate for the wedding. "Let's get on with this. You've got a kingdom to save, you know. Have you forgotten that the magic cannot be returned to Tir Na nOg until the marriage is consummated?"

Connal smiled, a slow, burning smile that sent a wave of love and desire coursing through Erin's soul.

"No," he whispered as he bent to brush his lips against hers, "I haven't forgotten for a minute."

Epilogue

The baby lay in a basket woven from the tenderest branches of the lavender Ledara trees. She was wrapped in a silken quilt stuffed with dandelion fluff, delicate embroidery depicting flowers and rainbows across its soft folds.

Peace had come again to Tir Na nOg, the magic restored after Connal had made Erin his bride. Lodan's forces had been driven back by the combined armies—and the combined magic—of the king and Prince Tynan. Connal had taken her on a whirlwind trip to Ireland and Scotland and shown her places she would dream of forever. Two months later she had joyfully announced the news that an heir would be born to the house of Tain. She'd never once regretted leaving the Outerworld. Even Ireland paled next to the wonder of Tir Na nOg.

"It's almost dawn," Connal said softly. "You should sleep."

"Isn't she beautiful?" Erin whispered to her husband.

The Fairy Bride

She lay in the cradle of his arms, tucked tightly against him. Erin closed her eyes and snuggled against Connal, her hair waving across them both. He held her as gently as if she were made of fragile butterfly wings, yet gazed down at her so fiercely, with such love in his eyes, that she thought her heart would shatter if another drop of joy were added.

"She is as precious as her mother," he said, kissing Erin's forehead reverently. "Her hair is spun from sunshine and her skin is kissed with dew."

"Did you see her little wings?" she asked. "So tiny, and lavender of all colors."

"The same color as her eyes. She's an angel, my love. Thank you for giving her to me, to Tir Na nOg." He gazed down into Erin's eyes, and for an instant the lavender aura shimmered so brightly it was almost silver. "What shall we call her?"

"Heather," Erin said promptly. "To remind us of Ireland."

"Heather it shall be."

Erin turned over and let one hand trail into the basket beside the great bed on which she lay. The baby stirred, opened her rosebud mouth in a yawn, then sank into slumber again.

"To think, someday she'll rule Tir Na nOg," she whispered. "I hope she'll rule wisely, justly."

"With a mother like you to guide her, how could she not?" Connal said. "The people of Tir Na nOg will love her as much as they love you."

"Will Moragh teach her as he taught you?" Erin asked.

"Yes, and don't forget Tynan." Connal chuckled. "He brought a present for her this afternoon. Don't worry, my love. With all of the adoration that will surround our precious daughter, how can she help but grow up to be the most perfect child in the world?"

"This world or the Outerworld?" Erin teased, trailing a row of kisses down his jawline.

"Either," he said, and shivered at her touch. "Both."

"And will she have to marry a mortal?"

"Nay, but nevertheless she will be happy." Connal twisted one long strand of Erin's hair between his fingers, curling the silken mass around his hand. "Remember, this is the land where dreams come true, and where love holds the greatest magic of all."

"You are my every dream come true," Erin whispered.

The lavender glow twinkled around them as husband and wife held each other tightly and drifted off to sleep in one another's arms. In the little basket near the bed, a small, sweet sigh of contentment broke softly against the dawning day.

GLOSSARY

Tir Na nOg (*CHEER na nohg*): Land of Youth. A country in the Otherworld said to be populated by the Sidh.

Sidh (*She*): The fairies and beings who live in the Otherworlds, among them Tir Na nOg.

Connal (*KAHN-ul*): The present-day King of the Sidh.

Moragh (*MOR-ahk*) The High Wizard of Tir Na nOg. He's a little absent-minded, so the wizard's magic is not what it used to be.

Ekalb (**Eky**) (*EE-kahlb and EEK-ee*): A miniature dragon raised in captivity by the king of the fairies. One of Connal's hobbies.

Ydroj (*EE-drawj*): One of the more ancient dragons in Tir Na nOg, once a good friend of the king, now separated from him by a silly misunderstanding.

Lodan (*LO-dun*): The Goblin King, sworn enemy of Tir Na nOg.

Dagda (*DY-dah*): Father of all the Celtic gods.

Futuristic Romance

Golden Prophecies

Pam McCutcheon

She is the Golden Pythia, the most accomplished oracle on her planet. Yet Thena doesn't foretell the danger one Terran man will bring to her world—or the storm of desire he will arouse in her heart.

Sent to Delphi to prevent an interstellar war, Lancer refuses to credit Thena's power of prophecy, but he can't deny the strength of his growing attraction for the silken beauty.

Enchanting believer and charming skeptic, Thena and Lancer soon learn that the wandering stars aren't the only heavenly bodies that cross in the night. But unexpected perils and deadly enemies stand between them and the sweet, sensual delight of golden prophecies.

_52005-2 $4.99 US/$5.99 CAN

Sweet Summer Storm

AMY ELIZABETH SAUNDERS

Bestselling Author of *Forever* and *Wild Summer Rose*

Christianna St. Sebastien has always fantasized about marrying a wealthy nobleman who can pay for her luxurious life in Marie Antoinette's court. But revolution dashes her hopes and sends her fleeing to an English farmhouse far from proper society. And the penniless girl's nightmare is made complete by the amorous advances of a farmer—a man who looks like a Roman god, but acts like a common peasant.

Rude, snobbish, and affected, Christianna is everything Gareth Larkin despises. And he doesn't want anything to do with her—but she's the most breathtaking creature he's ever beheld. Determined to steal the beautiful aristocrat's heart, Gareth sets out to teach her that the length of a man's title and the size of his fortune are not necessarily his most important assets.

__3650-9 $4.99 US/$5.99 CAN

TIMESWEPT

Only In My Dreams by Kimberly Raye. Night after night he calls to her. Each night she feels his touch, relishes his kiss, then watches him burn to death. Each night she tries unsuccessfully to save him. Then suddenly Kat Barringer finds herself in 1842, and the man of her dreams is all too real. Some say he is the devil, but Kat needs only to look into his emerald eyes to know his heart is pure, that he is merely a man. And she realizes that she has been sent through time to rescue him.

___52206-3 $4.99 US/$5.99 CAN

Circles In Time by Tess Mallory. Investigative reporter Kendra O'Brien knows it's a dream, so when handsome Navarre de Galliard charges up in chain mail, she does what any modern career girl would do. She caresses his cuirass. But to Navarre, Kendra seems a sorceress. And worse, the enchanting woman is the prophesied salvation of his enemy, King Richard. But as his love for the mysterious miss deepens, Navarre realizes that Kendra isn't Richard's salvation, but his own.

___52201-2 $5.50 US/$6.50 CAN

Heart's Magic

Flora Speer

Bestselling author of *ROSE RED*

In the year 1122, Mirielle senses change is coming to Wroxley Castle. Then, from out of the fog, two strangers ride into Lincolnshire. Mirielle believes the first man to be honest. But the second, Giles, is hiding something–even as he stirs her heart and awakens her deepest desires. And as Mirielle seeks the truth about her mysterious guest, she uncovers the castle's secrets and learns she must stop a treachery which threatens all she holds dear. Only then can she be in the arms of her only love, the man who has awakened her own heart's magic.

___52204-7 $5.99 US/$6.99 CAN

Dorchester Publishing Co., Inc.
65 Commerce Road
Stamford, CT 06902